Finding Love

The Lost & Found Series

Kristen Casey

Finding Love

GALLANT FOX
PRESS

The Lost & Found Series

About This Book

A year ago, he gave her his heart. Now he wants it back.

Meg never expected to find the love of her life sitting in a coffee shop. It wasn't like life was good right then, and she knew she wasn't any great catch. But handsome Edward, with his sexy British accent and irresistible kisses, was very persuasive. Meg handed over her heart without much resistance and expected it to be for keeps. When Edward suddenly disappears, however, she is forced to confront her deepest fears. Has she been a fool?

Months later Edward's brothers appear, begging for Meg's help and telling a story that is almost impossible to believe. Caught between the love she remembers and Edward's new, agonizingly different persona, Meg is faced with a choice. His family is counting on her to get through to him, but only she can decide whether to stick it out, despite the uncertain outcome—or cut her losses and move on.

Can Meg break through Edward's barriers, and remind him of all that they've lost? Or will he refuse her help, and force her to live a life without him?

Prologue

MEGHAN FLYNN PULLED the packing tape across the top of the final box, the harsh scraping sound of it echoing loudly in her apartment. She rocked back on her heels and dragged her forearm across her face. That was the last of it, all the remaining vestiges of her sister's things, sealed tightly into neat brown cardboard cubes and bound for a new, romantic life in New Zealand.

In a way, Meg was happy to be done with it, since her big sister's possessions had been making her feel like an intruder in this apartment for months now. But as she surveyed the scene that surrounded the stack of boxes, she realized that the absence of Morgan's detritus made the studio look virtually uninhabited.

And that was *not* a situation Meg anticipated would change in the near future. She'd used eight dollars to buy that damn tape, which meant that she currently had two dollars left in her wallet until Friday, two days away. With a sigh, Meg gazed at the boxes and realized with a sinking pang that she had no idea whatsoever how she was going to transport the boxes from her living room to the shipping store. She had no car, and truth be told, she rarely needed one. But there were certain times, like when she attempted to drag a month's worth of groceries home on the T, that she really wished she had one. And *now*—now was another time.

She'd considered asking a coworker for help, but that probably wasn't an option. The only two amenable ones had already done her favors. One had driven her to pick up a cheap unfinished wood dresser from the furniture store near work. The other helped Meg haul a nearly new mattress sold by an exchange student at the end of last semester. Which meant that Meg would have to use the decrepit dolly stored in the mail room to ferry the boxes downstairs in the elevator, and then hope for a cooperative cabbie. She'd have to tip well, and if she could manage to take two or three boxes at a time, she might get it all done in…four trips. Another hundred dollars in all likelihood, before she even paid for the overseas shipping. Morgan had understood this from the outset, had insisted that Meg only send her the sentimental, irreplaceable things. And Meg knew that Morgan was good for the money, it wasn't that. The problem was coughing it up in the first place. It might be months before she could get all this stuff sent. *Damn it.*

The simple fact was she couldn't afford to live here much longer. Morgan had been much more established than Meg, with a better job and money from her divorce, so living alone in a historic studio apartment right on Commonwealth Avenue had been no hardship for her. Then, when it became clear that her sister wouldn't be returning to the States any time soon, Meg had been happy to take over the lease, thrilled at the chance to finally live alone and have some peace and quiet after years of dorm rooms, sublets, and odd roommates. True, it had been a shock to realize that her sister had only rented her pretty furniture, intending to furnish the studio permanently sometime after she returned to Boston from her safari. The rental company had come to pick all of it up just two months after Meg had moved in. Now, she owned one futon sofa she'd discovered behind the building last night when she dumped her trash, one unfinished wood bureau, and one slightly-used mattress. Meg fervently hoped that none of her neighbors had witnessed her graceless efforts to maneuver the futon into the freight elevator and down the hall, but there you had it. It pretty much summed up her decor.

The notion of going to her parents for a dime was just laughable. And Meg steadfastly refused to ask her sister for help, even if she was married *and* someone's mommy now. For the love of God, how had *that* happened? Meg had always been the more social sister, the one with the string of agreeable boyfriends. Hadn't everyone always assumed she would be the first to settle down? Somehow Morgan had managed to find not one, but *two* husbands before Meg, though to be fair, her first husband Chip had turned into such a jerk he could hardly be counted.

Meg entertained a brief fantasy of sealing herself up in one of the tidy boxes and shipping herself off to the other side of the world. Maybe her sister could fix things for her, where she hadn't been able to do it for herself. She was twenty-six years old and stuck, absolutely *stuck*, in a bizarre limbo between college graduation and the start of her real adult life. She was so broke it was painful, buried under a mountain of student loans and debt accrued as she worked her way through college. It had taken her six years, but she'd done it, the price she paid to have autonomy from her parents and their dubious methods of interference. But two years later, she was still working in a dead-end job on the Boston University campus, in the same office she'd worked in as a student. It wasn't as if she hadn't looked for better jobs—she had. She *did*. Maybe it was her lack of suitable business attire, or the means of acquiring it, that sunk her every time? Or her lack of connections, perhaps—most of the friends she'd started school with had moved on or moved home by now. Or, she frowned, the stench of desperation that probably clung to her. There was that.

Even so, she marched into each new interview head held high, trying to be confident and amenable. Her transcripts were good— her grades had been terrific. Even though she'd done no internships (who could afford a non-paying job for months?), she had a few references, and they were all glowing. Each time she got a call, she went into the meeting with the certainty that she was exactly the person they needed for the job. The only problem was, she hadn't been right yet, and so far, those companies had been able to make do without her just fine.

So, Meg reported back to her dismal, depressing office week after week. She performed her tasks on autopilot. She crushed on her balding, paunchy boss's voice, that of a New Orleans native who could make "show me the budget reports" sound dirty in the best possible way. And Meg read the emails from her sister in New Zealand, filled with anecdotes and photos depicting spectacular scenery, a handsome new husband, and impossibly adorable baby Oliver. She heard from her old college friends, too, most of whom were progressing in their careers and lives, having weddings and babies in distressing abundance. Hell, even her best friend from high school had gotten married last year, and she had sworn herself to a life of celibacy. Not that Meg begrudged any of them a single ounce of happiness—they'd all earned every second of it, and she was honestly pleased for them. Happy for their accomplishments, and their loves, and for each of their particular joys.

It was just that...Meg felt bereft. She felt left behind, disappointed, and so very disillusioned. In the last couple of years, she'd had to come to grips with a very painful truth, and it had been an especially difficult one to swallow—she was a has-been. She'd grown up thinking that she was pretty, and smart, and funny, and that nothing in life—*nothing*—was barred to her. No boy, no adventure, no dream was unattainable. And how could it be? Despite her ineffectual parents, Meg herself was a force of nature, and it was a heady feeling to know it. She'd never taken it for granted, though. Like Morgan, she had still worked as hard as she possibly could in school and at jobs, laying what she hoped was a rock-solid foundation for her future, independent of her family. For a while, that method had seemed to work splendidly. She had gotten a college scholarship without her parents' involvement, and had hung onto it, even though it took her longer to finish school. She had graduated with honors, just like Morgan.

When Morgan had landed a guy as successful as Chip, it had felt like a personal victory to Meg, too. But then that marriage had turned poisonous. Morgan's pregnancy had ended too soon, and Meg's disconsolate sister had ended up in Africa of all places, where happiness had improbably landed right in her lap. As for Meg, she had not managed to land a real job after graduation. She stayed as broke as she was through college—a grinding paycheck-to-paycheck existence from which she couldn't seem to break free. It had a way of wearing a woman down, sucking the spontaneity and fun right out of her. And based on the way she looked in the mirror each morning, Meg suspected that any prettiness she'd once laid claim to was being leached from her face step-by-step, too. None of her short, half-hearted flings had turned into real relationships, and given the way she felt about socializing these days, she wasn't holding out any hope that they would.

Morgan might have turned the tide, but by now Meg understood her own hard reality. She no longer possessed the beauty or charm of her friends, not in any way a nice, decent guy might recognize. Her intelligence and work ethic seemed to be of little use to her, since no company yet had been impressed with them. And while her sister had somehow managed to get herself safely settled, it seemed that Meg was incapable of doing the same. She just didn't know how she was supposed to move forward from here. The long, lonely, empty evenings stretched ahead of her like an image in a funhouse mirror, reflected and repeated into eternity. She would splurge for the Sunday Globe, so she could work on the crossword. She would spend her free time reading romance novels from the library that, half the time, made her want to cry from the sheer impossibility of it all. And she would scheme about how to smuggle a forbidden pet into her apartment, just for some companionship. Meg would do all that, until she was as old on the outside as she felt on the inside—and that scared her witless.

She heaved a sigh that sounded alarmingly like a sob, and sat heavily down on the nearest box, realizing as she did so that she probably now had her sister's new address emblazoned in black Sharpie across her rear end. Something had to give. It *had* to.

Part One

Chapter One

MEG'S EYES POPPED open. Saturday. Her very favorite day, one of the few bright spots in an otherwise dreary week. Even better, she'd been paid just the day before, so she *felt* flush, though she knew most of it would go toward bills eventually.

Despite the chill in the air, she slid out of bed eagerly and padded toward her small bathroom. After she showered, she'd get dressed and head over to the coffee shop. On Saturday mornings, she treated herself to breakfast out—a small indulgence, but one that felt big because of how few and far between luxuries were these days.

She loved sitting there with her bagel and coffee, reading the paper or a library book, listening to the hum of other conversations and to the cool music. For a couple hours, she could stave off the oppressive quiet of her apartment, and pretend she was some better, more capable version of herself. For a while, she could feel that sense of *possibility* that she almost never felt anymore. And maybe...maybe if she was lucky, *he* would be there.

She'd started to notice him a few months ago, another regular, who always sat at a table behind, and just to the right, of hers. They made eye contact only occasionally, but the first time they had, it had given her a little thrill, a little stutter, right in the center of her chest. He hadn't appeared to be similarly affected, and he wasn't always there, but he'd begun showing up with increasing regularity. She was disappointed, she had to admit, when he didn't show, though it meant she could actually absorb what she was reading. And not sit there wondering how her hair looked from the back (and slightly to the right). Her neck positively prickled with awareness when her mystery man was in attendance, every brush of her hair across her neck and shoulders feeling like a caress. It was unnerving and exciting—about the only thing in her life these days that she could say that for.

So, Meg paid particular attention to her hair that morning, and chose her clothes with care. She shifted around on her feet waiting impatiently at the T stop, but she barely noticed the ride itself: three stops to her old stomping grounds near BU's main academic buildings. As she hurried up the sidewalk, she searched through the big front window of the coffee shop. It was busy, as always, but she didn't see him in there. Not yet. Meg tried to stay optimistic. There was still time, and after the week she'd had—hell, the *year*—she could use a little flirtation. Even if it was all in her head. She pushed inside.

Mentally she girded her loins, so to speak, preparing to face off and do battle with the young woman behind the counter. Each week, it was the same. Meg came here, to this café. She hovered like a vulture until she snagged her favorite table, then dumped her stuff there before reluctantly approaching her nemesis, who, it seemed, had not worked a different shift in at least a year. Her name tag said, *Poppy*. Meg couldn't conceive of a less-apt moniker. Poppies were cheerful, happy flowers. This Poppy was decidedly *not*.

The girl in question eyed Meg across the beat-up expanse of the wood counter, cracking her gum and examining Meg from head to toe through her thick black eyeglass frames. Her disapproval was apparent, as usual, and Meg brushed at her bangs absently, feeling unaccountably dorky.

"What can I do for you?" Poppy inquired, with her customary sardonic tone.

Meg had to clear her throat. She'd been eyeing Poppy's new hair color, a rather vivid deep purple, with fascination. She wasn't ready.

"Oh! I'll have um…an everything bagel. Toasted, with cream cheese."

"Do you want butter, too?" Poppy interrupted impatiently.

"Yes. Thanks. And also some sliced tomato and onion."

Poppy knew all this, of course, having taken Meg's order probably forty or more times in the last year. And every week, she still managed an expression that singed Meg with her contempt. She didn't *quite* raise one eyebrow, but it was certainly implied. Meg wasn't entirely clear what was so wrong with her usual breakfast— it didn't seem to be so much worse than anyone else's, and the butter had been Poppy's suggestion to begin with. But she did feel the need to defend her eating choices, to explain that she ate healthy the rest of the week.

Poppy had turned away, done with her rendition of customer service.

Meg blurted out, "Wait." It came out sounding calm, she thought.

"Can I get you anything else?" Poppy inquired, saccharine-sweet and deadly.

"I'd like a cappuccino, please."

Poppy nodded and began to pivot again.

"With cinnamon," Meg added.

Poppy's eyes narrowed. "Anything *else?*" The threat was clear.

Meg glanced down and grabbed a tangerine from the bowl on the counter.

"Just this," she said.

Poppy stared at the little orange fruit, looking for all the world like she'd like to kill Meg with it.

"Will that be all," she growled.

Meg nodded, but only because it forced Poppy to look up and meet her eyes, and she knew that would irritate the other woman.

Poppy stabbed her finger at the screen of the register with a little more force than was strictly necessary, then muttered, "Twelve fifty."

It was more than her order usually cost, but Meg had her money ready. She took her receipt and moved away, feeling satisfied with the way things had gone. Not too bad, all things considered. And the extra expense of the fancy flavored coffee and the fruit had been so worth it, just to tweak Poppy. But, for all her surliness, the woman apparently had *some* pride in her work, because Meg knew her order would be perfect. It always was. And while she might have expected Poppy to poison her by now, it hadn't yet happened. So that, too, was good.

Meg parked herself at her table and arranged everything the way she liked it. She spread the first section of the *Globe* out, but didn't do more than scan the headlines. Until her food arrived, she liked to people-watch. There were the other regulars, like herself, though by mutual agreement they didn't really acknowledge each other with more than the barest of nods, because—routines. All the creatures of habit had their routines. There were also the occasional tourists, and the harried students and professors. And, naturally, if the day was promising and the stars aligned just right, there might, gloriously, be *him*.

She glanced quickly around the café again. He still wasn't there. Her cappuccino arrived, and she took a quick gulp, scalding her mouth. Her knee bobbed restlessly, up and down. Why was she so antsy today? She couldn't seem to settle down. And now, she had to pee.

Meg sized up the girl at the next table, taking in her unhealthy pallor and enormous textbook. Deciding she was likely a pre-med student, Meg leaned over and asked her to watch her stuff, then threaded her way through the other tables toward the back wall, and the restrooms. As she paused for a departing knot of boys to gather up their backpacks and cups, Meg's eye was caught by the instantly recognizable pink pages of the *Financial Times*. Uh-oh. She furtively peeked down at the table next to her. Right into her mystery man's face, raised to hers in inquiry. Meg was stunned. He was there? *He was there!* How had she missed him? He smiled a little, and she felt herself flush beet red. Meg forced her feet into motion, hurrying back to the bathrooms in numb shock. She'd made eye contact with him. He had smiled. And now, she'd have to go back *out there*. Why was she such a wreck all of a sudden? It must be because he'd startled her, that was all. Oh God. She was being such a nerd. This was what she *wanted*.

Meg second-guessed her entire lavatory visit. Was she rushing? Was she taking too long? What would he think if she took too long? And when she finally admitted to herself that she had to get back out there before someone ate her breakfast or stole her stuff, she felt like her legs had been removed and reattached wrong. She walked clumsily past him, her movements feeling jerky and awkward. She stubbed her toe on a chair leg, recoiled, and bumped the corner of his table. In her peripheral vision, she thought she saw him reach out to steady his coffee cup, but she couldn't look at him. She just couldn't. Finally, gaining the sanctuary of her table, she slumped in her chair, and was never more thankful to be facing away from him. Her cheeks were flaming, and the fraternity guy next to her had swiped her paper's sports page.

"Sorry," he grinned guiltily, trying to return it.

"No, it's okay," she said, flustered. "You keep it." She lifted her mug, peered into it and decided it looked unmolested, then took a deep gulp.

Right then, she felt a soft touch on her shoulder, and heard a polite little throat clearing. Just behind her. And slightly to the right. Meg closed her eyes, said a silent prayer, and forced herself to look up. Up, and not at the belt buckle situated disconcertingly right at eye level.

Even prepared, it was still a shock to see him standing there at her elbow, smiling warmly down at her. He was even more attractive up close, with thick light brown hair and tawny hooded eyes that crinkled charmingly at the corners. His eyelashes seemed preposterously long for a man.

Meg realized with a start that he must have just spoken to her and she had no idea what he'd said. She was too busy staring like a loon, for God's sake. She blinked at him in confusion, speechless and tongue-tied. Willing herself to speak, to say something, *anything*, to acknowledge his presence. She only got as far as opening her mouth to speak. Sadly, no sound emerged.

Gamely, he tried again. "I said, I'm sorry to bother you, but," he shrugged, adorably. "The curiosity is killing me."

Meg was momentarily stymied by the fact that he sounded British, but it was an odd enough opening gambit that she discovered she actually knew what to say to him. "About what?"

"For weeks, I've been back there," he gestured to his accustomed spot, as if she didn't know exactly where it was, "Wondering how a girl who looks like you developed the taste in literature that you have."

Meg frowned slightly, glancing down at the book on her table. *Slowness*, by Milan Kundera. "Uh..." she stalled. There was a lot going on in his statement, and she was trying to decide which part to tackle first.

He continued standing there, waiting, for an excruciatingly long minute. Then he looked fleetingly, but significantly, at the chair opposite her.

Meg smiled and nodded, then managed a polite little, "Please."

Happily, he settled in, arranging his coat and bag against the wall without a second's hesitation. A server arrived then, and Meg was relieved by the further delay, so she could *think*.

He looked up, and the other girl melted before Meg's eyes. "She'll have another..." he peered into her cup. "Cinnamon latte?" She nodded, amazed that he'd gotten even that close. "And I'll have the same." He turned to her. "Have you eaten yet?" he asked, solicitous and elegant with his fancy accent and impeccable clothes.

"Not yet," she replied. "But I already ordered."

"What did you get?" he asked, just as Poppy stalked over to hand a plate to the server.

She dropped it unceremoniously on the table, right on top of Meg's newspaper, before intoning robotically, "Everything bagel, toasted, butter and cream cheese, with tomato and onion." So it wasn't just Poppy, thought Meg, they *all* hated her order.

Her mystery man looked quizzically at her plate, then up at her. Meg shrugged and nodded, as if to say, *Sure. It's not like it'll kill you.*

"For you?" the server asked, pulling his attention back to herself, and preening a little once she'd secured it.

"Oh, why not? I'll try one, too," he smiled up at her.

"How did you do that?" Meg breathed, once the server had left with a swish of her ponytail. "The rest of us mortals have to order at the counter."

"I know," he admitted, bashfully. "I've seen you."

"Am I really that obnoxious?" Meg asked, pained, suddenly, by her behavior with Poppy earlier.

"Not at all," he demurred. "Just...noticeable." He looked away for a minute, then seemed to collect himself. "Now, about these books you've been reading."

Considering last week's edition of *The Highlander's Reluctant Bride*, Meg was grateful that today's volume was a tad less dazzling. Frantically, she tried to remember every other title she'd read in the past year, but couldn't think of any. "Yes?" she said.

"At first, I suspected a literature class of some kind, but I can't imagine one that would encompass the scope of what's crossed this table," he began.

Inside her head, Meg was screaming *what is his name,* but she managed to find her normal voice somewhere. "I'm still stuck back on what you meant by *a girl who looks like you,*" she admitted. It was shameless fishing, she knew, but what did he expect when he dropped bait like that into the water?

He raised an incredulous eyebrow at her. "Surely you've had your appearance commented on before."

There was something so easy-going about this guy, and he seemed so utterly cheerful about whiling away the morning with her. Meg felt herself relaxing steadily, and with that, the words came easier.

"Well, I have, on occasion, been called cute," she began. When he started to look a little smug, she hurried on, "*But,* never with your particular emphasis. And to be precise, you didn't exactly specify *what* I looked like."

"No, I did not," he agreed. He smiled at the server who sidled up, thanked her for their fresh cups of coffee, then handed her Meg's empty one to take away.

Oddly, the girl didn't seem to find that annoying, even though patrons were generally expected to bus their own tables here. "Your bagel will be ready in a minute," she purred, before departing again.

He shot Meg a look of exasperation. "So, you're taking a class..." he prompted.

"Nope," she said.

"Are you a book reviewer of some kind?" he persisted, studying her.

"No." Meg was enjoying this, but she knew she couldn't drag it out forever.

"Then...?" he prodded.

Meg shrugged. "I just really like to read. Literary stuff," she glanced helplessly down at her book, a favorite of hers. "And I like a lot of genre fiction, too." She turned pink. The highlander's bride hadn't *exactly* been that reluctant last week, and she wouldn't have been either, given his skill set.

"I see," he said, looking unconvinced.

His bagel arrived, delivered by yet another server, this one a pale blonde Russian girl new this semester. Apparently, the kitchen was going to send out all its big fish in an effort to snag him. He didn't appear to notice, paragon that he was. Meg turned back to study her own plate, wondering how to consume something so large and messy with a modicum of delicacy. But he dug into his with enough gusto that she decided to give up on dignity and just go for it. She was starved.

He winked at her, licking his lips in approval, and said around a mouthful, "It's not bad."

Meg blinked, chewing mightily. Even with his mouth full, he was so beautiful it was actually a little difficult to look him in the face for very long. And the way he was searching *her* face, eyes roaming intently over her features as they ate, was incredibly unnerving. Suddenly, he snorted.

"Oh God, I am such an arse," he groaned.

Meg was confused. "You are?"

"I'm Edward," he grinned, wiping off his hand and holding it out to her. "Edward Hughes."

"Oh! Hi," she shook his hand, his fingers long and graceful, and broad palm warm and strong. "I'm Meg. Flynn. Meg Flynn."

"Meg," he repeated. She had to admit, her name sounded really, really good on his lips. "I'm sorry. I should have led with the introduction."

"It's okay," she allowed bashfully.

They finished eating, and an awkward silence threatened to descend. It wasn't lost on Meg that he had deftly managed to change the subject of her appearance, even though he'd been the one to bring it up in the first place. Who only knew what that might mean? As he busied himself paying the check Svetlana brought him, Meg gazed out the front windows at the glorious fall day underway out there. He hadn't asked for her number, and she was a little discouraged that things looked like they were wrapping up here. She only realized she had zoned out for too long when she felt his disconcerting eyes trained on her face once more. He turned in his chair to look outside too, then turned back to her.

"I expect you probably have other things to do today, but…" He paused, trying to gauge her mood. He seemed to steel himself, then continued, "I don't suppose you'd like to take a walk down to the Common with me? It looks wonderful outside."

Was he serious? They couldn't do that. Except…her mind flickered briefly to the desolate afternoon that would otherwise be looming before her. If she went shopping, she couldn't buy anything anyway. If she went home, she'd end up doing something riveting, like dusting her nonexistent possessions. So, with barely any hesitation, she found herself shrugging yet again.

"Sure," Meg agreed. And handsome Edward looked as pleased as he could possibly be.

As they gathered their things, Meg realized that a walk that long, especially if they went as far as the Common and back again, meant she'd be spending a good part of the day with him. Her heart picked up its pace, and she exhaled slowly, trying to stay calm.

Edward kept stealing looks at her face as he held the door for her, and they stepped into the sunshine. He was wearing a very expensive-looking navy blue wool coat, she noticed. Meg was wearing a jacket she'd gotten at the Army-Navy surplus store. She loved it but was suddenly very aware of the fact that it was at least six years old, probably more. Its fashionableness was debatable. It had cost her a whopping fifteen dollars back then, but at least it was warm.

Maybe he'd noticed her discomfiture, because he commented quietly, "As for your appearance, I think you're really rather lovely." As if that was just an unimportant aside.

The complete preposterousness of it made Meg think that she must have misheard him. But just in case, she whispered a soft, "Thanks," anyway.

Chapter Two

THEY AMBLED DOWN Commonwealth Avenue, Edward keeping his eye out for Brookline Ave, where they'd be able to cut over to Newbury Street. He figured all the lovely shops there would give them plenty to talk about on the way to the park, and if not, he'd be reasonably close to home, and could stick Meg in a cab and bail out gracefully. It was one of his favorite walks to take around the city, though, and the thought that today he'd get to have this girl for company was almost too good to be true.

He risked another brief peek at her face. Never in a million years would he have anticipated that today would be the day that he'd finally talk to her. *Meg.* Now, he knew her name. It suited her. Her soft-looking, pale skin with its smattering of light freckles across her nose. Her fine, straight nose, and expressive mouth. Her sparkling eyes—he'd thought, from his vantage point a few tables away from her, that her eyes were brown. Up close, he'd discovered that they were something closer to a mossy green. *And* light brown. Hazel, he supposed that was called. And Meg's hair— he loved her hair. Dark blonde, almost brown, and straight as an arrow, with lighter blond streaks next to her face and on the ends. He'd spent far too much time staring at the back of this girl's head, wondering how to approach her, just so he could stroke that hair.

But then, today, she'd brushed against him. She had stopped right next to him, close enough to touch. And, wonder of wonders, she had looked down into his face with an obvious jolt of recognition. Edward wasn't an overly superstitious chap, but that had seemed like a sign if ever there was one. He was tired of waiting any longer for an opening, so when Meg returned to her table, he grabbed his coat and bag and went after her. He hadn't thought what he would say beforehand, but whatever he'd blurted out had worked like a charm. She'd invited him to sit, and then she'd let him stay. He still felt warm from the triumph of it.

Hesitantly, Edward raised his hand and touched her back lightly, guiding her around a restaurant sign perched on the sidewalk. Her hair was just as soft as it looked, and cold from the brisk air. He let his hand linger only a moment before he forced it away again. There would be time. If they were meant to be, if he played his cards right, there would be time for everything he wanted. So Edward matched his longer stride to hers, and just enjoyed it all. The music of her shy voice, her hesitant smiles, her smaller frame next to his. He was already half in love with the poor thing, and he'd only known Meg's name for a couple of hours. He was already plotting how soon he could hold her hand, or tuck her under his arm. His infernal brothers would be having a field day with this if they knew.

Up ahead, blocking most of the sidewalk in front of them, was a homeless woman swathed in colorful shawls and shabby, too-large snow boots. Her overflowing shopping bags surrounded her, and she'd propped a large, hand-lettered placard up against them for passersby to read. She muttered continuously to herself, not paying attention to the people walking by her on the street, but to the conversation transpiring in her head.

As they inched by her, he paused to squint at the sign, reading aloud, "*Ask me what's wrong with the world!*" Even with his proper British inflection, so starchy here in America, he managed to give it a bit of a carnival barker's flair.

Meg grinned and giggled a little. Edward looked at her, then back to the lady, who still hadn't acknowledged them.

He started to walk on, saying "Right. I'm less frightened of you than of her, so I'll ask you instead. What's wrong with the world today?" If he hadn't delivered it with a disarming smile, she might have found the question a bit pretentious, he knew. But she played along and answered him.

"Lack of dignity." She stopped walking, and added more emphatically, "Lack of *shame*."

He raised his eyebrows at her, startled. "Shame? Can that possibly be a good thing?"

"Don't get me wrong. We were correct to get rid of some of our *misplaced* shame. Shame for being gay? We're better off without that. But being ashamed of reality TV? We probably should have held on to that one. Why does every detail of a life not count, unless it is broadcast to the masses? I mean, seriously, what happened to living a life of quiet dignity? An imperfect life, lived by a mere mortal where at the end of eighty-odd years, the sum of the parts adds up to something greater? Something...noble? You gut out the rough patches, you try not to humiliate yourself or others...not too often, at least..." she trailed off as she watched him, turning an endearing shade of pink. Meg obviously thought she'd done it now, gone off on a soapbox tangent for which he'd judge her badly. And now, she was trying to see how much damage might have been done. God, he could read her like a book—it was amazing.

Edward inhaled, considering how to reply. He gazed up at the sky, his eyebrows knit together, a half-smile playing at the edges of his mouth. Meg probably thought she sounded crazy. She cleared her throat and began examining the sidewalk, likely in the off chance that it might have mercy and swallow her whole. Which meant Meg *wasn't* expecting to find his lips so suddenly on hers. But she was so damnably pretty, he just couldn't resist. He leaned down and planted a firm kiss squarely on her lips, and held it there for one long, perfect instant. Her eyes drifted closed, and the street spun away, and when he pulled back to gauge her reaction, he heard her whispered protest. "*No.*"

No, he agreed, he wouldn't stop. Had he said that out loud? Her eyes flew back open, and Edward saw something far less uncertain in her eyes. The second time he kissed her, she saw it coming, and was ready for it. Very ready, the little minx.

When they eventually pulled back from each other, he scanned her face, then reluctantly withdrew his hand from the side of her warm neck. He missed that warmth, and the different warmth of her mouth, immediately. Had he really done it? Jumped the gun so precipitously? What was he, some kind of caveman? If so, there was definitely something to be said for it.

"Sorry," Edward apologized. He didn't exactly sound sincere. "Uh, had to be done." Meg still looked a bit dazed, so he seized the moment and placed her hand in the crook of his elbow. They began walking slowly up the sidewalk again.

After a tortuously silent few moments, she breathed giddily, "You should *not* apologize for being able to kiss like that." Expectantly, she watched him smile, but he kept his eyes trained on the street in front of him. Funny, he'd been thinking close to the same thing, though it was her hidden talent that he'd noted.

After a few more minutes, in which he struggled to calm his galloping heartbeat, he said, "Greed and tabloids." If he expected to make it through the whole day with her, and Lord help him he planned on dragging this out as long as humanly possible, he was going to have to refocus himself.

"What?" Lost in her own little reverie, Meg clearly was not expecting *that* to emerge from his mouth.

"In answer to your prior question," he explained. "Greed and the tabloids are what have happened to lives of quiet dignity." He grinned at her, waiting for her to catch up.

She laughed, in a full-throated burst that Edward instantly adored. He couldn't believe he'd been worried about approaching her. Everything was just going swimmingly, and he was a bloody genius for inviting her to come with him today. He was ecstatic that it would take them a nice long time to walk all the way up Newbury to the public garden, and to the Common beyond that. Strategically he thought ahead, planning which shops he'd like to take her in, and where they might stop for tea, later. It seemed like it might be pushing it to hope for dinner with her, too, but the way things were going so far, anything might happen. He'd been carrying a torch for this girl for what felt like an eternity, but he had talked to her. Hell, he'd *kissed* her. *Meg*. And it had been incredible. All the things he wanted to know about her crowded into his head, and he considered what he could ask her next.

She beat him to it. "So…you have a little bit of an accent there," she mentioned casually. Her hand waved vaguely toward his face.

"Noticed that, did you?" he smiled. He probably looked like a fool, but he couldn't seem to *stop* smiling around her.

"Are you from England?"

"Yes," he admitted. "That obvious?"

"Only a little," Meg said tartly, but she winked to soften the sting. She squeezed his arm. "What part are you from?"

"Cambridge," he told her. "Have you been?"

"No, I haven't been anywhere," she replied forlornly. And Edward wanted to take her absolutely everywhere at that. Places where he could kiss her on street corners. Places where she could wear a *bikini*. He wrestled his wayward thoughts back on topic.

"Are you from here, then? Boston, I mean?"

"Connecticut, mostly," she answered. Edward had a vague notion that the state of Connecticut was nearby, but he was a bit hazy on the exact geography, so he just nodded. Meg didn't have the distinctive pronunciation of a true Bostonian, so it couldn't be too close.

She continued, "What brought you here? It's kind of funny that you ended up living so close to another town named Cambridge."

This part was easy enough. "My dad was a visiting professor at Harvard for a bit, so the rest of us kind of tagged along to finish up university here, instead of back home." No need for her to know who his father was just yet. This once, Edward was relishing being judged on his own merits. Though admitting that he'd also graduated from Harvard could either help him or hurt him, depending on the girl.

She skipped over the question of what his father taught, and even over where he'd attended school himself. Instead, Meg asked, "The rest of you?" with a certain amount of alarm.

She was right to feel it. "Yes, well, there's myself, of course, plus my three brothers. And also our mum." Edward spotted a place up ahead that he wanted to go and angled her toward it.

"Oh my gosh. Four boys? Your poor mom," Meg groaned.

"You have no idea," he laughed. Pointing down the short stairway to the basement shop, he asked, "Mind if we pop in here?"

"Sure," she said agreeably.

The bell over the door tinkled softly as they moved inside, and he watched her take in the shelves of rustic urns, bowls, and platters that he so loved. Quiet music played—Edith Piaf, unless he missed his guess. The proprietor moved out from behind the counter and came to greet him.

"My lord," he said, "So nice to see you again. Looking for anything in particular today?"

Edward shook Hathaway's hand. "Not today. We're just browsing," he explained, shooting a look at Meg. Had she heard the appellation? He'd hoped to delay that particular tidbit—Americans could be even odder about titles than the British were. Edward sidled up to where Meg stood entranced by a lovely muted gray pottery bowl, thick and rustic, with a delicate little gold bee embossed in its center.

"This is some of the most exquisite French pottery and porcelain available in the area," he murmured, taking in the scent of her hair as he looked over her shoulder. He hoped that he didn't sound as pompous as he feared. *Exquisite?* Really?

"It's beautiful," she whispered back. Then, before he could warn her, she turned the bowl over to look at its price. Gasping, she set it back on its shelf with trembling hands. "Apparently, *really* beautiful," Meg said shakily.

Edward smiled and nodded at her. As he trailed behind her, he deftly pulled the bowl she'd been admiring from its shelf, and handed it back to Mr. Hathaway, a well-known antiques dealer in addition to an importer of French pottery. Meg didn't see him. Edward gestured with his hand to have it wrapped up.

Hathaway commented casually, "I expect your order to be in later this week. Will you pick it up all at once?" He looked pointedly down at the bowl he held in his hands, before setting it into a box and covering it with tissue.

"Yes," Edward said, definitively. "Will you ring me when it's ready?"

"Of course," the man assured him.

Meg was now staring at him. "Your order?" she asked.

"For work," he clarified. "Sometimes my brother and I help our clients find things for their homes once we've finished with them."

"And you do...what, exactly?" Her eyes were wide, guileless. He thought about making something up, something average and unremarkable and involving an office, but found that the thought of lying to her didn't sit well. Also, he was proud, so proud of what they had accomplished in so short a time.

"Well, we restore houses. Historic properties, all over the city. But especially here in the Back Bay and up on Beacon Hill."

"Really?" Meg asked, impressed.

He nodded at her, then again at Mr. Hathaway, before ushering her out of the shop and up the stone steps to the street. She seemed curious, but a normal sort of curious. Some girls he met found out he ran a business like that and got disturbing little dollar signs in their eyes, and some of them had heard of his father, or caught wind of his title, even if it was just a courtesy one. Some of them had done a bit of internet research to find out more about the bottom line of his and George's company. All of the girls changed with the knowledge, in subtle ways and obvious ones. Edward found himself yearning to hold that moment off as long as possible with Meg. It was just so lovely to be taken at face value, and he didn't want to give it up yet. He didn't want to give *her* up yet.

They strolled along, occasionally stopping in quirky shops to look at things like vintage cowboy boots, and hand-carved model whaling ships. The conversation ambled along as well, ebbing and flowing agreeably, with soft spells of quiet that felt comfortable, rather than awkward. Meg made him laugh, witty and clever as she was. And her innate sense of curiosity and wonder about the world around them made him view this familiar street with fresh eyes. When they hit Arlington Street, they waited for a lull in traffic before running across to enter the public garden. The swan boats weren't out at this time in autumn, but the willows still trailed their long fronds in the water, and the ducks still swam around hoping for crumbs. They meandered along the paths, kicking their feet through the scattered, colorful leaves, Meg's hand tucked in his elbow. Edward had to admit, as many times as he'd walked through this park, over its bridge and along its lanes, it had never seemed quite as picturesque as it did today.

By teatime, he was starving. He imagined Meg had to be too—he'd dragged her halfway across town in the last few hours. Soon, the sun would be going down, and if she lived anywhere near the coffee shop, she'd have quite a distance to go after dark. Still, Edward reasoned that a short stop for tea would be acceptable if he hailed her a cab to bring her home afterward. He waited until he had her right outside the front windows of the bustling French patisserie that faced the Garden before he suggested it. Warm bursts of fragrant air kept sweeping over them, each time a person entered or left the place. Meg eyed the tables inside, and the pastry chefs rolling out dough in the open kitchen at the back. He could see her wavering, and he wasn't above begging.

"Please," he cajoled her. "Don't make me fight for a seat in there alone." It was a mad crush inside, he had to admit. It was obviously a popular time to visit. "And I'll get you a cab after, I promise," Edward added. "My mum would be furious with me if I didn't."

Meg bit her lip, hesitating. What was the sticking point? Dining with him twice in one day? He couldn't decide, and she wasn't giving him any clues. Edward was reasonably certain she was having as good a time as he was, but maybe he was daft. Maybe she was dying to be free of him.

"Come on, love," he urged her. "My treat. And come to think of it," he continued, another thought occurring to him. "You'll have to share the cab with me, too. I left my car up on Commonwealth Ave."

She was caving, he could tell, and a wave of satisfaction washed over him. He grinned, perhaps a tad prematurely, and Meg snorted in amusement.

"Oh, all right," she huffed. "God, you're impossible."

"To refuse?" he asked cheekily, hauling the door open and ushering her inside. That earned him a swat on the arm, but he didn't mind. It gave him the perfect opportunity to sling his arm around her in the queue and hold her close while they waited their turn. It was warm inside. *He* was warm inside. And happy. So happy.

Chapter Three

ON SUNDAY, MEG awoke, as she usually did, to the sound of light traffic rushing by down below on Commonwealth Avenue. A pigeon landed on the fire escape outside her window and she listened to its cooing, to the fluttering of its wings and the click of its claws as it hopped around on the metal landing. The sun streamed in through the discolored plastic blinds and warmed her face. She had stayed up too late the night before, reliving the incredible events of the day over and over in her mind. They'd sat in that patisserie for another two hours before Meg had insisted on going home. If she hadn't, Edward might have managed to get her to go to dinner with him, too. He'd been hinting, and she probably would have agreed. As it was, he hadn't released her until he'd solicited a date for next Saturday night. When she'd exited the cab outside her building, he'd gotten out with her and dropped another brief kiss on her lips before continuing on his way. Meg touched them again, remembering the warmth of his mouth in the cool air. Yesterday had been possibly the best day of her entire life. It still felt like a dream. And there was no way in hell today would compare—she had a whole week of her real life to endure before there was even the hope of another day like that.

She contemplated the silence inside her apartment with a little trepidation. When it got too quiet, she could be prey to any number of irrational fears and anxieties. On weekday mornings, it was easy—the rush to get ready for work on time kept her moving, and her thoughts out of depressing loops. But the weekends were different. She didn't get out of bed on the weekends because she had anywhere particular to be, she did it because the oppressive loneliness required definitive action on her part, lest it drown her. She needed to turn the radio on to NPR and fill the kitchen with some clattering and *life*. After a while, that was not enough, and Meg had to escape this cloister of hers. She assigned herself trumped-up tasks to accomplish on both days so she would have both a purpose and a destination. So many things in her life felt beyond her control at this point. She couldn't control who would hire her. She couldn't control what people thought of her, and she couldn't control who would ask her out. But somewhere in her brain, controlling the order in her apartment and concocting a routine for herself seemed to help.

Meg opened the blinds, then leaned down to the floor and switched on her clock radio. According to NPR, there was trouble in Lahore. She was hungry, but knew she had no food to speak of in her kitchen. She should have gone shopping yesterday, but given the choice between spending the day with Edward and the chore of hauling heavy groceries home on the T, Meg thought she'd made the right choice. Maybe she'd grab some essentials later today. Maybe not. Today just felt...different. Better. There was no hurry. She leaned down again, and turned the radio dial, ending on another AM station from which Billie Holiday warbled "Dream a Little Dream." Meg smiled. Perfect. A little Billie Holiday, a little cappuccino, and thou.

She fluffed her pillows behind her and sat propped in bed. She fished last week's Sunday crossword off the floor, but realized she had already finished it. That was okay, there were other puzzles on the same page to work on while she enjoyed the warm sun pouring through the window next to her bed. Meg was feeling reluctant to set foot onto what she knew would be a very cold floor, hunger or no. Eventually, she'd need some caffeine, too, but she wasn't desperate for it yet. Maybe her next purchase would be a freaking rug of some kind. Somehow. Or perhaps she ought to just move her coffee maker from the kitchen to her bedroom. *There* was a thought.

Then came a noise that was so far outside the realm of possibility, it took a moment or two to process what she'd heard. Had someone really just knocked on her front door? Meg was baffled. Who the hell could it be? She knew exactly none of her neighbors—except maybe the med student next door, and him only in passing because she signed for his care packages from home sometimes. She wasn't expecting a soul, and besides, the foyer door downstairs was locked. No one could get in the building without a key. The knock sounded again—louder and somehow more...authoritative. So, she wasn't hallucinating, that was a plus. Meg groaned. She had to at least get up and peek out the peephole to make sure it wasn't the building's super or something.

But, oh God. It was freezing out from under the covers. Where the heck was her robe? Meg yelped as she skipped across the room. *Cold floor!* And she had to put *something* on in case she had to open her door—she just had on the tank top and old soft boxers that she'd slept in. But her robe was nowhere in sight, damn it. Meg's eyes fell, then, on the long, gilt-trimmed box laying in the corner of her living room. She'd kept it there, trying to determine what to do with it, and its contents beckoned to her now. Inside was a gorgeous, long black shearling coat, given to her by one Li Wei Wong, Chinese exchange student with a hard-on for American girls. He had hounded her relentlessly for the entire second half of her senior year. Meg had finally gone on an ill-advised date with him only a few weeks ago, during which he'd forced a kiss or two on her, and then sent the jacket to her office to underline what he could do for her if she agreed to "date" him regularly. She *had* been freezing that night, that was true. But it was his fault for making her stand outside the clubs on Lansdowne Street for hours, while it gradually became obvious he was trotting out his newest blond acquisition for all his ex-pat friends to see. None of them seemed to think American girls were much more that prostitutes, and extended her about the same degree of civility and respect. Needless to say, Meg didn't intend to ever date him again, and she'd told him as much. But that meant she would have to find some way to return the coat to him. She was just reluctant to have to actually *see* him again to do so.

Regardless, there was now a third knock, and to her mind, it seemed like an *"I'm giving up now"* knock. Meg flung off the top of the box and grabbed the heavy coat. Slipping her arms into the sleeves, she peered out the peephole, only to see Edward standing there holding two cups of coffee and a very promising-looking brown bag. *Edward.* He looked searchingly at her door, as if he could somehow divine why she wasn't answering. And then, he started to turn away.

"Wait!" she blurted out. "I'm here!" She hastily pulled the coat tighter around herself (geez, it was so soft against her skin, and really, really *warm*), and yanked at the deadbolts lined up above the knob.

Meg pulled the door open with a grin on her face. "Hi. What are you doing here?"

Edward pivoted back toward her. His eyes took in her unexpected attire and bare feet, and he raised startled eyebrows at her.

"I would ask if you were headed out, but I expect you might want some shoes for that," he commented. Meg backed up, and he followed her inside. He stood awkwardly just a few steps inside her door, likely because there was no real place for him to sit.

"Sorry. I know. I wasn't expecting anyone, and I couldn't find my robe. Come in."

He was already in, and she sounded jumpy even to her own ears. Well, now he'd know, she supposed. There was no finessing her spartan apartment—she didn't think anyone would live like this if they didn't have to. With a pang, she realized that this was, in all likelihood, the beginning of the end for them. He was so refined, so cultured. And she was...*this*. Meg swallowed, trying not to feel crushed. Trying not to feel ashamed. His eyes drifted around the living room, and the large alcove that passed for her bedroom. They rested for only a moment on her messy bed, then came back to her. His expression was unreadable.

"Nice coat," he murmured.

His eyes flicked down to her bare toes again, and she was very happy that she had painted her toenails a deep brownish-red late last night while she thought of him. *Vixen*, the color was called. It suited a woman standing in front of a guy wearing skimpy pajamas and a different man's gift, she mused.

"It's not mine," she explained, then realized how that might sound. "I mean…it was supposed to be mine. It was a gift of sorts, but obviously I can't keep it."

"You ought to," he said. "It suits you."

"Thanks, but..." she peered down at herself with a frown. She loved this coat to an irrational degree and returning it would sting like hell. "Too many strings attached," she explained. Searching for a change in topic, she asked, "Did someone let you in? Downstairs, I mean?"

Edward nodded. "I hope that was okay. I come bearing gifts," he told her with a hopeful little smile, raising the cups and the bag he held.

Meg grinned, feeling giddy. "I was really, really hoping that one of those was for me."

His crooked smile warmed her. She gestured weakly at the low futon sofa and said, "Have a seat and I'll just go put something on." She blushed. Could he tell the futon was someone else's trash? Hard to say.

At Edward's stunned expression, she realized that he probably thought she had nothing on under the damn coat, and she blushed even brighter. "Something *more* on," she added, but noted that it hadn't helped much. She hesitated as he looked down at the futon. Meg hadn't noticed it herself, but surely someone must have cut the legs off that thing? It probably wasn't supposed to be so close to the ground like that. "Um—if you need anything in the kitchen, help yourself," she added, pointing the way. "I'll just be a minute."

Edward seemed to take the hint and walked into the kitchen. She took the moment of privacy to dart into her bedroom and grab a bra, T-shirt, and some sweatpants from her floor, then dug in the tiny closet for a hoodie and some socks. She glanced in at him putting things from the bag onto a plate, then rushed into the bathroom to change, brush her teeth, and comb her hair. After a moment, she decided to hang the coat on the back of the bathroom door, next to her formerly-missing robe.

When Meg emerged from the bathroom, he was sitting on the futon, with the paper cups of coffee and the plate of danishes on the floor near his feet. And he was staring intently at her bed.

"I'm sorry," she said again, flustered at the sight of him perched in the middle of her home. He dragged his eyes back to her face and smiled. Meg gestured around and realized how weird it would be if she tried to park it next to him on the small futon. Instead, she sank cross-legged to the floor nearby and reached for the cup he handed her. "I don't really ever have visitors," she told him, in utter humiliation.

Edward looked around, noting the last two packed boxes across the room and the hissing radiator under the windows. "Did you just move in?" he asked.

She winced and forced a smile. "Not exactly."

"Ah," was his only reply. He took a long slug of coffee and examined the plate before extending it to her. Edward was watching her carefully, but she didn't *think* she saw scorn there. It was hard to tell. His face was impassive.

She accepted the plate from him, and tried to explain in a rush, "This was my sister's place. She moved away kind of unexpectedly, so I was taking care of it for her. But now that I've sent her most of her stuff, I haven't really managed to get much of my *own* stuff yet." Well, that was the truth, mostly. Meg might have managed "getting things" better if she could actually afford it, but he didn't necessarily need to know that. She grimaced at his long legs splayed in front of him. "I am so sorry. You don't look very comfortable."

But Edward leaned back casually, resting his cup on his thigh and his arm along the top of the futon. He looked so fresh this morning. So clean and handsome. And suddenly, he seemed utterly at ease. "No, it's great. Are you all right over there?"

Meg nodded with a smile, and bit into the corner of the cheese danish she'd snagged.

"Thanks for this. What a nice surprise." She couldn't keep the question from her voice. She was still wondering what he was doing there. Her apartment number was next to her name in the mail room, but still. He'd said next Saturday. And here he was the next *morning*.

Now Edward looked sheepish. "I think I should apologize to you. I was standing in the queue at the coffee shop, and this seemed like a really brilliant idea at the time. But maybe I'm imposing on you. It was rude of me to pop in like this, like I'm some kind of stalker." He laughed, but his eyes kept drifting over her—over her face, and her hair, and her clothes. Meg was utterly mortified. She must look like a wreck.

"I should have called first," he said. "Or, errm, waited until Saturday, like a normal bloke."

"I must look terrible," she blushed again, running an unsteady hand over her hair. He was shaking his head before she'd even finished her sentence.

"No, you look..." he shook his head again, at a loss for words. But his face went soft. He murmured, "You look amazing."

She smiled and stared at the floor, feeling her cheeks burning. "Thanks," she whispered.

"What's the story with the coat?" Edward asked, and Meg knew the answer was important to him. He was trying too hard to sound casual, and it came out sounding anything but.

"Well, so there was this guy in one of my classes last year. A foreign exchange student, from China." Meg began.

Edward made a noncommittal noise in his throat, nodding for her to continue. She was trying not to inhale her danish too fast, but man, she was famished. She always was in the morning, once she woke up a bit.

Meg went on, "He kept pestering me to go out with him, so finally I went. Just the once. I didn't really—I don't know why I went, to be honest." She flushed again. How must this sound to him? Like she was desperate? Loose?

"Wore you down, did he?" Edward smiled warmly.

Meg nodded, relieved by his tone. "Yeah, I guess," she agreed, not sure how to proceed.

"So, what happened?" he prodded.

"Well, he picked me up and it rapidly became clear that he was more interested in parading me around to his friends than in actually getting to know me. He wanted me to be a trophy, a—a toy—that he could use however he wanted." Meg shuddered. The memory of how demeaning that had felt still rankled. "It was pretty uncomfortable."

Edward was scowling now. "And the coat?" he inquired, his clipped accent making his inquiry even sharper.

Meg sighed. "It was delivered to my office the next Monday. I tried to call and tell him I couldn't accept it, but once we got to the part about me not seeing him again, he hung up on me. I think he may have blocked my number," she added self-consciously.

Edward blinked, taking this in. He opened his mouth to say something, but she cut him off.

"I don't know where he lives, so I can't leave it there. And I already called the store to see if I could return it, but they won't accept it without a receipt."

He snorted. "Do you even like the thing? If it's real, it must be worth a fortune."

"Oh, trust me. It's real. And as far as liking it..." Meg thought of its weight and softness. The toasty warm luxury of it. She'd never owned a thing like it. Ever.

He raised his eyebrows at her, a smile playing at the edges of his gorgeous mouth.

"I love that stupid coat so much, and I really wish I didn't," Meg admitted in a rush. "Everything it represents would make my skin crawl if it weren't so freaking gorgeous."

Edward laughed out loud at that. "*You're* freaking gorgeous," he retorted, grinning. "I can see why the poor bastard pulled out the big guns on you."

Meg shook her head. "Be serious. He was such a jerk. If that's the best he's got, he's going to be lonely a long time."

Edward was still smiling at her. "Oh come on, Meg. It was a great honor to hit the town with—what was his name?"

"Li Wei."

"Yes, with Li Wei. You should be grateful," he said, sardonically. Even if Meg wasn't already smitten with his face and his tall lanky build, that crisp accented voice of his would be enough, she thought, to win her over.

"Well, I'm *not*," Meg muttered. She could feel her stomach starting to grumble. Somehow the coffee and danish had just woken things up in there, and she was even more hungry than before. She clenched her core muscles, hoping to stifle the sound.

Edward said, "Then the only thing left, I suppose, is to consider the coat due compensation for enduring His High Petulance for a whole evening, eh?" He brushed off his hands, clapped them together, and stood. He reached down to help Meg to her feet, and said cheerfully, "Right, then. I'm starved. There might be another coat in it for you if you make me breakfast, woman."

At her startled laugh (and probably also her slightly panicked expression), Edward relented. "Just kidding. Come on, get your things. Let's go grab something else to eat."

"Umm," Meg stalled, making rapid calculations in her head about her appearance, and the cash, or lack thereof, currently residing in her wallet. She'd had to do the same yesterday afternoon, at the patisserie, and she hated it.

"Please," he urged. "It's on me, for barging in on you like this when you only just got rid of me sixteen hours ago. There's this dodgy place called Mal's not too far from here. Let's eat copious amounts of eggs in honor of Li Wei and his generous bribing habits."

"Okay," Meg caved, as susceptible to the lure of Mal's greasy, salty fare as the next girl. Had Edward actually just counted the hours since they'd parted yesterday? God help her, but Meg was sinking fast here. "But would you mind just waiting like ten minutes so I can hop in the shower really quick? I promise I'll go fast," she said.

Edward sighed dramatically and slumped back down onto the futon. "I suppose, if you insist on being *clean*," he huffed, as if it were the ultimate imposition. "I think you look, and smell, fine."

Meg's stomach rumbled, too loudly to ignore this time. She yelped, "Sorry! Thanks!" and bolted for the bathroom.

"Hurry up. By the sound of things, we don't have much time," he laughed, shooing her away with both hands.

Meg locked herself in the bathroom and got to it.

EDWARD SAT ON the low, hard couch and waited. So far, things had gone better than he'd hoped for. He'd sweet-talked his way into Meg's apartment with coffee and treats and managed to get her relaxed and talking relatively easily. She was so funny, so sharp when she let her guard down. Edward adored it. She hadn't seemed thrilled to have him in her space at first, but now she was comfortable enough to leave him sitting here alone while she got cleaned up. That had to be a good sign. Also good? He'd confirmed that there were no other serious contenders vying for her. Poor Li Wei seemed to have never stood a chance with a girl like Meg, and thankfully appeared to have thrown in the towel without much of a fight. He didn't love seeing another bloke's gift on her, but it did appear as if she deserved the thing. Li Wei sounded like a wanker.

Edward glanced around her apartment, a large, bright, airy studio. Good light. High ceilings, lots of old, ornate molding trimming the rooms, and gleaming parquet floors. And the feel in here was incredible—it was lazy and serene, welcoming, peaceful. He wanted to examine every last artifact in the place, every last possession that might tell him more about this woman—what she liked, what she cared about. He was undeniably what his mum would call gobsmacked. Edward stared at the bathroom door, behind which he could hear the rushing water of the shower. Meg was in there, and almost certainly naked, wet, hot...he jerked his gaze away, before it burned a hole in the door. The only problem was, when he looked in the opposite direction, he was faced with an equally problematic sight: Meg's messy unmade bed, beckoning from its sunny alcove to the right. He took in the pillows stacked against the wall, the open blinds, and the folded newspaper and pen lying amongst the blankets. He tried to picture Meg propped there, gazing out the window. No—looking at her front door, where some lustful Englishman stood knocking, begging entry. Oh, God. *That* image came all too easily.

Edward stood up quickly. Distraction, that's what he needed. The water in the bathroom had stopped running, but now the whir of a hairdryer had clicked on. Did she dress before she dried her hair, or was Meg standing in there in her lacy under-things blowing her hair all around? He shook his head. She was turning him into a masochist, torturing himself at every opportunity. Desperately, he cast around, but there wasn't a lot to look at. Except there, on the far wall, he spotted a small bookcase, crammed to the edges with CDs, and topped with a small stereo. Edward strode over, and stared resolutely at each and every title, until he heard the bathroom door open behind him. He'd opened the top of the player to investigate which music she'd been playing last, and when he turned, he still had the CD in his hand. Nina Simone. This girl was a goddess.

And the sight of her, fresh-scrubbed and damp around the edges, confirmed that assessment. Edward was inordinately pleased that he'd acted on impulse and showed up here this morning, instead of waiting around for a week like he probably ought to have done. And the notion that he now got to spend at least another hour gazing at her and talking to her over plates of eggs and sausages had him feeling triumphant. He set the CD carefully back in its tray and walked closer to her. Breathing in deeply her clean, sweet scent, he forced himself to smile. The alternative, such as it was, was to tackle her and pin her in that bed for the foreseeable future.

"Shall we?" he inquired, holding out a hand to her.

She blinked uncertainly, and inhaled a huge breath, but she moved toward him anyway. Grabbing her bag and keys from a shelf tucked behind the front door, Meg smiled her sweet smile, and they were off. Sundays. Next to Saturdays, they were Edward's favorite, absolute favorite, day of the week.

Chapter Four

MEG SAT AT her desk Monday morning, fingering the petals of a floral arrangement while her computer booted up. Nothing as obvious as roses, she mused, not for Edward, though as she peered closer, she did spot a handful of those, in a nice deep red color. No, this arrangement was loose and informal and gorgeous, and seemed to capture his personality perfectly. And the fact that it had appeared on her desk within moments of her arrival this morning just tickled her more. *Best weekend EVER*, the card had read. Meg would have to agree.

From the office across the hall, Meg's boss called out, "Meg, darlin', will you bring me last week's department transfers?" She grinned, but had to admit that drawl of his lacked a certain something this morning. Her taste in accents was veering in a decidedly new direction.

"I'll be right there," she said, calling up the appropriate files and sending them to her printer. She had, of course, already given Mr. Boudreau these reports last Friday, but the man was forever losing things in the wilds of his desk. Once she fished the reports off her paper tray, she sorted and stapled them, then walked them over.

"Here you go," she sang, dropping them on the corner of his desk.

As he reached for them, he glanced up at her, then did a double take. "You all right?" he inquired, looking perplexed.

"Sure. Never better," Meg assured him.

"I can see that," he murmured, his rich molasses voice flowing over her. "Caught my attention."

Meg smirked at him and waited silently near his door.

"All right, you just play it cool," he chuckled. "I'll find out eventually." He winked at her and shooed her out. A shameless flirt, that man was, though Meg knew he was 100% harmless. Still, he must have been a force to be reckoned with when he was a young man, with more hair and no paunch. And no wife. She shook her head.

By late afternoon, time was beginning to drag, but every time Meg looked at those flowers, her heart lifted. Saturday night. She'd get to see Edward again on Saturday night.

At four thirty, her phone dinged faintly from where it was still buried deep in her jacket pocket, hanging at the side of her cubicle. Meg dug it out hopefully and looked at the text.

You're spectacular. Feeling smug I finally talked to you.

She bit her lip and grinned, then typed out a quick response:

I get that all the time.

Edward's reply was long moments in coming, and reluctantly, Meg tried to refocus on her job. Just in case, though, she silenced her phone and moved it close to her keyboard, where she would see immediately if it lit up again.

May I have the names of the last 5 people u got that from plz?

Meg giggled, then quickly stifled it and glanced over her shoulder. Mr. Boudreau was on the phone, loud and boisterous as usual, though she could tell it was his fake cheer and that he did not actually know or like the individual he was talking to. No one else seemed to be around. Another text came in, hot on the heels of the first.

Also did I mention I used 2 be in the Army? I'm a dab hand w/ a
rifle.

Her cheeks were beginning to hurt from smiling so much. He
was just messing with her, obviously. But...

Really??

...she tapped. Because, seriously, the thought of that gorgeous
man in a uniform was almost too much to handle. Seconds later,
he texted back.

Yes! More on Sat. Gotta run - XO

Meg quickly thanked him for the flowers, added a dorky
winking emoticon, then sighed in happiness. She stared blankly at
her computer screen until she heard the pointed sound of throat-
clearing from behind her. Spinning around quickly, and apparently
guiltily, she spotted Joe Boudreau leaning against her doorframe,
looking between her and the flowers. He didn't say a word, just
handed her a folder and raised one inquisitive brow at her. Meg
felt her face flame in an instantaneous hot flush. Her boss dimpled
at the sight, pushed off from her doorway, and sauntered off,
whistling merrily.

Damn. Busted.

On Tuesday, Edward only made it until two p.m. before he
texted her.

Is it my imagination or is this week excruciatingly long?

By Wednesday, he'd thrown in the towel. His text came at nine
a.m. sharp, and read:

I can't wait till Sat. Meet me 2nite after work?

So here Meg was, having barely made it through her day
without losing her mind, walking the three blocks to the Japanese
restaurant he'd chosen near her office. He'd wanted to pick Meg
up outside her building, but after the ribbing she'd been getting
from her boss all week, the thought of Joe spotting her getting into
a car with Edward just couldn't be endured. Somehow, Meg just

knew Edward would be the chivalrous, door-holding type. Actually, wait. She did know that for a fact—he'd held doors for her all weekend, for crying out loud. When Meg had demurred on the ride, Edward came up with this restaurant, as close to her office as it could possibly be while still having edible food. She'd stopped in the ladies room on her way out to touch up her makeup. It was tricky, this time of day, to hit that golden middle ground between hung over and trying too hard, and Meg had no clue whether she had managed it.

When she approached the front of the restaurant, Edward was there waiting, watching for her expectantly as she rounded the corner. His face broke into a huge smile when he spotted her. In three long strides, he reached Meg and hauled her into a tight hug.

"Hey. Thanks for meeting me," he said into her hair, as if she was the one doing him a favor.

"Of course," she laughed. "Thanks for the invite."

He pulled back and planted a loud kiss on her, before touching her back to usher her inside the restaurant. Meg had to say, this guy was checking all the boxes in the affection department, and she *loved* it. Her parents were cold, reserved types, but not her big sister Morgan. Morgan had always been a hugging and kissing fool, lavishing sloppy affection on Meg from the day she was born. And now that Morgan was gone, Meg realized that she'd been missing that physical connection with someone. She squeezed Edward's hand, and was rewarded with an instant, happy expression and his arm slung across her shoulders.

Meg smiled and looked around. The restaurant was like a dark little oasis, its warmth welcome after her chilly walk here. Soft music played, and other than the quiet murmurs of the other diners, the only sounds came from little tinkling fountains set among the plants lining the half wall of the entry area. Now that the sun had gone down, the temperature outside was dropping and the front windows were beginning to fog up, totally cutting off the serenity inside from the rush hour traffic speeding by on the street. Meg hummed in happiness. This was the perfect end to her day.

Edward was casting sidelong glances at her as they were guided to a table in the corner.

"You look great," he said, gesturing to her work outfit.

Meg looked down at herself. It was always a bit of a challenge to cobble together appropriate outfits for work from the odds and ends of clothing in her closet. She was glad that she had worn one of her better get-ups today. Edward, as usual, looked effortlessly polished in a button-down shirt and nice wool pants. As she watched, he unbuttoned his cuffs and rolled his sleeves up his forearms. Her mouth went dry. *Why would that be such a turn-on?* Meg wondered. It wasn't like he was stripping over there. Still, the effect of it was striking. Intimate. His eyes glowed as he studied her face expectantly.

Right. She was supposed to say something back. "Oh! Thank you," she blurted out. "Um, you too." God. Could she be any worse at this?

But Edward remained unperturbed, going about ordering and making small talk as if Meg was the most interesting woman in the world, and he was just lucky to be sitting here with her. It boggled her mind, and she struggled to keep up. He asked her questions, he made comments, and Meg...reacted. If she didn't get her head straight, she was never going to find out the answers to any of the burning questions that had been keeping her up at night.

So at the next lull in conversation, Meg gathered her courage and launched her (admittedly weak) offensive.

Clearing her throat, she said, "So, the Army, huh?"

Edward looked up from admiring his beautifully arranged plate of sushi. His eyes crinkled at the corners, amused. He nodded in encouragement.

"And you're a crack shot?" Another nod.

"Wow. That's impressive. Did you join up..." she frowned, trying to work out the logistics. "Before or after college? How did that work?"

"I did four years at university as an undergrad, then two years in the service. Then I came here with my family for grad school."

Meg nodded. "And your job was—rifles?" she fumbled. This wasn't exactly her area of expertise—she didn't even know what to ask him.

"Essentially. My particular regiment has a tradition, a history so to speak, as sharpshooters," Edward told her. "Most of it was ceremonial stuff," he explained. "I didn't see any action or anything."

"Still, I'd love to see a picture of you in uniform," Meg admitted bashfully.

"Would you?" He brightened. "I have a few. I could show them to you on Saturday."

Saturday. She'd been wondering about Saturday. But if she admitted that, would she sound too eager? The more she learned about Edward, the more Meg liked him. And the more she liked him, the more she worried that she was going to mess this up and lose him. It was no way to conduct a budding relationship, she thought grimly, but sucking at things was rapidly becoming her specialty.

"That sounds good. Do you still want to get together then?" There. That had sounded nice and casual. Not desperate at all.

Edward scowled comically at her. "Of course, I still want to. You didn't think tonight was *instead* of Saturday, did you?" He pointed his chopsticks at her accusingly.

Meg shrugged, embarrassed. "I wasn't exactly sure."

"Well, I'm sure," he declared hotly. "I'm very sure."

"Okay. Fine. Where should we go?" Meg smiled, to placate him. Her worry over affording any of these outings was starting to wane a bit. Every time she offered to pitch in, he turned her down flat. He wasn't even willing to negotiate, and the more she insisted, the less well he took it. So, she'd resolved to accept his generosity with some semblance of grace. Even if he was really cute when he was disgruntled.

"I'd thought Italian," Edward mused. "There's a great place near my house. Would you like that?"

"Yeah. That would be great," Meg agreed.

"And then after, maybe we could walk over, and I could show you my house if you wanted." His knee was bobbing up and down under the table, and he toyed with his little porcelain cup of tea. "I could show you those photos."

Meg examined him. He looked…nervous? Edward, nervous? The possibility that she wasn't the only one reeling from all this giddy wonderfulness drifted into her mind. It didn't seem likely, but the evidence certainly appeared to be there. It gave her the bravado she needed.

"Not your etchings?" she teased.

"Not my—" he choked out a laugh. "No. I promise—no sordid etchings."

"Okay, then." Meg grinned.

Edward grinned back. "Okay." Then, he seemed to be steeling himself for another risk. He cleared his throat, stretched his neck, and added, "And, uh, maybe before dinner we can meet up with my brothers for a drink." He delivered the last few words in a rush, as if he'd had to force them out before they got stuck in his throat.

"Your brothers?" Meg squeaked. "All three of them?"

"Well, only George and Charlie. Freddy's a bit young to be haunting the pubs."

She gaped at him.

Edward turned slightly pink. "I, uh, might have mentioned you." He coughed, unconvincingly. "Once or twice."

Meg's brain had staggered to a painful halt, as it caught up with what was transpiring. Edward had just invited her to his house after dinner Saturday. They'd be alone. In *private*. If she was lucky, maybe there would be more kissing. More *other things*. She gulped down some water. But before that, she had to meet his brothers. Curiosity warred with panic in her brain, short-circuiting rational thought. Edward jumped into the breach.

"Don't worry, they will adore you. They always hounded our mum for a sister, believe me," he reassured her.

As he paid the bill and they gathered up their jackets, Meg knew there was only one response to be made.

"Okay. Yeah. Sure," she managed, somewhat inadequately.

Edward beamed. "Brilliant."

In a blast of frigid air, they were out the door and standing on the sidewalk. He pulled her close. "Let me drive you home. It's gotten cold," he murmured in her ear as she shivered.

Right on cue, a T rattled by on its tracks, windows glowing bright in the darkness. The thought of waiting for the next train at the lonely stop across the street was not an appealing one.

Edward's hot breath tickled her ear. "Please," he urged her.

What was she worried about? Her intuition about people wasn't *that* skewed.

"That would be nice," she admitted. He led her up the block, and as they walked, she said, "Oh! I meant to tell you. I called over to BU today. Guess who has returned to China?"

"Not Li Wei?" he asked, fake horror coloring his features in the dim light.

"I'm afraid so," Meg confessed. "I got one of the kids working in the registrar's office to tell me."

"That's terrific. Now you can wear the infamous coat on Saturday for our big date. It's supposed to get even colder." Edward pulled his keys from his jacket pocket and hit a button. The lights of a gleaming black BMW blinked, and its alarm chirped. He walked up and pulled open the passenger door for her, giving her a hand as she lowered herself into the seat. He trotted around the front of the car and slid in beside her.

Meg gazed at him. This absolutely beat the train, hands down. The engine roared to life. "Very nice," she remarked, as her tan leather seat began to warm up, and the vents blew hot air at her feet.

He glanced at her, then checked his mirrors before he pulled out into traffic. "Thank you," he replied, distracted as he cut across the lanes and turned to head in the opposite direction.

"I mean, it's no T, I'll tell you. But it's a really close second," she joked.

"Naturally," he laughed. "I guess I figured, Boston is one of the most frightful places to drive. Why not be comfortable?"

"Yeah, why not?" she teased.

He didn't pick up on her sarcasm. "Rome is worse, of course, but still..."

Meg had to laugh. This guy was too much. "Have you driven in Rome?" she inquired.

"Tragically. It was a trauma I hope never to repeat," Edward said sorrowfully.

He executed a U-turn across the train tracks cutting up the median, and moments later they pulled up in front of her building. Meg was amazed at how short the trip had been—it took much longer when she had to ride the train.

"Where are you?" He pointed up, eyeing the imposing stone structure that took up most of the block. "Third floor, right?"

"Yup," she agreed. "I'm over there, on the side. Front corner."

He nodded, studying the building as if scouting it for an ambush. "It looks different in the dark."

He walked her up the wide front steps of her building, then followed her into the vestibule as she fished around in her bag for her keys. When Meg looked up, he was closer than she'd realized. And he had a smoldering look in his eyes.

She smiled and bit her bottom lip, swaying closer to him. She'd been looking forward to this all night. He slipped his hands inside her jacket and gripped her waist, pulling her against him. Leaning down to her, his eyelashes looked outrageously long against his cheeks.

"May I kiss you good night, Meg Flynn?" he breathed, just inches from her lips.

In answer, she raised up on her toes and closed the distance for him. The air was cool, but his mouth was warm. His lips pressed to hers slowly, as if he was lost in some languid, erotic dream. And then he opened his mouth and slid his tongue along hers, savoring the taste of her. Edward didn't lose his head, and he didn't kiss her for long. But what he'd done had been plenty sexy. When he stepped back from her, Meg's knees were weak.

"I'll see you Saturday evening, then?" Edward confirmed.

"Yes. Saturday," Meg conceded, all aglow. She unlocked the foyer door and stepped through. He dropped one more urgent kiss on her, and then he was gone, trotting down the steps and waving as he got in his fancy car.

Chapter Five

EDWARD COULDN'T RESIST. The texting had gone so brilliantly for him earlier in the week, so on Thursday he'd sent Meg one that said,

Longest Thursday in the history of time.

It had felt that way, anyway, and his desire to be coy about his feelings for her had gone out the window a full week ago. And then on Friday:

Light at the end of the tunnel. I'd kidnap you 2nite but working late.

That was true, unfortunately. His father had set up a meeting with some colleague he'd rounded up at an architecture association fete. The man had a new, younger wife, and together they'd purchased an old place up on Beacon Hill. According to Edward's father, the seller was an elderly widow who had let the place fall into near ruin, and the buyers were hoping for an entire overhaul. Even so, Edward was looking forward to taking a peek at it. As he understood things, it was over one hundred and fifty years old, with many of its original trimmings. George had been all but drooling at the chance to get his hands on the place. And the meeting had gone smoothly, despite the couple's initial discomfort with his and George's relative youth. Still, the commission they'd walked away with was likely due more to their father—he'd genially insisted on sitting in on the meeting, and that seemed to assuage the couple eventually.

We just loved what you did with that Denver property, Mrs. Anderson had cooed.

Yes, well, Beacon Hill has quite a different scale, wouldn't you agree? their dad had deflected. *My head's full of futuristic rubbish, but my boys here know what they're about when it comes to an historical place like yours.*

The Andersons had accepted that graciously enough. They seemed the type to name-drop about who had re-done their house, and now they could.

Saturday had passed by at a crawl, even with the distraction of picking up his order from Hathaway, the pottery dealer on Newbury Street. He didn't know yet when he'd give Meg her gift. Probably soon—he wasn't getting high marks in patience these days. But he'd bought himself something, too, on a whim. When his eyes had fallen on the huge, rough-hewn bowl, he couldn't help remembering how her fingers had trailed along its edge last weekend. And he'd wanted it, wanted to keep remembering the sight, every time he looked at it. Edward envisioned it placed right in the center of a low square coffee table in his front parlor, where the light would stream in the bay window, illuminating every lovely imperfection in the surface of the pottery. He didn't exactly have the table yet, but eventually he would. And maybe Meg would have a hand in that, too.

He'd been thinking of all that when he showed up too early at her house Saturday evening. Thinking of her delicate fingers, and of her kisses. Once again, he'd had no trouble slipstreaming through that locked vestibule door. When he knocked, ten minutes earlier than their appointed time, Meg hadn't looked terribly surprised.

"How did you get in *this* time?" she huffed.

"A very nice old lady let me in, once she spotted these," he admitted, handing her the blowsy, fragrant bunch of peonies he held. They'd cost him a pretty penny, out of season as they were, but Edward could easily picture them on the windowsill next to her bed.

"I'm beginning to think the security at this place is not what it could be," she had murmured, burying her nose in the blooms.

"No, I'm just really charming," he'd teased, moving in on her. It was a good thing they had time. Actually leaving her apartment proved challenging. Driving was even worse.

But now, finally, he had Meg's small hand in his own as they walked up the block. She looked spectacular as usual, in a soft black turtleneck sweater that zipped up the front, straight black wool skirt, and high caramel-colored boots. The narrow sliver of skin he'd spotted between the hem of her skirt and the top of the boots had been driving him half mad the whole drive here. The pale skin flashed again now, as they descended the stairs to the pub, teasing his peripheral vision. She'd grown quiet as he parked the car down the block and looked nervous as hell.

"Don't worry," he whispered. "Our dinner reservations are at seven. They can only torture us for an hour at most."

Perhaps "torture" wasn't the ideal word choice. Meg looked a little ill. But the pub was loud and crowded and warm inside, Irish rock thumping and glasses clinking. It was hard not to feel festive. George and Charlie spotted them right off and beckoned from their stools at the bar lining the brick wall. And there was Freddy...Freddy? What was Fred doing here? Fred was twelve bloody years old. They were all three grinning like Bedlamites. Suddenly, Edward wasn't so sure about this. He turned and shielded Meg with his body, so they couldn't see her yet.

"This will be fine," he assured her loudly, so she'd hear him over the music. "Just follow my lead." He hoped he sounded believable. Frankly, he wouldn't put anything past those lads, though it would surprise him if they were outright cruel. He didn't think they had *that* in them, but even so, Edward was abruptly feeling protective.

Meg nodded and gripped his hand, ready to face the wolves.

"Oi, Ed!" Charlie yelled, keeping a low profile as usual. "Over here!"

George raked Meg with an appreciative, assessing gaze when they approached, before folding her into a half-hug. "You must be Meg, then. Pleasure to meet you. I'm George."

She was flushed, Edward noticed, whether from the warmth of the room or from shyness, it was hard to say.

"I'm Charlie. How do you do," his other brother bellowed. He leaned forward. "Here you go, sweetheart." He handed her a sweating pint that looked enormous in her hand. "You look like you could use this."

Not to be outdone by the older lads, Freddy leaned in and stuck his hand in Meg's face. Edward told her, "And this is Freddy. I am not entirely clear on what Freddy is doing here. Apparently certain individuals have lost their bloody minds."

"*Freddy* is here to spy for *mum*, you arseface," Freddy retorted, as if that were a perfectly reasonable explanation for his presence. Turning back to Meg, he added, "Our mum always wanted a girl, you see. Do you think you might stick around? Edward's a bit bossy, but he grows on you."

Meg coughed out a surprised laugh. "Yes, I'd noticed that," she told him. "How old are you again?"

George and Charlie chimed in together, "He's twelve," at the same time Freddy said, "Thirteen." George and Charlie were looking supremely pleased with themselves, despite Edward's efforts to glare them into submission. Freddy wasn't noticing a blasted thing, what with the way he was dividing his attention between Meg's legs and the drunk girls carousing at the end of the bar. Edward was readying himself to wade into the fray and try to keep this from getting even more cocked up than it already was, when his bloody father showed up.

"Hey, mates," his dad said, sidling up to the group, casual as you please. "Anyone want to explain how you got Fred in here?"

Suddenly George and Charlie weren't looking so smug. Their father hauled his youngest son off his stool with an iron grip on his bicep, picked up the boy's glass and sniffed at its contents, and then, only then, did he look at Meg. And look again. Edward bumped him with his shoulder to get his attention, and possibly to keep him from making a royal arse out of himself.

"Right, then." The man seemed to gather his wits, without releasing his hold on Freddy. "And who have we here?" He looked from Edward to Meg and back again.

"That's Meg, Dad. Edward's new lady friend," Charlie explained. George had turned aside to field a come-on from a woozy looking brunette.

"Ah. Just so. Lovely little thing, aren't you? Pleased to meet you, Meg," he declared, as if this were all some pleasant surprise, instead of a carefully orchestrated tactical assault by Edward's entire family. He glanced toward the front door warily, expecting his mum to whisk in at any moment, Burberry scarf thrown about her shoulders, and a Hermes bag dangling from her elegant wrist.

"You too, sir," Meg replied, her hand engulfed in his father's large paw. She looked a little shell-shocked, poor thing. Edward *should* have anticipated this.

"Meg, this is my dad," he began, not entirely sure how it would play if he called him "Alistair Hughes." His brothers would certainly smell a rat and would be all over him for it. He extricated Meg's hand from his father's, since the man hadn't seen fit to release her yet.

"Call me Westbroke," his dad interjected cheerfully, before Edward could finish. As in, *The Earl of.* Bugger it. Edward was going to have to cry uncle and end this farce before things got any worse. One stray "my lord" from Charlie, and he would have to break someone's face. He took Meg's untouched beer from her other hand and set it on the bar.

She turned to him, perplexed. "Didn't you say your last name was—"

"All right, well that's that," Edward blustered, refusing to make eye contact with any of the tossers claiming to be his relations. "We'll have to get going if we're going to make dinner on time."

"Yes, well, we were about to leave too, weren't we, young Fred?" his father inquired dangerously. Freddy was looking a bit green around the gills, now. At the moment, Edward was rather glad not to be him.

Bless her, but Meg wasn't going to argue the point. "Sorry," she sang, not sounding sorry in the least. "Nice to meet you all!"

Charlie chuckled. "Cowards," he barked merrily. George had disappeared, presumably to slink off with the brunette.

Edward leaned down to growl in Meg's ear, "Out. Before it's too late." Behind her back, he made an exceedingly rude gesture at his brother, then chivvied her along toward the door. Fred might have managed a retaliatory kick to the back of his leg, but Edward wasn't sure of it—the place *was* an awful crush.

Little Meg needed no encouragement. She towed him along behind her, plowing a path through the crowd like she was parting the Red Sea. Once they'd breached the door and dashed up the stairs to the street, Edward had calmed enough to stop her flight. He turned her toward him, and her expression was absolutely priceless. One part amusement, four parts astonishment. She laughed, a crazed, panicked sound.

"Oh my God," she gasped. "What the hell was that?"

Edward just shook his head in resignation. "That," he told her, "Was my barmy family. My apologies."

She just shook her head, then thought to look at her watch. "Oh geez, what are we going to do for the next forty minutes?"

He kissed her with no small amount of desperation, pointed her down the street toward the restaurant, and herded her along. "Come on, love, we'll sit at the bar. I need a damn drink."

"Man after my own heart," Meg muttered.

Chapter Six

MEG HAD NO idea how she'd made it through dinner. When they arrived at the restaurant, Edward had knocked back a scotch at the bar with somewhat alarming alacrity. Once he'd done that, he seemed to shake off the mood his family had left him in, and he leveled his laser-like focus on her. Meg was glad she'd worn the outfit she had, one of her sister's castoffs that she hadn't needed to mail to Christchurch. It made her feel more grown-up than she actually was, like maybe she belonged here in this swanky place. Belonged across the table from this incredible guy. He was gorgeous in the soft candlelight, the planes of his square jaw illuminated, the line of his nose straight and elegant. His cologne, too, was driving her a little crazy, making Meg want to bury her face in his neck and stay there. The soft tawny gold of his eyes was hard to see in the dimness, but the expression in them wasn't that difficult to decipher. Meg had no doubt what he had in mind for when they decamped to his house. If her head hadn't already been reeling from whatever had happened in that pub, it would be from the smoldering looks he'd been sending her way.

She inhaled her pumpkin ravioli, barely registering how delicious it was. Edward ate something with fettuccine, she thought, and maybe veal. Now he sat across from her, pushed back from the table and drumming his fingers as they awaited their coffee and dessert. Meg hadn't thought she could wait another second to have this agony over with, but when the server asked if she wanted anything else, the words had come barreling out of her mouth. Panic, she supposed. Stalling. She was both desperate to be alone with him, and desperate to delay the moment when he might discover her wanting. A head case, over-thinking everything as usual. She needed a distraction.

"So, you didn't mention where you live. Is your place somewhere on Newbury Street?" *Well, that was subtle*, Meg castigated herself. *He'll never guess what you're thinking now.* She blundered ahead before he could answer, "I've always loved those places—I don't know why. It would be so cool to live upstairs from one of the shops, don't you think?"

Edward smiled at her. "Absolutely. Unfortunately, a lot of them have been split up into smaller units, some studios, some offices, that sort of thing. My place is a couple blocks away. I bought it last year, and we've been trying to fix it up in between the paying jobs. I hope you don't mind—it's still a mess," he explained. "We've gotten most of the utility room issues sorted, but it's still a bit dusty while we shore up the plaster work. After that, we'll refinish the floors, and I can start getting some furniture in there." He eyed her expectantly, and Meg thought about what he'd said. A warning, she assumed, that his bachelor pad would be untidy and lacking finesse. But who was he kidding? He'd seen her place. What could be worse than that? And then she had another thought. Edward had bought the place, he said. *Bought* it. As her mind mapped out the neighborhoods a few blocks from Newbury, it occurred to her that maybe his warning was of a different sort entirely. Because Meg had a sneaking suspicion that even in the throes of renovation, his place would be much, much nicer than hers.

Their dessert and coffee arrived, placed before them with flourishes by a waiter wearing a long black apron tied around his waist. Edward didn't seem inclined to linger, though. Before the man could leave them alone, Edward tapped his arm and requested the check. And moments after Meg's last bite of tiramisu had crossed her lips, Edward was up and out of his chair, holding the notorious shearling coat for her to slip on. They bypassed his car as he explained that his garage was currently full of tools and equipment, leaving it parallel parked on the street while they walked the few blocks to his house hand in hand.

And, Meg was stunned to realize, it did appear to be a *house*, not a condo as she'd assumed. He strolled up to a red brick brownstone trimmed in dark, chocolate-colored stone, unlatched the fancy black wrought-iron gate, and waved her through. The small front yard was filled with ivy on both sides of the walk, and large, ornate planters of orange chrysanthemums flanked the tall double doors. A stained-glass fanlight stretched across the top of the entry, and polished brass hardware gleamed from both sides of the double doors. Meg swallowed back her sudden flash of intimidation and followed him slowly up the steps. Edward held open one black lacquered panel for her, then shut it behind them, closing out the outside world. Meg crowded up against him in the small black-and-white tiled vestibule, taking the opportunity to slip her arms around his waist and inhale another lungful of his enticing scent. It calmed her a little. Edward had some kind of strong magnetism, something that urged her to draw in close to his gravitational pull. He chuckled and fumbled the key at the lock, breaking her reverie when he dropped his key ring with a clatter.

"I don't think I ever noticed how, uh, *close* it is in here," he murmured, leaning down to grab his keys.

It wasn't that tight a fit. There was plenty of room for both an umbrella stand, and a small carved wood bench, Meg saw. But she was enjoying turning the tables on him, after he'd had her so riled up during dinner with his heavy-lidded gaze. "It *is* very intimate," she agreed.

Edward had the door unlocked now, but his head dropped back as he peered up at the ceiling.

"God, you smell amazing," he breathed. He turned suddenly on her, scooping her into his arms in a tight embrace, and stroking his tongue hotly into her mouth. He kissed her like a starving man, and though he'd caught her off guard, she wasn't about to complain. Meg held his face in her hands, trying to get her bearings as he delved deep to taste her. But by the time he'd spun her around and lifted her across the threshold, she'd given up taking things slow and had wound her arms around his neck to hold him close. They stood that way for long minutes before Edward finally pulled back and set Meg's feet on the floor of the foyer. He gazed down at her face, breathing hard, then blinked and looked around. He looked nervous, all of a sudden.

"Well. Here it is," he said, voice brisk. "Shall I show you about?"

Meg gaped as she looked around. The front hall was lit softly by a pair of antique sconces flanking the door. The place looked huge, possibly because it appeared to be entirely devoid of any furniture whatsoever. It was, however, dripping with wide white moldings and wainscoting everywhere she looked. The wood floors seemed to be parquet, but they were very dusty and scratched, and Meg couldn't be sure. To their right was a big front room with a wide bay window. Light from the streetlamps spilled in, and Meg spotted a large, shallow stone basin sitting on the floor in the corner of the room. What in the world? Who needed a bowl, but not a couch? She shook her head, turning to where Edward stood shifting on his feet, hands in his pockets. Behind him was another large, empty room—a thick black wire dangled down from the center of an ornate carved medallion on the ceiling in there. Meg could just make it out behind Edward's head.

"Oh my God. It's beautiful," she told him, amazed. And it was—it had a ghostly, otherworldly beauty to it, all stark outlines in hazy shades of gray. "This is all yours?"

He nodded, looking uncertain. "What there is of it. Come on, the kitchen's back here."

Meg toured the formal dining room, with its own bay window to mirror the one in the front parlor (and the black wire evidently where a chandelier would hang), a small guest bath, and a family room at the back of the house, overlooking the river. One floor up, she saw the rooms that would become his home office and a wood-paneled library. None of it took terribly long, since all of the rooms were largely empty, and she noticed that he hadn't yet taken her up to the third or fourth floors, where she presumed the bedrooms must be. But as they went, Edward explained what he and George had done so far, and what he hoped to accomplish next. According to him, there was a basement area too, that fronted the garage bays, but he was uncertain as yet whether to keep it as storage or turn it into a rec room, or even a wine cellar. Meg was flabbergasted that someone her own age could possess something like this. But the feeling was rapidly supplanted by her awe at how much Edward clearly revered the place. By how proud he was of their accomplishments thus far. Even if Meg wasn't inclined to love the house on its own merits, she'd have to love it for what it meant to him. A home like this *should* belong to someone like him, she thought. Someone who would appreciate it, and care for it.

Eventually, they ended up back at the narrow galley kitchen. Edward casually lifted her up by the waist and set her on one of the stools pulled up to the bar, then rounded the half wall to pour her a glass of wine in the kitchen.

"Sorry I don't have a couch for you to sit on yet," he apologized. He slid a glass across the bar to her, then toyed with the stem of his own glass, watching her.

"It's okay," Meg reassured him. "I mean, come on. You've seen my place." His little kitchen, at least, was still decidedly pedestrian. She imagined it wouldn't stay that way for long.

He nodded, smiling. "Maybe you can help me pick out some stuff sometime," he told her.

Meg took a sip of the smooth red, then set the glass down with a clink on the old, pitted marble. "I'd like that."

Edward rounded the counter to come stand next to her. "I've never brought anyone but my family here before," he admitted softly.

That gave Meg a little burst of pleasure. "Really?" she asked him.

His hand dropped down to caress the side of her boot. He looked thoughtful. "I don't know. It's odd. I wanted to bring you here almost right away. I feel…comfortable with you, I guess."

"Comfortable enough to kiss me again?" Meg whispered.

He jerked his head up from where he'd been watching his hand move over the leather covering her calf. "You better believe it," he breathed.

He gripped the counter on either side of her, then slanted his mouth over hers. Without the obstacle of being in public, his kiss was akin to dropping a lit match onto a pile of dry kindling. Meg was going up in flames before she even thought twice about it. When Edward finally pulled back from her, his chest was heaving. He rested his forehead against hers, and his lips were just inches away. Meg slid her fingers from where they were twined in his hair to rest on his shoulders, but some masochistic part of her decided to leave her leg hooked around his knee.

"I'm sorry, Meg, I'm having a little trouble controlling myself. I'm really, wildly attracted to you," he laughed, his breath rushing hot across her lips. "God, I've been thinking about Wednesday night all week long," he admitted.

Meg closed her eyes and thought, unsure what he was trying to tell her. Was this an *I want you, but I shouldn't* kind of apology? Or was Edward just looking for some kind of a sign from her, some hint of what she wanted?

"I don't think I want to control myself," she said quietly.

He drew back, looking hopeful. "Are you sure?" he asked, his accent seeming stronger now.

Meg nodded, and he closed the distance between them again, kissing her soundly. After a moment or so, she broke off, gasping, "There's just one thing. No—two things."

Edward looked concerned. "Okay." He held himself back, but his fingers still gripped her waist tightly, ready to pull her close as soon as possible.

Meg felt herself flush a little. "Any, um, diseases or anything, that I should…"

Edward was already shaking his head. "Clean as a whistle," he smiled, eyes creasing at the corners.

"Me too," Meg said.

"And?"

"Oh. Well, I don't know if you have any, uh…" she trailed off, and he looked confused. "What I mean is that I'm not on anything. I'm not, um, protected," she managed to squeak out. Yeah, she was a real romantic, Meg thought, groaning to herself. It was a wonder the dudes weren't dropping like flies at her feet. But still— it had to be done.

His furrowed brow smoothed out as understanding dawned. And then, charmingly, he flushed bright red, too.

"I hope you don't think I'm too presumptuous," he began, managing to reach over to their coats piled on the counter and freeing his wallet from his jacket pocket. "But I allowed myself a tiny bit of hope that you'd be willing sometime soon." He withdrew two condoms and dropped them on the counter next to her.

"Oh, I think it's safe to say I'm willing," Meg laughed, hugging him to her.

"That's two of us," Edward snorted. His fingers played with the tab of her sweater's zipper, and he began to inch it slowly down. His eyes watched avidly, as each new inch was revealed. When he'd freed the last edge, he slipped his palms in against her neck and pushed the two sides wide. Meg shrugged it off her shoulders, letting the thick, warm cashmere slip down her arms to hit the floor. Edward was studying the lacey camisole she wore underneath, even touched a finger softly to one thin strap, but apparently decided against removing it for now. Instead, he crouched in front of her, and took one booted foot onto his thigh. He eased the zipper down along the inside of the boot, then slipped it off her foot and placed it beside him on the floor. He glanced fleetingly up at her, then smoothed her high wool knee sock down her leg as erotically as if it were a silk thigh-high stocking. Edward repeated the action with her other leg, then held her calves in his warm hands as he smoothed his thumbs over her tattoos, one on the inside of each ankle. Based on the hungry look on his face, Meg's guess was that he liked what he was seeing.

"Nice," he told her, rising to his feet. "Could you *get* any more perfect?"

Meg bit her lip. "Now you," she said, studying his crisply pressed dress shirt and trying to imagine it gone.

Edward was a clever man. He took one look at her face, then wrenched the shirt up and out of his waistband. He fumbled with the buttons at his cuffs, then attacked the ones marching down the placket with his long, elegant fingers. Meg slid her foot along the side of his wool pant leg, urging him closer with her heel. He had his pristine white undershirt up and over his head with lightning precision, then was reaching for her with lean, muscled arms.

Meg didn't have much chance to ogle what appeared to be a finely chiseled torso, sprinkled with assorted tattoos across his upper chest and biceps. He enfolded her in his arms and tilted her head so he could suck at her neck, sending a jolt of desire straight through her. Edward shoved her skirt higher on her thighs, pushing his way closer between her legs. Meg, feeling very helpful, wrapped them around his hips, and he rewarded her with a slow and sexy grind against her. She sighed. It didn't get much better than a classy, smart guy who was secretly kind of dirty.

Edward's lips were hot against her ear. "I dreamed about you on Tuesday," he murmured.

Meg was concentrating on the way his hand was sliding high up her leg. The best she could manage was, "Hmm?"

"You were here, walking through the house in front of me," he continued. "You kept looking back over your shoulder at me, laughing and smiling, and I was following you, trying to catch you..." He nipped at her earlobe, then sucked away the sting. "It was such a good dream, Meg, I..."

Meg forced a sound from her throat, but she didn't think it was an actual word. She tried again. "Like tonight? Was it like showing me around tonight?" Did her voice sound lower? Huskier?

He shook his head and lavished some more attention on her neck and collarbone with his mouth. "No, not like tonight. There was furniture in the house, and other voices." He paused, clearly editing, "I could hear them in the other rooms. And I knew that you and I..." he trailed off again, searching for words.

"You and I—what?" Meg breathed, dying to know.

"We knew each other better," Edward finished. He looked into her eyes, and the heat there set Meg to burning, too. "I find you exquisite," he said intently. "In every way."

"You, too," she whispered.

"This is probably going to sound totally Victorian, but—will you come upstairs with me?" he asked carefully, biting his lip. "I want to make love to you."

Meg nodded. "I thought you'd never ask," she grinned.

Edward growled. He *growled*. The sound of it shot straight to the heart of her like a bolt of lightning. And then Meg was airborne, slung over his bare shoulder laughing her ass off, as he charged with her up the winding back stairs. Two flights, without even getting winded.

"Wait!" she shrieked. "Do you even have a bed?"

On the third floor, he turned toward the back of the house and maneuvered them into a large bedroom containing a mattress and box spring made up in the corner, and a rickety-looking chair off to the side. A small lamp, set on the floor near the head of the bed, burned dimly once he flicked the light switch.

"Here we are," he said cheerily. "I think I'll just set this right here." With that, Edward dumped her back on the bed, and Meg landed with a hard *thump,* right in the middle of a down and flannel cloud.

She gasped out a laugh, gazing up at him towering over her.

"Oh, wow," was what he said. He looked around the room, letting out a big breath, then back down at her.

"What it lacks in…in…" he gestured with his arm, an all-encompassing arc.

"Utility?" Meg offered.

"In *everything*, I plan to make up for with ardor," Edward told her. He extracted the condoms he'd shoved in his pocket and tossed them on the floor next to her head. Regarding her with blazing eyes where she sprawled smiling in the middle of his bed, he began divesting himself of the rest of his clothes. By the time he'd gotten down to his boxers, Meg's eyebrows felt like they were hitting her hairline. Edward, it turned out, was quite the male specimen. Taut and lean and muscled, the colorful tattoos on his chest standing out vividly against his pale skin. He crouched down and crawled toward her, taking the time to slip off her skirt and camisole on his way to her neck.

He planted hot, avid kisses up the underside of her jaw, before taking her mouth with his own. But he'd obviously remembered her lingerie, because he broke off suddenly to admire it.

"Ardor's good," Meg managed to gasp out, watching him trail his fingertips along the ivory lace edging her bra, before he moved down to caress the lace along her waistband. She'd found this set just last month, at Filene's Basement. It had seemed like an irresponsible waste of money at the time, but she'd been so taken with the way the darker taupe silk contrasted with the light-colored lace. It had seemed so decadent. So pretty. Meg had *yearned* to have it, and now—now she knew why. Edward's admiration of it was making her heart pound in her chest.

He rolled her gently over onto her stomach, and she shivered as his fingers released the clasp of her bra. She raised herself up, kneeling on the soft bed to slip off the bra and toss it aside. Meg reached down to slide off her panties, and immediately felt his large hands cover hers, helping her out of them. And then his palms returned, covering her breasts and pulling her back against his chest as he pressed his hot, hard length against her rear. He'd lost his boxers at some point, and the feel of all that scorching male skin against hers was inflammatory. Meg dropped her head back against his shoulder and sighed, the sound echoing loudly against the bare walls. Not having to look him in the face was helping her let her guard down. Without having to see his expression, his reactions, she didn't feel the need to evaluate the effect of her every move. She could just feel.

Edward groaned, "*Meg*. God, Meg," into her ear. With one hand, he cupped her chin, turning her head so he could kiss her again. And then his other hand dropped down to slip between her legs. Meg jumped at the sensation, and Edward chuckled into her mouth.

"Like that, do you?" he murmured. "So do I."

His fingers dragged across her folds, and she heard him swallow loudly. "You're so beautiful, Meg. So soft and hot. And…wet," he breathed. His voice had gone deep and husky.

He reached to the side of the bed, and Meg looked down to see him grabbing for one of the condoms. Her back felt cool without him pressed against it, and she shuddered again, unable to stop it. But suddenly Edward was there, flopped on his back next to her, eyes shining as he pulled her down on top of him. And it was the most natural thing in the world to grip him with her knees as he slid into her. The easiest thing, to arch against him and take him deep. Edward groaned and squeezed his eyes shut, his hands sliding to her hips with unerring precision. He gripped her tight as they found their rhythm. Meg couldn't take her eyes off the sight of such a self-possessed man, so utterly lost. For her, *because* of her. It seemed unfathomable, but there it was, splayed out beneath her in glorious disarray.

Edward might not have been quite as lost in the moment as she'd thought. Or maybe he'd sensed her galloping thoughts and wanted to rein them in, because in the space of a heartbeat, Meg was mystified to find herself flipped flat on her back with a hulking, arrogant Englishman buried deep inside of her.

"Hullo there," he smirked down at her. "Fancy meeting you here."

Meg's reply was incoherent at best, since he'd followed that comment up nicely by driving into her with long, hard, steady strokes, forearms propped beside her head. Before long, they were both tearing across the finish line, their guttural cries loud in the empty room. Edward collapsed heavily against her, rolling to the side to spare her his weight, but clutching her close to his chest. They tried to catch their breath, heartbeats thundering against each other as they lay tangled side by side.

Finally, Meg recovered enough to say, "That was..." She stopped helplessly, unable to summon an adequate adjective.

Edward smiled and peppered her face with quick, light kisses. "That *was*," he agreed.

Chapter Seven

EDWARD KNELT ON the edge of the mattress and gazed down at Meg, sound asleep with one arm flung beside her head. He set down the two steaming coffee mugs he held, placing them on a magazine on the floor. Then he sat back on his heels and just enjoyed the view. It wasn't often he got to do this. If he stared too long and she realized, it embarrassed Meg terribly. She would blush a furious red, and while that, in and of itself, charmed him, he did not much enjoy her obvious discomfort.

Edward had plenty of time to enjoy the sight of her now. Between the lack of sleep the night before, and the soporific effect of his bed, Meg wouldn't be waking any time soon. God love her, she hadn't batted an eye to find, last night, that his mattress and single lamp both rested on the bare wood floor. And though he had a chair, one chair only, it was a dodgy wood one that he'd discovered in the basement, and had to be over a hundred years old. As yet, there was no other furniture up here, much like the rest of his house. Much like her own apartment, for that matter.

However, Edward had managed to pick out a splendid mattress set, and down pillows and a comforter. He had figured that out after four uncomfortable nights in a sleeping bag on the floor, his first in the house. He'd been that enthusiastic to move in, to soak up the light and the feel of the place before he decided what he wanted to do to it. His darling mum was not to be outdone and had outfitted him with thick flannel sheets once the weather had turned. She'd added in a coordinating flannel duvet in navy blue plaid to complete the effect she wanted for him. Edward had to admit the woman knew her bedding, and always had. The resulting cocoon was deliciously warm and cozy, as every bed she'd ever made for him had been, back in Britain. Edward loved sleeping in this bed and despised the chilly gray mornings that required him to leave it. Except now, when his days held the promise of seeing Meg—that helped dramatically in the waking-up department. However, actually having her *here* in his bed with him might make it difficult to get anything done elsewhere ever again.

He eyed Meg's arm, so pale against the dark sheets that she seemed to glow. An ethereal goddess, sent to him as some unearned, but no less appreciated, prize. That soft, light brown hair of hers had a silvery sort of cast to it at this hour, a fairy glint that accentuated her otherworldliness. The lighter blond streaks glinted like frost. Suddenly, he was dying for her to wake up. Edward wanted to see her eyes, her smile, *now*. Wanted, in that moment, incontrovertible proof that this vision of Meg was *real*, and not just something he'd conjured up.

He lay beside her and fitted himself along her back, brushing her hair aside, and putting his lips near her ear.

"I am so happy you're here," he purred.

She shifted and murmured back, "I'm happy to be here, too." At least, he thought that was what she said. It was hard to understand, what with her face mashed into his pillow.

She seemed inclined to lapse back into sleep and he didn't want that, so Edward asked, "Really?"

Meg moved her head to the side. "Really," she smiled, but she didn't open her eyes. Yet.

Being tangled up with her long, soft limbs, warm beneath the covers, was an enticement no sane man could ignore. In Meg's company, Edward was decidedly *not* sane. In fact, he couldn't remember ever being this mad for a girl.

He whispered in her ear, "After all those nights laying here hard and restless, and thinking of everything I wanted to do with you, this is a nice switch."

"Mmmmm," she hummed. "I don't know, I caved pretty quickly."

"And then," he barreled on, "There were all the mornings where I woke up *still* hard and restless, and thinking of the things I wanted to do with you."

Meg tried to placate him. "We did things last night. Lots of things," she mumbled.

"There are more things," Edward informed her agreeably. "Lots more." He pressed against her in emphasis. She had to feel the state he was in—regardless of his pajama bottoms, she was still bare as the day she was born.

She contemplated that, eyes still resolutely closed, before inquiring, "Is this the part where you explain morning erections to me?"

He chuckled. "Heard about those, have you?"

"Once or twice," Meg admitted archly.

"It's a real thing," he argued.

"I believe you," she countered.

Edward didn't think that she did, but he kissed her anyway. His Meg was obviously not a morning person, and God only knew why he found *that* so ridiculously endearing.

After a few moments, Meg managed to pry her eyes open. "These *other things* that you mentioned," she began.

"Yes?"

"Do any of them involve coffee? Because I could swear I smell coffee," she commented.

Edward grinned. He might have, in his enthusiasm for her presence here, neglected a solid night's sleep last night for the both of them. But he just couldn't resist one more salvo.

"What's it worth to you?"

Meg snorted in amusement. "A *lot*. You fiend."

"Then kiss me," he offered.

"In a minute," she retorted, squeezing her eyes shut again. The sun was slanting in the windows, reflecting off the tops of cars in the alley, or maybe even the Charles flowing past the back of the house, and making patterns on his ceiling.

"Alright," he relented. "You stay right here. I'll be back in a sec." If he was going to harass the poor thing into kissing him some more, the least he could do was brush his teeth first. "Oh, and the coffee is right next to you."

When he emerged again, Edward's breath lodged in his throat. Meg stood at the window in her knickers and camisole, coffee cup balanced on the radiator, while she gazed out at the crew shells cutting up the river. He knew they were out there—he'd just been looking at the same view from the bathroom window. But she was…she was a vision this way. He exhaled in a rush.

"Blimey. That's an image that will stay with me forever," he said softly.

Meg looked up with a smile in her eyes, but also with a bit of disbelief. Which was it? Edward wondered. Did she think him some kind of loose-lipped Casanova, dropping compliments like rain? Or was it herself she didn't think much of? Something to discover, he thought. Another fact about her to add to his growing collection.

"Can I just hop in there for a minute, too?" she asked, setting the cup up on the wide windowsill and coming toward him self-consciously.

"Of course," Edward answered, and gestured her into the lavatory. "Make yourself at home." He'd left a set of towels folded on the counter for her, as well as a new toothbrush he'd bought, just in case. And he enjoyed the vision of her from the back nearly as much as he had the front.

When Meg returned, he was propped up in bed, drinking his coffee and fielding a flurry of texts, from both George and Charlie, that had rolled in around one o'clock that morning. There was also one from his mum, but he was steadfastly avoiding reading it. Meg hurried across the floor, scooped up her cup, then tucked herself next to him under the covers.

"Oh my God," she gasped, laughing. "It's chilly in here, isn't it?"

He grinned and set his cell aside. "That was on purpose. I'll warm you up, darling."

She turned to him with a smirk, sitting cross-legged with the covers up around her shoulders. Her lovely eyes drifted from his face to his chest and shoulders. Lightly, she touched his biceps with her fingertips.

"Tell me about these," she said.

What was there to say? Edward felt exposed. Too vulnerable. He knew what was coming, knew he wouldn't feel right dissembling with her if she asked him a direct question. But he didn't feel ready, not yet, to stop being Edward to her. *Only* Edward. So, he shook his head and shrugged his shoulders, in the weakest deflection ever attempted.

Meg started out easy, though, tracing the design on his left arm. "This one—there's a crown, and a…powder horn?"

He laughed. "That's a bugle, and St. Edward's crown, ironically. It's the symbol of The Rifles, the Army unit I was in."

"And this? What happened here?" Meg pressed on the streak of shiny pink skin two inches below the tattoo.

"Ah. Well, it was nothing. I just got grazed a bit with a friendly bullet. Not so *Swift and Bold*, as it turned out."

Meg drew back, narrowed her eyes at him. "I thought you said what you did was mostly ceremonial."

"It was. Mostly. Especially after they sent me home for getting shot." He didn't add what effect the ire of a countess had on the situation. Talk about a cock-up—his mates had never let him live it down.

Meg studied him in silence for a long, uncomfortable moment, before deciding that story could wait for another day. She moved on to his other arm.

"This looks like a crest. And there's a word. *Shurso*. Is that Latin?"

Edward steeled himself. This would be where it all fell apart. He took a long draught of his tepid coffee, then launched himself over the cliff.

"No, it's not Latin," he said, hating this. "It's a name."

"Someone you knew?" She traced the crest, peering at it closely.

"No, love. Someone I am," he muttered. God, did he have to sound like such a prick?

Meg frowned. "But your last name is Hughes, I thought. Is it like a nickname? As in—"

"As in, Viscount Shurso," Edward cut in briskly.

Meg's mouth snapped shut, and she sat there blinking rapidly at him. It didn't take long for the other shoe to drop—Edward had no time at all to wonder if she even knew what a bleeding viscount *was*. She poked a steady finger at his chest, at the other family crest he'd so rashly immortalized on his skin. What *had* he been thinking? His mum had been apoplectic when she'd learned of it.

"This one says, *Westbroke*. Who is that?" she inquired. Like a dog with a bone, Meg was.

"That would be the crest of the Earl of Westbroke," he explained stiffly.

"You?" she squeaked, apparently reduced to monosyllabic utterances by the shock.

"My father. As the oldest son, I am his heir. As such, I hold the courtesy title of Viscount Shurso," Edward clarified. "When he dies, I will be Westbroke." He didn't want to look at her, but he couldn't help it. He peeked at her face—Meg was still staring at his chest and seemed to be trying to master her expression.

Finally, she lost the battle and burst out laughing. Laughing? Wait...

"Are you serious? That's hilarious," Meg sputtered out between guffaws.

"It is?" Edward blinked at her. Had they both gone mad without him noticing? Edward peered into his mug. Something in the coffee, perhaps?

"Yeah, kinda," she assured him, grinning from ear to ear.

He took in her loopy expression, and the fact that she seemed wholly unimpressed with his revelation. Edward felt something tight within his chest begin to unknot, and he smiled back, incredulous. He'd expected many things, but humor hadn't been one of them.

"Well, Miss Flynn," he drawled haughtily, "Comical or no, I've still enjoyed making your acquaintance." He gave her a stiff little bow, just for good measure.

"And it's been a *pleasure* to meet you, my...honorable...lord?" she giggled, inclining her head and offering him her hand. He rolled his eyes, but Edward still kissed her hand, gratitude and fervent relief flooding his system.

"Oh, God, please don't do that. It means nothing, I swear," he complained.

"Whatever you say, your honor," she teased, mischief glinting in her eyes. "Oh my God! That's why the guy in the pottery store called you *my lord*," she gasped, the memory coming back to her. "And why your dad told me to call him Westbroke, instead of Mr. Hughes!"

Edward advanced on her, annoyed that she had not only heard, but remembered those details. "Seriously, Meg," he said, narrowing his eyes. "Stop screwing around. It's nothing." Or rather, he *wanted* it to be nothing. At least to her.

She edged her way off the mattress and was backing toward the door, trying not to grin.

"As you wish, your high holiness," she said, executing a sloppy curtsy before a huge chortle burbled out of her.

"That does it," he growled, rising and stalking after her. Meg was taking the main stairs warily, backing down them one at a time, so she could navigate the turn without stumbling. She didn't take her eyes off him, though, just felt for each step with her pretty bare feet.

"Okay, Sir Lofty," she howled, turning and taking off down the staircase at a dead run once she made the turn. "You're the boss," she called up to him, laughing her gorgeous ass off.

"I'll give you Sir Lofty, you little minx," he muttered, adjusting himself in his pajama bottoms and taking off after her.

It hadn't taken *too* much effort to seize his wayward woman and drag her back to his lair. But once he had her there, secure in his bed, she proved…not terribly amenable. By her fourth, or possibly fifth, uninformed and rather ridiculous question about the peerage, Edward knew it was time to call a halt. The sheer enormity of her American-ness was staggering.

"Meg, sweetheart, is this pillow talk or an interrogation?" he inquired, laying a finger on her smiling lips.

Naturally, she kissed it. "Fine. Ask *me* some questions," she declared, raising her chin. "Edward!" she squeaked, exasperated when he took the opportunity to gain access to the delicate skin of her neck.

"All right, let's see," he conceded. "Do you prefer dogs or cats?"

She rolled her eyes. "Cats."

"That's unfortunate," he replied, thinking of his mum's beloved Papillon, and his father's pack of hounds back home. "We'll have to work on that."

She frowned at him. When her stomach growled loudly, she frowned harder.

Edward paused, trying not to laugh, then asked, "Do you often find yourself excessively hungry in the mornings?"

Meg turned so red she was almost purple. "*Yes*," she answered. "And technically it's not still morning."

Edward was aware. In fact, he was somewhat famished himself. "How about some brunch, then? There's a lovely little place around the corner that does an incredible seafood crepe."

"Good Lord," Meg groaned. "I'm going to be enormous by the time you're done wining and dining me."

Edward eyed her very slim frame. "Nonsense. You'll look just as smashing with a few more kilos on you. Now then, up you get," he urged, grabbing her hands and pulling her to her feet.

With a few stops and starts of the *very* enjoyable variety, he managed to get them both decently dressed and down to the kitchen. Meg perched fetchingly up on his counter while he rinsed out their mugs and turned off the coffee maker. It had only now occurred to him how lucky they were that George had not elected to pop in this morning, Mum in tow. Perhaps Edward's violent and threatening texts earlier had some effect after all. Edward had only a moment to contemplate this, though, because when he looked up at Meg, her eyes were hot. Scorching, in fact. She laughed softly.

"What's funny?" he murmured, crowding close and wrapping his arms around her.

"Not much," she admitted softly. "The smell of you is all over me, in my hair, on my skin…the taste of you is in my mouth, and it just seemed a little comical how much of a turn-on the aftershocks alone are to me," she confessed guiltily. "What are you *doing* to me?"

If Meg had been trying to work him up again, she was stupendous at it. Edward yanked her skirt up her thighs, all the way to her waist. "At the moment? Taking what's mine. Again," he informed her. Shooting her a look that would likely melt a glacier, he relieved her of her panties, held her face still with one hand so he could ravish her mouth, and thrust his other hand between her long, lovely legs.

Several stops and starts after *that*, these of the ecstatic, crying out the Lord's name, variety, Edward managed to get them both re-dressed and out his front door.

"Please tell me I can have you all to myself today," he begged, glancing at his watch. "What's left of it, anyway."

"I have no plans," Meg smiled dazedly up at him. Would that he could keep that expression on her face for the rest of their days. It was bliss personified.

"Brilliant. Food first, then you can help me find a damn couch." Her eyes were positively dancing as she grinned up at him. They headed toward the bistro around the corner.

Edward succeeded in keeping his filthy paws off of her long enough for them both to eat the famous lobster crepes at Marabel's. He was able to regain enough of his wits to realize that she'd probably like to change into a fresh set of clothes, probably even to shower. She'd probably like for *him* to shower as well. And, really, they ought to be good citizens and conserve water by taking one shower. Together. He omitted that last salient detail from his suggestion, though, and before long they'd collected his car from the street and were heading toward her apartment. Edward could feel her eyes on him as he drove, navigating the gauntlet created by the other Boston drivers and their selective interpretations of the rules of the road. Finally, stopped safely at a red light two blocks from her apartment, he turned to her, and his heart stopped.

"Meg. You *cannot* look at me like that when I am trying to operate a motor vehicle," he scolded. But Edward couldn't resist leaning over for one heartfelt kiss before the light turned again.

She turned to stare out her window, but a smile still flirted at the edges of her mouth. "Sorry," she murmured, but she was clearly anything but. Edward's shower idea was looking better and better.

Chapter Eight

IN THE END, Meg and Edward had made it to exactly one furniture store, a large chain whose offerings she often coveted. It was nearly time for dinner by the time they got there, and neither of them were in the mood to listen to the eager sales pitch of the employee who cornered them, or to rifle through his seemingly endless supply of fabric swatches. When Meg happened to mention her collection of home-store catalogs, Edward was quick to suggest they grab a pizza and go peruse them. One quick pit-stop for wine later found them as they currently were: sitting cross-legged in the middle of her living room floor, the pizza box and wine bottle between them, and open, ear-marked catalogs fanned out around them.

Edward pecked away at his laptop as he chewed, and Meg assumed he was making notes about the furniture and other accessories they found. Every so often, as they flipped through the glossy pages, they would show each other what appealed to them, and what they thought would work in his house. He'd been quick to notice her own notations on some pages, and soon they were conferring on the things she had picked for herself, too. Not that he needed to know how far off in the future those acquisitions were, or how unlikely.

Even so, it was all very fun—the pizza was good, the wine was better, their flirting was constant…Meg was in seventh heaven, and she thought Edward might be, too.

So when his cell phone buzzed on the floor and he glanced at it, only to recoil as if it were a venomous snake, Meg was perplexed. She peered down at the screen, shamelessly reading the text displayed there.

Report to my home Monday evening. Bring the girl. XO

She darted a quick look at Edward's face, which seemed to have gone a bit pale.

"Bugger it," he muttered, shaking his head. Pulling himself together, he squared his shoulders and looked back at her with resolve now glinting in his eyes. "Meg, love, I don't suppose you're available tomorrow night?"

"Sure. Why?" she asked, despite the reason being on vivid, backlit display on the floor nearby.

He looked green.

"Edward?" she prodded.

"Uh, *right*," he said briskly. "My mum apparently smells blood in the water. She's asked me to bring you by."

"Seriously?" Meg asked, incredulous despite the forewarning.

He nodded. "I blame my brothers," he added morosely. "Freddy especially. He leaks information like a bloody sieve."

"Wow," Meg breathed. It had only been a week, and she was meeting the parents? Or rather, the *other* parent?

"Too weird?" Edward asked. He looked ready to champion whatever weak excuse she might manufacture, but of course, she'd already accepted. No chickening out now.

"No." She said again, more emphatically, "*No*. I'm sure it will be fine."

Edward gave her a look that spoke volumes. "Like meeting my brothers was *fine*?"

Meg felt herself blanch. "Oh God." Oh. *God*. His mother was a…*countess*.

"I think I liked it better when I was making you say that in my bed," Edward commented.

"I think I liked that better, too," Meg agreed sorrowfully. What in the world was she going to *wear*?

"Might as well be hung for a sheep as a lamb, as they say." Edward snatched another slice of pizza and ate half of it in two bites.

"What does that even mean?" Meg wailed. This was not dignified. She had to get it together. Panicking would solve nothing.

"It's not as if I'm ashamed of you," he continued. "Or her, come to think of it. This might be a tad…precipitous," he argued. "But it was bound to happen eventually."

"Right," Meg said, mind reeling. *It was?*

"Right," he agreed, grinning at her. "I expect I'll need to console you. What with the shock and all."

"You know what? You're obnoxious, that's what you are," she teased. "Are you done eating?"

Edward nodded, then gestured to another small pile of catalogs she'd put to the side. "What're all those?"

"Oh, nothing, just clothes and stuff," Meg said dismissively. Beautiful pages of beautiful things that she would probably never own, especially if the job search continued in the same vein it had been. The last thing she needed at the moment was Edward asking her why she didn't just order all the things she'd circled. Somehow that ranked right up there with screwing up the meeting with his mother—both rampant with humiliation.

Meg jumped up and stretched, then gathered up their plates and the pizza and carried it all into her kitchen. Once in there, she decided to take a minute to wash the dishes, in the hopes that she could calm her racing heart. It would be okay. She would wear something classic and modest, and she would not be ashamed of being who and what she was, even if Edward's mother was snooty and condescending to her. Meg snorted. It was hard to imagine the lady who had produced a man like Edward being anything but kind, but she *was* a countess, after all. Maybe being a snob was some sort of prerequisite.

Edward cleared his throat as he leaned against the door jamb. He had an indulgent smile on his face.

"Let me guess," Meg said, rolling her eyes. "Barefoot in the kitchen is a thing for you?"

"No, I don't think so," he said cheerfully. "But we can certainly discuss the whole sexy librarian angle if you'd like."

"Maybe some other time," Meg said, shaking her head and drying off her hands.

"Could you be any cuter, singing away in here?" he asked, pulling her toward him.

Meg squinted. "Was I singing?" She hadn't even realized. One of the perils of living alone.

"Like a bird. Something from *Chicago*, if I don't miss my guess," Edward commented.

"Ah. Mama Morton. I love her—she's one of my favorites," Meg explained, trailing behind him. He'd cleaned up all the catalogs and stacked them neatly in the corner. He also seemed to have turned off a light or two.

"She certainly seems earthy," he laughed, pulling her toward her bed.

Edward had lit a couple jar candles and set them on a magazine on the floor next to her bed. It actually made her bare-boned accommodations seem romantic.

"I know we have to get up for work tomorrow, but I hate to say goodbye just yet," he said softly, encircling her in his arms.

"You don't *have* to leave," Meg told him, wondering how he'd take it. Good God, they'd just spent the last twenty-four hours in each other's pockets. He must be sick of her by now, right? Still…"You could stay if you wanted. We could just get up earlier, so you had time to get home and get ready." She chewed on her lip, waiting to see what he'd do.

Edward's whole face lit up. "Excellent. I'd love to stay. Besides, my first appointment isn't until ten, so no worries there." He plopped down on the end of her bed, then dragged Meg between his knees so he could embrace her. Burying his face between her breasts, he sighed happily, "I know I said this before, but I adore the way you smell. It's not perfume, is it? It's just…you. Lovely you."

Meg smiled down at him, charmed beyond reason. But she just couldn't resist asking, "What if she doesn't like me? Your mom, I mean."

He grinned up at her, merriment crinkling the corners of his eyes. "Mum? Are you kidding? Even if you weren't spectacular all on your own, she'd love you because you make me happy. Please don't worry, Meg."

"If you say so," she hedged. But she had to admit, she did feel a little better. The countess didn't sound *so* bad.

"I do. Now, it's been hours and hours since I kissed you last. Shouldn't we be doing something about that?" he grumbled.

Something, as it transpired, involved a number of things. It included a rather loosely adjudicated game of poker, some actual kissing, and some other activities that Meg's sister would have termed "canoodling" with one eyebrow arched high. Finally, she and Edward nestled together under her covers, and he stroked softly at her hair while they whispered to each other long into the night.

IT WAS NO wonder Meg overslept. Monday morning came fast and furious, even with the incentive of Edward's sweet efforts to awaken her in lieu of her usual blaring alarm. The air was brisk in her apartment, the clanking radiator taking its own sweet time to warm things up. Apologizing profusely, Meg directed a sleepy Edward toward the kitchen and her coffee maker, before rushing into her bathroom to shower and get ready. She was flustered and in a fog, her usual efficient routine thrown off by the dreamy haze of their weekend together, but also by his gorgeous, disheveled presence there tempting her.

Moving as fast as she could, Meg blew her hair mostly dry before tossing it up into a loose bun. If she was lucky, it would dry in loose waves that would look semi-normal at his parent's house later. She slapped on some light makeup, then tossed a few things into a cosmetic bag so she could touch her face up before leaving work. Finally, she burst out of the bathroom, hoping that he'd had the sense to get himself dressed, too, so they could leave soon. Meg peered at her watch—if she caught the next train, she would just make it. It didn't leave time to eat, unfortunately, but she could put her coffee in a to-go cup, and she'd be golden. She darted to her closet and grabbed a mulberry-colored cardigan of her sister's, with three-quarter length sleeves and a ruffled neckline. Paired with her gray trousers and soft white shell, it was the best she could do on short notice. Not terribly fashionable, perhaps, but she *did* have to spend the day in the office before meeting Edward's mother. *Edward.*

Meg wheeled around, searching for him. And then she caught the scent of bacon.

"There you are," he said, emerging from her kitchen, plates in hand. "Come sit down and have breakfast."

Damn it. There was no time to eat. Edward must have caught the expression of alarm tightening her face, because he winked.

"It's okay. You have time. I'll drop you by the office on my way home," he urged. "I promise to drive very fast."

Oh. Of course. Why on earth would he make her take the T when he was going right past her work anyway? Meg hadn't even considered that. She looked at her watch again. Taking that into account, she probably could afford to sit for a minute and eat. She took a deep breath and settled herself carefully on the low futon. Edward handed her a plate and a napkin, then settled onto the wood floor across from her.

"Thank you," she told him, studying the bacon and egg sandwich on her plate. It was more than she usually had time for, but it smelled amazing. "This looks great."

"You need to eat more," he replied, swallowing his mouthful. "You're always hungry." He devoured another bite, chewing industriously.

That was true, but it was embarrassing to have it stated so plainly. Meg was used to partitioning out every last dime as well as she could. But to have it so apparent to others, to Edward especially, stung. She didn't answer him, just shrugged and tucked into her breakfast.

When they'd finished, he whisked her plate away while she went back into the bathroom to brush her teeth. Edward handed her two travel mugs of coffee, and they were off. As promised, he pulled up in front of her office building with five minutes to spare, having done his best Mario Andretti impression. True, Meg's heart might never be the same, but still. He'd promised, and he'd delivered. The man had earned a reward.

When he came around the car to help her out, she stretched up on her toes to plant a kiss on him. "Thank you," she breathed, right against his lips. "For everything. I had an amazing weekend with you."

"And you," he murmured back. Whatever he'd been about to add, though, was cut off by a firm thump on his back. Edward pulled away, disconcerted.

"Shut it down, young man," Mr. Boudreau grumbled as he strode by. "She's gotta earn a living now, you hear?" He breezed into the building, not seeming to notice their two sets of eyes glued to his retreating back.

"I'm sorry," she winced. "That's my boss."

Edward nodded, looking nonplussed as he double-checked that the other man was truly gone. "So, I'll pick you up at six?" he confirmed.

"Okay. See you then," Meg said brightly. Surely she could develop some courage by six. She had more than eight hours to figure it out.

She turned to go, jumping when Edward smacked her hard on the rear as she went. Meg glared over her shoulder at him.

"See you," he grinned insolently, watching her the whole way into the foyer before he got into his shiny car and took off. The hound.

Meg sighed happily. Could this even be happening to her? It was hard to believe it was real.

Chapter Nine

MONDAY PASSED AT a crawl, but at last it was time to leave, and Meg was *almost* relieved. Mr. Boudreau had greeted her arrival in the office that morning with a mischievous grin and an exaggerated wink. And while he hadn't actually *said* anything untoward about what he witnessed that morning, he did spend much of the day beaming goofily at her. For heaven's sake, it was Monday. Who did that? As nervous as Meg was about meeting Edward's mother, it almost seemed a welcome diversion from enduring her boss's good-natured, but relentless, teasing.

Meg stood on the sidewalk out front, holding her sweater and jacket over her arm, and fanning her face. The crisp air was refreshing after feeling overheated all day—whether because of nervousness, the blasting furnace in the building, or her eight long hours of blushing, she wasn't sure. Edward pulled up at ten to six, parallel-parked up the block, then came striding toward her. He trailed his cool fingers down her bare outer arm, then linked his hand with hers. He began speaking with no preamble.

"It's almost as if someone asked me to lay around for three days dreaming up my perfect woman—which I did, mind you, in lavish detail." His eyes were warm, gazing down at her as his other hand rose to graze the delicate skin at the hollow of her throat. "Then, at the end, they said, *Right, then. She's all yours.*" A smile teased the corners of his mouth as he kissed her lightly.

"I'm all yours," Meg whispered, shyness making it hard to meet his eyes. Having to be perfect felt like a lot of pressure, especially tonight.

He studied her face, his smile growing wider. "I accept." He lifted her hand and kissed it, then led her to the car.

They reached his parents' home with disconcerting swiftness. Meg hadn't realized they lived so close, on a shady side street in Brookline, just across Commonwealth Avenue from the BU campus's western edge. The area was dotted with pretty little parks—in nice weather, Meg would walk to the closest of them on her lunch break to slip off her shoes and read while she ate a slice of pizza she bought on the way. The lane they turned onto now was lined with huge old trees and large, stately, well-kept homes. She'd walked by dozens of them before, but hadn't really ever considered who might live in them.

Standing on the front step while Edward rang the bell, Meg marveled that this was the kind of residence a woman would choose as a temporary home. Two of her sons were grown and already living on their own. And her husband was only a guest lecturer, albeit at Harvard. Perhaps they were planning on settling in the U.S. longer than Meg had realized. Still, it seemed entirely too much—too large, too elegant, too *everything*. A breeze wafted by as they waited, swirling the dry leaves on the sidewalk. Meg caught a whiff of the decaying blossoms on the rose bushes beside the stairs, just as the front door swung open.

"Ah, we're standing on ceremony, are we?" the woman said abruptly, wearing the same sardonic half-smile Edward was always flashing at Meg. She stood on the threshold in her bare feet. Meg noticed her perfectly manicured toes immediately, but not much else. "Welcome," she called over her shoulder as she left the door ajar and moved deeper into the house.

Edward shot Meg a quick, bracing smile, then pulled her inside. The foyer was dim in the evening gloom, despite the elaborate transom over the door and the narrow sidelights marching up either side. Edward's mother seemed to be a thin, mousy woman in a dowdy brown sweater and wool pants, heading up the hall toward a well-lit room at the back of the house. In the hallway, she stepped into a pair of shoes mid-stride as Edward and Meg followed her, then turned to greet them once she entered the brightness of the family room.

As she came closer, Meg realized that her first impression had been inaccurate. The woman facing her was classically beautiful, refined and sophisticated, and belonged in this house and neighborhood without question. The brown sweater turned out to be an exquisite cashmere confection that offset her long auburn bob perfectly. The wool pants fit her slim, athletic frame flawlessly. Her hair, makeup, jewelry…it was all tasteful, understated, and obviously expensive. No faux baubles for the countess, it seemed. Meg stood in thrall, tongue-tied. The woman's accent, in particular, sounded so much posher than Edward's, on whom it just sounded like sin incarnate. Meg discovered she was holding her breath, for fear of being coarse just by breathing wrong. She let it out in a big gust, and Edward chuckled beside her.

That's when she calmed enough to notice the warm smile on the other woman's face, and the way her eyes crinkled at the corners, just like Edward's. When the countess smiled, she didn't look nearly as intimidating.

"I hope you had no trouble getting here? No?" she asked Edward. Then, clearing her throat meaningfully, she inquired, "And who do we have here?"

Edward twinkled at his mother, clearly enjoying her impatience. "Mother, I'd like to introduce my girlfriend, Meghan Flynn."

Girlfriend? Meg's head whipped around to blink at him, stunned. Apparently, they weren't going to be pulling any punches tonight.

His mother extended her lovely hand, bracelets clinking at her wrist. "Meg, this is my mother, Violet Hughes," Edward said, completing the introduction without using her title. Surely Meg wasn't expected to curtsy, but was she supposed to use some sort of special honorific?

The countess had a firm grip. Meg settled on, "It's a pleasure to meet you."

His mother held onto her hand, squeezing it and saying, "The pleasure's mine. Please call me Violet," before she released Meg and gestured to the couches arranged around a large fireplace. "I believe you've already met these scoundrels?"

"Hey, Meg," George said affably, standing up and shoving his hands in the pockets of his jeans.

Charlie set down his beer and lounged back. "Going to be a tad harder to run off now, isn't it?" he asked brazenly. Edward snorted and bumped her with his shoulder, his mother watching the whole exchange with undisguised interest.

Hesitantly, Meg set her purse on the floor next the couch and straightened. Edward's mother lurched forward and snatched it up in dismay.

"Oh, don't leave your bag there, love. Pippa will gnaw on the handles and empty it of everything you hold precious," Violet exclaimed, setting it instead on a side table that looked like an antique.

Just then, a small brown and white dog trotted into the room, her pink collar studded with rhinestones, and a bow clipped to the fur beside one ear. The ears themselves were too large for her body, pointy, with long, comical tufts of fur spraying out from them. She wagged her tail once, then sat near Violet's feet with a little huff, staring up at her mistress.

"Pippa, darling, be *polite* to our guest please," Violet intoned sternly.

Pippa rose and trotted dutifully to Meg, nudging her hand and giving her a quick bark before returning to her position. Violet smiled, then leaned down to balance a small biscuit on the dog's narrow nose. Pippa waited patiently for her signal, tail swishing back and forth across the floor. When Violet snapped her fingers, rings flashing in the lamplight, Pippa jerked her head up and tossed the treat into her mouth, crunching on it happily. Violet laughed in delight.

"Well, Pippa. Looks like we'll be able to run off to the circus after all," she chuckled.

"Run off?" Charlie sputtered from his seat. "Why bother? This *is* the circus, mum."

Violet sighed, and gestured Meg and Edward toward the couches. "Well, he's not half wrong about that." She hoisted a tray of glasses from a sideboard and brought it to the coffee table, offering one to Meg. "Wine?" she asked.

Meg accepted gratefully, sitting next to Edward on the loveseat, while Violet shooed Charlie over to share the couch with George. Violet perched regally in the side chair angled near the hearth and crossed her ankles, raising her own glass to her glossy rose lips.

"It's lovely to have you here," she told Meg. "The boys were always after me and their father to have a sister for them." She turned to George and Charlie with a narrow-eyed look. "Completely ignoring the fact that our exorbitantly large brood would then have five—*five*—children in it."

"Exorbitant?" George inquired softly.

"Now, of course, they've decided the thing to do would be to adopt some unfortunate little baby to be their sister, from God knows where. Honestly. At my age, can you imagine?" she rambled, looking to Meg for support.

Meg shook her head, blinking.

"And do you know why they want a baby sister so badly?"

Meg shook her head again, though no answer seemed to be required.

Violet plowed on, "For help with girls! They want a sister *for the advice* she could give them. Have you ever heard such a thing? Never mind the fact that it would be at least fifteen years before she could offer them the slightest bit of help. They'll be pitiful by then," Violet scoffed.

"Hardly," Charlie grumbled, scowling into his beer.

"I don't know why none of them considered dating an actually suitable individual before. For more than five minutes, I mean." She turned back to George and Charlie. "It helps to figure things out for yourselves once in a while, lads."

"It's harder than it looks," George groused.

"Being British only takes one so far, Mum," Edward murmured, smiling at Violet.

"Actually," Charlie interjected, "The accent helps more than you'd think. I'm a boy *magnet* once I start talking," he boasted.

Meg cocked her head and glanced at Edward for interpretation. Violet caught the gesture and leaned forward conspiratorially.

"Charles is a homosexual, darling," she explained.

Charlie's cheeks turned pink, but he didn't look away.

"Is that what we're calling it?" George snorted, earning an elbow in the ribcage. He shoved back at his brother, but both managed to retain their pleasant expressions in the face of their mother's assessing gaze. She raised her brows at them, and they both went still.

Edward cleared his throat. "We thought we'd keep him, regardless," he said, winking at Charlie.

Charlie looked at Meg, uncertainty clouding his expression. Meg smiled back at him, with what she hoped was reassurance.

"I would think adding *more* males to the mix would just complicate matters," she teased.

Violet bit her lip and let out a little laugh, and Edward grinned at his younger brother.

"Really a foregone conclusion with Charlie," George snarked, leaning over to ruffle his brother's hair.

"Bloody hell," Charlie complained, but his shoulders lost some of their tension and he looked more at ease.

"Language," Violet intoned. "Charles, darling, I would think around here you'd have better luck with an Irish accent, rather than a British one." Her eyes twinkled at him. "Boston does love its Irish, doesn't it?"

George told Meg, "Happily, half of you Yanks can't tell the difference."

Charlie punched him in the arm. "Except for some of the blokes in Southie. *They* know. But then, they're too far in the closet for words. Who's got the time for that kind of project?"

George muttered, "Certainly not you."

"Certainly not," Charlie rejoined.

Mrs. Hughes, if one was allowed to call her that, was smiling at the interchange. She had bustled out of the room and returned with a tray of appetizers.

"Canapé?" she inquired, proffering the selection of tidbits.

Meg thought maybe a change of subject was in order. She turned to her hostess.

"Your sons seem to be such good friends," she commented. Their interplay was entertaining, to say the least. "You must enjoy that."

Violet glanced back and forth among them and nodded. "Trust me, there were days I didn't think they would let each other live to adulthood," she said cynically.

"There's still time," Edward murmured beside Meg.

More loudly, George observed, "To be frank, we're a little amazed *you* let us live."

"Yes, well," Violet demurred.

"How we squeaked by Father remains a bit of a mystery, as well," Charlie remarked, shifting on the couch.

Freddy came stomping into the room, clearly already a party to the conversation. He plopped on the arm of the loveseat next to Meg and barked, "It's because we're kings, you dolt."

Maintaining an innocent expression, George began to hum the first few bars of *We Three Kings*. Charlie joined in, with more vigor of course, and next to her, even Edward chuckled.

"Do I even want to know?" Meg asked, looking around, puzzled.

"Impudent," Violet stated, pointing her finger at each of her sons. "Meghan, my children seem to find it amusing that they all share names with kings," she explained. "Not that any of them act particularly kingly."

"Says you," muttered Charlie, earning another jab from George.

"Not very royal of you, Charles," Edward admonished him.

"I heard that," Violet huffed. "I'd just like to remind you cheeky little upstarts that we could easily have named you Basil. Or Neville. Or…or…*Phineas*," she warned them.

Charlie popped up from his sprawl on the couch to plant a sloppy kiss on her flawless cheek. "Thank you, Mum, for not naming me Phineas," he declared gravely.

She managed to wince only slightly at his token of affection.

"Or Basil," piped up Freddy.

"Or Neville," added Edward, grinning merrily at Meg as he did so. Obviously, this was a well-rehearsed exchange.

"You lot are just like your father," Violet pronounced. "Too charming by half." She was fighting to keep her expression impassive, but a smile of her own clearly loomed.

Meg silently repeated the word *half* in her head, fascinated by Violet's aristocratic inflection.

In the pause that followed, the sound of a door opening and slamming shut reverberated through the room. All heads swiveled to the side, watching the doorway for the new arrival. Meg counted heads and realized who it must be. Then she availed herself of the rest of her wine.

Edward's father, the earl, strode in, looking harried.

"Hullo," he exclaimed, looking around at their collected faces. "What have I done now?"

Violet rose from her chair and set her glass down. "Ah, there you are, darling." She pecked him lightly on his proffered cheek. "I was beginning to think we'd have to send out scouts for you."

"Nonsense," he sputtered. "I'm right here. Merely," he peered at his watch. "Ah. Half an hour late. Sorry, love."

Violet rolled her eyes good-naturedly. "No harm done. The lads have just been…" She gestured airily. "Doing what they do."

Edward's father looked alarmed at that. He turned to Meg and met her eye, but apparently didn't detect any serious damage. "Miss Flynn," he blustered. "So nice to see you again!"

"And you," Meg smiled.

He turned back to his wife, who was waiting expectantly at his side. "I'll just, erm…" Now he motioned vaguely, this time in the direction of what Meg presumed was the kitchen. "Check on supper, shall I?" he inquired. There was a euphemism in there somewhere, Meg was sure, but she'd be damned if she could figure out what it was.

Violet nodded and patted him on the arm. "As you wish," she piped. "Don't take too long." Her husband made his escape, and she returned to settle on her chair.

"Now then, Meghan," she stated efficiently. "You have a lovely name. Is it a family name?" She asked as if Meg's family traditions could be counted in generations, rather than…well, rather than months. Whatever perfunctory efforts her parents had made were rarely repeated and did not last long into her adolescence, and Meg had determined that she would have to create her own traditions if she wanted to have any at all. She just hadn't come up with any yet. But the holidays were coming, so what better time?

Meg refocused on the countess. "No ma'am. Actually, my mom and dad just wanted my sister and I to both to have M names."

"I see. And why is that?" she inquired.

"I have no…" Meg coughed. "…idea," she finished. She had almost blurted out "freaking idea," but had just managed to choke it back. Just.

The look on Violet's face was wry. Meg got the distinct impression that Violet had not only heard the unspoken pejorative, but she also *approved*. Edward moved his leg slightly on the couch next to her, pressing it against hers in a silent move of support. She wanted to look at his face, wanted to gauge how she was doing in his eyes, but Meg didn't dare. Freddy, for one, didn't miss a trick, and he was eyeing her like a hawk.

Across from them, Charlie had slipped his phone out of a pocket and begun texting furiously. George nudged him, but it was too late. Violet had already risen silently from her seat. She leaned over the back of the couch to deftly pluck the offending device from her son's hands with two long, elegant fingers.

"Charles, George. Please join me in the kitchen. I need your assistance."

"And me?" Freddy asked.

"And you," she confirmed. "Please excuse us a moment," she told Meg. She wrapped an arm around Freddy's shoulders and guided him away.

"Bollocks," Charlie muttered, hoisting himself to his feet and scowling after her. George shoved him forward, none too gently.

Edward watched them all parade out with an amused smirk on his face, then waited another full, awkward minute before finally turning to her. Leaning in, he affected his most ridiculous Count Dracula accent and murmured in her ear.

"At last, I have you alone," he drawled. "I thought I'd have to waylay you in the loo to get a kiss out of you."

Meg giggled, swiveling in his direction, only to find his face much closer than she anticipated. No sooner did that register than his large hand gripped the back of her neck and his mouth descended on hers, hot and desperate.

Drawing back only far enough to whisper against her lips, he said, "*God*, Meg, you're adorable when you're nervous."

"Was it that obvious?" she asked him quietly.

"No, not at all. You're doing great," he assured her. "What about me?"

"What do you mean, *what about you?*" she demanded, bewildered.

"Could you tell how nervous I was?" Edward elaborated.

"Oh, stop. You weren't nervous," she told him.

"I was. I've never brought a girl home before," he claimed, looking virtuous.

"You haven't?" Meg challenged him.

He shook his head and smiled his little sheepish smile. "I told you, you're different."

"Oh," she whispered, peeking guiltily over her shoulder to see if they were still alone.

"Are they too horrible for words?" Edward asked, searching her face. "We could make an excuse, try to break out of here before supper."

"No, they're fine," she assured him. "Your mom is…" Meg struggled for an adequate description. "And your brothers. Wow."

"She likes you," Edward broke in. "*They* like you. All of them."

"How can you tell?" Meg laughed. "I hardly said anything."

"Because they aren't being fussy with you," Edward explained. "Or too polite. They are just being themselves."

Meg contemplated that. "I almost died when she blurted out that your brother is gay. Poor Charlie. He must be so embarrassed when she does that."

He looked at the ceiling, frowning. "We've determined…" But then Edward smiled. "We believe she is trying to help, by weeding out any undesirable people who might judge him badly for it. Right from the beginning, so to speak."

"Your mom isn't what I expected," she admitted.

"No," he agreed softly. "She's better."

Meg nodded, and from the other room, right on cue, Violet called, "Supper!"

"After you," Edward grinned.

Meg squared her shoulders and prepared to face the wolves. Again.

Edward held her chair for her as they all took their seats. When they'd settled, Meg was startled to see a large structure made of popsicle sticks gracing the center of the table, instead of the expected floral arrangement or bowl of fruit. Upon closer inspection, it appeared to be some unfortunate combination of barn, planetarium, and Greek temple. And not a very sturdy one, at that. Everyone else appeared to be as transfixed as she was.

"Ahh…" she began, casting around for a suitable comment. There was no question that *someone* had to acknowledge it.

Naturally, Violet leapt to the rescue with a regal smile. "I trust you'll excuse Frederick's school project, Meg dear. The glue isn't quite dry yet, and we were a little afraid to move it."

Meg turned to Freddy, who was scowling at his creation with a critical eye. "What class is it for?" she asked. She smoothed her napkin over her lap, but noted that no one else had so much as picked up a fork.

"Introduction to Engineering," Freddy told her. "Once my teacher met Father, she decided that we had to have a big building design fair at the end of the semester. It's really stupid," he added, dripping disdain as only a teenager could.

His mother cleared her throat and cast him a meaningful glance, then turned toward her husband. "Alistair is to be one of the judges," she beamed.

Meg smiled at him, thinking he seemed like a very good sport. "Did you help Freddy with it?" she inquired.

He looked embarrassed. He murmured, "Well, certainly, I…" at the same time Freddy blurted out an affronted, "No!"

"At times, Fred allowed me to wield the glue gun," the earl admitted.

Satisfied with that admission, Freddy turned to Charlie and George, demanding, "Well? Did you bring them?"

A flurry of activity ensued, as both brothers got to their feet and enacted a farce of pocket searching and irritable recriminations. At last, George procured the requested items from some pocket or another and proffered them to his youngest sibling on an outstretched palm. Freddy stood as well, carefully placing the two small LEGO figures on what seemed to be the front porch of his project. One small man was outfitted in a toga and laurel crown, and the other looked to be a farmer, complete with overalls and pitchfork. Edward and his mother took in the new additions with identical, quizzical expressions, tilting their heads to the side in the same curious way.

"Lovely," the countess murmured. After a careful pause, she reached for her salad fork and leveled a gracious smile at her assembled family. "Shall we?" she inquired.

Once she'd taken her first dainty bite, the rest of them grabbed their forks and tucked into their food heartily, as if they hadn't eaten in weeks. Under the table, Edward bumped her leg with his, and when Meg peeked at him, she could see his eyes crinkling at the corners merrily. The lunatic was enjoying this, damn it.

Chapter Ten

WHEN EDWARD USHERED Meg into the dining room, Freddy and his father were already seated, and George, Charlie, and his mum were busily ferrying in dishes. His mother had put out place cards, he saw, and he was relieved to note that she'd placed Meg between herself and Edward. It was probably safest that way. George faced Meg, another safe choice, and Freddy and Charlie flanked his father, where they might inflict the least amount of damage. Edward was hopeful that his mother's consummate skill as a hostess would keep things from getting too out of hand, but she could only do so much. He'd have to do the rest, get Meg through what was sure to be a barely veiled inquisition by a panel of bickering court jesters.

"Now, then," his mother said, once they'd dispensed with the explanation of the peculiar centerpiece. Both of his parents were looking around the table with cheerful, expectant faces, but none of his brothers seemed willing to take the bait. Freddy was tearing into his roast like the rabid wolf he was, Charlie toyed with his water goblet, and George fussed with the napkin on his lap.

Meg, who didn't appear to suffer silences well, turned to his father. "So, Edward tells me that you are a professor at Harvard," she began. It was as good an opening as any, and he squeezed her knee lightly, under the table, to bolster her. He still wasn't sure if she knew who his father was, but after the way she'd handled the whole hereditary title bomb, he was feeling pretty relaxed about her potential reaction. Of course, the wine had helped. He'd had plenty.

"Just a guest, I'm afraid," his father replied. "I'll be finishing up at the end of this semester. Thank God."

His mum smiled indulgently at her husband down the length of the table.

"You aren't enjoying it?" Meg asked.

"Well," his dad hedged. "Let me put it this way. Edward told us you attended Boston University, is that correct?"

"Yes, sir."

"That's a much more *plebian* atmosphere, I hear," the earl commented. "Not necessarily ivory tower academia, as it were."

Meg looked like she was trying to decide if that was an insult or not, because who was more peculiar about class distinctions than the British? And who was more sensitive about their lack of nobility than the Americans? Edward shifted in his seat, preparing to dive into his role as cultural moderator.

His father had more to say, though. His eyes were alight as he went on, "I'd much rather teach in that sort of environment, I think. Have a more collaborative learning experience instead of just going through the exercise of fawning and idol-worship. And name-dropping. Good Lord, all the name-dropping," he complained, before stuffing a heaping forkful of meat in his mouth. Chewing industriously, he made a noise of pleasure in his throat, and said, "Violet, dear. This is quite good."

"Thank you, Alistair," she replied, making a little motion with her fingers to urge him to wipe his mouth. Edward knew that his mother's housekeeper had likely prepared much of the meal, but it didn't seem quite cricket to point that out right now.

"I prefer a modern aesthetic, as you know," Edward's father expounded. Edward doubted Meg did, but she didn't appear ready to contradict him. "Not a thing modern about Harvard, I'll tell you that," he chuckled. "But perhaps it would be the same anywhere. Hard to say—I shouldn't be critical."

Meg made a small sound of amusement and turned to his mum when she spoke.

"Alistair was astonished, to say the least, when Edward and George decided to eschew his spare, clean-lined vision, and…"

"Wallow amongst the millwork and moldings," George and Charlie chimed in together.

Meg sat there wide-eyed, hands resting beside her plate, and seemed uncertain of how to respond. Edward decided a little explanation was probably in order. He took a deep breath, wondering how little he could get away with telling her, and immediately felt guilty. Meg wouldn't be odd about it, would she? Not after last weekend, certainly.

"My father is a prominent architect," he clarified carefully.

"He's quite famous," Freddy boasted, between bites of beef. "Everyone knows him."

"When George and I decided to restore historic properties, I think we offended every progressive bone in his body," Edward continued, trying to ignore his youngest brother.

"Nonsense," his father protested loyally. He hadn't been insulted so much as flummoxed, that much was true.

"And then there are all the wankers who want to get to him through us," George commented dryly. "That's always great fun."

"George," the countess huffed. "*Language.*"

Meg's eyes had been bouncing back and forth between his family members like she was at Wimbledon. At last, they came to rest back on him. Edward tried his best to look reassuring.

"So you and George studied architecture, too?" she asked politely.

"I did," he agreed. She had barely touched her food. Did she dislike it? He wondered if he ought to offer her something else. *Somewhere* else. As always, Meg smelled distractingly divine. Sitting so close to her, but not being able to touch her, was driving him a little mad. He couldn't seem to concentrate.

"But not me," George told her, setting down his own fork. "I was a business major."

"It's a useful degree," his mother soothed automatically.

Meg focused on Charlie, who had been uncharacteristically silent. "What about you?" she asked him. "What are you majoring in?"

Charlie brightened, clearly happy to be included. "I'm doing graphic design," he told her. "It's brilliant, actually. Something finally makes sense to me." Meg furrowed her brow at that, and he rushed to explain. "Dyslexia," he told her. "Took us a bit long to figure out what my problem was," he groused. "By the time we got it, I was already entrenched in the art and design stuff."

"Because of all the hijinks," Freddy said, leaning forward to catch her eye. "They just thought he was naughty, for years and years."

"He was always intelligent, but art was the language he truly understood," his mum said softly. "Thankfully." She smiled mistily at Charlie down the table, "Darling boy."

"Charles, you must show Meghan some of your work after dinner," his father said. He fixed Meg with his intent gaze. "He's quite talented."

Meg smiled at Charlie, who flushed with pleasure. "I'd love to see it," she told him sincerely, and his brother looked delighted. God, he loved him, even if he was a pain in the arse. He'd developed a smart mouth and quick fists to counter his struggles in school, throwing up the world's greatest smoke screen to obfuscate his vulnerabilities. Edward didn't think his parents would ever forgive themselves for letting their second-youngest child languish as long as they had.

"What did you study at university, my dear?" the countess asked, redirecting smoothly.

"Oh, I was an International Relations major," Meg told her. This was news to him, and Edward eyed her with interest. He thought of her nondescript office building on the BU campus, and couldn't imagine that matters of global importance were being solved there, but who was he to judge? They could be spies, for all he knew. Ensconced where they were, no one would suspect them.

His parents both looked blank, though, which didn't seem to throw her off. She hurried to clarify, "It's sort of a combination of Political Science and History."

"Not the easiest field in which to find employment," his father commented dryly. Edward rather thought he'd like to stab him with a salad fork.

"*Dad*," George hissed, looking chagrined on Meg's behalf.

"Well, it was very interesting," Meg said, her voice upbeat. "But you're right. I think most people end up doing graduate work to narrow their focus. You know—the foreign service, law school, that sort of thing."

"And is that something you might pursue?" his mother inquired. Edward assessed her. A fork might not be quite adequate to handle Violet—she was cagey. Still, he was curious to hear Meg's answer.

Meg hesitated, then admitted, "Yes, I've definitely considered it."

Edward remembered the thick sheaf of papers she had slipped into her bag when she got in his car today. *Tulane University Law School*, the seal had read. A neon sticky note affixed to the top read, *As requested, JB*, scrawled in a man's firm, slanting hand. He'd better discover where that was, and soon. It would take her two days at most to pack up that sparse apartment of hers, and then she could be gone. He swallowed painfully. He'd only just found her—he didn't want to have to let her go yet. He could just ask her about it later when he dropped her off, but Edward wondered what she'd tell him, given her tone just now.

When Meg didn't elaborate, his mother guided the conversation in a new direction, but not an entirely welcome one.

"Will you be visiting family over the holidays, Meg?" she inquired, as gracious as always.

Meg blinked, considering. The winter holiday was more than a month away, though he supposed the American Thanksgiving might count too. Shifting in her chair, Meg appeared to be stalling.

Before he realized what he was about, he blurted, "They're in Connecticut, are they not? Or do you have family elsewhere as well?" He shouldn't have done it. Meg blanched and seemed even more uncomfortable with his prompting. What was that all about?

"Well, my sister Morgan actually lives in New Zealand now," she reminded him, completely sidestepping the matter of her parents. "But no, I think I will be staying here for Christmas." She stared at her plate, seemed to recognize how little she'd eaten, and made a half-hearted effort to stab an au gratin potato with her fork. Edward felt guilty. Meg was getting *more* uncomfortable, not less, and it was his fault. He'd subjected her to this. But truly, he'd known her for such a short time, he could hardly be blamed for not understanding where the landmines were.

"Ah. I see," his mother responded neutrally. There was no hint of her opinion in her words, though Edward had to imagine she was wondering what kind of person might decline an opportunity to see her parents at Christmas. "We're quite looking forward to our own trip home. The boys don't have to be back for the start of the semester until the middle of January, so we'll have a nice long visit," she said.

Damn. Edward hadn't mentioned the month in the U.K. yet. Nor had he told Meg about the…

"Even longer for Edward and I," his father put in helpfully. "What with the conference."

"Of course, I'd quite forgotten," Violet exclaimed. She turned to Meg. "Edward and his father must leave for London two weeks sooner than the rest of us, for an architecture conference. Naturally, Westbroke is the keynote speaker," she explained smugly.

"Oh, how nice," Meg responded faintly.

"Then we'll just pop over to Cambridge and open up the house for the rest of this lot," his dad finished happily.

Edward could almost see the gears turning in her head. She wasn't daft, she'd easily add up that he'd be gone for a full six weeks while she was here alone. The question was, how could he make it up to her? With everything so new between them, Edward wasn't sure what Meg would expect. He didn't even consider asking her to tag along with them, though that was by far his favorite idea. Meg would never agree to it, her pride too large to countenance such an offering from him so early in their relationship. He had only to remember Li Wei's coat gaffe to realize that. The alternative was to give her some other really smashing (but appropriate) gift and stay in close and frequent contact. She wouldn't forget him or take up with another man, if she believed he would come back to her. Counting the week they'd already had together, Edward would have a month and a half to convince her he was worth waiting for. Easy.

Resolved on that course of action, he tried to tune back into the conversation flowing around the dinner table. Plans were being discussed for his mum's upcoming birthday, and it seemed that a restaurant he rather fancied had been decided upon. Catching his mother's eye, he let his primary question linger in his gaze. She gave him her answer swiftly: a curt nod and a look that wondered if he'd gone soft in the head.

"Meg," he asked, draping his arm around the back of her chair. "Won't you come along? I'm sure we'd all love to have you."

"But…it's your mom's birthday," she stammered. "You don't want me there for that." Her eyebrows drew together, and she fixed him with a pleading gaze. He almost hated to do it to her, but he wanted her there, and he was feeling possessive.

"Don't be silly," Violet said firmly, beside her. "Of course, we want you there. I won't hear of you declining, darling. You *must* come."

Meg swallowed, struggling to see a way out. Her lovely hazel eyes flew to Edward's in disbelief when he echoed, "You must."

Charlie guffawed, from his place down the table. "You're caught now, sweetheart," he bellowed. "Good luck!" His father and other brothers just sat there, grinning from ear to ear like a troop of baboons.

"Okay," Meg breathed weakly. "Sure." She shrugged, clearly understanding that resistance was futile. He squeezed her shoulder, happy. His family might be mad as hatters, but when they'd set their collective mind to something, there was no stopping them.

Chapter Eleven

MERCIFULLY, THE EVENING with Edward's parents wound down soon after Violet served dessert. Meg had been so nervous, she'd only managed to pick at her food, and the fact that she couldn't force herself to eat normally only served to make her more anxious. As Edward disappeared to get their coats, Meg stood awkwardly at the side of the kitchen and wondered again if she'd made a total mess of the night. The brothers were trying to rope their father into a game of cards, and Violet stood by, sipping daintily from a tiny cut crystal glass of sherry and eyeing them fondly.

When Meg reviewed her performance, she had to acknowledge that she had not tripped or spilled anything, had not barfed at the table nor burst into tears. Conversely, she had eaten like a bird and barely managed complete sentences, much less charming, witty conversation. And now, thanks to her treacherous new boyfriend, she'd have to do it all again in two weeks. She wanted to strangle him.

But then he waltzed back into the room, looking handsome as could be in his wool coat. He held her own coat up for her to slip her arms in, and his fingers were light on her neck as he pulled it over her shoulders. She shivered. It was hard to stay mad at the man, when she was so darn enamored of every move he made. Meg gave a wave and a smile to the men when they called their goodbyes, and allowed Edward and Violet to shepherd her to the front door. Edward stepped outside, but before Meg could follow him, Violet had grabbed her and enveloped her in a fragrant embrace.

"Meg, darling," she said softly, "I know we can come on a bit strong. But you must know our Edward lights up like a theater marquee when he looks at you. It's difficult not to get…enthusiastic. He's been so *moody* lately." Meg felt her face get hot and tried to conjure up some proper reply to that. But then Violet added, "And as for this birthday to-do they are planning, you needn't bring a thing, you understand. Just yourself. They've had me outnumbered for some time now, you see. It will be marvelous just to have another woman there." With that she gave Meg a reassuring nod and released her to Edward. Meg knew that she'd sooner impale herself on a dull butter knife than show up empty-handed to this woman's birthday party, but still she nodded and thanked her.

Edward took Meg's hand in his own, leaned in to kiss his mother on the cheek, and moments later had tucked Meg safely into the soft leather seat of his car. Once Violet had shut the front door and he'd gotten the heat going, he turned to look at her.

"Well, love? How bad was it?" He was smiling, but as Meg peered at his face, she realized he was possibly as unsettled as she was.

"I was about to ask the same thing," she smiled back. "Did I embarrass you?" She winced, remembering the look George and Charlie had shared when she bluffed about considering law school. The truth was, Mr. Boudreau had insinuated that Meg ought to be looking for something better during her last performance review, four weeks ago. After an hour of luxuriating in his smooth, honeyed voice, Meg had blurted out some nonsense about looking into Tulane Law to deflect the man. Because of course she knew she should be aiming higher. She'd been *trying* to aim higher, for

God's sake. And then Joe had gone and dropped the application packet on her desk this afternoon with a wink and a nudge, and a *Not sure if you still want this, honey, but here ya go. Let me know when you apply—I know some folks there.'*

Edward looked confused, though. "Embarrass me? No. Why would you think that?"

How to say it simply? "I didn't say much," she tried. And, "I'm very…American, compared to your mom." It sounded so ridiculous out loud that she had to chuckle along with Edward.

"I think you did splendidly," he assured her, dropping a soft kiss on her mouth. "My God, how many girls have to meet the family after only eight days of dating? It's completely odd. But what I'm wondering is what you thought of them. Did you like them?"

Meg thought about the various people there tonight—his lovely, refined mother, who still managed to be warm and kind. His genial father, with that absent-minded professor quality to him that Meg found so endearing. And his three brothers, like a rowdy, adorable pack of puppies. And then she thought of her own parents. The heavy silences during meals. The way her neck ached with tension after half an hour in their company. The way that nothing she or Morgan did ever seemed to satisfy them.

"Yes," she told Edward, then. "I really did. You're very lucky."

"I am," he agreed, his eyes crinkling at the corners in the way that she loved. "And even luckier now." With another quick kiss, he pulled away from the curb, and Meg just caught the shift of the curtain in his parents' front window when she looked back.

WHEN THEY REACHED her building, Edward circled the block for several minutes before he found a tight parking spot on the side street. He killed the ignition, then peeked at her.

"It seems like a shame to waste such a good spot," Meg smiled. "Do you have time to come up for a bit?"

"For you? Always," Edward said. He was up and out of his car, and then opening her door as swiftly as ever. She had to admit, she could get used to a guy who was so into her.

He trailed her casually, glancing up and down the street as they climbed the stone steps of her building, holding the vestibule door for her, and waiting with his hands in his coat pockets while she dug out her keys and unlocked the lobby door. When she pressed the elevator button, he gave her a devilish little wink, but otherwise leaned innocuously on the wall and waited. It wasn't until the doors slid shut behind them and he had her alone, that he made his intentions clear.

Edward crowded her up against the wall of the elevator and leaned his forearms on the wall near her head. Nuzzling up under her jaw, he pressed urgent kisses to her neck before devouring her mouth, hot and hungry.

"I think I rather hated being so close to you, and not being allowed to touch you," he growled.

"Don't look at me," Meg gasped, running her fingers up into his hair to hold him close. "It was your great idea."

"Actually, it wasn't," he complained against her lips. "My ideas all involve getting you alone and bare-arsed."

The elevator bell dinged for her floor, and they jumped apart. Edward dragged her off the elevator and down the short hall to her apartment. As Meg tried to unlock her door, Edward pushed aside her hair and breathed deeply against her neck and ear.

"I could barely look at you either," he told her. "Every time I tried to admire those blushing cheeks of yours, my mum would get this really alarming, calculating look on her face."

Meg laughed, pushed into her apartment, and turned to face him. He slammed the door shut behind him and scrutinized her with a hot gleam in his eye.

"Well," she breathed, "It seems you've got me alone, milord."

He narrowed his eyes and stalked nearer, brushing close as he circled her.

"Now for the naked part," he declared.

With startling efficiency, he stripped off her clothes, dropping each article onto the floor in a heap near her feet. Meg shuddered in the chilly room and wrapped her arms around herself while Edward shucked out of his coat. Neither of them had hit the light switch, and she was glad for the darkness, feeling self-conscious standing there without a stitch on while he studied her in the glow of the streetlights filtering through her blinds. He didn't undress himself, though. Instead, Edward sank to the futon and pulled her into his lap. Meg curled into his hard chest, and he wrapped his arms around her, warming her and holding her tight.

"Shall I tell you what your blushes were doing to me tonight?" he inquired, the soul of civility.

"Okay," she told him, burrowing close. "Lord knows I did enough of it."

His voice rumbled in his chest when he spoke. "When you blush, Meg darling, it turns out that you look exactly like you do when I've got you all hot and flushed and ready for me in bed."

He pried her off of him and faced her forward in his lap, pressing her back to his chest and dropping his head down to murmur in her ear.

"So when you sat so close to me, smelling so damn good," he told her, smoothing his palms down her legs and draping them wide over his thighs, "And you looked so cute and pink and lovely, all I could think about was how much you love it when I do *this*." He had her spread wide, the cool air brisk against her skin. Meg held her breath, but he didn't touch her there yet. He cupped her breasts in his hands first, squeezing her nipples between his fingers and nipping at her neck. Meg sighed, shifting in his lap and feeling the hard length of him beneath her bottom. He stroked his hot hands down her ribcage, gripping her waist and nudging her with his hips. Meg let her head loll back on his shoulder, giving him better access to her neck while his hands smoothed over her stomach and down the insides of her thighs. They pushed her knees even wider, then travelled up again to trail lightly between her legs. Meg jerked on his lap, startled by his touch, and Edward laughed darkly in her ear.

"And naturally, the redder you got, the more I wanted to taste you," he confessed. Meg whimpered at his admission, the glances he'd been tossing her way all evening suddenly cast in a different light. He gripped her chin in one hand, turning her head so he could kiss her. When he dropped his other hand to cup her, Meg moaned. He caught the sound with his mouth, swallowing it and delving deep with his tongue just as his fingers dragged across her slick folds to push inside her. Edward held her pinned like that, his mouth possessing hers, his arm locked across her chest and his hand filled with her breast. And working her body with his fingers until she was slick and burning, quivering on his lap. Meg dug her hands into the futon and flexed her legs, pushing against his hand, marveling at the strength of the thighs that held hers wide, at the solid arm that kept her trapped against his chest, at the hunger of the mouth that sucked at her and had her wound so tight. Her gorgeous man, so proper everywhere else, so naughty with her.

"*Now*, Meg," he insisted hoarsely. "Come for me." He pressed his thumb harder against her, sinking his fingers deep, and the tide broke, shuddering through her in a great unruly wave. Meg felt his rumble of appreciation clear through her chest. The light, crisp scent of his cologne hung in the air around her, and she breathed it deep.

When she'd stopped shaking and her skin cooled, Edward shifted her sideways. He hooked one arm behind her back and the other under her knees, heaved to his feet, then brought her to her bed. Setting her down, he pulled back the covers so she could crawl under them. He stood staring down at her, still wearing his dress pants and soft v-neck sweater.

"Stay," Meg told him softly. She couldn't stand the thought of him leaving just yet. Not without her getting to lay beside him, looking into his beautiful tawny eyes, stroking his hair, and tracing the planes of his face with light fingertips. She loved to follow the curve of his lip, the straight line of his nose, the fringe of his long black lashes. He held still when she did this, didn't seem to mind her perusal of his features. And she wanted to reward him for what he'd just done for her, wanted to repay those clever, skillful hands with some adoration of her own. He nodded, jaw set in stark, sharp relief as he began to disrobe.

"I'll have to leave really early," he told her, toeing out of his shoes.

"It's okay," Meg assured him.

She pushed herself up to kneel at the side of the bed, caressing each inch of skin as he revealed it. She pressed her face to his chest, inhaling the aroma of his skin, flicking her tongue out to taste him. In the last few days, she'd learned a thing or two about what got to this man, and Meg referenced that knowledge now, teasing and pushing him as far as she dared. She took him in her hands, and then in her mouth.

Edward certainly reveled in her, but no matter what she did, Meg couldn't seem to get rid of the restless edge she sensed in him. He'd found his completion and had pulled her over the edge again with him, but even though he now lay spooned behind her, his body still thrummed with energy. Meg knew they should sleep, but couldn't imagine being able to do that as long as he was like this.

"Edward?" she asked softly, turning to face him. "What's wrong?"

He shook his head, denying it. His hair, cropped close on the sides and longer on top, was gorgeously disheveled.

She traced the tattoo on his chest, and his pectoral muscle twitched under her fingers, like a skittish animal.

"*Edward.*"

He sighed deeply, pulling her closer. "Meg. It's nothing wrong, not precisely, it's just…" he trailed off, searching for words.

"Was it something I did?" she asked carefully. Her voice sounded small to her ears. She *felt* small, suddenly.

"*No.* God, no," he laughed. "How do I tell you?" He thought about it, considering, and she stayed quiet and waited. Hoping it wasn't the end somehow.

"Most girls I've met," he said. "They're all fur coat and no knickers, if you know what I mean."

Meg giggled. She couldn't help it. "I don't. Is that as trashy as it sounds?"

At least he smiled at that. "Yes. No. It means they're all flash. All…veneers, with nothing solid to back it up."

"Oh," she breathed.

"In Britain, the society birds were all after the title, or barring that, the money. And here…I found out soon enough that if it wasn't money they were after, they were angling for access to my dad. There didn't seem to be anyone who gave a rat's arse who I am," he explained grimly. "But not you. You're…" he stroked her hair back from her face, tucking it carefully behind her ear. "Meg, I didn't think there could be someone like you. I didn't think there could be a woman for me, a woman…a woman like you. That's why it took me so long to work up the stones to talk to you. I developed this whole fantasy around you and I really dreaded having to learn that you were just like all the rest of them."

Meg swallowed, unsure of what he was saying. The words were encouraging, but the tone seemed…sad. She had never once thought a man like him existed, either. Or if he did, that he would look twice at a loser like her.

"Meg," he breathed on a sigh, resignation heavy in his voice.

"Yes," she whispered, in case it was the last time she got to say it.

"I'm terrified that I'm going to overwhelm you. I've spent so much bloody time on guard, I've realized I have no idea how to be when I'm not trying to be careful. Am I moving too fast for you?" Meg shook her head and he plunged on. "I don't want to freak you out and drive you away. I mean, seriously, I took you to meet my family after only dating you for a week. That's, like, *barking* mad." He rolled on his back and threw an arm over his face. He sounded a little disgusted with himself.

"Edward, no. It's okay. You're not doing that," she told him. She pulled his arm away from his face. "I really, really like you," she added, staring down at him. *Really*, she added mentally.

"Meg, I'm arse over teakettle crazy about you," he informed her. "Just so we're clear."

"I'm good with that," she said carefully, holding her breath. "Are you?"

"Right as rain," he assured her, finally dimpling at little at her.

With his worries assuaged, his actual exhaustion seemed to overtake him quickly. He yawned hugely, then turned to pull Meg close again. Edward made a small hum of appreciation deep in his throat, and before long Meg felt his body relax beside her. She lay that way, ensconced in the circle of his strong arms for a long, long time, blinking in the darkness and trying to process what she'd heard. The notion of being someone's salvation, someone's lucky find, was inconceivable. If anyone had needed saving here, it was her.

EDWARD WAS GONE when Meg's alarm woke her the next morning. The din from the traffic on the street below was already ratcheting up, signaling the onset of rush hour. He didn't leave a note, and the only sign that he'd been there at all was the pile of her clothes they'd left in the middle of her living room floor the night before. Meg smiled, stepping around them across the cold wood floor. She tried to hurry so she would have time for breakfast, but it was so hard to shake off the languid haze she was in. Once she finally drifted off last night, she'd had long, convoluted dreams, faintly erotic, stream-of-consciousness things that never seemed to go anywhere. It had been disappointing to find her bed empty this morning, and Meg wondered when, exactly, Edward had left. Turning the shower water hotter, she wondered when exactly she might see him again.

He'd told her that he would be busy for the next couple of days, and that it might be hard to get together. But they'd made a date for Thursday night, and he'd already made suggestions for things they could do over the weekend. Meg wasn't worried. Somehow she knew it wouldn't be long before she heard from him. As it turned out, it was no more than an hour.

She rode a packed train into work, glad for the warmth of the swaying car after her frigid wait at the T stop. Then, as she sat at her desk and booted up her computer, Edward's first message hit her cell phone. Enlarging the photo he'd sent, she realized he must have taken a selfie of them before he left. The image showed their profiles, forehead to forehead, nose to nose. Meg thought she was asleep, and Edward's eyes were closed, too, but the faintest hint of the dimple in his cheek told her how pleased he must have been with himself. Her neck and shoulder were bare. His shoulder was bare, too, and flexed as he held the phone high above them to snap the picture. She sighed and held the phone to her chest, wondering how hard it would be to get a poster made out of the image. She didn't think she'd ever seen something so romantic in her life.

Chapter Twelve

EDWARD WONDERED HOW long it would take her to decide on an image to text back to him. Meg had kept it light for days, texting and calling back and forth with him, flirting in that lovely, snarky way she had for most of Tuesday and Wednesday. He'd been stuck in meetings with their new clients, trying to ignore the longing looks the architect's young wife kept sending his way (and George's too, when she thought Edward wasn't looking). It was no small feat to keep the husband on task. He seemed intent on impressing them with his "vision," but didn't appear to be entirely clear on the limitations of a historical restoration. It was all very irritating, but never knowing when his cell would buzz with a note from Meg kept things endurable. He knew she'd be looking for a way to trump that photo he'd sent—the anticipation was making him jumpy. He wanted to see her again, but short of a late-night booty call, Edward didn't see how he could make it happen before Thursday.

He had things to give her. He'd decided how he would present the pottery bowl to her, to begin with. And his mum had gotten in on the act, calling him from some mall to inquire about Meg's shoe size, of all things. Edward wondered if it had been a motherly sort of test, because she'd been startled when he rattled it off easily.

Then later, when he returned home, he'd found a shoe box on his counter and a note for him to pass them on to Meg when next he saw her. It seemed safe to say the countess had liked her.

Come to think of it, he'd soon have more things to give her. He'd snatched up several of her girly catalogs when they were perusing the home ones, and snuck them home with him. Meg had a good eye for what would suit her, and laying in his bed studying the things she wanted for herself made him desperately want to see her wearing them. Because she didn't seem to like him for his money, Edward perversely found that he wanted to buy her *everything*. It was clear she didn't have much money to spend on those sorts of frivolities, but pragmatic as she was, she'd circled sizes and colors anyway—he'd only had to pick out the things he loved best. He hadn't been able to resist the impulse to dress her up like a damn pet, even though he knew it would probably prick her pride.

Edward had toyed with whether to set up a closet for her at his place, or whether to gift wrap it all and mail it to her. In the end, he'd split the difference, arranging to send half to her and half to himself. If all went according to plan, his presents would begin descending on her just after he'd left for Britain, and continue arriving throughout his absence. He only hoped he'd be able to sweeten her up enough beforehand that Meg would agree to keep the stuff—and to model it for him when he returned.

Edward feared she might suspect what he'd done. Twice already, she'd asked him to check for the missing catalogs, saying she wanted to look for something to wear to his mum's party. He'd played dumb. Just this once, Meg could hit the shops or the internet like the rest of humanity.

Finally, Thursday morning, she got her revenge. Edward was sitting in the passenger seat of George's truck, heading toward a tile distributor's warehouse in Somerville, when his cell went off. He drew it from his jacket pocket, called up the text, and choked on his coffee. The steaming liquid blazed a trail down his throat, but he pressed the phone to his chest as he coughed anyway, shielding it from George's laughing eyes.

When he could speak, Edward choked out, "Tell me you did not see that."

His brother eyed him quizzically. "And what if I had?"

"Well, for starters, I would have to murder you," he told him.

"For starters?" George asked, chuckling as he watched his lane. They were heading over the Harvard bridge, and some dimwit in front of them was weaving a bit, eliciting honks and rude gestures from the cars around them. "What comes after fratricide?"

Edward didn't reply, trying to decide how to get a better, closer look at his cell screen without George noticing.

"You would never kill me," George bluffed. "I'm your favorite."

"You *were* my favorite," Edward informed him. "Now you are perilously close to becoming my victim."

George just shook his head and laughed harder. "Stand down, Guv'nor. I didn't see shite."

Thank God. Edward angled his body toward the window and took another gander at Meg's photo. She was lying in bed, hair mussed all around her head on the pillow, bare arm thrown back next to her head. The sheet had slipped to her waist, and she was wearing a lacy little top that didn't obscure much. And her *face*. Meg was looking at the empty pillow next to her with an expression of such erotic longing, Edward was half hard just glancing at it. The little vixen. How had she managed it? He'd like to get it blown up into some stupendously huge size, then plaster it on the wall across from his bed like a mural, so he could wake up and fall asleep, and it would be the first and the last thing he'd see. And he'd do it too, except he never wanted another soul to see this picture but him. He'd be committing homicide right and left if it ever got out.

Thoughts of criminality aside, Edward *was* rather enjoying having a saucy bit of skirt in his life, one who sent him photos of herself while he was sitting in meetings bored to tears, or eating dry takeaway at his kitchen counter at ten at night. He was enjoying it rather a lot.

George cleared his throat. "Meggers did something right this morning, did she?"

Edward nodded. Yes, she had. He loved her to distraction already.

"I like her," his brother commented benignly.

Edward nodded again, that seeming to be his safest option.

"And you, mate…you *more* than like her," George added, braking abruptly as he spotted their turn-off, then squealing the tires a bit as he made his left.

It wasn't a question, not really, and therefore Edward didn't feel compelled to answer. Chattiness might not be George's strong suit, but he'd never had any trouble making himself understood. Edward studied the photo she'd sent him again. Somehow, that little camisole made it sexier than if she'd been bare. He wondered how many tries she took before she got it right. Edward himself had eleven versions of the image he had texted her on his phone. Eleven attempts before he had it the way he wanted. He liked to look at them all in a row—it almost felt like he was still there, basking in the morning-after happiness.

They got out of the truck and strolled toward the open bays of the warehouse, their breaths clouds of steam in the cold morning air. Edward dropped the phone in his pocket, clapped his brother on the shoulder, and received a rough shove in return. The Honourable George Hughes was wearing a thick khaki Carhartt jacket and steel-toed work boots today. Not the clothes of the aristocracy, but those of a common laborer, and they suited George perfectly. There was something to be said for inhabiting your own skin with aplomb. George had always gotten it right, even as a child, and never made apologies for who or what he was. The last time Edward had felt comfortable as himself had been years ago, boxing for the company's team in the Rifles. And he *might* be getting it right, just now, again.

"Good for you, Ed," George said softly, clearly inclined to wrap things up and get to business. There were clangs and shouts emanating from the building before them, and George's eyes were trained on the interior. He had darker hair than Edward, hidden under his Bruins ball cap, and their mother's eyes. Edward had never wanted for a better friend.

In a flash, he thought of the Anderson couple, Carl and Anjelica, their newest high-maintenance clients. Carl wanted only to restore the glaze on their master bath tile, but Anjelica would settle for no less than radiant heat and marble mosaic under her pampered, nouveau-riche toes. That's why he and George were here, to find a work-around if possible. Because Anjelica always got what she wanted, it seemed. Edward worried for his brother.

"Don't sleep with her," he blurted out in a rush. "Mrs. Anderson, I mean."

George sent him a disgusted look. "I may be randy, but I'm not *daft*. When have I ever fancied mutton dressed as lamb?"

"She's on the pull, you know. It might get tricky," he told his brother. This whole project was starting to seem like trouble. A small-time architect determined to prove his street-cred via a celebrity's children. And his younger, hot-to-trot wife, keeping every one of her options open.

"It takes two to tango, Ed," George groused, indignant. "And you know I hate to dance."

George stomped ahead into the receiving area, grumpier than usual now despite the enormous coffee Edward had given him. He had no concerns about George's judgement, but now he felt more comfortable that he'd be on guard against anything Mrs. A might try to pull. Mr. Anderson did not seem the type to laugh off such an indiscretion. Anjelica, after all, was his fourth wife and the youngest yet, if their dad was to be believed. It was bound to make an aging man feel antsy.

With George several feet ahead and diverted, Edward shoved his hand in his pocket and stole one more peek at Meg's photo. Tonight. He'd see her tonight in all her glory, taste her, smell her.

Glancing at the tiny clock at the top of the screen, he sighed. Only…ten more hours to go.

Chapter Thirteen

MEG TRUDGED TOWARD the T stop up the block, hitching her tote bag higher up her shoulder. This part of Allston was always so ugly this time of year, gray and cold and dingy. She'd taken off work early today, wanting to make this trip before dark. Meg glanced around, wondering how safe she was, despite the fact that it was still broad daylight. It was the only time she would visit her old roommate Molly anymore. It had been different, a few years ago, traversing these streets at night to attend rowdy house parties. Then, Meg had been one tipsy coed in a crowd of them, and she'd felt confident and safe all over these neighborhoods, no matter what time it was.

After their freshman year together, Molly had moved off campus, and had sublet a succession of rooms in these big, shabby old Victorians. Meg had always found the group homes inexpressibly cool, filled as they were with bevies of independent, artistic types. She used to love to hang out with Molly, soaking it all up, Solo cup in hand. Now, Meg was a smaller, more scared version of herself, and visiting her friend felt like a bigger deal. She felt…vulnerable.

Fresh from this last visit, Meg found that she felt depressed, not invigorated. Some of the residents were young professionals now, but still didn't seem keen on growing up yet. Some of them didn't appear any closer to graduating than they ever had. And in the cold light of day, their tattered hand-me-down furniture, packages of expired tofu, and quirky ukuleles just looked sort of sad.

But Molly was still her friend and was trying to eke out a nice life for herself. Molly had eaten up every last detail Meg had shared about Edward, with her usual infectious enthusiasm. And Molly, conveniently, remained a total clothes horse. She had so many gorgeous clothes, and always had. She knew exactly what looked great on her, had a knack for finding the stuff for a pittance, and most importantly of all, she loved to share. Once Meg had realized that her missing catalogs were gone for good, and that if she was honest with herself, she didn't have the money to spend on a new outfit anyway, she'd picked up the phone and begged.

That brought her here, two days before the countess's birthday party, hauling home a bag full of clothes that Molly insisted looked terrific, and were perfect for the brunch the boys were planning. Meg prayed she didn't get mugged before she made it home. She didn't know how she'd replace what she'd borrowed—the cashmere turtleneck alone must have cost Molly a fortune, even on sale. Throw in the tweed pencil skirt and the designer black suede wedge booties, and that was probably enough to pay Meg's rent next month. It might be akin to putting lipstick on a pig, but at least Meg thought she'd look appropriate.

It didn't solve the problem of a gift, though. Meg bit her lip. She'd been agonizing over what to get the woman. Violet had specifically told her not to bring anything but herself, but she'd be damned if she showed up empty-handed. She might be having trouble getting her life off the ground, but she did have *some* standards. Meg clearly didn't have the money to buy the woman something nice enough. Any sort of perfume or apparel, or even stationery, to which the countess might be accustomed would come at too high a cost. Which left…God only knew what. Good manners were all fine and well, but Meg was going to have to be very, very clever about this.

She shivered. It had gotten colder, a brisk wind kicking up and turning her fingers to ice. And there went the T, rattling by the stop up the street without even stopping. She sighed. As mopey and dejected as Meg felt, it would still be better to keep moving—she'd freeze if she waited at this stop for the next train. So she turned at the corner, and walked toward the next platform a few blocks away.

That was when she spotted the store. A dingy little thrift shop, on a block she'd rarely been on. She had time, and on a whim, Meg decided to duck in. It would be warm, at least, and maybe she could find a cheap rug or something for her apartment.

She wandered around the crowded space, her coat brushing the warped shelves packed with dusty green cut glass. She trailed her fingers over boxes of old records, discarded electric typewriters, and grungy old clothes. Nothing here was quite old enough to have any retro cachet to it. It was just cast-off junk. Threadbare chairs. Battered side tables. Meg wove through the collection anyway, her eye roving, waiting for inspiration to strike if it planned to. It was stifling in the store, and she was getting impatient for some fresh air. She didn't want to forgo another train, either, and have to linger in this neighborhood even longer than she already had. The sun set early this time of year.

Meg almost missed it. She had passed it by at least twice, nestled as it was among a grouping of tacky, dated artwork. But something about the antique sheen of its ornate gilt frame kept drawing her eye. Finally, she stopped and really looked at it, and her heart began beating double-time. She glanced around to see if anyone else had noticed it, was even now making a beeline toward the little painting to snatch it from her grasp, but Meg was still alone. It was just as quiet and dusty as before. Too dim, with the low hum of an oscillating fan pushing the hot, dry heat around the room.

With shaking hands, Meg extricated the painting from the pile, blowing at the cobwebs clinging to the frame. It was small, the actual image measuring only about 5x7 inches or so, but appeared to be a real oil, not just a print. The frame itself added at least another three inches to each side. But it was the people depicted that took her breath away. A tall old-fashioned woman stood at the center, her soft wavy brown hair pulled back on her head in a bun. In front of her ranged three little boys, obviously brothers, bearing various expressions of mutiny and mischief. The mother had her slender hand on one boy's small shoulder—the other hand rested on the head of the shortest child. Meg imagined she'd had to do that, to keep them in place long enough. The third boy looked as if he would submit to being restrained by no one, and his face was, of course, the most compelling. The woman's eyes, though, were the very best part. Soft, warm, with a faintly amused expression to them. It was Edward's mother to a tee. Who were these people, and how could their picture have ended up here?

Meg ran her fingertips carefully across the surface. This was definitely an original, not a reproduction. The frame felt solid, too, and even though it was small, Meg feared for what something like this might cost. She looked around. This was no antique shop, though—it was better described as a junk emporium. Meg prayed both disinterest and a general lack of shrewd dealing would be in evidence. She approached the elderly man dozing behind the counter as casually as possible.

Meg held her breath and plopped the painting down as if it were just a piece of meaningless ephemera. Then, for good measure, she pulled a pack of gum from the rack nearby and tossed it right on top. She swallowed, and waited. Then cleared her throat. The old man startled in his chair, peered up at her, then at the edge of the gilt frame. His chair was a low one, and Meg wondered if he could even see the painting itself. She wasn't about to point it out to him, and toyed with how to ask its price without seeming too eager. But then he turned to his ancient register, pushed his bifocals up on his nose, and punched a few keys.

"Ten fifty," he barked.

Meg blinked, stunned. Her poker face had never been good.

He turned grumpily toward her, snatched the painting, gum and all, and wrapped the thing in thick brown paper.

"Look kid," he snapped impatiently. "It's a good frame. I gotta make a living here, all right?"

Meg was already trying to pull the cash from her wallet, but her shaking fingers were clumsy and uncooperative. Surely she had that much on her?

"It's okay," she said, finally slipping the money free. "Here." She had three singles left for the rest of the week. That meant, for lunch tomorrow, she could either buy two slices of pizza, or one slice and a drink, but not both. Who cared? This was worth it. *This* was the inspiration she'd been hoping for.

He took her money and turned away without another word, the drawer of his register slamming shut with a weak chime. Their transaction was clearly at an end. Meg caught the quiet sound of a baseball game coming from the radio under the counter, though the Sox had been eliminated from the series weeks ago. She grabbed the bundle, cradled it to her chest, and high-tailed it out of there before he could remember her and change his mind. Before he could suspect that something was up.

Meg nearly danced to the train stop, and waited only a couple moments before one trundled up. On the T, she shielded the bundle on her lap, protecting her find like precious treasure the whole ride home, even though her train car was mostly empty.

Once she'd made it to her apartment, Meg unwrapped the package with giddy anticipation, Molly's clothes tossed aside and forgotten now. In good lighting, the painting was even better than she'd dreamed. She had feared it would lose its magic somehow, that she had made an impulsive mistake, but no—it was perfect. This was a miracle. Meg never had this kind of luck, she mused, settling at her table with some cotton balls to carefully clean off the frame.

It was all Edward, of course. Because of him, she was different. Better. Because of him, she was going to get her life back on track, and she was going to be worthy of him. She might love him for a thousand other reasons, but she'd love him for that one, especially. Tomorrow, instead of buying lunch, she'd use her last three dollars at the campus convenience store to buy a pretty ribbon for this gift. The next day, she'd wear her borrowed clothes to his mother's party with her head held high. She would be the very best Meg she could be for Edward, now and for as long as he'd have her. And she wouldn't dare think about what might happen to her if he decided to move on.

MEG HARDLY REGISTERED anything for the next couple days, she was that excited to give her gift. But she'd made it through work, and she'd managed to keep the secret from Edward, difficult as that was. Her viscount, it seemed, was fully prepared to fight dirty to find out what he wanted to know. He just hadn't ever come across an adversary like Meg before. She smiled down at her gold-edged plate of lobster salad. Holding out on him had been about as fun an afternoon as she could've imagined. Her cheeks flamed, and she dared a peek around the elegant table again. It was a lovely, serene, sunny restaurant, and they had been seated in a private side alcove containing just their group. The boys were exhibiting reasonably good behavior, so far. Violet was, as expected, everything gracious at the head of the table. And Edward's mother was lifting her gift from the pile beside her right *now*. Oh, God.

Meg's head snapped up and she held her breath, waiting for the moment of truth. She *knew* she had gotten this right. She just knew it. But would the countess understand? She'd already received perfume, a Hermes scarf that she said she already owned, and a CD of some woman Meg had never heard of, but who Edward assured her was on Broadway. There was another small box from Edward's father that Violet set aside—it was obviously a piece of jewelry. No surprise there. After a quick admonishing look at Meg, Violet slid the ribbon and paper open with careful fingers.

Edward's mother froze, and the whole table fell silent, watching her expression as she studied the painting. Meg rubbed her suddenly damp palms on the starched white napkin in her lap. She had never attempted to open the frame at the back of the painting, or tried to determine the name of the artist. Should she have?

When Meg took a breath to speak, it seemed awfully loud in the room. "I hope you like it," she said into the silence. "It made me think of you." Violet looked up at Meg, darted a quick glance at Edward, then stared back at Meg again. She was blinking furiously.

Setting the painting gently to the side, she rose from her chair. Edward's father leapt up to pull it out for her, and to hand her around the corner of the table. Violet strode over to Meg with determination, then pulled Meg up out of her chair when she reached her. She took Meg's face in her hands.

Leaning in, the countess announced, "Of course I like it. It's absolutely smashing, you brilliant girl." She kissed Meg lightly on the forehead with cool, dry lips. "Thank you," she whispered. She nodded once at Edward, then turned away.

"I'll be just a moment," she called over her shoulder, before making her way towards the restrooms behind the bar.

"Nice job," Freddy barked crisply into the ensuing silence. "You made Mum cry."

His father hushed him with only a look, but softened that by ruffling the boy's hair. "Clearly, my wife is quite sentimental," he murmured, with a fond glance in the direction she'd gone.

George and Charlie were standing and peering down at the painting now. They snorted, almost in unison.

"That one's you," Charlie told his older brother, pointing down. Meg wondered which of the boys he'd indicated. They passed the frame to the earl and Freddy, who, after perusing it, passed it along to Edward.

He studied it for long moments, then gazed up at her with a faint smile on his face and a look in his eye that she didn't dare try to interpret. Was he proud? Disappointed? In love? It was hard to tell, and she put her confusion down to nervousness. She'd done her best to be thoughtful, Meg knew. Whether it was good enough was out of her hands. But at the moment, she wished she were better at reading people, and wasn't always trying to decipher what their hidden thoughts might be. Her gift had made the light-hearted lunch turn heavy, somehow, and she wished she could talk to Edward privately, to ask for reassurance. She'd thought his mother had seemed sincere, but surely a countess possessed consummate tact. Meg gripped her knees tightly under the table, her appetite for the delicate fare gone. Was she so untutored and naïve that her no-name little painting was a gaffe of some sort? One she wasn't even aware of?

Meg groaned to herself. She always did this, she knew. Second-guessed herself. Second-guessed other people's perfectly plain comments and reactions. It was over. The gift given. No take-backs now. She reached for the painting, wanting to get one last look at it, wanting to affirm her original, delighted impression. But Violet returned just then, plucking it from Edward's hands and marching back up the length of the table.

"I'm very excited, Alistair," she commented briskly. "And I know just where I'll put it."

Charlie raised his eyebrows at Meg. "There goes my last school portrait," he grumbled. "She'll probably tack it on the fridge now, next to Freddy's."

George casually pushed the scarf he'd given his mother closer to her, but his parents had their heads tipped close together, contemplating the painting in their hands. They didn't notice him. "Upstager," he grumbled, shooting Meg a foul look that made her giggle.

Edward scooted his chair closer, then squeezed her knee under the table. He leaned in next to her, turning away lest anyone else at the table read his lips. Putting his mouth right against Meg's ear, he breathed, so quietly that she barely heard him, "God, I love you."

Chapter Fourteen

EDWARD LOOKED AROUND the front parlor and decided that he adored his new couch. Meg had turned out to have lovely taste when it came to furniture, with a keen eye for what would look perfect in his house. She'd helped him pick this comfortable sectional, after all, as well as the large, antique wood canopy bed upstairs, and several other pieces scattered around. The fabric they'd decided on for the couch was exactly what he'd envisioned, but hadn't been able to articulate without her help: a cool-toned taupe color, and a soft microfiber that may as well have been velvet. It fit the room exceptionally well, making a perfect corner around the low square coffee table George had just made him. It also picked up the grayish clay undertones of the large pottery basin he'd bought right at the beginning of his relationship with Meg—he'd parked that right in the center of George's table, just as he'd imagined it. Meg had christened her own smaller version of the bowl a satellite to this one, immediately upon his presenting it to her. Edward had to admit, his iteration was, in fact, as large as a planet. It was brilliant. Her lacy underthings, which he'd just tossed aside, had caught on the rim, and were currently draped fetchingly over the side like a decadent bunch of black grapes.

Perhaps his favorite aspect of the new couch, though, was the way one end of it extended in a long chaise. And the way Meg was currently helping him christen it this afternoon. He held her tightly to his chest as she straddled him, her face buried in his neck, her mouth warm on his skin, and the rasping of their breath loud in the room. He squeezed his eyes closed and urged her on, trying not to clutch her too closely, trying to draw it out. How many more times might they come together in this room, or in any of the others? How many times to feel her exquisitely soft skin against his, or to taste her lips? He ran his palms up her back, feeling her spine and ribcage beneath her skin. He was leaving for Britain in one week. The time had seemed to stretch ahead of them for ages, giving them all the hours in the world to get lost in each other. But not any longer. Now he could almost count the time left on one hand, and he *hated* it.

Shaking his head, Edward tried to throw off his odd mood and refocus on the gorgeous woman he was holding. Meg. He could still taste her on his lips. They had barely made it through the door today before he'd sat her on this chaise, tossed her knickers aside, and buried his face between her thighs. It was always like that between them, the urgency that flared up out of nowhere, but he shouldn't cling to her like a drowning man. Because how adolescent was he? He was only leaving her for six lousy weeks. Just a month and a half. He'd go to the conference with his dad, she'd get Edward's gifts in the post, he'd celebrate the holidays with his family, he'd text and call her like the worst sort of stalker.

And somewhere in there, he planned to work in a visit to the jewelry store to buy this woman a diamond. That decision had come easily enough, once he'd realized he was in love with her. Easier than he'd ever thought it might be. Then, once that was all accomplished, he could return here, present Meg with the ring, and explain to her why any future separations were not in the cards for them. Why any future that didn't include her by his side was really no future at all. It seemed so logical. So black and white.

Simple, really. One would think that he'd be calm about it. It wasn't as if he had any doubts. He'd found the woman he was meant to be with for the rest of his life, and that was that. Or, it should have been. But the closer Edward's date of departure came, the more foreboding he felt. It was completely juvenile. One quick trip. No one was dying or going off to war. No one was going to cheat on anyone. It wasn't the end of the world. He held Meg in an iron embrace as she shuddered around him, her body encasing his so sweetly, her lips perfect against his neck. Edward stared across the room. He didn't want to let himself go and finish. He didn't want it to be over yet, any of it. Saying goodbye to her next week felt like the worst sort of error a man could make. He trusted her, and he trusted himself. So what in the bloody hell was his problem? He was shagging his cute little minx in the middle of his front parlor. He was more in love with her than he'd ever thought possible, and was nearly certain she felt the same. And here he was, brooding like an idiot, when he should be losing himself inside her as many times as possible before he left.

"Edward?" Meg murmured softly. He wrenched his eyes back, and found her studying him curiously, at close range. "Are you okay?"

Damn. She'd noticed. He nodded, then leaned in and took her mouth, her warm, willing mouth, hoping to distract her.

Edward kissed her, and held her, and let her heat melt into the chill in his chest. Gave in to it. Meg raised her hips, and lowered herself slowly over him again and again, and finally, he couldn't hold off any longer. He grabbed her tightly as she came apart again, holding her steady so he could thrust into her faster and deeper, then, blissfully, Edward tumbled over the precipice he'd been teetering on.

Meg had gone boneless in his arms. He fell backward on the chaise and brought her with him, draping her across his chest, her legs tangled with his. She sighed quietly, the sound vibrating through him, right over his pounding heart.

"I don't want to go," he told her.

"I wish you didn't have to," she admitted.

"You'll wait for me?" Edward asked her. Pathetically, but he didn't even care.

"Of course," Meg reassured him. She raised up on her arms to look down into his face. "I'll be right here when you get back." His eyes took in her expression, and he despised how fragile she seemed.

Edward's throat closed up, and he couldn't say another word. So he nodded at her, again. Then he kissed her again, too, hoping that his kiss would convey what his words could not. He'd be back. And then he'd never leave her again.

Chapter Fifteen

EDWARD LEFT AT the end of November. He hadn't wanted Meg to come to the crowded airport, though she'd offered. The day after he flew out from Logan, she struggled through a tepid version of Thanksgiving with Molly and her housemates. And the day after that, Meg received a lovely handwritten note from Violet, thanking her for the painting and expressing a wish to see Meg again once the family returned to the States in January.

For four days, Edward texted and called Meg with all of his usual affection and charm. Meg floated around the city on cloud nine.

And then, inconceivably, everything just…stopped.

She kept texting and calling him well into December, but he never responded. When the packages began arriving, she opened the boxes to discover gift wrap and Christmas messages inside. So Meg dutifully piled the gifts in a corner of her living room, the growing stack becoming more festive, and more incongruent with each passing day.

Christmas loomed at the end of the month. Edward and his family were due to arrive back within weeks, but Meg didn't know the specific date. Edward had said he would let her know. It couldn't be too far away—second semester would start for both

Freddy and Charlie sometime after New Year's. But Edward's email and voicemail boxes were full. Her texts to him were now flagged as undeliverable. It was impossible, really, to comprehend.

Meg fielded a phone call from her sister at the crack of dawn on Christmas morning, then took a cab to church for mass. She returned home, sat alone in the middle of her wood floor, and opened each and every gift he'd sent her. Each and every item she had circled in catalogs all those months ago, tagged with varying expressions of love and desire from a man who'd gone silent as a stone. While it explained what had become of her missing catalogs, it did not do much to explain her missing boyfriend. She looked around her apartment, and she did not understand. Meg's gift for Edward rested on her windowsill. He had wanted to wait for it, so she could give it to him in person. So he could *thank* her in person. Meg didn't want to look at it anymore. She got up from the floor, took the small box and set it on the top shelf of her tiny closet, refusing to think about the engraved gold cufflinks inside. Each one was inscribed with their entwined initials—they'd cost a fortune, but the jewelry store had agreed to finance them for her. Meg was paying them off a little each week and would be for months to come. At the time, she'd thought it was worth it.

January came, descending on the Boston area with a fierce nor'easter that dumped ten inches of snow on the city. Meg staunchly ignored New Year's Eve and went to bed at ten o'clock. In the basement laundry room the next day, she washed and folded the gifts that fit. In her apartment, she boxed up for return or exchange the ones that didn't, and superstitiously refused to wear a single item until he came back. Edward would come back, because he'd promised her, and Meg was *not* that much of a fool. At least, she didn't think so. Something must be wrong.

She did not take a step without her cell phone, keeping it with her every second of the day and night. That was not pathetic, it was just being prepared. One day, back at work, Meg was staring at its dormant screen and trying not to pick it up when she finally thought she figured it out. Grabbing the thing, she called up her contact list and scrolled through it. All those names and numbers—friends, coworkers, family members, all alphabetical and orderly, programmed in for ease of dialing. She did not have a single one of their numbers memorized. If she lost this phone, how would she call anyone? As the thought registered, Meg sagged with relief. Of course—*that* was what had happened. Edward must have lost his phone. He probably couldn't have searched for her number online either, because Morgan had made the landline unlisted after her divorce. And...*yes*, Edward would come back in the next couple of weeks, and he would feel awful when he explained it all to her. Probably almost as awful as she'd been feeling without him.

Meg did manage to survive the rest of January, but sometimes it felt like a near thing. The weather was hideously cold and snowy, so she hibernated at home, reheating canned soup in the microwave and getting jittery from too much tea. Edward did not email, text, call or return to town. Meg did not cry, sleep, eat, or give up. The website of his and George's restoration business bore a new home page emblazoned with a warning: *Not accepting new commissions at this time. Our apologies.*

Before Meg knew it, it was February. It was even colder and grayer outside than before. As barren as the city looked, her heart felt worse. But some of her numbness had moved aside to make room for a tiny kernel of doubt. Of anger. Had she been played? Callously manipulated and then left? Meg hadn't suspected that she was such a terrible judge of character. None of it added up, but then, it had never made sense to her why he wanted her, of all people, in the first place. She probably shouldn't be surprised. Maybe it was all a great big lark to him. Still, Meg woke up one day, steadily dismissed the fact that it was Valentine's Day, and embraced her inner Nancy Drew.

In the morning, she called over to Harvard from her desk at work. After being redirected a number of times, she reached a departmental secretary who starchily informed her that, "Professor Hughes was only a guest lecturer here, and is no longer with the university." Meg nodded, not particularly shocked by that. During her lunch hour, she wrapped her neck in the thick wool scarf Morgan had knit her for Christmas, donned Li Wei's heavy shearling coat, and set off for Brookline in the bitter, freezing wind. When she found herself, half an hour later, standing in front of Violet's home, it was as she anticipated. Dried leaves were piled in drifts in the corners of the front stairs, matted down with ice and dingy snow. The top of the driveway and the front walk were totally iced over as well, and didn't look like they had been shoveled at all this winter. There was even a sodden newspaper lying in the front yard, a pink *Financial Times*, no less, cowering and wilted within its weather-beaten bag. Meg allowed herself to look for only a minute before she forced herself to turn around and walk back to work. Once there, she fired up her search engine and looked for all their names, discovering only a bare bones listing of the family tree in a Wikipedia entry on the British peerage.

That afternoon, Meg called the alumni office of BU, and registered herself for the next LSAT being given on campus. She stopped at the campus bookstore that night after work, bought a used, dog-eared study guide, and began reading it on the train ride home.

She procrastinated for weeks before she could do the final, hardest things. She had turned into some sort of numb robot that barely resembled a human, but Meg had still held off on the last two tasks, dreading what she'd find. Her sister Morgan was calling more frequently, disturbed by Meg's desultory conversation. Molly had been inviting her to literally every event in town, trying to rouse her. But March brought with it a weird sort of resolve. She took the LSAT in a utilitarian campus classroom, and presumed she'd done well enough. It wasn't like she'd had anything to do in the evenings but study, anyhow. On the way out of the testing room, she had stopped at a large bulletin board, and pulled off the number of a girl searching for a roommate. Meg's lease was up next month, and the landlord had already sent a letter informing her that her rent would be raised. She would have to move somewhere cheaper—there was no question anymore.

After the long hours of the test, Meg hopped on the crowded T, rode three stops, and then disembarked two blocks from Edward's house. She didn't want to see it, but she still couldn't quite admit what was happening. She couldn't give all the way up, not yet. What did she want? To find it cold and desolate, like his parents' house? Or warm, and blazing with lamplight? Meg didn't know, but either way, she was going to be thorough in her agony. She walked to the gate in front of his house, stood still, and looked up. His brownstone was silent, dark and empty, the flowers in the planters long dead, the ivy in the yard overgrown and reaching through the wrought iron fence. Curtains were drawn over the front windows. When had he gotten curtains? No smoke drifted from the chimney. Even though it was ostensibly spring, there was ice and snow everywhere inside the gate, all the way to the threshold. No one was home in this house. Meg choked back her yearning and locked her jaw against the tears that wanted to come. No. She wouldn't. Not yet. She returned home, called the phone number on the slip, and arranged to meet Mayu, the girl seeking a roommate.

April came. How had it happened? Meg still had not cried even once. She had ached, for weeks and weeks, but she had not let herself shed a single tear. Morgan, her deliriously happy sister, informed her in no uncertain terms that she would be visiting next month, husband and baby in tow. But Meg was tired, so tired all the time. And she didn't care what a single person thought of her. It was oddly freeing, being a zombie. Nothing mattered. Meg had three job interviews and agonized over none of them. In April, she filed her taxes, and rolled her eyes when the government refunded her a whole two hundred dollars. In April, her boss Joe and his wife helped her move into Mayu's spare bedroom, in a sterile new high rise in Kenmore Square. Meg knew Edward would have hated it. Hell, she hated it, but it was cheap. Mayu was almost never home, focused in equal measure on her graduate Art History work and the clubs on Lansdowne Street. And Meg's sparse furniture filled up her small bedroom nicely. She used part of her tax refund to pay the application fee for Tulane University Law School, and refused to consider how hard it would be for Edward to find her again if she left town like he had.

In April, Meg sat in her little room, fired up her computer, and allowed herself to search one more time. The *last* time, she thought. Just this once, and then…no more. She typed Edward's name into the Google search box and sat stunned when she received an instant hit. A *new* hit, one she hadn't seen before. Clicking on the link with shaking fingers, she held her breath as the new site loaded. Then she scanned down the page of the architectural society newsletter, searching for Edward's name. Finally, she found it, an italicized blurb outlined at the bottom of the page.

> *The 76th Annual London Architectural Design Conference has been delayed this year, out of respect for the Hughes family of Cambridge. Lord Alistair Hughes, Earl of Westbroke, and his son Lord Edward Hughes, Viscount Shurso, were involved in an auto accident last December which left both men in perilously critical condition. Westbroke, an industry superstar, was to be this year's keynote speaker. Conference organizers note that when the conference resumes in March, Westbroke will be replaced by Dr. Reginald Plimpton as keynote. Dr. Plimpton is widely admired for his groundbreaking work on the Balboa Contemporary Art Museum (Spain), and his visionary reinterpretation of the country train station concept here in Britain. Final dates for the conference will be announced shortly.*

Meg sat back in her chair and stared. Frantically, she scrolled back up to the top, and noted that it was the February issue of the digest. She opened a new window on her computer and made her fingers type the words: Death, Obituary, Accident. Edward. She found nothing though, as usual. And the tears, dammed up for so many months, came then. Maybe the better word was *gushed*. They flooded her. Drowned her. Meg sat at that computer and cried until she was so empty that she was certain she would never feel a single emotion ever again. She crawled into bed and didn't come out, calling in sick to work for four days straight, and subsisting on oatmeal and bottled water only when she couldn't endure the ache in her stomach for one moment longer.

Even without the specific confirmation, Meg forced herself to accept it—Edward must be dead. There could be no other conclusion. Even if he had been lying paralyzed in a hospital bed somewhere, surely he would have found some way to reach her. He had told her he loved her and had begged for her to wait for him. She had found something good in this world, something fine, but she had lost it. Why should she be surprised, or hurt? That was what losers did, wasn't it? Lose the things that mattered? She had called Edward Hughes her own for only one month and four days. He had probably been dead for five times that long. True to form, Meg had kept her head in the sand for as long as humanly possible, but it was time to face the truth now. And it was time to move on.

Part Two

Chapter Sixteen

EDWARD FLINCHED, AND shifted in his sheets. He had been awake for approximately thirty seconds, and he was already irritated. As much as he enjoyed this bed—probably because it was one of the few things he (mostly) remembered buying—he was beginning to hate it, too. Like he despised this town. Like he hated his life. This bed made him think of what he did not have, and that feeling was both unpleasant and unwelcome.

Edward was also starting to loathe that huge round stone basin in the front parlor, because every time his eyes fell on it, it made him think of ladies' knickers. Specifically, it made him think that the bowl ought to be full of knickers, and the fact that it wasn't, the fact that they were missing, bothered him. So much so, that he actually wondered if there had been a burglary in his absence. What kind of pervert might that have made him? Did one call the authorities, when ones' bowlful of panties disappeared? Was he a man who actually *wore* ladies' underthings? Or a man who collected the panties of the legions he seduced, and kept them in a huge bowl on his coffee table? Edward shuddered. Neither option bore contemplating.

It wasn't as if he could ask Mr. Hathaway, the dealer who had purportedly sold him the bowl. And he refused to ask his brother George. The man could not be relied on to know the answer to anything important. What was more, Edward gave too much away about the state of his mind and his emotions when he asked questions like that. It was more efficient for all of them if he pretended to be doing fine. Because most of the time, the memory loss was manageable. The blank oblivion that met him so often here in Boston could be endurable, comfortable even, when it was about, for example, a restaurant he didn't recall going to before. If he didn't remember what his usual order was, he could experience the ambience and the menu as if for the first time. And that was all well and good, as long as some blighter didn't *say* anything to him about it. People themselves were trickier, of course, though Edward was mostly able to finesse those situations, too.

But Edward had these *feelings*, and he couldn't stand to ask about them anymore because no one ever had an answer that appeased him. All the vocal prods in the world from his family hadn't resulted in a single retrieved memory more recent than about six months ago. Last September to sometime in February had been completely lost to him. Edward just couldn't shake the notion that he was forgetting something big. Something *important*. The frustration was driving him off his rocker, and young Fred, especially, had been outspoken about Edward's personality change.

He didn't care that no one found him very nice anymore. He just…needed to figure out what in the bloody hell he was missing. Edward was not a man who lost things, this much he understood about himself. And whatever it was that was missing right now was critical enough that he felt it in every cell of his body. But Edward also understood that he was tenacious. Whatever it was, he would find it, and he would get it back. The only trick was in discovering what he was looking for. It was something valuable, something tangible, something…gone.

Why did he long for it in this blasted bed? At night, when he couldn't sleep? In the gray dawn, when he hated to get up and face another trying day. Why, when he texted on his new mobile, or took a snap with the camera app? Whenever he looked at his damned kitchen counter for more than one minute? Good God, the clues were all around him, but none of them fit together or made sense. The answer was right there, at the edge of his awareness, but he just…couldn't grasp it. It was enough to make a bloke crazy. And no one understood. They just wanted him 'normal' again. They just wanted him to remember the things that served their own ends.

Christ. And as for George and Mum, they kept nattering on about some chick from before that Edward ought to find. Like he had even an iota of time or energy to devote to a girl right now. It was one more note of insanity in a whole bleeding symphony. One more nail in the claustrophobic box he was in. Edward thought of the engagement ring he'd discovered in his things when they released him from hospital. He'd brought it with him here to Boston, but he still couldn't decide what to make of it. It had been a mistake, some sort of misunderstanding, he was nearly certain. He was probably doing a favor for a friend, someone from the Rifles about to get hitched, no doubt. The man would come calling for his property soon enough, given the value of that stone. There was no way it belonged to Edward, even if he did have the receipt for it.

Edward had only been dating someone for a month or so, they said. Forget about what his lunatic family had claimed about her, there was no way in hell he had fallen that fast for a woman here— he didn't even *like* American girls. What's more, it usually only took about that long before any girl's ulterior motives revealed themselves. Edward reviewed the classics—his title (both current *and* future), his money, his father. The Big Three reasons why women couldn't be trusted. Honestly, how special could she have been, if no one even knew how to get in touch with her?

Edward shook his head violently, dismissing it all. He had a mystery to fucking solve here. And if unravelling it turned out to be the key to unlocking his tortured, screwed-up psyche, so much the better.

Chapter Seventeen

MEG STOOD ON the sidewalk and contemplated the façade of the café in which she'd found and met Edward for the first time. She had not set foot in it since Christmas time, and was not so sure it was a good idea to do so now. She peered down at her nephew once more, snug in his stroller, clutching his fleecy blanket. Oliver blinked his large round eyes at her and hurled his stuffed animal at her feet. He didn't cry or fuss, though, leaving that one gesture to stand as his sole expression of displeasure. They needed a break from the mid-May sun, she needed a ladies' room, and he needed a fresh diaper. Both of them could use a snack. And Meg could do this, because Meg didn't care anymore. Why should whole establishments be off limits to her? She needed coffee and bagels as much as the next woman, and it was stupid and pathetic to limit herself only to places she'd never been with Edward. She glanced up and down the block again. There was nowhere else open this time of day, anyway.

Meg was tired. She and Oliver had walked and walked this morning, enjoying the warmth of the spring that had finally graced the city of Boston. Last night, over linguine in the North End, Morgan and her husband Owen had discussed their sight-seeing plans for today. Meg had met the eyes of her young nephew and made the offer to watch him without even thinking. He was a sweet, calm baby, and Meg had the surreal sense that he understood her and didn't judge. It was crazy, but it made her love him even more. Besides, how hard could it be? After Morgan and Owen had shared one long, speaking glance with each other, they'd agreed. They transferred Oliver to her care on the sidewalk in front of her new building at nine a.m. this morning, both of them shooting looks over their shoulders as they walked away. But if they'd had second thoughts, they didn't act on them. Meg was grateful for it—she wasn't sure the small measure of pride she had left would've survived if they'd come running back to snatch her nephew away from her.

Pushing the heavy stroller was work, that much was true. More physical activity than she'd had in a long while. In addition, Meg had not calculated how being back on this street would affect her. The emotional weight of her sorrow dragged her further down which each and every step. Sitting down for a few minutes seemed a mercy, even if it had to be in here. Meg hiked up her sleeve and checked her watch. They still had plenty of time before they had to meet Morgan and Owen at their hotel in Copley Square. Steeling herself, she picked up the stuffed elephant and returned him to Oliver. She yanked the café door open, wedged her hip against it, and maneuvered Ollie's stroller inside. They threaded their way through the jumbled tables with difficulty, then took care of business at the bathroom in the back. It wasn't until she left the bathroom and pushed Oliver toward the counter that Meg realized with a sinking heart who was working. Oh God. Not today. Why did Poppy have to be working today?

Meg shuffled up to the counter with downcast eyes, but before she could mumble her order in the same flat tone she used for everything else these days, she heard Poppy clear her throat impatiently. Meg glanced up, and something in her expression seemed to register with the other woman. Poppy held up a hand and rattled off Meg's old order with brisk efficiency. Meg nodded, but she didn't have the energy just now to register even a smidgen of triumph. There was no one around to witness this victory, anyway. Oliver certainly wasn't going to be telling tales. So she dug in her bag for the cash, all the bills lined up carefully in her wallet as usual, facing the same way, ordered from smallest to largest. Meg snorted. The largest she ever had was, like, a ten, but hopefully that was going to be changing soon. She'd gotten a call back on one of her interviews.

Poppy spoke, and oddly, it wasn't sardonic or brusque. "So...no more lover-boy, huh?" Her eyes, heavily lined in black, shifted between Meg and the stroller curiously.

Meg swallowed, her eyes filling with tears so easily it shamed her. She couldn't say the words aloud, so she just shook her head, staring into her wallet. How much was she supposed to be handing over? Shit. She couldn't think.

"I'm sorry, dude," Poppy said sympathetically. "You guys were pretty cool together."

Meg's hands were shaking. She couldn't seem to grasp the bills with her fingers, much less count them out. Was it six dollars? Eight?

Poppy laid her white hand over Meg's, with short navy-blue fingernails and a small anchor tattoo that Meg had never noticed on her wrist. She carefully extricated a five and three ones, then unzipped the outer pocket to retrieve some change. She pushed the wallet back at Meg and numbly, Meg tucked it back into her bag.

"He'll come back, you know. Something obviously happened, but he'll come back," Poppy said. She looked down at Oliver again. "Especially, if…"

The last thing, the very last thing Meg needed was false hope. On top of everything else, it might very well destroy her for good.

"I don't think that's going to happen," she croaked out quickly, cutting her off.

"Yeah well, I guess you didn't see the way he looked at you," Poppy retorted, some of her usual acerbity creeping back into her voice. "I saw it. Poppy sees alllll," she said mysteriously, gesturing around the café like a loopy medium before turning away to work on Meg's order.

Meg stared at her back for a long moment, unable to move despite the customers behind her. When she finally forced herself to take Oliver and go sit at her regular table, she noticed the change in the music. The peppy Bollywood tunes that had been playing upon their arrival had segued into mournful Billie Holiday selections. Dream a Little Dream? Cheek to Cheek? *Jesus.* Was Poppy trying to help her or kill her? She cracked open the bottle of apple juice that Owen had given her and poured it into a clean sippy cup for Oliver, then fished out the baggy of Cheerios that was stashed in the diaper bag for him.

Poppy's words spun around and around in her head. Edward wasn't coming back. Meg *knew* he wasn't coming back. Once people died, they tended to stay that way. She would be the worst sort of fool to torture herself over it. Oliver slammed his pudgy palm against the stroller's tray, catching her attention. Cramming a handful of Cheerios in his mouth, he gave her a tentative smile, as if he wasn't certain it was okay to do it. Lord, he was adorable. A miracle of sweetness. When Meg grinned back, unable to resist him, he extended his precious elephant to her, offering to share. She took it and nuzzled that mashed, faded head, kissing his toy with a loud smack, before tucking it into the pocket of the diaper bag where he could still see its face.

"You are an excellent sharer," she told him. "And Auntie Meg loves you. Do you want to read a story now?"

Oliver sucked on his fingers and blinked at her, bouncing in his seat as he absorbed her every move. Meg took that as agreement, retrieved the small board books from the basket of the stroller, and threw herself into entertaining her nephew. Her food arrived, delivered by a new waitress she'd never seen before, and Poppy disappeared into the back room, apparently on break.

By the time she was done reading and eating, Meg had formulated a plan of sorts. She was still a reasonably young woman. She had her first real job prospect in ages, and a new home that wasn't colored with memories. True, it was a small, soulless room, but it was affordable. She was also making reluctant plans for the future. She had managed to take the LSAT and had sent in that Tulane Law application. Maybe she'd even apply to other places, too, in other exotic locales. Like…Alaska, or Canada. She would be okay if she weren't dead inside, her soul tethered to a ghost.

So what Meg needed was an exorcism. And today seemed as good a day as any. She had a sturdy companion in Oliver, who wouldn't chastise her for being a masochist and tell her to get over it already. She had just enough time to complete her mission before she had to bring Oliver back to his parents, so there was no time to wallow. And, it was a beautiful spring day with buds on the trees and hyacinth, crocuses, daffodils and tulips cropping up in flower beds everywhere.

Meg was going to start in this place, this genesis of all she'd had with Edward, and she was going to walk the route they'd taken that first day. She was going to stand in front of his house, the place she'd allowed herself to dream in, and she was going to say goodbye, once and for all. Meg was going to put her fantasy to rest, then she was going to turn around and walk away and try to never be a loser again. It was the plan of last resort, but she was praying it would work. Nothing else had helped—Meg was still in love with a dead man.

IN THE END, Meg was amazed at how far a walk it had been. True, it had not taken her nearly as long to navigate it power-walking behind a stroller, but it still had been one heck of a hike. She hadn't even lingered anywhere on Newbury, and once it became clear that Oliver couldn't care less about the swan boats or the ducks, she'd made short work of the Common, too. Now, though, her calves were burning, and her nephew was decidedly groggy. That was good, Meg thought. If he had a long nap now, before they met his parents, maybe the adults would have enough time to enjoy a late lunch somewhere. She checked her watch again. So far, so good on the time. When they reached the end of this block, they would be facing Edward's brownstone.

Meg trailed her fingers along the wrought iron fence that surrounded the small garden here. It felt cold and oddly clean for something exposed to the traffic and weather day after day. She was being pulled along the street by an invisible cable, with odd tunnel vision focused only on the houses slowly being revealed to her at the end of the street. It hadn't been like this when she'd visited in the winter. Now, she wasn't aware of taking steps to bring her closer—she might as well have been flying there. But slowly. More slowly, the nearer she got. What was she expecting? To see both everything and nothing, all at once? To experience some cathartic shift that suddenly enabled her to survive again?

And…there it was. Meg stood with Oliver across the street and leaned against the black metal fence boxing in all the flowers in the little bed there. Oliver had been quiet as a mouse most of the morning, gumming the ear of his ragged stuffed elephant, and blinking up at her with his huge, brown, knowing baby eyes. She glanced down at him now, seeing his long black lashes resting on his cheeks for longer and longer intervals. He'd be sound asleep soon. Perfect. If Meg was stupid and ended up crying, she wouldn't upset him. And she'd have plenty of time to get herself together before she had to face her sister's happiness.

Meg looked back to the house, noticing that the stairs had been swept free of debris, and the big stone urns cleared of the dead mums from last fall. The ivy in the yard was trimmed and neat, and the lacquered front doors gleamed. And then, then—just as she was steeling herself to walk away for the last time, the unthinkable happened. The front door opened, and a man stepped out. She knew at a glance that it wasn't Edward, he was both shorter and burlier than Edward had been. But there was enough similarity there that Meg still did a double take, even though this arrangement of features didn't pierce her heart in nearly the same way. That's when she realized…*George.*

The blood drained from her face, and she wheeled the stroller around as fast as she could. Apparently the emotionally numb did still have survival instincts, because her feet were moving quickly up the pavement before she'd even made a conscious decision to flee. Meg was reeling. She wanted to run, but she also wanted to grip him close, to demand recourse. Help. *Anything.* She'd hesitated one second too long, though. George had seen her.

"Meg!" George hollered. She heard his boots running. "Oh God. Meg, wait!"

She felt his hand land on her arm, and knew she was caught. Reluctantly, Meg stopped, and turned to meet his eyes. George looked positively green, staring down into Oliver's little sleeping face. Meg realized in sickening flash how it must appear.

"He's not…he's not Edward's," Meg told him, forcing the words out. "He's my nephew."

George seemed to slump in his clothes at that. She knew what he was going to say, that Edward was dead. How sorry he was that no one had called her, that no one had thought to tell her. But she'd stopped listening to whatever he was frenetically babbling, because the front door of the brownstone had opened again. A slimmer, sterner Edward stepped out. Her breathing registered the fact before her brain by entirely ceasing to function. Meg swayed, catching herself on the black metal railing. Edward looked over at them with irritated detachment, strode down the steps, then got into his gleaming black BMW, parked right in front of his home. All with no acknowledgement of her whatsoever. Apparently, that critical car accident she'd read about hadn't been quite so critical. Meg opened her mouth, but since she had stopped breathing, no sound emerged—she was screaming, pleading, and sobbing only in her mind.

George looked frantically back and forth between her and Edward's car. In some of Meg's worst, darkest moments (mid-February, give or take), Meg had thought herself utterly unlovable. After all, the people who were supposed to do it kept abandoning her. Her parents, through sheer self-absorption. Her sister, all the way to Africa and New Zealand, for God's sake. Morgan's visit here had largely worked to dislodge *that* destructive, insidious idea. Her sister plainly still loved her, and now came equipped with a handsome husband and son who both seemed prepared to love Meg, too. But—Edward. Edward, who she had loved more than all of them after only one month, Edward had vanished into thin air. Edward had *died*.

The trouble now was this: if Edward was still alive, that meant he had *chosen* to leave her. He had used her for what he wanted, lied blithely to her face over and over, and then he had left her without one backward glance. The money he had thrown around must have been pocket change to him, a way to obfuscate what was really going on. To blind her to his real motives. And Meg, so desperate for love, for one good thing to happen to her in life, had fallen for it hook, line, and sinker. She could see it all now. The sheer enormity of the betrayal cut her off at the knees.

"Oh my God," Meg managed, before turning and making herself move again. Edward was just sitting there in his fancy car, scrolling perfunctorily through his phone as if she was just a shrubbery. She would never have guessed it of him—to love and leave, and then pretend like it had never happened. She was such an almighty fool.

"No! Wait!" George pleaded, grabbing her arm. She looked down at his hand and he slowly removed it. "It's not what you think, Meg. Let me explain."

"I *thought* he was dead," Meg said flatly. She had mourned him. It had been agony.

George's eyes bugged. "What? No, he's…"

Edward hit the button on his car door to lower the window.

"*George*," he barked. "We'll be late." He glanced at Meg like she was an insect, then retreated into his cave like the monster he was.

His brother gave him a placating wave, but George looked desperate. If Meg had been seeking closure, it didn't come much more obvious than this. She couldn't seem to tear her eyes away from the shiny driver's side window of that car, reflecting leaves and flowers back at her.

"Look, Meg, he doesn't remember you," George blurted out, grabbing her arm again. "He doesn't remember…*anything.*"

That caught her attention. She stared at him, not willing to give George even an inch of leeway. She had thought Edward dead, and that knowledge had killed her. But the truth was much, much worse. His family had known and done nothing. Edward was alive, and he'd left her in the dust.

"Amnesia, George? Really? You expect me to believe that?" she asked him.

"Yes. Well…sort of. More of a short-term memory loss thing. TBI. There was an accident, and…"

"I know about the accident." Meg could still see that computer screen when she closed her eyes, superimposed over the lovely spring day.

"You do? Oh. But then how…why didn't you…" he stammered. George scrubbed his hands through his hair, cropped shorter than his brother's, as always.

"*No.* Why didn't a single member of your family," At this she looked pointedly back at Edward in his car, revving the engine impatiently. "Call me even once? Not once, in the last six months," she asked George. The anger was there, back, and curdling in her gut.

"Meg, listen. I can explain everything," George insisted. "Just say you'll meet me tomorrow." He cast a worried glance back at his brother, then turned his traitorous, very sincere-looking eyes back on her. "I have to go now. Just say you'll meet me. *Please,* Meg."

Meg shook her head and looked down at Oliver's sweet sleeping face. She couldn't let these awful people hurt her again. She couldn't…

"*Meg,*" George begged, his voice cracking. He hadn't struck her as the type, before. But what did she know? She was apparently a horrible judge of character. He thrust his cell phone into her hands, made her close her fingers around it. "Give me your numbers. It's really important that you hear me out."

"Why?" That was all she could come up with. Why her, why now, *why*.

"I promise it will all make sense if you just hear me out," George told her.

Some of George's words were beginning to worm their evil way under her skin. TBI? Memory loss? Her hands were shaking as Meg tried to decide what to do. She stared at the cell phone she held. George had already pulled up the screen for her to enter her contact information. All she had to do was type in the numbers.

Across the street, Edward tapped his horn. Living, breathing Edward, only steps away from her, and inexplicably as rude as can be. Meg swallowed and began typing.

"Fine," she muttered, feeling stupid and pathetic and weak, and a host of other loser-like attributes.

"Oh, thank you baby Jesus," George murmured in a rush. Grabbing his cell phone, he kissed her fervently on the cheek, then took off running toward Edward's car.

"I'll ring you later," he called, waving at her once before ducking into the BMW. In moments, Edward had driven off, speeding up the street.

Meg stood there, shocked, for what felt like an eternity. Finally, gathering her wits, she peeked at her watch and realized they'd have to hurry if they were going to meet Morgan and Owen on time. It was important to her that they thought of her as a responsible baby-sitter. The best aunt ever. Still, she shook her head and let her eyes run over the façade of that brownstone one more time, trying to understand.

"What the hell was that?" Meg breathed, then wheeled Oliver's stroller around and headed back the way she'd come. Wherever they ended up for lunch had better serve her a drink. Or four.

"WHAT THE HELL was that?" Edward complained, when his damn brother had finally gotten in the car. "I didn't have breakfast this morning. I'm hungry as hell."

George blinked at him, wide-eyed and looking stunned. "Me, as well," he said.

"Well, if you'd stop trying to pick up Yank nannies on the sidewalk, maybe we'd have more time to fucking eat," he bitched, trying to navigate the worsening traffic. Edward hadn't calculated sitting on his ass all the damn day waiting for George to make time with some girl when he made the appointment with the guys in Newton. "Or was that her kid? I thought we were avoiding married women *and* mothers, George," he snarled. He was acting like a dick. He knew it. But honestly, they only had so much time to grab some lunch, and at this rate, he'd have to inhale something on the fly if they were going to make it.

George, never verbose on a good day, seemed at a total loss for words. "She isn't…that wasn't…" he tried. After that, he just threw up his hands and gave up.

Just as well. Edward didn't need to hear it, whatever it was.

"Look, I'll just call in to that sub shop in Brighton for some takeaway," George muttered, pulling out his phone. "We can pick it up on the way."

"Whatever, mate," Edward drawled. "I'm over it." He *was* over it. He was so over all of it.

George stared out the windscreen, looking haunted.

"Bloody hell," his little brother whispered.

Edward might have found that alarming, if he weren't feeling so pissy about everything else. It wasn't like that kid in the pram had been George's—Edward was certain he'd never be so careless. So how bad could it be?

Chapter Eighteen

MEG WAS LINGERING in the hotel bar with Morgan when George finally called. Owen had graciously offered to take Oliver up to the room to put him to bed, so the sisters were using their time alone to catch up. Meg had just finished explaining to the other woman what had happened with Edward earlier that day. And Morgan had just begun explaining that even if George never called, Meg was going to be okay. When the cell began buzzing across the polished wood of the bar top, both women jumped, staring at it as if it was a cobra.

Morgan recovered first. "Oh my God, Meg, it's him. Answer it!"

Meg stared at her sister in panic. "I don't think I…"

Morgan grabbed the phone, stabbing at it with her short, manicured nails. "Hello? No, it's not. Hang on, she's right here." With that, she shoved the phone at Meg's face, daring her to refuse.

Meg did not need any reminders of what her big sister was like when she was angry. Meekly, she took the phone in trembling fingers, holding it to her ear as if it might burn her.

"Hello?" she squeaked.

"Meg! Hi," George said, clearly relieved. "I wasn't sure you'd answer."

"Neither was I," she admitted. "So my sister did it for me." She glared at Morgan.

"Ah. She's…your sister from Africa?" he asked hesitantly.

"Well, New Zealand, now, but yeah. She's here for a visit."

"I see. Right. That's good," George replied.

Meg sat there, saying nothing, until Edward's brother seemed to remember the reason for his call.

"Listen Meg, Charlie and I need to see you. As I told you earlier, we have a lot to explain," he told her.

"I can imagine," she offered, filled with the liquid courage that came from two large glasses of excellent pinot noir.

"Can you meet us tomorrow morning? Before work? There's a Starbucks, right at the start of Newbury Street."

"Umm," Meg hedged. She didn't have to work tomorrow, having taken time off to visit with her sister. But she didn't want to look too easy, either. That seemed important right now, but maybe it was just the wine talking.

"You know the one? Not on the park end, the other end, near Mass Ave."

"I know the one you mean," she said, mostly to get him to stop talking so urgently. Meg felt a headache coming on, but she didn't think she could blame *that* on the pinot, much as she'd like to.

"So, will you? What time works? Charlie isn't in class until ten, and all my appointments are after lunch," George urged.

Morgan had been leaning her head close to Meg's, trying to listen in. At this point, she shoved her little sister on the hip, nearly dislodging her from her barstool. The bartender was ignoring them, watching baseball reruns on the television mounted in the corner while he absently rubbed at glasses with a towel. No help from that quarter.

"Uh. Okay," Meg finally agreed. "How does…8:30 sound?" No more than an hour to sit through their spiel, and then she'd be free again. It seemed doable.

"Perfect. And Meg?"

"Yes, George?" Meg asked in resignation.

"You're really going to show, right? You're not just saying you will?"

"Yes, George," she sighed.

"All right. Cheerio," he said, then cut the connection.

Meg turned to her sister.

"Dear Lord, you look terrified," Morgan told her, pulling back with a frown.

"I am," Meg admitted.

"Owen and I better come along," Morgan decided, in her brisk, big sister way.

"I'd better have another glass of wine," Meg said. "Maybe two."

WHICH WAS HOW, the next morning, Meg ended up with a cappuccino in her hands, a hangover in her head, and agony in her heart. She sat in a crowded coffee shop listening to the most incredible story she'd ever heard, while her well-intentioned family observed everything from three tables away. Meg kind of wished she had Oliver's nappy little elephant to hold on to now. It seemed like it might be helpful.

"I'm serious, Meg," George was saying. "You mustn't take it badly that he didn't know you yesterday. Edward genuinely doesn't remember anything from about mid-September until sometime in February."

Charlie sat there looking pained and shaking his head in confirmation.

"But he knew all of you?" she asked, for about the fourth time.

"Yes, once he'd woken up and gotten most of the meds out of his system. As I said, the doctor explained that those sorts of memories, older ones, are stored differently in the brain, so they're easier to access again when there's been an injury."

"But..." Meg was having trouble processing everything they had told her. Edward and his father had been driving a rental car in London mere days after their arrival, on roads that were turning icy as night fell. Despite the slick conditions, they had managed to stop at a red traffic light without skidding. The car barreling toward the intersection in the opposite direction, however, had not been so lucky. It was impossible to comprehend, like a bad soap opera. "Your father," she tried again.

The brothers seemed to understand that they were going to have to repeat themselves a fair amount with her, but neither seemed inclined to begrudge her.

Charlie said, "Father's legs were mashed a bit, among other things. We weren't sure if he was going to be able to walk again for several weeks there."

"Your mom must have been beside herself," Meg whispered, trying to imagine it. A husband and a son, in intensive care an ocean away. It was unthinkable.

"It was better, once we got all our tickets changed to fly home sooner. Once she could see them for herself, see that they would make it, she rallied," George said.

"But why…" Meg shook her head, trying to order her scattered, half-formed thoughts. "Why was Edward…but not your dad?"

They seemed to understand. "It's probably because of the way Ed was sitting," George told her, fidgeting with his cup. "He doesn't remember anything of the accident, but Dad said he thought Edward was trying to find something in the glove compartment just before. The doctor said if Edward was bending down on impact, he might have hit his head badly enough to cause the TBI."

"TB…?" she asked again, feeling foggy. Clearly, more caffeine was needed here.

"Traumatic brain injury, remember?" Charlie offered. "Blimey, Meg, I'm beginning to wonder if you have it, too."

"Charlie!" she protested, at the same time George spat out, "Charles."

George scowled at his little brother. "At the beginning, it was especially rough. He was unconscious for days, and when he awoke, Edward couldn't remember little things, like the fact that he'd just eaten lunch. Or he would ask us over and over what time it was."

"God, that was irritating," Charlie commented.

"Most of that sorted itself out, eventually," George explained. "And his other injuries healed fine—broke his arm and a couple ribs, probably from Dad being thrown into the side of him. I don't think any of that bothers him anymore."

Meg sat and thought about what they were telling her. Tried to envision what it must have been like, the hospital, the disorientation. From across the room, her sister gestured. Did Meg need help? Was she okay?

Meg shook her head. No to both things. But something about George's words snagged her attention.

"Is there something that *is* bothering him now? Besides the obvious, I mean," Meg asked.

The brothers glanced at each other, their gazes searching.

"He's been…a bit testy," Charlie admitted.

"I don't think he's sleeping well," George added. "And he has headaches, here and there."

Meg waited a minute, making sure they were finished. Feeling a bit testy and tired herself.

"Explain to me, please," she choked out, "Why not one of you thought to tell me all this when it happened? To call me, to write me, why didn't you think I would want to know?" Her hard-won composure cracked right down the middle, and Meg felt the tears start to pool in her eyes. She couldn't stop them, she knew. But she didn't exactly care anymore.

"*Meg*," George began. He looked as agonized as she felt, and he gazed at his younger brother for reassurance. Charlie nodded at him, urging him to continue. "You have to know we tried. Once we could think straight, we thought of you straight away. But none of us had your number. We tried to search online for it, but…" he shrugged helplessly.

"Do you have any bloody idea how many Meghan Flynns there are in the city of Boston?" Charlie groused. "Not to mention in all the surrounding towns."

Meg tried to blink away the tears. "You wouldn't have found it anyway," she admitted. "My number was unlisted. But Edward's phone—couldn't you have looked in there?"

George was shaking his head sadly. "Edward's cell was in the center console of the car. It was destroyed in the crash. That wasn't an option." Just as she'd guessed, all those months ago.

It seemed impossible. All of it seemed impossible. Meg sifted through their words, trying to find the lie. Sorted through every interaction she'd ever had with these people, looking for dissonance. Something came to mind, a small detail, from the time right after Edward left.

"Your mother—she wrote me a thank you note, after her birthday party. Clearly, she had my address," Meg pointed out.

Charlie was nodding in agreement before she'd even finished. "Yes, she remembered that, too, once we moved Father and Edward home to Cambridge. Took her a long bit to uncover it, but she did mail you a letter."

Meg might be hazy now, but she knew she would remember such a thing. "I never got anything like that," she said flatly, denying it.

"No, you wouldn't have," George agreed. "It came back as undeliverable. She called and told us, after we'd already returned here."

"I moved," Meg whispered. She'd moved, and it had taken her weeks before she remembered to have her mail forwarded. What an idiot she'd been.

She took a deep breath, filling her lungs with the cool, coffee-scented air, then released it. She wished she could blow out all of the pain of the last six months along with it. Not just hers, it seemed, but Edward's family's, too. She realized with a jolt that she actually believed what they were telling her. But strangely, that knowledge didn't make it hurt any less.

"One thing I still don't get," Meg said quietly. "Why did you come back? If your father still isn't doing great, and your mom and Freddy stayed in England with him, why did the rest of you bother coming back?"

"Well, *some* of us still have to go to college," Charlie said acidly.

"I didn't mean you," Meg gritted out, her patience wearing thin.

George understood. "Can't you guess?" he asked softly.

"The business?" Meg replied, being deliberately obtuse. She refused to consider any other option. Not when she thought she might break into a million pieces at any moment.

"Meg, Edward's not the same," George began.

"He's an arse now," Charlie interjected.

"True. He's not himself. The doctors thought he'd have remembered everything by now. The fact that he hasn't is worrying them—they say if he doesn't get it back soon, he might never. And if he's in what they call a fugue state, he might remember last fall, only to forget everything since then."

Meg blinked rapidly, the thought of that making the tears come faster.

"You think *you* miss him?" Charlie challenged her. She nodded faintly. "Well, we miss him more. He's our bloody big brother, damn it."

George was doing a better job of treating her gently, but it was clear he agreed with Charlie. He nodded. "The thing is, Edward knows he's fucked in the head. He was bitching about "missing something" constantly before we dragged him back here. And we thought if we brought him back, it might help jog his memory. The doctors agreed it was worth a shot."

"And?" Meg asked carefully. "Did it help?"

"Well, he stopped complaining so much," Charlie commented. "But he's still being a dick."

George mused, "I think it's still bothering him. I think he's frustrated that it's not getting better, and I think he's pretending he's fine, because he doesn't want us to worry."

Meg hadn't noticed her sister approach the table, but Morgan spoke now, standing behind Meg's shoulder. "And how does any of this affect my sister?" she inquired.

George and Charlie did not look the least bit perturbed. In fact, this seemed to be the question they had been waiting for. Charlie leaned back in his chair, looking satisfied that the reason he'd come here was finally reaching the fore. George smiled tentatively.

"We don't just miss our old Edward," George told Meg, looking intently at her. "We miss him most the way he was with you."

"Mum, especially," Charlie pointed out. "She never shuts up about it."

"True," George said, smiling wider.

Meg lost it at the mention of the countess. "Jesus. What do you expect me to do about it? You saw him—he looked right at me yesterday and didn't even know me!" She intended to go on, but found herself choking on the words in her throat. Morgan laid a placating hand on her shoulder, squeezing gently.

"We thought if we could set up a meeting between you two, sort of reintroduce you, so to speak…that might help. He was crazy about you, Meg. Surely when he talks to you for a while, he'll be able to remember," George begged. He was desperate, and not trying to hide it anymore.

"Christ, Meg, you're like, our last bloody hope," Charlie grouched.

"Guys, you don't understand," she forced out of numb lips. "When Edward disappeared without a trace, it…it *leveled* me. I was ruined." She sobbed out the last word. Everyone waited patiently for her to recover enough to continue. "I don't think I would be able to sit there with him and pretend I didn't know him. That there was nothing between us. I'm not that good an actress, believe me. He'll know something is up."

"But that's bollocks, Meg. Don't you even want him back at all?" Charlie was disgusted.

George was kinder. "Will you at least think about it?" he asked quietly. "I can call you again, in a week or two, and we…"

Morgan had crossed her arms over her chest and was surveying the table and its occupants like an avenging angel.

"That won't be necessary. Meg will do it. Name the time and place and she'll be there," she decreed.

Meg was aghast. "Morgan! I don't want to!"

Morgan shook her head. "Nope. You pipe down," she told her outraged sister. "What did you have in mind?" she demanded of George.

"I'd thought a group outing at first, so he wouldn't suspect right out of the gate what we were about," George offered. "Meg could bring you, or a friend."

Meg thought the distinction between her sister and the term "friend" was an apt one at the moment.

"And what if the new Edward likes my friend more than me?" Meg inquired crankily. "Did that occur to any of you?"

George didn't pause, he simply retorted, "If she's a good friend, she'll have no problem acting like a psycho to prevent that."

Meg rolled her eyes. She had exactly one friend who still lived in town, and Molly was both gorgeous, and notably *not* psychopathic. "But you keep saying he's different," she said. "What kind of *psycho* are we talking about here?"

Charlie snorted. "Loud and clingy ought to do the job nicely," he laughed. His brother nodded eagerly.

"You're right," Morgan nodded briskly. "Good idea. Text Meg the details and I'll make sure she gets there."

"Er, thanks," George said, clearly wondering if the interview was at an end.

Owen sauntered up, bouncing Oliver on his hip. He looked his wife up and down with a smirk on his face. "Got it all sorted over here, have you?"

Morgan raised her eyebrows at Edward's brothers, who both nodded readily, taking in the brawny new backup that had arrived.

Meg sat sullenly, dabbing at her eye makeup with brown paper napkins, and refused to look up.

"Excellent. Well, we'll be taking our womenfolk off, then, if you don't mind," Owen told the brothers. He extended a hand down to Meg, then hauled her to her feet and tucked her under his free arm. Morgan pulled Oliver from his other arm, and the four of them swept out the front door, leaving George and Charlie looking shell-shocked at the table.

"I thought that went well," Morgan chirped, looking satisfied. Owen squeezed Meg around the shoulders, and she wound an arm around her brother-in-law's waist, letting herself be comforted by his tall, solid frame. What in the hell had she gotten herself into now?

Chapter Nineteen

FUCKING GEORGE. *GEORGE* was making him go out again tonight, Edward thought, scrubbing at himself in his shower. He didn't want to go, he never did. He didn't want to go *so* much, that even the idea of wanking off in the shower did not appeal to him. Not that it usually did anymore, anyway. Edward barely cared. The ancient pipes clanked and groaned in the wall. George had told him they replaced most of the pipes in the basement soon after Edward had purchased the house—there had been signs of water damage down there when they inspected it. But Edward didn't think the pipes up here, behind the wall, had been touched. If they hadn't, George and the crew would need to take a look at them. That, at least, was a question Edward could ask his brother without feeling weird. Something solid and normal.

As for tonight's outing, his brothers had tried to be nonchalant, and sell it to Edward as some casual get-together. Some meet-up with Charlie's friends. If that was really the case, they'd end up going to some gay bar in Jamaica Plain. Instead, they were going to a touristy Irish tavern near Quincy Market, and it was not the sort of place either one of his brothers hung out in regularly. If George had left the bulk of the lying to Charlie, then Edward *might* have been taken in—Charlie was the best dissembler they had. But being the oldest gave one certain advantages in a family of boys, and one of them was that Edward could always, *always* smell a rat when George was plotting something. And George was definitely plotting something.

Edward supposed it probably involved a girl. There'd been a few pointed remarks in the last week or so, along the lines of Edward needing to get laid. George clearly assumed Edward's issues could be sorted with something as basic as a proper bit of fluff, since that was the method that apparently worked for George. It wasn't as if Edward didn't *know* it had been a while since he'd shagged someone. As far as he could determine, it had probably been six months or more. He just hadn't expected that fact would be obvious to anyone else. Or that anyone one else would care quite so much. But leave it to George—he had an innate ability to determine Edward's tender spots, and to drive his daggers right in. Clearly, this was a talent that went along with being a *younger* brother.

As he toweled off, Edward wondered what she'd be like. Surely George wouldn't be so gauche as to suggest Edward hook up with a college girl Charlie's age? But he was curious as to what sort of woman his brothers *would* dangle in front of him. A Yank? A brunette? Perhaps a foreign girl—with all its universities, Boston was certainly awash in Eurotrash types. Edward, through long years of experience, had learned not to put anything past his brothers. He supposed he ought to be charitable, to a certain extent. The woman, whoever she turned out to be, was likely an innocent bystander in all this. Edward pulled a starched button-down shirt from a hanger and resolved to at least be polite. It wasn't her fault this was a set-up, and she hardly needed his brothers' foolishness to be compounded by Edward's surliness. That, he could keep all for himself.

Standing in his closet with damp hair and bare feet, he let the shirt hang from his hand. When he'd moved back into this place, he had gone through almost everything inch by inch, praying for a flash of some sort. Some recollection, some recall, *something*. In the privacy of his own home, he had allowed himself to feel hope, but Edward had been disappointed. He'd felt like a failure when he'd come up blank, as inadequate as he ever did lately, when the people around him wanted him to remember something he couldn't. However, he *had* found something surprising. Why had it been this, and not whatever he thought he was missing?

Edward looked at it now. For some unknown reason, he had a whole shelf in his walk-in closet full of women's clothes. All the same petite size. All very pretty muted colors. He'd initially assumed they belonged to the purported former girlfriend, though it seemed awfully presumptuous of her to leave so much stuff at his house after only a month of dating. Lord knew he'd instantly thrown out the extra toothbrush he'd found in the loo. He wondered if she even cared—after six months, she would have had to concede that she wasn't getting her things back.

It had taken him a few days before he could work up the nerve to actually touch the stuff, to hold it up and try to get a sense of the kind of person she might have been. What her style had been like. That was when Edward found the tags on everything. It was all brand new, never washed or worn. Perplexed, he'd laid it all out on his bed, piece by piece. Nothing fussy or flashy, all of it stylish and elegant, and judging by the price tags, all high quality. Edward had run his fingers over soft lace and cashmere, warm wool and velvety silk, intrigued despite himself. He'd like to meet the woman who could pull off this look, he thought. He'd like to hold her in his arms, her warm body inhabiting these clothes. Edward folded everything up and put it neatly back where he found it. And then he also put aside all the things troubling him and let himself picture one good thing. He'd had no problem jerking off *that* night, imagining her.

Edward shook his head, dismissing the thought and checking his watch. If he was going to be ready when George came by to pick him up, he was going to have to get moving. There would be a different girl at the bar tonight. Maybe she would be pretty. Maybe Edward would feel something like desire for her. He wasn't so confident that she'd be able to inspire passion, not like he'd had with…*someone* before. He couldn't think when that had been, or with whom. Edward sighed wearily. Another thing he had lost. Focusing, he reordered his thoughts. Maybe the girl would like him. Maybe she would even want to kiss him at the end of the night. It was easier, these days, to speculate about the wishes of others, and to leave his own emotional wasteland out of it.

THEY ALL CONVENED at McGillicuddy's in Quincy Market, and through strength of numbers managed to commandeer a table large enough for most of them. After an urgent debriefing, Meg had brought Molly instead of her sister Morgan. Charlie brought several friends, including two young men named Sean and Cal, who had obviously heard one too many enticing stories about Charlie's brothers. George showed up last, a bored and reluctant-looking Edward trailing behind. Meg steeled herself at the sight of him and was helped in her efforts by Molly's hand surreptitiously squeezing hers.

"This is going to work," her friend hissed in her ear. "Just wait." Meg wasn't quite so optimistic. The sight of her hadn't had much effect on Edward the other day, and if they were shooting for familiarity doing the trick…she looked around. This wasn't exactly the sort of place she and Edward might have gone. When they'd been able to get out of bed, that was.

After a fair bit of jockeying for position, the boys managed to get Meg into the seat next to Edward. He looked grateful for it. Molly had done her part, lighting up like a Roman candle at the sight of Edward, whom she'd never met before. She made a beeline right for him and began laying on the corny come-ons with her very first words. She'd dressed to impress, and was giving her over-the-top persona of the evening all she had. Meg was relieved to note Edward was already recoiling from Molly's performance like the plague. Charlie was enjoying it immensely, however. Given the way the two had begun whispering, Meg suspected he was giving Molly tips on how to annoy his brother. It didn't seem to matter—once Molly had draped herself on Edward after their introduction with a seductive *"Hello, Handsome,"* he'd made it clear he would rather have a root canal than pursue any further conversation with her. The band was loud, and the drunk crowd of students, half of them looking very underage, was even louder.

"So, how do you lot know each other?" Edward managed to yell over the din.

George caught her eye across the table. Somehow, in all their handwringing earlier in the week, they hadn't anticipated this most obvious of questions.

However, Charlie was alert and quick on the draw as usual. "Meg used to work at my school," he shouted across the table. "We met there."

Edward seemed to accept that explanation without question. He raised one of his aristocratic brows at her, mildly curious. Leaning in, he inquired, "Oh? And what did you do there?" She didn't think he really cared about her answer, but God, did he smell good. Just the same as she remembered. It was torture.

Meg blurted out the first thing that came to mind, "Property management. We tracked all the college-owned equipment on campus, like computers and tables and stuff." It was possibly the least interesting work in the world, guaranteed to kill any and every line of inquiry just by mentioning it. She knew this, because it had been her actual job while she was still in school herself.

Meg eyed Edward warily, trying to gauge his reaction. Would he remember that about her? So far he hadn't seemed to find her the least bit familiar, but if George was to be believed, a flash of recollection could come at any time. Nothing happened. Edward's eyes glazed over, then drifted away in a very predictable fashion. She was safe, for now.

He turned to George, calling out some innocuous work-related question across the table. Meg welcomed the reprieve and worked on shoring up her composure. Pretending as if she didn't know him was harder than she'd expected—trying not to reach out and touch him, or to smell his delicious neck. Molly kept trying to catch her eye, obviously hoping to see how Meg was holding up without giving herself away. Meg felt fragile. She suspected that if she had more than one drink tonight, she was going to find herself in the bathroom, with Molly mopping tragic tears off her face.

Thankfully distraction arrived, in the form of a very noticeable young woman weaving her way expertly through the crowd. Her glamorous rockabilly looks made her stick out like a sore thumb, like some sort of technicolor pin-up girl dropped into the middle of the bar. Meg's eyes were drawn to her vibrant blue and black hair immediately, and she wasn't the only one.

"That girl," she exclaimed. "I think I know her!"

Charlie turned to see who she was talking about. "She looks like half the birds in my school," he commented, unimpressed. His attention was being pulled toward the corner, where a huddle of fraternity guys was knocking back shots with grave determination.

"That way lies only heartbreak," Molly told Charlie with a wink. "Trust me—been there, done that."

Meg smiled, turning to Edward. He studied the girl in the crowd, his eyes narrowing critically. "She looks like a freak," he declared.

But George had the most interesting reaction of all. His gaze had zeroed in on the girl like a wolf scenting a very juicy steak. And once he had her in his sights, he didn't take his eyes off of her.

"George?" Meg called. Even Molly jostling his shoulder from the side with a loud, uncharacteristically brazen giggle didn't divert him. Reticent George had morphed into some kind of predator, intent on tracking his next meal.

Charlie's classmates, who had been unabashedly enjoying all the brawny British eye candy at the table, registered his expression and dissolved into well-dressed puddles in their seats. Meg half expected them to start fanning themselves and swooning.

"George?" Meg tried again, incredulous at his reaction. "I *know* her."

He turned back reluctantly, obviously not wanting to lose the girl's location in the crowd.

"I know where she works," Meg told him.

This piqued his interest. "Oh yeah?" he asked. He fished his phone out of his pocket and waved it at her. "Text it to me," he said. He turned away again to find Poppy in the melee, dancing next to the stage.

Meg shot another amused look at Edward, took her own phone out of her purse, and tapped out,

> Her name is Poppy, like the flower. She works Sat morns at Jazz & Java—coffee n bagel place on Comm Ave / BU West.

A moment later, George looked down at his phone, nodded, then stood and made his way through the crowd. When he reached her, there was only a sentence or two of conversation, before George pointed out Meg and Edward back at the table. Poppy's eyes bugged out behind her black-framed glasses, and she raised one hand to them in bemused acknowledgement. Meg waved back, wondering what the barista would have to say the next time Meg saw her. She shuddered to think, but guessed it would have to begin with, *I told you so.*

Edward turned to her in amazement. "You know, all this time, I think my brother has been hit on by every desperate housewife doing a renovation in Massachusetts. No wonder he was never interested," he chuckled.

Meg just shook her head. Was that an actual memory of his, or just something he'd been told? Across the bar, George was crowding up nice and close to Poppy. "I *never* would've guessed she was his type," she admitted.

Edward didn't seem to find it odd that she might know his brother that well. All he said was, "Indeed."

They watched the couple across the room, not even trying to disguise their fascination. George might have been anywhere—he had eyes only for Poppy. Poppy, on the other hand, kept glancing their way, seeming nonplussed by the interest of the people at their table. Meg wondered if they'd leave together. She hoped not—George had promised her he'd help her this evening.

After a couple minutes, Edward leaned over again. "Listen, Meg. As long as you have that phone of yours out…" he said in her ear.

She turned to him, heart beginning to thump strangely. He was only putting his mouth next to her ear because it was ridiculously loud in this place. Not because he was trying to seduce her. It didn't mean anything. She had to remember that.

"Why don't we exchange numbers?" he asked her. "It might be nice to talk somewhere quieter. Later this week, maybe? After work some night?" He looked…kind of interested, but Meg thought he'd be okay with her answer no matter what she said. Edward was not giving her much to go on. She didn't know what she had been expecting, but this tepid indifference wasn't it.

She swallowed with difficulty. "Yeah," she agreed, trying to sound neutral even though Meg thought she might be heading toward cardiac arrest. "That might work."

He handed her his phone—it was a new one, all right, and encased in a bulky industrial-looking black case that looked as if it could withstand a lot, though probably not a full-on car crash. Meg shuddered, but Edward didn't seem to notice. He was too busy entering his own details into her phone. When he handed it back to her, she was zoned out watching the crowd bobbing to the music. He reached for his cell phone, but when he noticed that Meg hadn't typed anything yet, he left it in her hand. Glancing between her and the stage, Edward leaned in and asked,

"Do you like to dance?"

Meg was startled. She hadn't noticed his attention. "Oh! Yes, but…I don't think I will risk it here," she laughed. "That looks treacherous." She felt ancient, suddenly, weighed down by years and years of angst.

He smiled. "Good thought. So, we'll go somewhere quiet and talk, and then later I'll take you dancing. We can waltz, or something. Very dignified."

Oh, God. Even when he was not himself, he was charming, Meg thought. This was impossible. She was wrecked by an image from *before*: standing in darkness in the middle of the night in Edward's bedroom, swaying slowly in his arms to a quiet song he played for her on his phone. Meg's eyes filled. She couldn't do this. Couldn't let herself remember. Couldn't pretend.

"Sounds very calm. And safe," she replied, forcing an answering smile to her face. She'd meant to be funny, but Edward must have picked up on her mood, because two little lines formed between his brows before he turned away.

"Exactly," she thought she heard him say.

It was going to be a long, long night. She wished the others hadn't abandoned them. George and Poppy had disappeared from view, and Molly and Charlie were being goofy with his friends over near the bar. And right now, Meg could use a wingman or four.

Edward stood up suddenly. "Right," he barked officiously. "Come on, then."

He grabbed her hand, pulled her out of her chair, and dragged her into the hot, gyrating crowd. Before she knew it, they were dancing, pressed tight against each other by the people around them, moving and gyrating to the thumping music in a way that they had never done in the past. Molly and Charlie appeared, laughing and pressing bright red drinks into their hands. Meg and Edward knocked them back, set the empty glasses on the side of the stage, and grinned at each other. It was…fun.

Chapter Twenty

EDWARD OUGHT TO wring George's neck. The reasons for it were endless. It had taken long moments last night to determine which woman was intended for him, but that had sorted itself out easily enough. The decoy girl had eventually sashayed off with his little brother, and then heartless George had pulled a vanishing act himself, sniffing at the heels of a woman who looked like she belonged in a carnival. Or...he struggled with the proper analogy. Painted on the side of a punk rock B-52 plane? Posing on the cover of some rockabilly motorcycle magazine? It boggled the imagination.

That left him with Meg all night. Poor Meg. She was so obviously out of her element, looking uncomfortable and shy, and if Edward didn't miss his guess, likely fresh out of a wretched breakup. Half of the time, he wasn't sure if she was going to break down crying, or kiss him senseless. He wouldn't have minded the latter—Meg was a pretty enough girl. Not flashy, more of a jeans and trainers type. A natural kind of pretty. He'd fancied her. And somehow, in the heat of the moment, he'd felt sympathetic and protective enough to ask her out. How had that happened? He'd recognized something of himself in her, he supposed, something barely held together. He hadn't meant to do it, but he wouldn't back out now. By the end of the evening, they had managed to have a decent time together. Edward figured she was safe enough to take out a few more times. The girl looked like she could use it. And if it turned out to that Meg felt grateful and wanted to reward him with physical favors…so much the better. He wouldn't turn her down. When he'd danced with her, he'd discovered a fetching enough body under those modest clothes. But his managing arse of a brother might have at least let him in on the plan beforehand.

Edward looked around his study, hands on his hips. Thoughts of prospective shagging partners aside, he needed to go through the stuff on his desk. Now. He'd been putting it off, knowing that George had already gone through everything a few weeks ago, to take care of the most time-critical bits. But Edward was still a full partner in their business, and he needed to get back up to speed if he didn't want to be dead weight. George had carried him long enough. He grabbed his travel mug of coffee from the top of the tall filing cabinet, dropped into his leather desk chair and set to work.

A few hours later, Edward felt like he'd made progress. He'd gotten up to speed on the company's recent history, and sorted the papers into piles for their few current clients. He had another group of papers that he thought might represent some prospective new accounts. He'd filed the paid bills, thank you brother dearest. All that was left now was a mysterious, plain manila envelope he'd found on the printer. Edward centered it in the middle of the desk and stared down at it. A normal man might not think twice about something like this. He might just tear it open and look inside, unconcerned about what its contents might be. But Edward was not normal, and Edward felt a fair degree of trepidation about what the envelope might hold. When one lost whole long months of one's life, the possibilities were endless. There were other mysteries, after all: the diamond ring and the women's clothes among them. His lingering, frustrating feeling of loss. His bowl full of phantom knickers. This could be anything from a bad business deal to a private investigator's report. Or the membership packet for an odd sex club. Edward blinked. Certainly not that.

He gritted his teeth, flipped it over and pried open the clasp. Inside were two photos, approximately 11x14 inches in size. He slid them free, laid them side by side on the desk, and stared. Two selfies, based on the angle of the pictures. One of him kissing a sleeping woman, and one of the woman alone, sprawled in bed. Same woman, he saw…Edward jolted in his seat, looking closer. Was that…Meg, the girl from last night?

Damn his infernal brother. It *was* her. It had to be. Which meant that George, the bastard, had just fixed him up with his former girlfriend, and hadn't even said a word of warning to him. No wonder George had been acting so squirrely earlier. Edward, blazing idiot that he was, had fallen right for it.

And Meg! She had come on so sweet and reserved last night, Edward would never have guessed who she was. No wonder she'd been so tragic—ruddy hell, half the time she'd had a face like a wet weekend. She and his brothers were con artists of the first order, it seemed. Edward dropped his head in his hands and held it there. Was there no one he could trust in this town? Every last person seemed to have a hidden agenda, and until Edward could regain his missing memories, he was at the mercy of all of them. He knocked his forehead on the desk top, frustrated. Why wouldn't it come back? All the doctors had thought it would by now. And he'd tried almost everything he could think of to jog it free. It was bloody hard not to get discouraged.

Except…he raised his head and examined the photos again. Here was a woman who had known him before. They looked so…hmm. Happy, he supposed. Had he printed these out, intending to frame them? That would be the mark of a man in love, as unlikely as that seemed. It would certainly support what his mum and brothers had told him. But now he'd met Meg. She wasn't exactly the sort to fire a man's passion, at least on the surface of things.

Or—another insidious thought intruded. Had she taken the photos and given them to him in an effort to curry favor, or force a connection that wasn't really there? Edward couldn't discount it, not after the way she'd hoodwinked him last night. He studied the pictures a moment longer, rubbing at the uncomfortable tightness in his chest. He'd better not destroy them, Edward thought. What if he'd kept them as evidence or something? He sat back heavily in the swivel chair and squeezed his eyes shut. He tried to imagine Meg—quiet, mouse-like Meg—as a thief, for example. She'd be perfect at it, if only because it was so utterly unbelievable. He had to wonder if *she'd* somehow stolen whatever it was he was missing. It bore consideration. The culprit, right there in front of him. She'd had the access, that much was obvious. The question was, what could she have taken? There were valuable things littered all over the house that she had presumably left unmolested. The bowl he'd begun to think of as Planet Knickers came to mind. He'd paid a fortune for that, but it might have presented too big a challenge (literally—it weighed a ton), spiriting it out and trying to unload it on the black market. No, a girl like her might have better luck with cash. Or jewelry. Like a large diamond ring. Which Edward had the foresight to whisk out of her reach by bringing it to Britain with him?

He cursed and slammed his fist down on the desk, wrinkling the photo of her lounging in bed. He tried to smooth it out, admiring the line of her bare arm as he did so. Now he was just getting fantastical. He snatched up his cell phone and dialed his scheming brother.

"George," he demanded when the man picked up, "Are you barking mad?"

"It's likely," George replied complacently. "Why do you ask?"

"Oh, I don't know. Maybe because you just fixed me up with a possible felon and didn't think to warn me?"

Edward heard a woman's voice in the background, and George's muffled response.

"George!" he shouted.

"Sorry," his brother answered insincerely. "Now, who do we think is a felon?" He clearly thought Edward had gone soft in the head. Or rather, *more* soft.

"Meg, for starters," Edward exclaimed, exasperated beyond all endurance. "Why didn't you tell me who she was?"

"Because you would never have agreed to go," George commented calmly. "But Edward…" he began, then paused. "Wait—how did you find out? Did she tell you?"

"I mean, what do you really know about her? She could have been doing unspeakable things to me, and now you've foisted her on me all over again. For all you know she was stealing from me. *She* could be the one who took whatever it is I'm missing." Edward's voice had gone a bit shrill. He forced himself to shut up and worked at regulating his breathing into some semblance of normal. He was clearly losing his effing mind.

When George started speaking again, his voice had gone deadly quiet. "Now who's gone mad?" he asked. "You listen to me, brother mine. Meg is no thief. She's a lovely person who has had a very rough go of it these last six months. Besides, when you met her last night, you plainly enjoyed her company," his brother explained reasonably.

"How would you know? You disappeared for half of it," Edward growled, cutting him off. He couldn't seem to tear his eyes away from the way his lips were brushing Meg's temple in the photo. Last night her skin had been soft. So soft, when he'd conspired to touch it.

"Edward, stop. You want to know about Meg? Here it is. You two were *mad* for each other. Like I've never seen. There is no way she was screwing you over, and you have nothing to be suspicious about. Now, be a good lad, call the girl again and take her out. You will not be sorry, I promise you."

His brother had not strung together so many words in a long time, possibly ever. Edward was amazed. "Are you quite sure?" he breathed, afraid to believe it. Because if he was wrong…

"Quite," George agreed drily. "But let me tell you another thing. If you intend to fuck around with this girl and then walk away like it means nothing, you can think again. She's been hurt enough," he warned. "Don't go out with her unless you're willing to really give it a go."

Edward sat there blinking, trying to process what he was hearing. His brother, defending a woman he probably barely knew? How many times could he and Meg have met, if she and Edward had only dated for a month? The amount of imagination this required was staggering. Meg must be one hell of a woman to inspire this kind of loyalty. He traced a finger over her face, lying there looking sublime on his desk.

"All right," he murmured. "I'll try. I promise."

"Edward," George said quietly.

"Hmm?"

"Did it ever once occur to you that the thing you might be missing…" he broke off, launching into another muffled conversation with whoever was there with him.

"What?" Edward asked, curious. Desperate, even.

"Never mind. I'll talk to you later. I've got to go now." With that, he disconnected.

Edward snorted, tossing his phone aside. Of course. Trust George to dangle a carrot like that before pulling a runner. It was classic. Now he was back to wanting to strangle him.

Would it be such a bad thing, trying to get to know Meg again? She was pretty and calm and nice. It couldn't hurt, Edward mused. Either they'd hit it off like gangbusters, which would be a win for all concerned, and had the added bonus of getting Mum and George off his case. Or, they'd discover they no longer cared for each other. She'd get closure, and he could move on with his life. Easy-peasy.

Edward reached for his cellphone and began twisting it in circles with his fingers while he thought about whether he ought to text or call. It was a new phone, with a new case his mother had picked out. It looked indestructible, like something that might be issued to a miner on the job, but it wouldn't spin on the desk for all the rubber and plastic encasing it. His old phone had spun in circles when he did this, and he wished he still had his old…phone. Edward froze. Was that a memory? A lost one? Frantically, he reviewed what he knew. He'd gotten the phone when they had upgraded him, must have been in July or August, because it had been hot as hell with no A/C in here. He used to sit right here working, spinning the phone around with his hand while he was waiting for…something. Edward grabbed up the phone and clicked into the photos. Disappointed, he realized—nothing there. Nothing except the handful of photos he had taken of his family in the hospital, when he was still worried that the memory of them might be taken from him, too. What else had he been expecting to find?

It wasn't enough to throw a parade, but Edward still felt as if something important might have just happened. They'd told him it might be like that. If he would just relax, think of other things besides regaining his memory, then suddenly, there it would be. He massaged his forehead, already beginning to feel the start of a headache. Nothing was guaranteed to tense up a person more than telling them, over and over, to *relax*.

I'm trying, he thought. God, I'm *trying*.

Chapter Twenty-One

EDWARD WAITED TWO days before he called her for a date. Meg wasn't sure he would, thinking maybe he had been caught up in the moment at the bar. After all, as far as he knew, she was a total stranger. They'd had a couple drinks, made each other smile a few times, and when they'd danced there had been a definite edge of something…hotter. Even though there had been no opportunity to be alone at the end of the night, when she might have gone so far as to kiss him if he'd seemed inclined, Meg still felt like a connection of sorts had been formed. She had no idea if he felt the same. After all, when it came to Edward, Meg's judgement was decidedly compromised.

Still, the delay in having to deal with him gave her a chance to bolster her defenses. She and Molly had thoroughly rehashed every detail, examining each moment for clues to his mental state. And then they'd debriefed Morgan and run through it all again. Meg had been drilled over and over on how to approach this new hell on earth. While she couldn't say she felt one hundred percent comfortable with the situation, at least Meg knew what her marching orders were. And the lure of getting Edward back was too great to turn back now.

When he did finally call, she was ready. He wasn't quite as gung-ho as he'd been at McGillicuddy's, though she tried not to read too much into it. There would be no talking and getting to know each other again in a quiet, romantic location. There wouldn't be any waltzing, either. Edward punted, and invited her to the movies. Not a romantic comedy either, but a blockbuster spy movie that already had three prior installments. Meg had to fight back her disappointment. She told herself that she would be sitting next to him, in the dark, for hours. He might even try to hold her hand. Surely that was better than thinking he was dead and buried? Meg met him at the theater. Edward didn't offer to pick her up.

When she spotted him, he was standing beside the ticket window, hands in his pockets and staring off into space. As she approached, Meg took in his appearance: jeans and a button-down shirt, rolled up above his elbows. Nothing unusual there. He didn't look nervous. Meg was, though—she had taken pains to look especially nice, herself. She smoothed down her hair and adjusted the straps of her silky, sleeveless, light blue top. She had changed her jeans four times before she felt satisfied with the way her butt looked in them. Damn, who was she kidding? She hadn't changed a fifth time, because if she had, she would have been late. And Meg didn't want Edward to be able to use lateness as an excuse not to see her again. Or for him to leave before she even got there.

She had to put herself directly in his line of vision before she could get his attention.

"Hey," she said cheerfully. "Fancy meeting you here."

It must have been the wrong thing to say. Edward frowned and looked panicked for a minute before he recovered.

"Oh, it's you. Hullo. Right on time, aren't you?" He checked his watch to confirm.

"Well, yeah," Meg replied stiffly. *It's you?* Who the hell else would it be?

He had already bought the tickets, and with characteristic politeness, Edward smoothly guided her into the snack bar line for treats, too. She went willingly. Meg didn't know too many women who would turn down chocolate, not in this kind of situation. She added a cherry cola and some popcorn, too, just to be contrary. Edward didn't appear to notice anything amiss. He got a small bottle of water for himself, and Meg, standing there with an armful of crappy calories, felt like an ass. Fitting, really.

The theater was only half full, since the movie had been out for weeks already. Any normal person with a halfway decent social life had probably already seen it. But she and Edward weren't exactly normal, were they? When he suggested a pair of seats in the dead center of the theater, Meg agreed. No extra-dark back row for them, which likely meant no canoodling, either. That was fine. That was really, completely fine. Meg had been wondering what would happen to the spy in the film anyway, since she was reasonably certain he had been killed off definitively at the end of movie number three.

Two and half hours later, when the lights came up, Meg knew a few things for sure. The chocolate-popcorn-cola combo had almost certainly added a full five pounds to her weight. Also, Edward still smelled as phenomenal as he always had. And, though Meg had rested her hand palm-up on her thigh for the whole damn movie, plowing through her junk food using only the other one, Edward had not made any moves to hold it. Meg was *not* so clear on whether the spy had miraculously come back to life—a new actor had apparently taken over the franchise, and she wasn't sure if he was meant to be an entirely new character or not. But, Meg was crystal clear on the fact that she and Edward had not made plans to do anything *after* the movie.

They shuffled out of the theater, blindly following the other patrons. Edward was glancing around the squalid street outside the cinema with a faintly desperate expression. She could not take it anymore, not one more second. Meg willed a chipper tone into her voice.

"Well, thanks again for the movie. This was fun," she smiled, setting a possible exit plan into motion. She felt like hitting something, and then crying about it. But Meg was a social butterfly.

No, scratch that—a *former* social butterfly, dragged low by life. Still, her instincts ran strong. After that salvo, Edward would certainly understand he should extend their night…or let her go.

She'd have to take the T home again—as usual she didn't have enough money for a cab. Meg wondered absently if she was going to get that job she'd tried for. They'd called her back for a second interview with two other people, but it had been a week since she'd heard anything else. She crossed her fingers, hoping hard. That bigger paycheck would be so freaking great right about now. Coupled with her recently lowered housing expenses, Meg might actually be able to live normally again.

Edward looked undecided about what he should do next.

"Yes, it was," he said. He looked down, jingled some change in his pocket. "We ought to do this again soon." He didn't look exhilarated by the prospect.

Ah. So the night *was* over. Perhaps she had misunderstood, Meg thought. Maybe this was not supposed to be a date, but just two friends hanging out. She nodded to herself. Right. Of course. She had just done some wishful thinking, that was all.

"All right, yeah. Give me a call when you're free," she hedged. Meg looked down the street, marking the nearest T stop. "I should, um…get going." She gestured weakly. Took a few steps away.

Her imminent departure seemed to spark something in Edward, though.

"Oh, are you leaving so soon? I thought we could, uh—pop in over there for a bit." At this, he indicated a weird little tea shop across the street.

Meg peered at it dubiously. This was not like Edward at all. There was no way he had chosen *that* place ahead of time—he was obviously playing this by ear. Oh well. In for a penny, in for a pound. George and Charlie were going to owe her, big time.

"Sure," she acquiesced. "Sounds good." Meg realized she sounded stilted, but she couldn't seem to recapture the easy, companionable rapport they used to have. Everything she said and did felt awkward. She could not possibly be expected to keep up this charade for long, Meg thought. It would be inhumane to all of them.

As she and Edward waited to cross the street, Meg surreptitiously mopped at her forehead with the sweater she'd brought. The sun had gone down, but it was still warm, and felt muggy enough that she wondered if they were due for rain. Wouldn't that just be the icing on the cake? To not only be a conversational reject, but a drowned rat, too? All with the man she was in love with, who didn't even remember her. Par for the course, really. Meg didn't know why she should feel surprised.

The light turned and they ran across the street, shimmying through the tightly parked cars on the other side. The tea shop was empty, but brightly lit. It seemed clean enough, and the small woman behind the counter waved them in impatiently when Edward stuck his head inside. He held the door wide for Meg, and she stepped hesitantly in. It smelled divine, the aroma of the teas filling the small space with their spicy fragrance. The air conditioning was blasting, too, making it more bearable to drink something hot despite the weather. Edward placed his hand lightly on her lower back and urged her forward. The counter was lined with many glass jars, each labelled in multiple languages and filled with loose tea leaves.

Meg skipped right past the row of flowery herbal blends—she hated those. The green teas looked more interesting, boasting fun names like "Happy Joy" and "Monkey Hug". Meg peeked at Edward's face, and was gratified to see as much amusement there as she was feeling. The lady at the register was watching them like a hawk. Neither of them dared laugh. At last, they'd progressed to the section of black teas. Meg was relieved to see some of her favorites: Darjeeling. Earl Grey. Prince of Wales.

She pointed, feeling very, very staid as she said, "I'll have the Irish Breakfast. With milk, if you have it." The woman sniffed in disdain, but she refrained from comment. She looked to Edward.

"The same for me," he told her. "Do you have it in decaf?"

"No decaf," the lady said.

"That's fine, then," Edward agreed, extracting his wallet, but looking put out.

He asked Meg, "Do you want a snack? Or some dessert?" He frowned at the menu board overheard, which had not been translated into English. "I'm not sure, but maybe they have food."

Meg had to laugh. "I just ate an entire box of Milk Duds," she said. "I don't think I need anything else."

Edward smirked. "Well, not an *entire* box. I snuck some out when you weren't looking."

"You ate, like, two," Meg protested, disgusted with herself.

But they were smiling at each other, and it felt relaxed and normal, almost like it used to. She let out a breath and tried to ease the tension from her neck. Maybe this would work after all.

Once they sat down and received their tea, though, a stiff silence seemed to descend on them. Meg, who'd once danced and partied her way through whole years of her adolescence, could not think of one single thing to say. It felt like her brain had frozen over. Her foot jiggled back and forth under the table. Maybe she shouldn't have come here. Edward took a large gulp from his cup and cleared his throat.

"So," he said over the whirring of the air conditioning unit. "George tells me we knew each other. Before, I mean." He toyed with his spoon and didn't seem able to look directly at her.

Meg felt her face drain of blood. She supposed it made sense to address the elephant in the room, but that didn't make it fun. Freaking George might have warned her this was coming. Cautiously, she responded.

"Yes. Uh, that's true."

The old woman reappeared, dropping a bowl full of glistening dumplings that they had not ordered on the table between them. They looked up at her in inquiry.

"Here ya go," she announced, "Eat 'em while they're hot."

They blinked at each other in confusion, but the woman had disappeared into the back, and the steam wafting from the bowl smelled delicious. Edward scooped two onto his plate.

"We dated? Before I left?" he asked Meg, sounding unsure.

She swallowed down the bile that rose into her throat. God, how could he not remember any of it? It was cruelty beyond measure. She didn't dare try to speak. Instead, she just nodded.

"And you agreed to see me again?" His laugh was more disbelieving than anything else.

"I'm here, aren't I?" she laughed back, but it sounded testy nonetheless.

"I guess I couldn't have been too much of a bastard, then," Edward tried to joke. It went over about as well as a lead balloon.

Meg wanted to say something light in return. Something carefree, so he wouldn't feel…whatever horrible thing he was currently feeling. She hated the expression on his face. But more so, she hated how totally inadequate she felt in the face of it. The jest just wouldn't come.

Instead, she took a deep breath and went for honesty. "No. I think it's fair to say that you were *not* a bastard to me." Meg smiled then, gently, at his uncertain expression. For whatever reason, it seemed to take the sting out of the fact that she knew so much more than Edward did about their past, their relationship. She wanted him to feel okay about continuing on like this, even if he was flying blind. She wanted him to know he was safe with her.

Meg remembered something he had said once, about the women he'd known before and their motives for dating him. If this Edward was a sort of throwback version, presumably he'd be sensitive to that sort of thing again. Meg would have to be careful not to throw any red flags in his direction, but it limited the scope of what she could talk about. References to his work might be construed as fishing for information about his dad or his money. Asking about his family could be viewed as title-hunting. She bit her lip. She was so bad at this.

"So…how are you feeling?" she asked him carefully. At Edward's alarmed expression, she quickly explained. "I mean, they told me you had some injuries—are you all healed up for the most part?"

He nodded. "Yes. For the most part." He winked, but it seemed more reflex than charm.

"And your dad?" Meg shrugged, trying not to look too avid, lest he misinterpret why she was asking. "How is he doing?"

Edward studied her. "Did you… meet him?" Okay. It was clear Edward did *not* want any more reminders of what he couldn't remember. She was making him *more* uncomfortable, not less.

She nodded. "He was really nice to me."

He processed that. Eventually, he told her, "He's doing better. He wasn't paralyzed, thank God, but it's taking a while for him to get full mobility back. It's a process."

"That must be so hard," she sympathized. He nodded. Poor Violet, Meg thought. Hard on her, too. But she didn't dare say that, for fear of making him more anxious. He might not recall that she had also known his mother.

Old Edward had been so inquisitive, she remembered. He had wanted to know all sorts of things about her life and her feelings, and his questions had made her feel vibrant and interesting. This Edward was prone to awkward silences and short, declarative comments. She felt dull just being in his orbit. As if all her pessimism were entirely appropriate.

Lamely, Meg tried again. "How's work?"

Edward did a sort of half nod / half shrug move that managed to be wholly dismissive. "It's fine. Now that we are back in town, we're trying to get our workload back up to its usual level. It shouldn't be hard. There was a waiting list before, so…" he trailed off, popping another dumpling in his mouth and chewing. "You should try one these. They're really good."

Meekly, Meg stabbed one with her fork and nibbled at a corner, just to appease him. She hadn't eaten dinner, but she had consumed enough calories at the movie to last her into next week. Her appetite would have been nonexistent, regardless. She had never been able to force down food when she was feeling nervous or upset. She had barely even touched that popcorn after the first five minutes, just slid it under her seat and forgot about it while she focused on her candy.

"How's *your* work going?" Edward inquired, once he had swallowed. "Property management, isn't that what you said?"

"Oh, it's…" Meg shook her head. "Boring. You know. But I had some interviews for a new job, so I'm hoping to get that." She set down her fork. Pretending to eat the dumpling was a wasted effort.

"Do you think you have a chance?" His eyes moved over her face restlessly. What was Edward seeing? Meg did not even want to hazard a guess.

"Who knows? I hope so, but…I'm not sure," she answered pathetically. "I haven't had much luck on that front lately." She felt like crying again. Did she have to come off like such a loser? Now? To him? Meg tried to peek around the perimeter of the room, looking for the bathroom in case she couldn't hold off the tears. When she glanced back at Edward's face, though, she was startled by what she saw there.

His gaze was locked onto her now, his former pallid expression gone. He looked compassionate. "Well, I hope you get it," he told her. "Is it important to you, then?"

Meg nodded. It sure was. He waited, but she couldn't manage to say anything else, her impression of a charmless clod reaching new heights of excellence.

"Meg, uh…" he finished off his tea in one gulp, then moved his sweating water glass around in a little circle on the table. "Do you think you might fancy getting together again next weekend? Maybe grab some dinner somewhere?" He checked her face from under his lashes, nervous. Edward rushed on before she could answer, though. "I know this was…odd, tonight. I was a bit thrown off when George told me about us, and I just…it was hard to get my sea legs back, so to speak. I promise I'll be better next time." He'd grown so quiet by the end that Meg had to strain to hear him.

She said, "I didn't know he was going to tell you." Then she thought about how that sounded. "Although, to be fair, I wasn't convinced that *not* telling you was the best idea, either. They sort of steamrolled me into that one."

"Yes, well, it's done now," he demurred, not appearing to hold a grudge. "I'd still like to see you again, if you're game."

Was she game? Meg wondered. It was hard to identify one overriding emotion from all the conflicting ones swirling around in her chest. Relief and gratitude that he was alive. Despair that he was changed, diminished. Desperation to restore what had been wrenched mercilessly away. Doubt that it could be done. Molly and Morgan had been clear, though. She had to hold the line and stick this out.

"Sure," she squeaked, with faux enthusiasm. "I'd like that. We can…" her throat closed on the words, but she forced them out somehow. "We can start fresh then."

Edward looked pleased. "Brilliant," he said softly, almost like he used to. But he also seemed to understand that she was tapped out this time around. "Shall we get going? I can give you a lift home if you like. I hadn't realized how dodgy it got around here after dark."

"Yes. That's perfect," Meg managed in reply. "Thank you."

Chapter Twenty-Two

EDWARD HAD DRIVEN Meg home after the tea shop, to a high rise near Kenmore Square that looked utterly unfamiliar. He parked in the turnaround under the watchful eye of the doorman, but it may as well have been Mars for how strange it felt. Meg seemed to understand his frown—without him even asking, she explained that she had lived in a studio apartment in Brighton before. Edward had felt grateful for the soft way she offered him that information. Beholden to her, for her gentle, undemanding perception. It was simple, really, to lean across the gear shaft and give her a goodnight kiss. Meg kissed him back, willingly.

It was effortless, too, to escort her to dinner the following weekend. Edward chose a new Italian restaurant, in the hopes that it would hold no latent memories for either one of them. He'd planned out some conversational topics beforehand, and that date had progressed far more smoothly. Edward held her small, soft hand on the way back to his car. And he had kissed her goodnight once more, outside her building. It had been pleasant, he thought. No screaming fireworks, not exactly. No compulsive desire to rip anyone's clothes off in a coat closet. But Meg tasted good, and he'd wanted to keep going. She'd matched him exactly, responding in equal measure to him. Never taking more than Edward offered, and never giving less than he asked for. He'd thought she might invite him in, but she hadn't.

Edward was…curious about what it would be like with her. It wasn't a clawing lust. But it *was* a healthy interest. He thought it might be nice—slow, and sweet. He thought she might be into it, too, but of course, she'd likely sampled the goods before. Meg would know what she was getting. She'd have expectations. Edward hoped he wouldn't disappoint her.

For their third date, he invited her over to his house, so he could cook her dinner. The third date was the social benchmark, wasn't it? A recognized time frame after which intimate relations could be in the cards? Edward was impatient to get past the milestone of sex with her, with anyone, really, and she'd explained about the situation at her place. Since Meg was only subletting a room, she wasn't sure how entertaining a guest overnight would be perceived. Edward understood. He'd hate for her to lose her home over him. And he thought she might be more willing if there weren't prying eyes and ears around. That was usually the way of it, with women.

Before she arrived, Edward sat at the desk in his study and pulled out the photos of Meg again. Studied them. His expression, and hers. Yes—Edward would see where it went tonight. If she wanted to, he could try to make her feel those things again. And if not tonight, then soon. Surely he could at least remember how to seduce a woman. In those photos, Meg looked very seduce-able. And he looked as satisfied as a cat that had found the cream. Who wouldn't try for that again?

When she rang his bell, he was keen to greet her, waiting in the foyer like an eager teenager. Edward shook his head. If he didn't want to put her off, he'd have to dial it back a bit. Maybe feed the poor thing before he tried to jump her.

"Hullo," he said casually, throwing the door wide for her. "Don't you look lovely?"

Meg flushed. "Hi," she replied, her eyes darting around. "Thanks. Am I too early? I got here faster than I thought I would."

"No, you're fine," he reassured her. "Did you take the T?" He moved to take her light jacket from her, but she wasn't quite ready for him. Flustered, she dropped her bag on the floor next to her feet and tried to wriggle out of it. It didn't go well. Her zipper seemed to snag on something, and then her arm got tangled up in the sleeve. Her total lack of pretension was oddly endearing. At least Edward had some confirmation that he wasn't the only nervous one.

"I did, and one pulled up right when I got to the stop," she explained. "I'm not sure that's ever happened to me before." Meg stood there, frozen awkwardly in place, while Edward went to hang her jacket in the hall closet.

"Dinner won't take long," he explained. "Would you like to sit and have a drink before I finish things up?" She was wearing a loosely-woven sweater with a tank top underneath, and a denim skirt. Her streaky blonde hair was tied up in a loose bun on the back of her head. All the glimpses of skin were excellent.

"Sure, that works," Meg agreed. Edward noticed her trying to look around without being too obvious. She noticed him noticing. "Um, the house looks really great," she said weakly.

"Oh, thank you," Edward said. "Would you like a tour? I could show you everything we've done since I bought it last year."

"Oh! Okay," she squeaked, seeming startled. "Yeah, I'd like that."

"All right. Come back here to the kitchen with me, and we'll fetch those drinks before we start." For fuck's sake. He was going to have to expend some effort if he expected to relax either of them enough to get starkers by the end of the night. A good wine could only do so much.

On some level, Edward knew that Meg had probably been here before, but when he'd decided to play it like this, he reasoned that perhaps a lot had changed in the interceding months. Besides, this seemed like a thing he might naturally do with a new date, and lately, Edward had been taking refuge in social niceties and correct etiquette. It helped him to maintain a calm demeanor, particularly since he'd returned to Boston.

He hadn't had quite so much trouble in the UK. Then, he'd been focused on getting well, and on monitoring the progress of his father's recovery. There hadn't been quite so much that was unfamiliar there, either. As his doctors had explained it, that was to be expected. The old memories were mapped in his brain in different ways, and were able to cling to life more successfully. The new memories were a different story, however. It felt as if a bomb had dropped in the middle of the autumn and winter, annihilating everything he'd lived through but somehow sparing his body. They weren't sure if any of it would come back to him, the longer he went without remembering. Edward didn't know if that mattered—he and his father were alive, after all, and surely that was the important part? But his family was anxious, and insisted that he return here to pick up the pieces.

However, in Boston his sense of calm felt like a very thin, very brittle veneer that had been pasted all over his skin. Inside was a riot of disorder—a churning cesspool of emotion, constantly threatening to boil free. Uncertainty and doubt and fear. Insecurity and anger. All writhing around inside of him in one big, debilitating miasma. He never knew when he'd bump into someone he "knew" here. And his family was the absolute worst. They wore identical expressions of sympathy and barely concealed hope, and it made his skin crawl. Because really, no one wanted to remember more than Edward. He had no idea if his life before was really so splendid that he was desperate to retrieve it. He was, however, desperate to be relieved of how he felt now. He felt…confused. Fuzzy. Out of joint. He felt like none of his gears or levers were aligned properly, and were chafing and grinding against each other in some mechanical parody of automation. And if he'd ever possessed a sharp edge (what man who'd been a boxer in his Rifles unit wouldn't have that?), it had been dulled now.

Edward wrenched himself back into the present. He'd been making a vague effort to show Meg around as his thoughts spun, and she'd been making an equally vague effort to appreciate things as she sipped at her wine. His glass, he noticed, was nearly empty. Now, they were ascending the stairs to his bedroom. Maybe it wasn't strictly proper to bring her up here to look, but he supposed it might not be the first time she'd seen it. Not if Charlie and George and his mum were right, and he had been close with this woman. Edward glanced over his shoulder and eyed her downcast face, watching the stairs as she climbed. Meg was pretty enough that he probably would have slept with her if he'd dated her for any length of time before. But perhaps they'd only hooked up at her old place—Edward did prefer to keep his home as a drama-free sanctuary, after all.

Not for the first time, he wondered if the engagement ring he'd found in his things had been meant for her. He still wasn't certain it was even his. After the accident, his mum and brothers had gone to the hotel in London to gather everything up and bring it to Cambridge. They'd dumped it in his rooms at home and left it there, likely forgetting it as they dealt with all the more immediate concerns for his and his father's welfare. Edward hadn't been able to unpack and go through it all until many weeks later. When he had, the glittering diamond, and what had been paid for it, had been a bit of a shock. He couldn't fathom not recalling an imminent fiancée.

He was not the sort of man to propose to some bit of fluff without knowing her or her family intimately. There were the titles to consider, after all. And all the difficulties of having a famous father. Surely, if he'd meant to settle down, Edward would be acquainted with the lucky lady for longer than a hot minute. So he had not mentioned the ring to his family, and had bided his time to see which women of an amorous persuasion presented themselves. Or which lucky groom of his acquaintance demanded his property back.

They'd reached the second-floor landing, and Edward dithered, pointing out the polished, carved wood banisters and the original plasterwork of the walls. So far Meg was the only romantic candidate to emerge, but the length of time he'd supposedly known her would seem to disqualify her as a contender. Edward rolled his shoulders, trying to dislodge his unease. The constant sense of missing something nagged at him, and he wondered yet again if he'd forgotten the real woman he supposedly loved. Maybe there was another one out there somewhere, one who was so tied to his heart and soul that the mere sight of her would jostle free the obstructions in his mind. That thought made him wary of Meg, made him reluctant to wholly commit to her. Edward was nearly certain she knew it. While she never looked at him with pity, he did catch rare glimpses of what appeared to be longing. Usually, though, she stifled that sort of thing, and approached him with exactly the same amount of reserve that he offered her. He liked it. It was comfortable. It was easy.

Meg never, ever prodded him with comments such as, *Don't you remember?* And he didn't think she was the type to manipulate him by trying to plant false memories in his head. (George had already attempted that, and it hadn't been nearly as funny as he'd intended. Nothing ever was these days.) Meg had a core of serenity that she carried around with her always. She was quiet and reserved, but somehow not cold. Edward found it *restful* to be around her, if nothing else. She didn't light any fires under him, but she didn't aggravate him, either. One could make a worse case for a potential wife, he supposed.

Although…what the hell? The woman in question seemed to be frozen in place, rooted to the floor at the foot of his bed and staring at the framed prints hanging over the headboard. She'd taken advantage of his inattention to wander into the room by herself, apparently maintaining the appearance of the house tour. He supposed George was right that she had not stolen from him— Meg didn't appear to be the least bit interested in assessing the value of anything around her. Up until now, she had drifted around the rooms of the brownstone in his wake, uttering polite (but neutral) comments and inquiries as he made his explanations. She gave no indication that she had been involved in any of the renovations or decorating. Edward had no idea, really, what stage in the process the house might have been in when last she was here. George had done things both after Edward's departure in the fall, and before his return this spring. He wasn't sure he *wanted* to know if Meg had been the one to pick out his dinner table, if only because he'd been using little details like that to help define himself in this new reality. *I'm a man who likes the rustic industrial look*, he could say to himself. And it was a small anchor in a huge sea of 'Who am I?'.

Right now, though, he was acting as her host, and had to break the ungainly silence blanketing the room. She'd clearly stopped listening several moments before he'd stopped talking, though what he'd been yammering on about was anyone's guess. Edward cleared his throat to catch her attention, and tried not to sound too pompous.

"Meg?" he asked. "Do you like those prints?" He shouldn't be surprised that she'd noticed them—they were the only shot of color in the whole neutral-toned room.

She took too long to turn to him and answer, and when she did, her face was ashen. Edward watched her fingers grip the footboard of his bed with white knuckles. He'd thought this might be a vaguely erotic interlude, seeing her here in his bedroom and anticipating being here later. But the look on her face right now made him feel ill.

After a couple failed attempts to speak, Meg managed to choke out, "They are…extraordinary. Where did you get them?"

Good. A question with a concrete answer. Edward knew what to say. "They're the work of my brother, Charlie, actually," he told her, looking between her and the prints once more. "He's in design school right now."

"Yes," she agreed. She'd known that. "I don't think I ever saw any of his work, though. Nothing like this, anyway."

Edward nodded, but Meg wasn't done. She pointed at the frames.

"What are they?" she asked, still not quite making eye contact. Did she know the answer to her own question? Was she testing him? Edward couldn't tell. Her normally open countenance had gone a bit flat.

"Pen and ink, I imagine," he replied absently. He knew he was being deliberately obtuse, but Meg was making him very uncomfortable suddenly. He hated it. She was the one who *wasn't* supposed to do this to him. Edward stalled for time, trying to decide if a hasty retreat was in order.

"I see. And what exactly do they depict?" she inquired. Meg stared at his face, and he'd have to be an idiot to miss the challenge in her voice. He supposed this ought to count as proof that he'd slept with this woman, because he now felt sure that she already knew the answer to her own question. Or, at least, part of it. Now, Edward had to discover if she had the answer to one of *his* many questions.

"The image on the left is the crest of the Earl of Westbroke. I think you know that I am the heir to that title?" he asked carefully. She nodded, so he went on. "I have it as a tattoo, right here." Edward placed a palm over his heart.

Meg couldn't see through his shirt, but she sure looked as if she was trying. When he didn't continue immediately, she prompted,

"And the other?" Her voice came out sounding rattled. Why, he wondered. *Why?*

"The print on the right is another tattoo, one I got after the accident. I, uh…when I finally woke up, it was in my head and it was—I couldn't stop thinking about it and it was starting to drive me crazy. I tried over and over to draw it myself, but I'm no artist. I ended up having to describe it to Charlie, and he was able to do it better. It gave me something to bring to the tattooist." A mysterious image of wolves and coins from the dark caverns of his mind, that had felt so deeply crucial that he had inked it permanently in his skin, without knowing what it meant. How did one explain that to another human being? Did Meg have even one tattoo? As he spoke, Edward watched Meg's face. He couldn't have described what was happening there for a king's ransom.

Meg made a little noise in her throat. "Where did you put it?" Her eyes ran over his person in quick perusal.

Edward was startled to realize his hand still rested on his chest. He moved it a little to the side. "Here," he told her. "Right next to the other one."

"Over your heart," she commented. Her nice voice had gone curiously hoarse.

Still, he nodded, and she turned back to the frames on the wall. "What do you suppose the second image represents?" Meg asked softly.

The wild notion to ask her that very question had certainly occurred to Edward. But she was acting so strangely, and the words just seemed to lodge in his throat. What if she knew, and the answer was something horrible? Or, worse than that, what if the answer was something bloody wonderful, and because he couldn't remember, it was lost to him forever?

"I have…no idea," Edward admitted to her haltingly. It was the best he could do right now. He prayed she'd understand. "Maybe it represents recovery, to me."

Her voice stayed quiet. "Why hang them here? Over your bed like this?"

God, she was perceptive. Edward thought about deflection, but decided understatement might work just as well. She'd be appeased, and he wouldn't reveal too much. "Westbroke reminds me of who I am, obviously, what's gone before and what's to come. The other…I may not ever know precisely what it is, but it makes me feel at peace. Can't ask for much more than that when you're trying to sleep, right?"

And then, because Meg appeared about to shatter into a million pieces (and that was a feeling he knew a little something about), he came closer. He put a hand on her shoulder and turned her to him. Edward knew he couldn't bear to see her eyes right now. He couldn't even begin to fathom the deep undercurrents of what was happening in this room. So he focused on her hairline instead, brushing a finger into the fine, silky strands. He knew how to make her questions stop.

"May I kiss you?" he whispered, for lack of a better option. He'd salvage their date from all of his weirdness, and Meg would feel better. She had to, because it would suck beyond measure if he dragged her down into the hole with him.

"Okay," she breathed shakily. Lord, if that sound didn't slay him. It almost seemed cruel to continue.

Edward hadn't made it this far in the last six months without perseverance, though. He shifted closer to her and pressed his lips to hers. Her mouth was cold under his. When he put his arms carefully around her, trying not to spill her wine, she was trembling. Edward would bet his last dime that Meg knew more about that wolf print than she was letting on. But she hadn't offered any information, and until he could decide why, playing dumb seemed the safest option.

"Are you okay?" he murmured against her mouth. Her eyes stayed resolutely shut, but she nodded. "Shall I stop?" he asked, discomfited by her unease.

"No, please. It's okay. Don't stop," she breathed.

When he kissed her again, she was prepared to return the favor. Meg kissed him back, opening for him when he tested the seam of her lips with his tongue. Her mouth was hot and tasted of the wine. She held her arms carefully around him, balancing her glass behind his back, and trying not to upset his where he rested it on the footboard beside her. Edward kissed her longer than he should have, but he felt like he was chasing something elusive. Something tantalizing, just out of reach. The taste of Meg's mouth, the feel of her tongue sliding over his, the sight of his bed stretching soft and wide behind her…there was more here than just this. *More.* He could feel it. He didn't want to let it go.

Meg was trying to tell him something, though. She murmured unintelligibly and pushed a hand against his chest.

"Sorry?" he managed, breaking off, dazed.

"I said, do you hear that?" She was blinking, too, equally bemused.

Edward did. A timer was going off in the kitchen, its shrill warning carrying all the way up the stairwell.

"Ah. Right. The dinner bell," he smiled weakly. "Got a little carried away," he admitted sheepishly, winking at her.

Meg turned pink, an adorable flush that crawled up her neck to spread across her cheeks. Then she bit her lip. It wasn't the best plan if she wanted to eat anytime soon. Coupled with the taste of her mouth, the sight of it shot a charge straight to Edward's groin. He clutched his goblet and whirled away.

"Off we go," he called, hitting the stairs at a brisk clip. "I'd hate to follow mauling you with burning your meal. Some insults just can't be ignored." He ran an unsteady hand through his hair, hoping Meg couldn't see how she affected him. If it was all desire in his eyes, then fine. But Edward suspected there was a healthy dose of puzzlement, too. Something had been happening there, with her, that was more than just making out.

Edward was relieved to hear both her footsteps and her startled laugh following him down the staircase. That was good. Whatever weighted moment had transpired up there with the prints seemed to have passed. As long as he could avoid triggering it again later, he'd be in good shape. They'd linger over dinner, he thought. Edward and Meg would finish cooking it together, then they'd eat. Slowly. They would have some dessert. Talk a bit. If he was lucky enough to bring Meg back up to the bedroom later, it would be well after dark. Neither of them would have to look at the frames on the wall, or think about what they might mean. Foolproof.

Chapter Twenty-Three

GIVEN HOW SHAKEN Meg was by the revelations up in Edward's bedroom, she was proud of how she handled herself once back on the ground floor. She helped him finish cooking and playing house with him only felt a little traumatic. After all, in the fall they'd mostly done things like cooking dinner at her old apartment, not here. The change in venue helped. Being surrounded by the things they'd picked out together did *not* help, even if she finally had the satisfaction of seeing how great everything looked in person. It was clear that George and his crew had been in the house working while Edward was gone. A lot had changed.

Still, Meg made conversation that was only slightly awkward—pretty commonplace as far as she was concerned. She tried not to get too emotional, looking into Edward's handsome face over the candlelit dinner table. But she had maybe one too many glasses of liquid courage, and Meg was feeling nervous about what she might do or say now.

To see a stylized version of her ankle tattoo, an emblem representing the Flynn coat of arms, framed on Edward's bedroom wall had been a huge shock. She'd stood there like a statue, stunned, completely clueless about how to handle it. Was she supposed to tell him flat out what it was? Strip off her boots and *show* him what it was? There was no freaking protocol for this kind of thing. And, after hearing his explanation of what it meant to him, Meg was even less certain of what she should do. He'd had the picture inked on his own chest, for crying out loud. It wasn't like she could keep it a secret for long. Eventually, if they kept dating, he was bound to discover what it was. And then, Meg could only imagine what he'd think. Disgust, that he was now twinsies with some chick he didn't even remember dating? Scorn, that he now had some other, less-noble family's crest emblazoned over his heart? Meg had wondered if he kept seeing her now out of some sense of obligation. How would this disclosure make him feel?

She peeked at him, trying to get a sense of his thoughts. Edward took the napkin from his lap, refolded it, and placed it carefully next to his coffee cup. Then he looked up and smiled. Before, Edward had been more open, but now, reading him was tougher. Meg got the sense that there was a lot going on under the surface that he was keeping suppressed by sheer force of will. What was it, though? He was beautiful to her, still. His light brown hair had gotten longer on top, though he still kept the sides tightly shorn. His jaw had the same angular line, the nose still straight, the eyes that same caramel color that she adored. When he smiled, he still had a tiny dimple at one side of his mouth, and his eyes crinkled at the corners. This Edward didn't smile much, though. This Edward did not kiss quite the same, either.

That had been the other shock. When Meg realized that he was about to kiss her upstairs, she'd been amazed. Relieved. Grateful. But it had been nothing like she'd expected. Meg had to admit, at least to herself, that she'd been expecting it to be the same earth-shaking gesture it had always been. She had to admit… she'd been expecting him to remember *that*, at least. But Edward hadn't. It wasn't as if the new kiss was bad, per se. It just wasn't the same anymore, and that broke her battered heart all over again.

Edward was into it, though. He had moved things along prettily handily before that kitchen timer sounded. She'd been thrilled for the respite, even if it was only temporary. Meg suspected, given the way he was eyeing her now, that the reprieve was over and Edward was interested in guiding things back in that direction. She didn't think she had it in her to say no, but she was very, very worried about what might happen if she said yes. At least now it was dark. If he didn't insist on having the lights on, she might escape the tattoo confession for another several hours, at least.

"That was delicious," she told him, lining her glass up with her plate. "Thank you for having me over."

"Thank you for coming," Edward responded warmly. "I enjoyed having you here."

His tone held a little something extra. Meg studied his face, but she didn't have to wonder long. He got up and rounded the table, coming to sit in the chair next to hers. He angled toward her, then slid gentle fingers across her cheek and into her hair.

"I hope you don't have to leave just yet," he murmured. He watched his hand as it freed the sloppy bun at the back of her head, then looked back into her eyes. He was close, so close.

"No," Meg whispered. "I don't."

"Good," he told her. "I'd like to kiss you again."

"Oh." *Yeah, look at her.* Smooth as she ever was.

He nodded, looking amused. "May I?"

"You're very polite," she stalled.

"I'd love an answer," he retorted, smiling.

"Edward…" Meg said. She had to ask him something huge, but she wasn't sure she should. She wasn't sure she wanted to know the answer. What did it matter, anyway?

"What is it?" He leaned back a little, giving her some space.

"I have to ask you something—something kind of personal." Meg gnawed on her lip, watched his eyes lock on her mouth when she did it. She stopped and licked her lips nervously.

Edward gave her a nod, signaling her to go on.

"Have you…um." Meg swallowed, praying for some finesse to come to her. "I just wanted to know if you've uh, *done* this. Since the accident, I mean."

"Done what?" he looked guarded now, and Meg had the sickening sense that she'd jumped the gun. Was she being presumptuous? Maybe New Edward had no designs on her person whatsoever.

Meg's hand moved spastically between them. "This," she said helplessly.

"Talking? Eating?" he asked her, eyebrows raised. "*Kissing?*" At her expression, he leaned back in his chair. "Other things?"

Meg nodded. He hadn't taken his eyes off her face, and she was kind of wishing he would. He blinked fast, mercifully shifted his gaze to look all around the room, and started to talk a few times before he actually made a sound.

"Are you asking if I've slept with anyone else since my accident? Since…you? Before?"

"I guess I am. I don't know why, it's just…I…uh…" she hemmed, before lurching to a halt.

"I can see why you'd want to know," he told her, face softening.

"You can?"

"Yes. And the answer is no, I haven't. What with my own recovery, and that of my dad, you know, it wasn't like I had time to hit a brothel, or anything." Edward was trying not to smile again. The fact that he was not taking this too seriously unknotted something tight in Meg's chest.

She giggled. "Do they *have* a lot of brothels in London, would you say? Because I might not have let you go so easily if I'd known that." She'd meant to lighten the mood, too, make a joke. But suddenly her eyes filled, and Meg swiped at them impatiently.

"Shh," Edward whispered. He cupped her face and brushed at the tears with his thumbs. "We'll figure this out, okay? I know it's probably hard."

"I never know what to say to you," she cried, giving in. "I don't know how I'm supposed to act."

He swallowed, hard. Meg watched his throat move, the Adam's apple bobbing up and down.

"I feel the same," he admitted. "I think you must have some expectations of me. But the fact is, I don't remember how we were. Until I remember, all I can do is take you as you are. Right now. I like you a lot. I think you're very pretty. And I—I liked kissing you a lot, too. I'd like to do it more."

"Would you?" Meg breathed. The heady combination of his cologne and *him* was as intoxicating as ever. It would be so easy to just accept what Edward was offering and melt into him.

Edward nodded. "Would you like that as well?" It seemed funny to Meg that he would ask her that, about something so innocuous. He'd asked her the same question before, of course, but about much dirtier things. *Would* she like it? Probably. But she'd probably hate it, too. So what was she supposed to do?

Meg drained her glass, noticing as she did so that the wine bottle itself appeared mostly empty. Between the two of them, they'd finished it. Edward wasn't exhibiting any major signs of impairment, though. He just seemed more relaxed. And possibly amorous. Once she'd set her glass down again, he leaned in to kiss her, slow and sexy, like he was savoring the taste of it. His hands came up and rested on her shoulders, under her hair. His fingertips brushed at the sensitive skin under her ears, tickled the fine hairs at her nape. Meg shivered. She'd never had a chance, not against Edward.

"I think so," she answered him on a sigh. His lips moved from her mouth to trail across her jaw and explore her neck.

"You're not certain?" he inquired. He kissed along the neckline of her sweater, nudging it aside to access more skin along her collarbone. Her eyes drifted closed, and before long, he'd pulled both the sweater and the tank top underneath lower. He licked along the lacy top of her bra, inhaling deeply as if he enjoyed the scent of her, too. His hands crept under the hem of her sweater, pushing up to rest against her ribcage, warm and gentle.

"Scratch that," Meg gasped. "I'm sure."

"Wonderful," he murmured against her skin. "That's two of us." Edward pulled back, grasped her firmly around the waist and lifted her to sit in front of him on the table. He spread her legs, shoving her skirt high up her thighs so he could get close, and wrapped his arms around her to hold Meg in place. When he kissed her again, there was new heat there. He stroked deeply into her mouth with his tongue, ratcheting up her arousal by careful degrees with his lips and hands.

Before long, he'd divested her of her sweater and tank top. Edward left her bra on, though, pulling down the lace cups to get at her breasts. The sensation of his mouth on her was welcome, but Meg retained enough presence of mind to note that it was different than it had been before. Each step Edward took felt measured, deliberate. Meg wanted to revel in the touch and feel of him, returned to her alive and well. But this was not Edward, not like he'd been. Her Edward was so consumed with need for her that he was urgent, desperate for her. This Edward wanted her. But he was perfectly willing to take his own sweet time. Meg sighed. Each method had aspects to recommend it, that was for sure.

Edward had nudged her back, to lay on the section of table he cleared with his arm. Rising slightly, he kissed her again, then pulled back to murmur, "If a lonely viscount wanted to get an innocent maiden up to his bedchamber, what might you advise he say to her?" His hands had crept up under her skirt, and Meg found herself lifting her hips to allow him to slip her panties down her legs. Well, at least some things remained the same. Edward, in any iteration, definitely had a thing for getting busy all over the house.

"Are you serious?" she gasped out on a laugh, as he moved back to kiss his way up the inside of her thigh. Meg relaxed, realizing that he was going to leave her low boots and socks on her feet. The tattoo stayed safe and concealed, for now.

"I'm asking for a friend," he chuckled, and then his mouth was on her. Meg didn't waste time comparing techniques this time. Both methods clearly had points in their favor. Edward dragged his tongue along her folds, then sucked at her before raising his head.

"Perhaps he could offer to show her his priceless Ming vase. Think that would work?" he asked, setting to work on her again.

Meg squeezed her eyes shut to avoid the glare of the chandelier dangling overhead. This Edward, this charming, cheeky Edward, was so similar to hers that Meg would give him anything he asked. Just to pretend, for a little while, that nothing had changed.

"Do you *have* a priceless Ming vase up there?" she managed to pant out.

He raised his head again, torturing her. "Actually, no," he said conversationally. "Do you think it matters?"

"I doubt it," Meg replied. She tugged at his head, trying to pull him closer again.

He didn't budge, smirking up at her across the expanse of her stomach. Edward gripped her hips with his long, elegant fingers, and his shoulders held her legs spread wide. Suddenly, Meg felt disturbingly exposed. She tugged up her bra to cover her breasts, like that would help.

Something flickered in his expression, and Edward's eyes narrowed. Now that he had his prey in hand, he wasn't going to give up so easily.

"Perhaps you noted the large and comfortable bed, while you were up there before," Edward commented. "Bit softer than reclaimed oak," he added drily, patting the table beside her.

"I seem to remember something like that," she agreed.

He nodded, rising from his chair and taking her panties from the table beside her. He shoved them in his pocket, grabbed her hands, and pulled her up.

"Up you get, there's a good girl," he said. Meg hopped down from the table and smoothed her skirt down over her bare skin, feeling herself blush. Edward dropped a quick kiss on her mouth, then purred, "Follow me." Meg grabbed her sweater and tank top and did.

He towed her behind him, two flights up the front stairs to his bedroom. Dim light filtered in the open curtains, cast by the streetlights down in the alley that bordered the river, and by the lights of the buildings on the opposite shore. There were no stars tonight, and no moon to reflect on the Charles, both obscured by the clouds of an impending spring rainstorm. Still, Meg could make out the soft gray walls, painted the color of clay. There was no mattress or box spring on the floor, instead, he had a large, carved wood bed that she knew was worth a fortune. It didn't look like an army could dislodge it. His bedding, she now remembered, had been changed. He no longer slept on the navy plaid flannel from the fall, but instead had crisp white sheets and a soft taupe linen comforter. Meg remembered seeing something similar once in a catalog. With a start she wondered—was this one of the things he'd ordered before his accident? From one of *her* catalogs? She swallowed, doubly grateful that the prints above the headboard were now reduced to indistinct blurs. She couldn't go through with this if she had to see those clearly, that was for damn sure.

Edward turned toward her and pulled her into his arms. When he kissed her again, Meg kissed him back. When he finished undressing her, she let him. She set her shaking hands to undressing him, too, peeling away the trappings of New Edward to reveal the same skin, the same musculature and bone structure of her lost, beloved man. She let herself fall into the feel of him, and deliberately pushed everything else away. Meg wondered if he was doing the same, packing all the worry into a box to examine later. For now, she wouldn't let it matter. For now, Edward was hers, and she'd take him in whatever form he came in. She let herself believe that it was all going to be okay. If there was reason to fear, Meg would handle it tomorrow.

"You're so lovely," he whispered to her. "So soft and pretty."

Edward drew her to the bed and pulled her down with him. He lay beside her, skin to skin, and kissed her again. Meg matched him, action for action, and waited for the moment when the fire would light. That flick of the switch when Edward went from dignified to uninhibited, that she remembered, and loved, so well. Surely that was such an elemental part of him that it would still exist? One couldn't lose their most basic, primal self, just by forgetting a few months, could they?

By the time Edward was settling himself between her legs, balancing on his forearms above her, Meg began to doubt that assumption. He was methodical, she realized. His actions in bed were the work of a man crossing all his T's and dotting his I's, but the result was leaving Meg cold. It was technique, stripped of the underlying feeling that would usually elevate the act to one of intimacy. Oh, this Edward clearly still knew his way around a woman's body. He was giving Meg just enough to keep her in the game. And she had no doubt that he did feel *something* for her. Affection, maybe, or just plain goodwill. But he wasn't burning for her, and at this point in Meg's life, she discovered she needed that. When she was doubting so much about herself that she used to take for granted, she needed her man to uplift her—to see her and want her so much that he was driven past the point of sedate deliberation. Meg needed Edward to be crazy for her, like he was before, and this new man was not. If she tried to stop him now, she wondered what he'd do.

She watched his face when he came. Eyes screwed shut, face serious, jaw set. A harsh, stark expression. Lost in the moment, he didn't seem to be aware that she hadn't finished with him. That was as telling as anything she'd experienced yet—her old Edward would never have missed that, not in a million years. Meg never would have been able to maintain such a clinical detachment with him. This Edward held himself in place for long moments before dropping his head to her neck as he regained his breath. Her heart beat steadily in her chest, as it always did. Her lungs continued to push air in and out. His hair was damp along his nape, and Meg raised a hesitant hand to stroke it. Edward lifted his head at her touch, and placed two careful, precise kisses on her lips.

"Are you okay?" he asked. Meg nodded, not trusting herself to lie with words.

Edward withdrew carefully from her, slipping quickly out of bed and into the bathroom to get rid of the condom. Meg lay where he left her, feeling cold and bereft. She gathered his soft new bedding close around her, desperate to feel the armor of clothing again. All of a sudden, being naked felt too damn vulnerable. When one person felt nothing, and the other participant felt too much of all the wrong things, Meg mused, what they'd just done together became a bastardization of what it was supposed to be. An abomination of what it was before. There was no way she'd be able to do it again with him. Not like that.

Edward emerged from the bathroom, the shape of him in the dimness so familiar to her. It was easy to keep getting fooled, thinking he was the same inside when he looked the same on the outside. But this had been a strict lesson on the danger of letting down her guard. Meg wouldn't forget how this felt, wouldn't be tricked again. When Edward slipped under the covers next to her, she shuddered at the feel of his cooling skin. His bare arm pressing hers, his bare flank against her hip—she couldn't endure it. Before he could pull her close, Meg fled, darting out of the bed on the opposite side and bee-lining for the safety of the bathroom.

"I'll be right back," she called hastily, before shutting the door and locking it behind her.

She approached the sink with some trepidation, certain she didn't want to meet her own eyes in the mirror that hung above it. Meg ducked her head and splashed cold water on her face, scrubbing it dry with the thick, soft towel laying on the counter. Then she looked around, stepped into the big claw-footed tub, and turned the hot water tap. She had to wash off the evidence of Edward's possession. It was all wrong. Meg couldn't stand the feel of him on her skin one second longer.

It took too long to work up the courage to return to bed. Meg hoped he didn't notice. Or, if he did, that he was sensitive enough not to comment on it. She was cold. She wanted to just get dressed and ask him to take her home, but it seemed callous to do it so abruptly. So instead, she dashed from the bathroom to the bed, and crawled back under the covers next to him. He laughed, startled when he felt her.

"God, Meg, you're freezing. What happened to you in there?"

"Nothing. I don't know why I'm so cold," she explained, shivering. She was reluctant to snuggle up to Edward, even though she could feel the warmth coming off him. She didn't want to give him any ideas. "Do you have a t-shirt I could wear?" she asked. That would help, she thought. Put a barrier between them, even if it was only a thin cotton one.

He peered at her, trying to see her expression. "Yeah, of course," he agreed. "Hang on, I'll get you one." Edward tossed back the comforter on his side and walked into his closet. At some point he had donned a pair of boxers, probably while she was lollygagging in the bathroom. Once he'd disappeared, Meg hurled herself out of bed, pulling her panties from the pocket of his jeans on the floor. She yanked them on and got herself under the covers again half a second before he reappeared. He stood nervously with a small bundle in his hands and didn't seem to notice she was out of breath.

"I, uh, found these," he told her, proffering what he held. "When I moved back in. I thought maybe they were yours." His voice was strange. He sat on the side of the bed and didn't move to lay down or get dressed himself.

Meg held up the garments, a camisole and loose, long bottoms in matte sueded silk. A woman's matched set of pajamas, expensive. Understated, but still sexy. She checked the label—her size. She couldn't tell the color in the darkness, but it looked to be another colorless gray or taupe like everything else in the room. Pajamas that matched the bedding. She'd never laid eyes on them before. Meg shook her head, but Edward already knew—she could tell.

"These aren't mine, I'm sorry," she said numbly. She tried to give them back to him.

"It's all right," he reassured her, pushing the clothes back at her. "Go ahead and wear them. They weren't anyone else's either. I cut the tags off just now."

"Oh," Meg whispered. She thought about the boxes that had arrived in the weeks after his departure. She remembered Christmas, sitting alone on her floor and opening each package while doleful carols played on her stereo. How devoid of life each item had seemed, without him. It had made her skin crawl to wear any of it, and she had mostly refused, not until he returned. Resting her fingers on the soft cloth of the pajamas, Meg wondered if this was part of that same shopping spree. Had Edward kept some things here at his house, to spoil her with later? It would've been exactly the kind of thing he might have come up with.

Meg wished he had just given her an old t-shirt, like she'd asked. Something that smelled like him, something she hadn't seen before, something that wouldn't force her to confront the devastation she was feeling now, more than ever. But he hadn't. And he was sitting there, expecting her to put this gift on. Meg really didn't want to. But she slipped the top over her head. Then she stood and pulled on the pants. Edward blinked at the sight of her underwear, but didn't comment.

Instead, he whispered, "Come here." He held out his hand, and Meg, weak-willed fool that she was, took it. He pulled her to the center of the bed, where he stretched out on his back and guided her head to lay on his chest. Meg draped her arm across his waist and listened to the slow and steady thump of his heart under her cheek, through the skin unwittingly stained with her family's crest. Meg felt the rise and fall of his chest as his breathing settled into sleep. She tried not to notice the slip of the silk over her skin, the way it made her nerves jump and twitch with unwanted titillation. She willed herself, with every fiber of her being, not to cry.

How long before she could slip out unnoticed? How long did she have to stay? She waited what felt like an eternity before she attempted escape. But Meg should have known nothing would be easy for her, not this time around. Edward awoke when she was only half-dressed. She'd been cursing the creaking boards of his antique wood floor, trying to find her clothes in the gloom. Before she knew it, he was up and dressed in sweatpants and a ball cap, leading her down to his garage, and driving quietly through the dark wee hours of the morning to take her home. In the turnaround of her new building, he kissed her hand (but not her lips) and thanked her. *Thanked her.* Meg marched inside, refusing to make eye contact with the ever-alert doorman, and saw Edward's car idling out there even as the elevator doors were sliding shut.

She reached the apartment, tip-toed through the living room and locked herself in her bedroom. There was light shining under Mayu's door, and she could hear the low, quiet murmur of a man's voice through the wall. Thank God Edward hadn't made her bring those beautiful, awful pajamas home. Meg dressed in a ratty BU t-shirt and a pair of old boxer shorts—Edward's, unfortunately. She hadn't dared contemplate it, but some part of her had thought Edward would remember. He would make love to her and he would *have* to remember. How could he not? Curled under the covers in the pitch dark, Meg finally let the tears come.

Chapter Twenty-Four

IF EDWARD HAD to inhabit this body and this brain for one more day, he was likely to go apeshit. He absolutely could not take it anymore. As of this morning, he thought he might actually despise himself. He turned his back on the tangled sheets, sat on the edge of the mattress, and dropped his head in his hands.

He didn't want to think. Didn't want to review what had happened, and how it played into his life right now, but the self-debriefing seemed like it was going to happen whether he wanted it or not. Images from the night before scattered in his pounding head. During dinner, Meg had picked up on his ambivalence about this blasted house. She'd been astounded that he didn't love it. He did, sort of, though it was certainly no bachelor pad. How could he have explained that it felt like a house for a family, and he was envisioning knocking around it all by himself for the next fifty years? It was pathetic.

He let her wear those silk pajamas he found, because giving Meg something of his own had felt too intimate for some reason, even after what they'd done. They fit her like a dream and felt even better against her skin. The trouble was, she hadn't recognized them—they clearly weren't hers. He had made a quick decision not to mention all of the other stuff in his closet, because her not claiming the pajamas meant he had a bigger problem. Edward not only had to figure out what was missing in his life, but now he had another woman, maybe even a fiancée expecting a ring, to find. One that no one but him likely even knew about. How the hell was he supposed to begin? All he knew about her was that she must be about the same size as Meg. And hopefully, better in the sack than Meg.

Jesus. What a disappointment that had been. Edward had been so hot to trot for her. He'd kissed her and charmed her, and by some miracle had gotten Meg into his bed last night. Meg, who had asked him point blank if he had shagged anyone else since last he'd seen her. Edward wondered: did Meg *know* of his other woman? Maybe her worry centered around the idea that she was in direct competition with another woman that Edward liked better. Little did she know. Any small flashes of desire he might have felt in the last several months had been easily dispatched with his hand and a hot shower. Banging women had been about the last thing on his mind. And now that he'd taken one shaky step back into the pool, he was not at all sure swimming was the right plan. Because last night...

He felt like a total bastard about last night. He'd been gunning for her, and she'd folded like a deck of cards. Of course she had. It was a no-brainer. The poor thing had been holding a torch for a bloke she'd thought dead and buried for months. Now he was back, and making the moves on her, and naturally Meg fell for it. But Edward had thought, with the history between them, that the actual act would be a bit more interesting. He had thought there might be fireworks, that her reserve and modesty would take a hike and they'd have a cracking good time. What a joke. He'd tried to get her invested, but he'd known, just under the surface, that Meg was a wreck. And he'd gone ahead with it anyway. Edward had used her, he supposed. Used her body and her complaisance to scratch an itch. That sort of transaction wasn't going to be rocking *anyone's* world. She'd tried to sneak out in the dead of night, for Christ's sake. If his floors hadn't been so bloody creaky, she would have gotten away with it, too, preferring to walk the dark city streets at three a.m. rather than remain with him any longer. No wonder he'd hightailed it to Britain after only a month with her.

Edward had a sudden unwelcome thought. Over dinner, he had invited her to the theater on Wednesday night. Well, fuck that. That wasn't going to happen. He'd have to cancel. He couldn't keep seeing Meg, not if he just cheated on his future wife with her. He had just let her wear his woman's pajamas, damn it, after sticking his dick where it didn't belong. Edward massaged his throbbing temples. And it hadn't even been good sex. Meg had clearly expected something different. *He* had expected something different. What a disaster. Nothing could be more of a buzz kill than coming in second to a *memory*. But…why would she have gone through with it? To try to stake a claim before his missing woman got a chance? Did Meg not only know *of* her, but actually *know* her personally? Hell, how long had Edward been juggling the two of them, hoping not to get caught? Or…maybe he *had* been caught and *that* was why he'd left? Why the fiancée was still missing in action? He wished he could ask George, but he didn't dare. If Edward had been that scurrilous, he probably had done everything possible to keep it from George and the rest of the family. His thoughts swirled in his aching head, none of them making sense.

Meg probably hated him. He certainly hated himself at the moment. He'd let himself get carried away by a momentary attraction, and he hadn't thought how it might affect the woman—women?—involved. As a gentleman, Edward probably owed her an apology. First thing Wednesday morning, he would text Meg and tell her sorry, something had come up and he couldn't go out with her. *Text* her. Like the dog that he was. Like a bloody coward. Meg wanted the Edward he had supposedly been last fall, but he'd likely never be that man again. Why had he even tried? It was foolishness in the extreme, and mostly, if he thought about it, George's fault.

There was one encouraging thought, though. Edward supposed it was likely that the thing he had known was missing, and the woman out there who he'd meant to marry, were one and the same. That meant he only had one thing to find, and not two. He ticked off the facts: a woman, probably about his age, about Meg's size, who was in Boston during the fall. With him, being irresistible. And who could at this moment, be anywhere in the world, believing him either unfaithful or dead. Edward groaned. Fuck.

He shoved himself to his feet and staggered down the stairs toward the kitchen. He needed some coffee and some aspirin, in any order. Why did he always feel so damn scatterbrained? He thought of himself as a practical, logical chap, but lately he had to wonder. Maybe that was wishful thinking. Maybe he was really just a spoiled, rich sot who couldn't think straight to save his life. There was definitely a precedent for that sort of thing. He'd consider becoming a drunk in earnest to seal the deal, if only the following mornings weren't so shitty. On the kitchen counter, his cell was vibrating.

Edward's heart fell, and he stared at it with a knot of dread in his stomach. All of the potential options sucked. His mum? No thanks, he already had a headache. Meg? *God*, no. She could leave him a message if she'd forgotten something here, and he'd drop it with her doorman later. Any work calls could wait a few minutes. And his brothers, all of them, could wait forever, as far as Edward was concerned. After all, George and Charlie were the arseholes who had hatched this scheme to begin with. As usual, they had gotten him into a mess that Edward would have to get himself out of. Fat lot of help they were, the little blighters.

Edward skirted around the phone and headed for the coffee maker, ignoring the wine glasses in the sink. The dinner dishes were still on the table in the other room. The table on which he'd selfishly molested his unsuspecting date last night. Lord. He had to get out of here. He couldn't stand himself. The cell phone fell silent.

He pulled open the cabinet next to the sink and fished out three aspirin for his head. He filled the coffee maker with water and beans, then washed down the pills with more water from the tap. He leaned against the counter and waited for the machine and the medicine to work their respective magics. Edward's cell began buzzing again.

"Ruddy hell," he grumbled, his foul mood growing fouler. He was going to have to take a run, he realized. Trying to sit in his study and work like this was obviously not going to happen for him. First coffee and probably some toast, to settle things down. A quick pop upstairs to wash off the scent of Meg's perfume. Then, a long, punishing jaunt down through the Common and back. After that, he might be human enough to play nice with others.

His phone shuddered itself right off the edge of the counter, landing on the floor with a thud. Edward lurched for it with a curse, but of course, his mum's case-from-hell had protected it from injury. All the same, he couldn't help but notice who was calling. *Damn.*

"Fred? That you?"

"Edward! Hullo! I thought you weren't there," his youngest brother said plaintively.

Edward checked the clock over the range.

"Freddy, why aren't you in class right now?"

"The tutor cancelled. He said he caught the stomach bug I had last week."

Edward frowned. "I thought you were lying about that?"

"I was, you arse. Which means he's lying, too. I told you he hated me."

"I'm sure that's not true. Where're Mum and Dad?"

"Out. He told her he fancied some fish and chips for lunch, and she told him if he wanted them, he'd have to drive there and get them himself."

"How's that going, anyway?" Edward asked.

"It still stinks. Every time she makes him do stuff, he complains for hours after that it's made him sore."

"I see." Edward did see. He still had a host of twinges and pains that cropped up when he wasn't expecting them, and his father had been banged up quite a bit worse than he had. Ironic, really, that Edward was the one who was the head case.

Freddy made a grunt of agreement, but didn't say anything else. Edward listened to the crackle of the phone line for as long as he could stand it.

"Fred?" he finally asked. "Was there a reason you were calling me internationally, or did you just miss me?"

"Um, right," Freddy hedged. "Well, Mum told me you saw her again."

"Who?"

"Meggie. I just…would you please tell her I said hi?" His brother suddenly sounded younger than he had in years. Freddy's voice had changed early, growing deeper the summer after he had turned eleven with hardly a crack. But the vulnerability in his voice right now made him seem like a little boy again, not like the thirteen-year-old half-man, half-beanpole that he was.

Edward hesitated. "So you knew her, too?" he asked. Had she met his whole family then? Why her and not the real woman he loved? Meg appeared to be quite the operator. Edward wondered, though, if he himself was the charlatan. A lovelorn, faintly evil con man.

"Yes, of course I did, idiot. I felt so badly for her, you know. I tried to help them find her, but then Mum took away my computer, so…there went that idea."

"The topless snaps of Princess Kate, wasn't it?" Edward grinned, unable to resist tweaking the kid.

"Don't remind me," Freddy groaned. "Anyway, will you? Tell her, I mean?"

"Of course I will, Fred." It was a lie, naturally, but Fred didn't need to know that. "Everything else all right?"

"Smashing," Freddy drawled sardonically. "I can't wait until we can come back there."

"Not long now," Edward reassured him. "Just…help Dad as much as you can, and kiss Mum for me."

"I will, Ed."

They both sat there and waited, listening to each other's breathing. Goodbyes had gotten tricky in the Hughes family.

"Love you, Freddy," Edward murmured, relenting.

"You, as well," his baby brother said, and then he hung up.

Edward sighed, poured himself a steaming mug of caffeine, and headed for the back stairs. Screw the toast. He'd eat after his run. He was bound to be hungry then.

FIFTEEN MINUTES LATER, Edward wrenched open his front door and hit the stairs, only to find George sitting on the stoop with a travel mug of coffee and a bag of fast-food breakfast sandwiches. Edward dropped down beside him to tie the laces of his trainers, while George peeled open a paper wrapper and began to eat. When George silently offered a sandwich to him, Edward accepted it with a sigh. Another delay. Edward would be lucky, at this point, if he was home by dinner time.

"What the hell are you doing here?" he inquired stiffly.

"I rang the bell. You must not have heard," George replied complacently, not answering the actual question.

Edward chewed, and kept his eyes resolutely on the fence of the garden across the way. The tulips were dying off. And this greasy breakfast was going to sit in his stomach like a rock once he got going. *If* he got going. It was salty and cheesy and tasted splendid. Now.

"Rough night?" George inquired.

Edward snorted, hating the universe that had given him this brother, especially. "You might say that." Resistance was futile. It always had been, from the moment his parents had brought George home from the maternity ward. That didn't mean Edward couldn't try.

"But I thought you were seeing Meggers last night," George asked, confused. "Filet mignon with béarnaise sauce, you said. Did you bollocks things up again?"

Did everyone in his family have a pet name for the woman? He hated to consider what his mother might have called her. "*No*, I did not bollocks things up. And the first time was hardly my fault," Edward snipped. Blimey. No sooner did he decide she wasn't for him, then every Hughes this side of Russia began lobbying for her. It figured. He rooted around in George's bag to find another sandwich.

"Edward," George said calmly. "What happened?"

Edward shook his head. "Nothing. Nothing happened. I just…" he trailed off. Shrugged. Sighed again. Good Lord, one might think he was becoming asthmatic.

"You slept with her?" his brother asked, looking off down the street.

"Yeah," Edward admitted.

"No good?"

"Nope."

George squeezed his eyes shut, and on a huge exhale pulled the brim of his Red Sox cap around to the back of his head. "Sorry mate," he told Edward. "I did not expect that."

Edward rolled his eyes and shrugged again. Neither had he. After it was over, he hadn't known who he felt sorrier for— himself, or Meg.

"George…" he began. No. He shouldn't. This was a terrible idea. But his mouth kept moving while his brain begged *Stop*. "George, I think there was another girl. Before. A different one, besides Meg. Did you, uh…did you know anything about that, maybe?"

George burst out laughing, a huge, blustering emission that sent fragments of egg shooting out over the sidewalk. "Edward! Jesus, have you gone mad?"

"More than the usual, you mean?" he retorted angrily. He hated being asked that question, especially now, and it seemed like it was becoming one of George's favorites.

"Yes. Yes, more than the usual, you prick. Of course there wasn't another woman," George exclaimed, staring at him.

Edward gazed stonily ahead, refusing to acknowledge George's incredulity.

"Edward, you're serious? What on earth could have given you that idea? You and Meg—Christ, you two were joined at the hip. You wouldn't have had the bloody *time* to have some piece of arse on the side. For fuck's sake—even if you did, you wouldn't have wanted to. You were in love, man. You had it bad."

Edward shook his head again and scrubbed his hands over his face. As unlikely as it seemed, it had to be true. George *must* be mistaken, because there was no other explanation. No other way that the pieces could fit together in any form that made sense. His brother just hadn't known about the other woman, that was all. For some inexplicable reason, every damn Hughes except him felt loyal to Meg Flynn. Well, they could have her. They didn't have to be the ones to…

"You thought you'd remember. You thought if you slept with her, it would come back," George accused.

Edward nodded, numbness settling over him.

"And Meg probably thought the same," George mused, staring at him.

Edward stretched his legs out in front of him, leaned back on his elbows, and stared up at the blue sky.

"I'm sorry, mate," George said quietly. "Sorry for all of it."

"Not your fault," Edward grunted.

"Not yours, either," George countered.

They sat in silence for long minutes, George polishing off the last two sandwiches, and Edward trying to focus on the warmth of the sun on his face. If he tried to run now, he'd likely be puking in a trash bin before long.

"Could you please not give up yet?" George asked him. "Just give it another try for me? Promise?"

Edward peered at his brother, taken aback by the pleading note in his voice. What the hell did George care? But George stared right back at him, not giving an inch, and Edward found himself unable to deny his brother.

"Yeah. Sure. I'll, uh, give it another go," he agreed weakly. Edward knew it was a bad idea. But his little brother was giving him a bit of a mindfuck with this noble attitude of his. It was like George had aged a decade in the last six months, and Edward hated that, too, along with everything else.

George slumped in relief, looking away and trying to gather his composure.

"Did you forget about our meeting with the Wilkinsons?" George asked finally.

"Yes, I did," Edward admitted, unsurprised. Of course he had.

George glanced at the time on the screen of his cell, which, inexplicably, now had a large red poppy bloom as its wallpaper instead of the usual cartoon hammer. "You have time to shower and change. I'll watch the game downstairs while I wait." He heaved himself to his feet, balling up the bag of trash and cracking his back. "Sox and Yankees," he commented.

"No telly yet," Edward reminded him.

George followed him up the stairs and through the doors. "Fucking hell, Edward," he complained. "What century is this for you?"

Chapter Twenty-Five

"MAY I SPEAK to Ms. Flynn, please?" the voice on the phone said.

"This is she." Meg had left her cell on the floor next to her bed last night, and at nine a.m. sharp this morning, it began ringing.

"Hi, Meg. This is Andrea Cooper from Waters Matheson. I'm sorry to bother you on a Sunday, but I really wanted to catch you before tomorrow. How are you doing?" Andrea Cooper was the woman Meg had first interviewed with several weeks ago, and she'd found her very friendly. Andrea sounded even happier now, not businesslike at all. Which could only mean one thing.

"Great, thanks. What can I do for you?" Meg asked, forcing herself to sound alert and professional, despite her throbbing head and cottony mouth.

"Well, I have good news—the partners have reviewed all the candidates for the open position, and they would like to offer you the job," Ms. Cooper explained. She sounded thrilled.

"That's terrific," Meg replied. And it was. *It was.*

"Okay, just one thing to keep in mind. I know the standard is two weeks' notice, but we have a training session starting here next week. Any chance your current boss would agree to share you with us for a couple days a week for the next three weeks? We'd love to get you up to speed as soon as possible, and that would be the best way to do it. If you want the job, I mean."

"Um, I'm sure he would be okay with that, but I'll double-check tomorrow, just to be sure." Poor Joe. He'd be happy for her, Meg knew, but he probably wasn't anticipating something quite this precipitous.

"I understand," Andrea said. "Kim from HR will be calling you in a few to talk about salary and benefits. Do you think you could drop me an email by close of business Monday to confirm your acceptance? Or would Tuesday work better?"

"Tomorrow should be fine," Meg agreed. "And…thanks. I really appreciate this."

"Of course. I'm so pleased, too—I was rooting for you," the other woman confided. And Meg realized that she likely was getting a new friend, in addition to a new job. Would wonders never cease.

The call from Kim came swiftly after the first. Meg, feeling an almost unbearable sense of relief and gratitude nearly accepted the first offer Kim extended. But some shred of business acumen surfaced, and she managed to negotiate herself an extra 10K a year. Meg didn't dare ask for more. It was already so much better than she could have hoped for. She could get her own apartment. And clothes. And *furniture.* Maybe even snag another studio like her previous one, in the same building she was before. Molly would go crazy for that, having her nearby again. By the time Meg hung up, she was trembling all over, and it wasn't from her hangover. The universe took away, all right, but some cosmic scale must have been tipped because it had just given her something huge back.

Meg hauled herself out of bed, wrapped herself in her robe and poked her head out of her door. All was quiet in Mayu's room, and in the kitchen. She darted on light feet toward the fridge, reheated a cup of leftover coffee in the microwave, splashed some milk in it, and retreated quickly to her bedroom. Her phone was ringing again.

As if she'd felt Meg thinking about her, Molly was calling. "I have good neeeews," she sang, when Meg answered. "I snagged an interview with that firm in Wilmington I was telling you about—they're flying me down next month!" She sounded elated. Meg smiled. She would hate to lose her friend to some place in North Carolina, but with her own new job…she could probably afford to fly down and visit Molly whenever she wanted.

"That's amazing. I'm so happy for you," she told her friend, and meant it. "Weirdly, I just got a call about the job I wanted, too." Meg bit her lip, waiting for Molly's reaction.

Molly squealed loudly, just as expected, and Meg found herself grinning. "Oh my God, that's awesome," Molly gasped. "You've waited *so long*."

"That's the truth," Meg agreed. "I kind of can't believe it."

Molly took that in quietly. Then she asked hesitantly, "So…why do you sound sad?"

Meg sighed. Why hadn't she ever learned to be a better faker? Or acquired less-perceptive friends? She took a long, burning gulp of coffee.

"I slept with Edward," she admitted dully.

"Yay!" Molly trilled again. When Meg didn't join in, she fell ominously quiet.

"No," Meg said into the silence.

"No? How, *no*?" her friend demanded.

Meg rubbed at her forehead. Why hadn't she ever noticed how *loud* Molly was before? Did she have to scream everything?

"*Meg!*" the other woman yelled.

Meg gave up. "It was awful, all right? Nothing like before. It was just…there."

"No," Molly gasped. "How is that even possible?"

"I have no idea," Meg whined. "I'm so disappointed."

"I can imagine. And he didn't…" Molly paused.

"Go ahead. Say it."

"He didn't remember *anything*? Even after that?" Molly wailed.

"Not a thing," Meg admitted. "Seriously. It was the worst." She swiped at her eyes. Damn it, she would not cry again. She had a new job, finally, and she was *not* going to wreck her morning by crying.

"Oh, *Meg*," Molly groaned, sympathy heavy in her voice. "What the *hell*?"

"I know," Meg agreed. What else could she say?

"Are you going to see him again?" Molly asked, horrified.

"We're supposed to go out Wednesday night after work. But honestly—I don't think I want to go."

"No, of course not," Molly agreed. "So…is that it, then, do you think? No more Edward?"

"I'm not sure. Maybe," she said, feeling frozen.

"I don't like this," Molly grumbled. "This is sucky and I hate it."

"Me too."

"Does Morgan know what happened?"

"I haven't had a chance to tell her," Meg explained. "The lady from Waters Matheson literally woke me up a few minutes ago."

Morgan would only be in town for a few more days, Meg realized with a pang. She'd missed her big sister something awful, and had not even realized how much until she was hugging her again. If her sister weren't so ridiculously happy where she was, Meg would be begging her to move back to Boston. But she couldn't, no matter how sad she was. Meg was already crazy about Owen and Oliver. She couldn't stand to take a thing away from Morgan, not after she'd endured so much to get where she was. Meg would have to do this alone, again.

"Okay, well…" Molly seemed uncertain of how to go on. "You'll let me know what happens?"

"You know it," Meg agreed, trying to sound casual.

"Okay," Molly said again. "Okay."

But it wasn't. It *so* wasn't okay. Meg hung up, throwing her phone on the duvet next to her. She cracked her lone window a couple inches to let in the cool spring breeze, then tucked her feet back under the covers. She cast a critical eye around the small room. She'd left that raggedy futon out by the trash at the old apartment when she moved here. Once she had a couple paychecks from the new job under her belt, Meg would start looking for a new place. Get a real couch. A bigger dresser, and maybe even her own television. If Molly didn't get that job down south, maybe they could even be roommates, in a big, sunny two-bedroom somewhere. Her life should feel full of possibility right now, but Meg had to admit—she might never feel normal again.

She had once lain in that big bed of Edward's with her back to his sleeping form. Watched big snowflakes drift down to melt over the river in the stark gray morning light of late autumn, and thought with joy of what the future held. She used to luxuriate in having the fragrance of him enveloping her, feeling the aftershocks of his touch across her skin each time his body brushed hers. But instead, last night, she had only wanted to flee. Ached to leave.

Meg felt both cold and numb at once—she wanted to stand under a hot shower for too long, try to scald away the guilt and sorrow. Here, in this aftermath, she judged herself harshly. Molly hadn't asked, but Meg knew she'd had a little too much to drink last night. And she'd come on to Edward a little too strong. She knew she was a fool, thinking if she could just get him to make love to her, he would remember her. Remember everything. She'd done it all right and look what it had gotten her. Edward had remembered *nothing*. It was as empty a transaction as Meg had ever experienced, devoid of meaning.

When she felt him stir beside her, Meg had panicked. She had tried to disentangle herself from his arms and his bed as quietly and quickly as possible. In her anxiety, she hadn't even realized until later that Edward didn't see the tattoo on her ankle, hadn't had the opportunity to make that connection between them. It hardly seemed to matter now. She still found him achingly handsome, in that old school leading-man way he had, with his soft brown hair and square jaw. But though she had looked and looked,

Meg had found very few signs of the man he was last fall. The man that she had loved.

If she was going to see him again, Meg knew she would have to assess his attributes clinically. Remotely. She would have to armor herself against his charms if she was going to survive this. The thought left her feeling even more bitter and soulless than before. What was the point? Why endure this charade, if she was only going to be scourged, with no hope of having Edward restored to her? But Meg knew the answer to that, and it made her feel wretched. She loved him, loved him completely, and even if he never realized that again, she wanted him to be well. Wanted him to have his past back, so that he could have a normal, happy life. Meg would do this for him, to honor what they'd once had. And when George told her that Edward was whole again, Meg would leave him to his future. She set her empty mug on the floor, braided her tangled hair down her back, and curled under the covers. Squeezing her eyes shut, she held still until finally, mercifully, Meg fell back asleep.

It was early afternoon when her cell phone woke her again, pinging with an incoming text. Mayu and her boyfriend were out in the living room, watching TV and bickering. Meg pushed down her queasiness—why hadn't she eaten something this morning?— and checked the screen. *George*. Of course. That man was stubborn as the day was long. Naturally he wouldn't be dissuaded by one date gone awry. Or by the feelings of the people he was manipulating.

About Wednesday night…

Meg frowned. What about it? She wasn't going to go, to begin with. She typed out:

???

It took George a moment to reply. Meg wondered if he was with Edward, if they were plotting together, or if the Honorable Mister Hughes had gone rogue. Finally, he wrote,

What do u think about a group thing instead? Maybe hit the pub and watch some football with friends?

So, Edward felt the same as she did, Meg mused. He didn't want to see her either, and his brother was trying to strong-arm him into something survivable. Trying to salvage his scheme from a painful death. Whatever. Meg didn't have to make it easy on him. She replied,

It's not football season.

George responded quickly, with an angry little emoticon rolling its eyes.

SOCCER.

Meg was impressed with his restraint. She'd expected something more profane, given his temperament. She also expected herself to stand firm for a few days, but here it was, only hours after her most recent heartbreak, and she was giving in again, despite her resolve.

Fine. Where and when.

George texted her the name and address of the pub, and Meg was dismayed to note that it was the very same place Edward had introduced her to his father and brothers for the first time. Of course it was.

Meg wondered how long it would take Edward to tell her himself their plans had changed. Would he call today? Wait until Wednesday? Still, she didn't have to go in without reinforcements. She fired off a group text to Molly and Morgan.

911- If u love me u will clear ur schedules Wed pm.

Their replies came fast and furious. Meg didn't have high hopes for the romantic possibilities of watching soccer in a pub, surrounded by prying eyes. But at least now she'd have backup.

As it turned out, Edward contacted her on Tuesday. Her boss had spent Monday telling her all about Andrea Cooper's call, days earlier, to check Meg's references. He'd wanted to tell Meg because he was so excited for her, but hadn't wanted to ruin the surprise. In between all of the man's loopy grinning, he tried to hide how much he was dreading having to replace her. By the next day, some of his fervor had worn off, but Joe was still standing in her office chatting happily when her cell pinged. Her boss took one look at her face and nodded, slipping out the cubicle doorway and retreating to his office.

Meg peered at the text screen. Of course, she thought acidly, Edward didn't even call.

> Sorry it took me so long to get back to u—George let u know about Wed?

She snorted in disgust. No mention of Saturday night, but who was surprised? Meg had slunk out before dawn as disgracefully as any tramp doing the walk of shame. She typed out:

> He did.

She couldn't think of anything else to write, and was suddenly thankful he hadn't called, after all. Sitting in silence on the phone would probably be even worse. At least this way, he might think she was busy at work. He waited to respond, probably hoping Meg would have more to say. But finally, he wrote back,

> That ok with u?

No, it wasn't okay. None of this was okay in the least, and Meg wished people would stop asking her that. But really—if this was a game of sorts, she had to play along.

> Sure. Sounds fun.

Fifteen long minutes passed. Meg set her phone aside and tried not to envision what Edward might be doing. What he might be thinking. A text came in.

> Shall I pick you up beforehand?

Meg scowled. That rankled. The fact that he even asked made her decide that he didn't want to, but felt obligated to offer. Well, screw him and his stuffy noble manners.

No need. I'm heading over with friends.

There. That ought to show him. Meg didn't need his ride, and she didn't need Edward's weak attempts to pretend he wanted to be with her. She didn't need him at all.

Ok. Let me know if u change ur mind—otherwise see u then.

Meg growled, irritated beyond belief by that finale. He couldn't be making it any more obvious how little he cared. Wham bam, thank you ma'am. *Fine.* Two could play that game. She turned off her phone, dropped it in her purse, and got back to work. Who needed Mister Full-of-Himself Edward? Not her. Definitely not her.

Chapter Twenty-Six

EDWARD SAT BACK in the scarred wooden chair and took in the scene around him. Almost everything about it was familiar and comfortable, even if they weren't back home in Britain. The pub was tricked out in the English style, all dark wood and dodgy lighting, a place their father had found for them to gather only days after they'd first settled in here in Boston. His brothers around him, a sweating pint in his hand and football on the telly—all was right in Edward's world. The feeling was rare enough these days that he took a moment to savor it. True, their father and Freddy were still stuck on the opposite side of the pond, but both of them had already started texting him with stats and gossip on the players, and the match hadn't even begun yet. Edward eyed the bartender, polishing glasses behind the gleaming row of taps. A transplant from Liverpool, he had somehow finagled a satellite showing of the Cambridge United / Peterborough game. It was just an exhibition between rivals—it meant absolutely nothing to the clubs' standings. Still, the taste of home was perfect. Edward smirked over at Charlie, sitting grinning in a knot of his mates that included the two blokes from the bar a couple weeks ago. He couldn't recall their names, but the starry-eyed expressions on their faces were definitely memorable.

There were *some* differences, of course, just enough to keep Edward from feeling entirely at ease. George, typically, had a slightly sketchy girl tucked under his arm. This latest one, however, was quite a bit more colorful than usual. If Edward didn't miss his guess, this was the girl in the crowd George had been gunning for at McGillicuddy's. It was a little difficult to be sure, since he was keeping her as close as a second skin, on the side away from Edward. While the thick black glasses were certainly the same, the colors in her hair seemed different. Had it been electric blue before? Now there was some hot pink and vivid red streaked through the black. Edward shrugged. Didn't matter—none of George's conquests ever lasted very long, and as territorial as his brother could be, Edward was unlikely to have to talk to her at all.

He took a long draw from his glass and frowned. The beer was pretty crappy, watery and tasteless. Charlie had ordered them a couple of pitchers, but heaven only knew what was in them. Edward would have to go get himself something that cost more than a dollar a glass if he hoped to enjoy it. That was what happened, when you left the ordering to the cheap college students. He pushed himself up out of his chair and was making his way toward the bar when she arrived. He'd nearly forgotten.

Meg. She blinked rapidly as her eyes adjusted to the gloom, glancing around before she spotted him. The smile she gave him was brittle-looking, and Edward swallowed, feeling his shoulders and neck go tense. She was holding a grudge, maybe, about the change in plans. Her hair was pulled back in a soft ponytail, the blonde ends swishing over her shoulder as she turned her head. A small piece of hair at her temple had worked itself free—Edward watched it drift across her cheek with an almost scientific interest.

Two other women pushed into the pub behind Meg, taking a moment to arrange themselves and their handbags before turning to face the room as a unit. *Ah.* So Meg was unhappy enough with him that she'd brought reinforcements. Edward couldn't say that he blamed her. As he made his way across the room to meet them, he took note of her friends. One he had met before, on the same night they'd all gone to McGillicuddy's—the decoy girl. The other was unfamiliar, but bore such a resemblance to Meg herself that she could only be a relation of some sort. A sister, he remembered, visiting town with her family. The expression they all wore was the same—a sort of grim resolution. Edward fought not to roll his eyes. He may not have been *exactly* as doting as he ought to have been, but it was hardly as bad as all that. And given how much happier he was watching football with his brothers than sitting in some dark theater making stilted conversation with an affronted Meg, well…these ladies could just stow the attitude. He'd offered to pick her up, at least. She was the one who had declined that offer.

"Hullo ladies," he greeted them. He laid a hand on Meg's arm to pull her slightly away from the pack, and planted a dry, chaste kiss on her cheek. They were supposedly dating, after all, and even though their first foray into shagging hadn't gone according to plan—now that she was here in front of him, Edward was remembering how good she smelled, and how soft and pretty she was. Maybe he *was* crazy, come to think of it. Could sex with this girl really have been so bad? Maybe they'd both had an off night. It happened.

"I'm Edward. Molly, isn't it?" he asked, shaking hands and pulling the name of the first girl out of the recesses of his sluggish brain. Her handshake was a touch firmer than was strictly polite. A warning, he presumed.

Meg turned to the second woman. "Edward, this is my sister Morgan. She used to live here in Boston before she moved abroad."

"Right, Meg's told me about you. Nice to meet you," he said, proffering his hand.

She shook it, murmuring pleasantries and examining him carefully as she did so. He wondered how much they knew about him. Had they met him before his accident, or were they only operating with the current set of information? It was hard to tell, based on their faces. While it was clear both women were there in a supportive capacity, it was less obvious to Edward what they actually thought about him. He didn't imagine he'd have to wait long to find out. The girlfriends always discovered a way to make their feelings known.

"Can I get you anything to drink?" he inquired. "I think the match is about to start, and I doubt the bartender will be much help once it does."

With slightly perplexed expressions, the three women gave him their orders, and moved across the room to secure chairs for themselves at the edge of the group. Meg did a double take at the sight of George's date, but otherwise didn't move to address the other girl. Edward placed the drinks on his tab, adding several snacks to the order when he spotted George pantomiming eating to him. No surprise there—George could probably eat a horse if he tried, at any time of the day or night. George, who was greeting Edward's erstwhile date rather…warmly. Charlie, too, extricated himself from his mates, planted a sloppy kiss on Meg's cheek and wrapped her in a bear hug.

Edward scowled, ferrying the glasses and platters over to the tables they were congregated around. His brothers would certainly not make a move on his girlfriend under ordinary circumstances, Charlie least of all. But this was not exactly an ordinary situation. And the Hughes brothers had made it eminently clear how they felt about the exalted Meg Flynn. Edward was not sure whether he felt jealous of their easy camaraderie with her, or whether he was irritated that they insisted on kissing up to a woman he may or may not even like that much anymore.

He plopped into his seat again, pulled out his cell, and fired off responses to the flurry of texts that had come in from Dad and Fred while he'd been sorting out Meg.

Next to him, Meg and her girls leaned in close to each other, murmuring too softly for him to hear. George kept his arm draped around his date, but cast worried glances at both Meg and Edward. Edward was beginning to feel restless. What was the sense in having a cute girlfriend, if she was intent on being disgruntled?

This was supposed to be fun. If she kept up how she was acting, she was going to ruin the first normal thing he'd done in ages. It wasn't as if he'd *hurt* her. He hadn't even been mean, as far as he remembered. He just hadn't done it for her in bed. Edward crossed his arms over his chest and glared up at the huge telly, waiting for the kickoff. So what. She hadn't exactly lit his fire, either.

After several minutes, Morgan pulled a chair closer to him and dropped into it.

"So," she said, elbowing him to get his attention.

He turned to her. She was a little older than Meg, he thought, a little blonder. But she had that calm about her that he associated with Meg, too. Was it simple self-possession, Edward wondered? Or a certainty that life hadn't managed to break you yet?

"So," he began, echoing her as he searched for a conversational topic. "Meg tells me you've come on holiday from New Zealand, is that right?"

"Yes, we live just outside of Christchurch. It's a long trip, especially for Oliver," she confirmed.

"Oliver is your son?" Edward asked, taking a wild guess.

"Yes. He was tired, so he and my husband Owen stayed at the hotel to watch rugby on the laptop tonight. Wonders of modern technology, right?" she smiled, gesturing toward the flat screen blaring the match up on the wall.

Meg had shifted closer, and now she asked hesitantly, "Is this an important game? Or, um, a team you guys follow?"

Edward nodded, eyes on the screen mounted up on the wall. "Cambridge United, in the yellow and black jerseys, are the club from our hometown. The team in blue are Peterborough—I suppose you could say they're our rivals."

Charlie was shouting profane suggestions at the Posh goalie, causing his friends to mock him for his incomprehensible British slang. George was deep in conference with his girl, urgently whispering back and forth, his head dropped down close to her ear.

"So, is this a playoff game or something?" Morgan inquired politely, once the furor had died down a little. She glanced back at Charlie, her brows raised.

"Ah, no, not exactly. I think we're always a bit like this," Edward admitted sheepishly. The U's made an early goal and he roared, leaping up and toasting his brothers and the telly with his glass.

He sat back down, grinning at the screen, and then at the girls. Molly, true to form if he recalled, was already cozying up to Charlie's friends and didn't notice. Meg and Morgan met his look with tentative smiles of their own, though they obviously didn't share his fervor. Edward checked on George and his date, but they had slinked off somewhere unnoticed. He tried not think about what they might be doing, though he could guess. He pulled a plate of soft pretzels and cheese sauce closer and offered it to Meg. His phone was blowing up with ecstatic texts from Dad and Freddy. Laughing, he tapped out responses, then refocused on the game.

No one said much else to him for quite a long while. He was relieved not to have to explain every play to the Americans. They had football here, he knew—soccer, Edward corrected himself— so it wasn't like the rules would be a mystery to them. Perhaps one or two of the girls had even played it in school. They could follow the match like all the rest of them, without a lot of hand-holding on Edward's part. He settled in with his ale, becoming absorbed in the flow of the match.

At halftime, Edward surfaced and looked around the pub again. Meg sat further off to the side, flanked by her girls and looking pinched. She was gnawing at her thumbnail, while the one named Molly rubbed at her back comfortingly. Hmm. His fault, probably. He had gotten pulled into the game, and sort of lost track of Meg and of making conversation. Between joking around with Charlie and the constant stream of texts flowing into his cell from Fred and Dad—it was all so ordinary and familiar. Edward had needed something like this, badly. But as dates went, he was not giving his best performance. He supposed dismissing Meg's girlfriends from mind had been an epic blunder. He'd have to try harder, right after the next play.

Suddenly Meg herself was standing next to him and clearing her throat. He'd barely registered her.

"So, we're gonna take off, I think," she commented, looking off across the bar.

"Really?" Edward started to stand up, confused. Had he missed *that* much time? It was a hard-fought match, certainly, but...Edward glanced at his watch. *Oh.* Right.

Meg nodded. "No, it's okay—you don't have to get up. Anyway, I'm sorry. I have a training at my new job tomorrow. I should probably get to bed early, and you know...be ready."

Edward checked his watch again. It was only 6:30. How early did one have to get to sleep for something like that? Then another thought intruded, as he tried to keep one eye on the screen behind her. "You got the job, though? Congratulations. That's good, right?"

"Mm-hmm," she affirmed. She didn't seem inclined to say more. His attention drifted.

Edward cursed feelingly at the screen. The U's had just let in another bloody goal, making it 2 - 1. Morgan, the sister, tossed a largish piece of ice at his chest in a gesture that he assumed was meant to be funny, but in reality kind of stung. He rubbed at the spot, giving her a wounded look that didn't appear to impress her.

"Okay, well, I'll talk to you soon, I guess," Meg muttered, turning away.

Edward wrenched his attention back to her. He leaned in to give her a half hug and another peck on the cheek, an arid twin to the one he'd greeted her with.

"I'll call you," he promised. "You can get home okay from here?"

Meg scowled. "Yeah, I think we got it. See you later."

As Molly passed, he was nearly certain he heard her mutter, "*Dickwad.*"

Edward refused to think about that, but he would not turn down another pint or four. After a while, the game wrapped up, a 2 - 2 tie. He pocketed his phone after promising his father he would email Freddy tomorrow, Freddy having been ushered humiliatingly off to bed some time earlier.

Charlie and his mates were clearly settling in for the long haul. George, too, had reappeared, sans lady friend and in the mood for scotch. With one gesture, he had the waitress at their table proffering a bottle of single malt and two tumblers. In all likelihood, George would have her number before long, too.

"Where'd she go, Ed?" George demanded, fixing him with a deadly glare.

Edward didn't bother misunderstanding. "She left," he told him. "I think her knickers were in a twist about something."

"Oh, you think, do you?" George sneered, tossing back the amber liquid a mite too fast. "D'you suppose it's because you ignored her all damn night? *And* her friends?"

"We were watching the game," Edward protested, but it was half- hearted, even to his own ears. "Besides, I don't want to give her the wrong idea."

"And what idea is that, numbskull? That you're going to be a ginormous arse now that you've gotten into her pants?"

Edward sat sullenly, refusing to answer.

George just shook his head. "If *I'm* appalled, Ed, just imagine what Mum would say," he reprimanded.

"Are you fucking kidding me, George? You really want to bring Mum into this?" Edward protested. How *was* one supposed to be a gentleman, anyway, when one should *not* have slept with someone to begin with? Lord.

By nine, he and George were both drunk, and Edward was beginning to feel sentimental.

"George, what happens if I want to do it with her again?" he inquired blearily, slumping toward the table. Meg smelled *good*. She *always* smelled good. It made him want to bite her.

His brother didn't bother asking who Edward meant. "What, get her kit off again? Because you had such a gasping good time the first go around?" Edward tried to remember if his brother had always been this scornful. He didn't think so, but it was a wee bit hard to focus.

"I've got to get you out of here," George grumbled, heaving Edward unsteadily to his feet.

They paid their tab and made their way out onto the dark street. George pointed him toward his brownstone and gave him a little push to get his feet moving.

"This way, mate," he said.

"No," Edward protested. "I don't want to go there." In some small, still-functioning part of his brain, he realized that he sounded like a two-year-old. He also didn't care. His brownstone was cold and dark and empty. It made him feel pathetic.

George squinted at him, this being an unexpected sentiment. He looked around the street, at the closed shops and sparse traffic. "Well, where do you want to go instead?"

Edward wheeled around in a circle, like a compass searching out true north. He could picture Meg's old building, the gray stone edifice of it stretching a full city block wide. He could picture the black and white tiled entry, and the small, cramped elevator. He wanted to go there, to slump boneless onto her hard futon sofa or her small lumpy mattress and pull her into his lap. But...

"Edward?" George snapped his fingers in front of his face, and Edward blinked slowly.

"Do you know where Meg lives now?" he asked, perplexed. "I have to talk to her. I have to tell her sorry I'm a bastard."

"What? *Now?*" George wanted to know, disgusted.

Edward just nodded, trying to look forlorn. *First* he would apologize, *then* he might lick her on the neck, right where she liked it best. But he couldn't tell his brother that, or he'd never take Edward to her.

George rolled his eyes and jammed his ball cap farther down on his skull, but he set off walking. Edward hurried to catch up, hoping he'd gotten his way.

Several long blocks later, they came to a halt in front of Meg's building. Or rather, the place George said was hers. Edward rubbed at his temples with the heels of his hands. He knew George was right—Edward had been here before, when he'd dropped her off. But it didn't *look* right—Edward was so sure it was supposed to be that other place. Meg didn't live there, anymore, though, did she? If he wanted her, she would be here, wrong as that seemed.

"Well, here you are," George intoned. "What's the plan, now?"

"I have to ring for her," Edward said, looking at the call box. At this time of night, the doorman sat inside, behind a small podium, studying his cell phone. Edward didn't move.

"And then?" his brother prompted, elbowing him.

Edward inhaled a great lungful of the cool spring air. Meg was ticklish, right along the backs of her knees. He smiled a little to himself, thinking of it.

"And then I apologize for ignoring her tonight," he responded dutifully.

George narrowed his eyes at Edward, smelling a rat. "Great. After that, you can come right back down here, and I will walk you home. Assuming she even lets you in. Assuming she's even *here*."

Edward glared back. "I don't know how long it will take."

"I'm. Sorry. There—it takes two seconds," George proclaimed. He pointed: "That bench. I will wait right there for you."

Edward stayed where he was. The doorman had taken note of them now and was giving them the skunk eye.

George huffed in irritation, then marched over to the large metal panel of hand-lettered names and little round buttons. He didn't see Meg's, and turned, frowning, toward Edward. Edward reached over his shoulder.

"This one," he said, ringing the correct buzzer, next to *M. Takai*. "She has a roommate now."

They stood staring at the call box for several laden seconds.

"Yes?" a small, disembodied voice asked, crackling through the speaker.

"Meg?" George called. "Edward's here. He needs to tell you something."

There was a pause, then the voice returned. "One minute, please."

Edward and George looked at each other. George yanked on the heavy glass door, but it remained locked. The doorman frowned harder at them.

The speaker fuzzed to life again.

"Hello?" said a second woman's dubious voice.

"Meg?" they both asked together. Edward shoved George aside. His brother crossed his arms over his chest, looking tough and defensive. Edward was, as always, unimpressed.

"Edward?" she bleated, sounding sleepy and panicked and horrified, all at once.

"Yeah. Hey, can I come up for a minute? I need to tell you something," Edward asked, careful to enunciate each word properly. He had to go a little slower, but he thought he'd managed it all right.

"Um," Meg hedged, lapsing into silence. The speaker cut off, and Edward began to wonder if she planned to just leave him standing out here like an idiot. He cast a worried glance at his brother, who just shrugged.

"Okay," Meg said, her voice sudden and loud in the quiet night air of the building's turnaround. "Hang on, I'll buzz you up. We're in 12B."

Edward heard the click and buzz of the door, and he pulled it open. George sauntered over to the bench, muttering. He turned to Edward as he sank down, holding up two fingers.

"*I'm. Sorry.* Two seconds," his brother mouthed.

Edward nodded, then hurried inside toward the elevators. The glass door clanged shut behind him. The doorman stared at him the whole way, just waiting for Edward to step out of line.

Chapter Twenty-Seven

ONCE SHE LET Molly and Morgan run out of steam, Meg had an easier time getting rid of them. After Edward's public snubbing, both women were on the warpath, and had an awful lot to say about it. Meg herself was too humiliated, she found, to muster up the proper degree of outrage to assuage them. But they'd had their say, Meg had a gloriously long hot bath, and now she was, mercifully, *alone*. In her pajamas, ensconced under the covers, and considering the escapism offered by the various 99 cent romance novellas in the digital bookstore. So many choices. Anything would do, anything at all that did not feature a British hero. A cowboy, perhaps. Or a shapeshifter. Any. Thing.

There was a soft knock on her bedroom door.

Meg disentangled herself and padded over. Cracking the door, she saw her roommate in the hall. Mayu had shed her usual designer gear for an old t-shirt emblazoned with the red dragon logo of a Japanese baseball team. Her thick black hair was a mess, sliding sideways in a loose ponytail on top of her head. She was also wearing big thick-framed glasses, which was startling all on its own.

"I think it's for you," Mayu said, indicating the crackling call box next to their front door.

Meg followed her down the hall. Her roommate had books and binders spread across the coffee table and couch, clearly studying for a final exam. Meg had promised she would be quiet in the apartment for the next couple of days, but Mayu still looked concerned, blinking like an owl from her nest of papers.

It was Edward. Of course it was. Meg closed her eyes and rested her forehead against the cool plaster of the wall as long as she dared. He was drunk, naturally, that being what soccer hooligans generally became while loitering in pubs half the night. What could he possibly have to tell her? He could have suddenly remembered something, she supposed, though she hated to get her hopes up. Still, the faintest possibility of that was impossible to resist.

Meg buzzed him up. Then, with a panicked look at Mayu, she bolted toward her room. She had to change, right now. In her peripheral vision, she saw Mayu turn to regard the front door with some alarm.

"It will only be for a minute, I promise!" Meg called out. "We'll be quiet!" In her bedroom, she threw on a bra and changed into a pair of yoga pants, then kicked her clothes from the bar under the bed. She jammed her laundry basket into the closet, straightened her bedcovers, and cracked the window.

His knock sounded just as Meg skidded back to a halt in front of the door. She whisked it open with a nervous glance at her roommate, who still sat watching with open curiosity. When Edward stepped in, her eyes grew even wider. He did look adorable, she had to admit, rumpled and delicious.

"Back here," Meg said, grabbing his arm and towing him toward her room. Edward followed unsteadily, giving Mayu a little wave as they walked past.

Once she had him safely behind closed doors, Meg took a closer look. Her room seemed smaller than ever with him crowded into it. He was disheveled and swaying, but looking around with obvious interest.

"You're drunk, aren't you?" Meg asked.

"A little," he admitted, running a hand back through his soft brown hair.

"We have to be quiet," she told him. "My roommate is studying for a test."

"Okay," Edward nodded. He was very serious, his hands on his hips, prepared. As if she'd just told him, *We have to fight a bear.*

Meg waited. He looked at her. She raised her eyebrows in inquiry. He snorted in amusement.

"Edward," Meg demanded, exasperated.

"Yes, *Meghan?*" he retorted cheekily, smirking.

"Edward, why are you here?" she demanded.

He blinked. His face fell. "Oh. Well, George and I were talking." He ran his palms up and down his thighs nervously. He looked around for somewhere to sit.

Meg pointed at the end of her bed, and he sank down gratefully. But that meant she was looking down at Edward's upturned face like a scolding parent. So she stalked over to the other side of the mattress and perched awkwardly on the side.

"And?" she prompted.

Edward leaned in and whispered, "And I realized that I was a royal arse tonight."

Meg rolled her eyes and exhaled in a rush.

"Shhh," he said, putting a finger to his lips. "Incidentally, you look really pretty right now."

"Oh my God, Edward, are you kidding me?" she exclaimed.

He shook his head.

"Don't tell me. You thought if you came and apologized for ignoring me, in front of my sister *and* my best friend, I might add," she fumed. "I would give you another ride? Is that it?"

"What?" he squeaked, but his sudden, lurid blush gave him away.

"This is a goddamn booty call, isn't it?" Meg shouted, furious.

Edward turned even redder. "I think you said to be quiet," he told her.

"Oh my God!" Meg cried, throwing up her hands. "You are *too much*."

"I really am sorry about before," he murmured, the soul of contrition.

"Why, Edward?" Meg questioned him. "Why are you so sorry?"

"I just didn't want you to think I was that kind of guy." She stared at him, and he shrugged. "You know—some kind of love them and leave them type. I feel guilty about that."

Meg chuckled in derision. "And so you downgraded our date and then gave me the cold shoulder once I got there?"

"That was mostly an accident."

"How do you figure?" she sneered at him.

"Well, the cold shoulder part. That was not on purpose," he tried to explain. "I had to watch the match." He looked worriedly at her door, as if he expected Mayu to come in at any moment to scold him.

Meg thought a moment. "That would imply that the date downgrade *was* intentional, Edward."

Edward was in no condition to be wily. He readily agreed, "Yes, well, I had to do that so you wouldn't get the wrong idea about us."

"Oh, Jesus," Meg muttered.

"It wouldn't be fair to you, you see. To let you get too attached again," Edward pointed out reasonably. "They said you've been hurt enough already."

Meg just shook her head, speechless. Edward wasn't through, though.

"Once I find my fiancée, we'd have to end things anyway," he elaborated, watching his hand smooth back and forth across her duvet.

"What did you say?" she breathed. In a rush, all of it came back. All of Meg's fears and insecurities. All of the reasons why someone like Edward would never look twice at someone like her. And all it had taken to get him to admit it, was one traumatic brain injury and some beer.

He peeked up at her through his eyelashes—those ridiculously long lashes and beautiful eyes, wasted on such a horrible man. "I think I was about to get engaged," he said softly. "Before the accident. I found a ring in my stuff, and some woman's clothes…"

"The silk pajamas," Meg interjected, skin crawling at the memory of them on her body.

"Yes. Exactly," he told her, as if he wasn't destroying her all over again. "Once I figure out how to find her, I assume that I…that we…" he fumbled to a stop and looked away.

"Are you saying—I'm sorry—you're saying there was someone else? Besides me? That it was all a lie between us?" Meg choked out. "Because you sent *me* stuff, too. A lot of stuff."

Edward shrugged. "I think so. Maybe."

"But…I don't understand. Why would George try to get us back together? Why would he do that to me?" Meg cried.

Edward gazed at her, and his lashes were damp. His Adam's apple bobbed up and down. "I don't think he knew," he told her. "About her, I mean."

Meg looked at him, this rare and beautiful stranger across from her. She'd given him too much power over her, she realized. She'd let him sneak in past her defenses when she was in a vulnerable spot, desperate for love and for something good in her life. Exactly the kind of victim a man like him might look for. Well, no more. Meg was no longer vulnerable, and she wasn't going to be at anyone's mercy ever again. Especially not this man's.

"You need to leave," she said, getting up.

"Right now? But it hasn't been two seconds yet," he protested.

Meg tilted her head at him, perplexed. Never mind. Didn't matter. What really mattered was, "Look, this is pointless. You obviously felt some sort of obligation or something toward me, but your heart just wasn't in it. You made a game effort, but clearly we aren't a good fit anymore, so here you go—*I release you.* Whatever you thought you owed me, it's over. We're done. Now please leave." Meg forced the words out haltingly, and while she spoke, she tried to decode his expression.

Edward sat quietly, inscrutably so. He didn't look relieved, but neither did he look despairing. He was merely…mildly concerned. And, as his mother would say, "Lord knew" that wasn't nearly a vivid enough emotion to convince Meg to persevere.

"Get up!" Meg shouted. "Go!"

Edward jumped to his feet, blinking and swaying a little at the sudden change in position. Meg stalked over to her door, wrenched it open, and pushed him out.

At the front door, he dug in his heels. "Goodbye, erm…"

"Mayu," her roommate offered. She had a pen stuck crazily through her ponytail, but didn't seem to be aware of it.

"Mayu," Edward repeated. He frowned comically, then turned back to Meg, his head bobbing as if he were counting in his mind. "Have you ever noticed that you know an awful lot of people with M names?" he inquired. "It's really quite extraordinary."

Meg unlocked the door, pulled it open, and urged him out. "Goodbye, *Milord*," she jeered, then slammed the door in his face. She slumped against it, sliding all the way down to the floor in a defeated heap. She blinked at Mayu, who stared at Meg from her perch on the couch.

"Oh no," her roommate said softly.

"Yup," Meg replied. *Who had it been?* Meg wondered, mind reeling. During all those days when she'd thought herself gloriously in love, who had Edward been wooing? Who had been grieving, too, all those months when Meg had thought him dead? Exactly how devious and evil were the women around her? Was it Molly, perhaps? Or Poppy? Or had it been someone else entirely, someone more suited to him—a sleek, refined, grad student who would make him proud with her every accomplishment? She wouldn't have an M name either, Meg thought. She'd be named something smart and British, like Kitty or Georgina. Meg choked.

Mayu stood up and took a step toward her, uncertain of what she should do. They barely knew each other, after all, despite living in the same apartment. "Can I do anything for you?" she asked.

Meg looked back at her, and remembered her resolution of moments before. She stood up, brushed off her clothes, and squared her shoulders. "Nope. I am absolutely fine," she told her, then strode back down the hall to her room.

EDWARD STARED AT the brass elevator doors for several long minutes, not wanting to press the down button and admit defeat just yet. This visit, hell this whole evening, hadn't gone the way he intended. George would be apoplectic. Especially if it turned out that George was correct, and Edward did not, in fact, have another woman waiting in the wings somewhere.

The bell of the left car dinged, and an older couple emerged. They cast suspicious frowns his way, skirting him like he was radioactive. Edward roused himself from where he'd been leaning against a nondescript laminate console table, and caught the elevator door just before it closed. He didn't want them calling the constabulary on him. The only thing that could make this evening worse was adding a drunk and disorderly charge to the program.

The ride down to the lobby was slow. He propped himself against the mirrored wall and tried not to look himself in the eye while his thoughts skipped around, landing haphazardly on things Meg had said. Edward had half a mind to turn around and go back to defend himself. Deny stuff. Instead, his brain landed on the one correct detail she'd mentioned. He *had* sent her things, he knew he had. He could see them in his head—a grey handbag with a long leather tassel hanging from the handle. A pair of bright pink suede flats. A whole rainbow of little cashmere sweaters, as soft and warm as Meg herself could be. What had she done with all of it? And would Edward have done such a thing if he hadn't really cared about her? He pressed his fingers to his eyes, his head beginning to throb again. One more image assaulted him: being propped in bed, his bare back against the chilly plaster of the wall, his fingers flipping the pages of a catalog, his lap covered in thick navy-blue plaid flannel. He started. *That bedding.* His mum had gotten him that bedding. Edward wondered where it had gone. He wanted it back, suddenly, with a soul-deep longing.

The elevator door slid open and he ambled out. The doorman, vigilant behind his little podium, watched his progress across the lobby with a disapproving scowl. Edward walked carefully, concentrating on looking as routine and sober as possible, but the man didn't appear convinced. It was a relief to finally push through the doors into the fresh air outside. The night was getting cooler, with just a hint of humidity that made him think they had some more rain in store for tomorrow. George was still on his bench, talking on his cell, but when he noticed Edward walking toward him, he quickly disconnected the call. Edward plopped down beside him, feeling scattered and weary down to his bones.

"Perhaps you don't understand how long two seconds lasts?" George inquired archly.

"Please. Not now," Edward said, massaging his temples.

George nodded. "Well? How did it go?" He leaned back and stretched his arm across the back of the bench, as if he had all the time in the world for Edward's answer.

"She dumped me," he told his brother. "Rather unceremoniously, I might add." *Like a trash bin*, Edward thought. Just like that. He might have even deserved it.

"What?" George sputtered.

"You heard me."

The doorman had left his perch and stood watching them through the glass wall of the lobby, hands on his hips. They weren't disturbing anyone, but that didn't mean he wanted them there.

"Now why would Meg do that, I wonder?" George asked, accusation heavy in his words.

Edward focused on the little landscaped circle at the center of the building's turnaround. The small tree planted there was in bloom, but in the darkness, he couldn't quite make out if the flowers were white or pale pink. Meg didn't like to wear light pink. She thought it clashed with her skin.

"Edward," George persisted. "Why did Meg dump you?"

"I don't know," he muttered. His head hurt. It was happening more often, he thought, though whether that meant anything significant or not was a mystery at the moment. He probably ought to ring up the doctor and find out for sure.

"Well, what did you say to her?" George demanded.

"Nothing," Edward protested. His thoughts were disordered. The picture of Meg yelling for him to leave all tossed together with images of blue flannel, and lacy women's knickers, and Nina Simone singing, and Mayu's round worried face.

When he spoke again, George's voice was deadly. "You wouldn't, perchance, have mentioned the *other woman*, would you have?"

"I may have done," Edward replied defiantly, gripping his shaking knees with white knuckles and preparing for violence. He really couldn't handle violence at this stage, though George certainly seemed to be heading in that direction. The thought of hitting something did have its appeal, but it needed to be something inanimate, not his goddamn little brother. Tomorrow, he ought to call around, see if he could find a boxing club nearby. Get back into it as a mental health measure, if nothing else. Hell, he could even hang a punching bag in his basement.

George had leapt to his feet. "Edward, Christ. Why did you do that? *Meg* is the other woman. She's both bloody women. She's *all* the women, to you!" he exclaimed.

Edward had been impressed, up to that point, with the way George was holding his liquor, but that last burst of logic had him wincing. He rubbed at his eyes again. The building's outdoor floodlights seemed very bright all of a sudden.

"What's wrong?" George demanded, his voice altering slightly.

"My head is killing me," Edward admitted. "I need to go home." He got to his feet too, and looked away. He didn't want to see his brother's expression change to pity. He couldn't endure that now, on top of everything else. His deficiencies were piling up, it seemed, and before long they were likely going to bury him. Edward didn't want to be the oldest anymore. He didn't want to be a business owner, and he didn't want to be the heir to an earldom. He just wanted to sleep.

George chucked him on the back, knocking him off balance, then slung a heavy arm around Edward's shoulders to steady him. "Off we go, then, Princess," he directed, relenting for now.

Edward was grateful for the insult. If he focused on that, the outwardly disdainful interplay of brothers, he could almost pretend that things were normal. That *he* was normal.

Chapter Twenty-Eight

EDWARD WOKE UP with a vicious hangover. He *had* to stop doing this. It was a Thursday morning, for God's sake. Grown men didn't do this sort of thing regularly, did they? How could they? It was bloody awful. Edward winced, avoiding the shafts of sun slanting through his windows like death rays. George had forgotten to close the blinds last night, when he'd dumped Edward into bed. *George.* Once again, Edward probably owed his brother. George, decent interfering chap that he was, had been handling a lot lately. Edward wondered if he'd stayed the night downstairs on the couch, or whether he'd decamped to his latest flame's house.

Now seemed as good a time as any to find out, so Edward hauled his sorry carcass to his feet. The room spun around him, but he gripped the thick bed post for a moment and it soon steadied itself. Right. Edward worked his way gingerly down the back stairs, picking up the sound of voices as he approached the main level. George, on speakerphone, or George, with a client? Edward paused to look down at himself. He was wearing the same undershirt and jeans he'd worn to the pub last night, though somehow he'd lost the button-down and his shoes. And his socks—his feet were bare, the wood of the stairs worn smooth beneath them by many, many years of footsteps. Edward shook his head, and immediately regretted it. Whoever was in his family room would have to deal with his current appearance. That's what you got, when you popped in without warning on people: their dark underbelly. It wasn't exactly the behavior of a viscount, Edward supposed, but he rather expected the aristocracy had seen its share of dissolution long before now.

When he rounded the last turn of the stairs, George was there on the floor, surrounded by thick black wires like garden snakes, hooking up a large, new flat-screen telly in the corner. Charlie was there, too, lounging at the kitchen island and chuckling at something on his cell phone.

"What in the bloody hell are you two doing here?" Edward asked, his voice raspy and deep.

"You're welcome," George growled. "I was happy to buy you a new TV this morning, Ed."

"Good morning to you, too, Sunshine," Charlie added. He cast a critical eye over his oldest brother. "You look like shit. There's some java, though." He gestured toward the kitchen, where, yes, Edward could smell coffee. He wasn't entirely sure how his stomach would receive it.

"Again—why are you here?" he tried once more, moving carefully past George's mess and bee-lining for the sink, in case last night's remains decided to stage a comeback.

His brothers shared a loaded glance, then George grunted and dipped his head behind the screen to plug something in.

"We missed you," Charlie said cheerily. Edward wondered what significant gene had bypassed him, that allowed his brothers to completely sidestep the aftereffects of hard drinking? It didn't seem fair, but then, what was, these days.

"That's bollocks and you know it," Edward retorted.

He quarantined himself in his small galley kitchen, pouring a mug full of coffee and sipping at the scalding brew, willing his stomach to settle down. His mind drifted, while George called Charlie over to give him a hand. Something from the night before filtered to the front of the scrambled eggs currently masquerading as his brain.

"What happened to my sheets?" he asked loudly, cutting into their murmured tête-à-tête.

Both of his brothers looked up from the thick installation manual they were consulting to stare at him.

"The blue plaid flannel ones," Edward elaborated, "That mum got me last year."

Charlie shook his head, and George looked wary. Neither seemed inclined to answer.

"I want them back," he insisted, like a petulant child. "Where are they?"

George cleared his throat. "I changed them out," he stated. "Mum said, when we got back here, that they would be too warm and I should change them out for you."

"Where did the new ones come from?" Edward asked, annoyed.

"From one of the boxes of stuff that got delivered while you were in the hospital. I assumed you ordered them before you left," George explained. "Things kept arriving for months after. The housekeeper we hired piled everything in the front room and I sorted it all when I came back in March."

Edward frowned, looking around the parts of the house he could see from this vantage point with searching eyes. How much had he done himself, and how much was George's handiwork?

"The flannel sheets are up in the linen closet, across from your bedroom," George added carefully, perplexed by Edward's suspicion, no doubt. "The housekeeper washed them and put them there."

Edward nodded. He would run the new central A/C if he had to, but he intended to sleep on that bedding again, tonight.

"Ed?" Charlie asked him.

"Hmm?" If he concentrated, he could almost feel the caffeine surging through his veins, clearing cobwebs before it and turning him human. Thank God. He was almost beginning to feel a wee bit hungry.

"When did you remember those?" George asked. It sounded as if he'd had to repeat himself.

Edward looked back at his brothers, who wore identical expressions of curiosity.

"What do you mean?" he inquired, baffled.

"Mum didn't get that bedding until at least October or so. I know because she gave me some too," George explained.

Charlie scowled, now. "But that's right in the middle of Ed's dead zone."

"Exactly," said George.

Edward looked at them. "That's what you call it? My dead zone?"

Charlie just nodded, and George looked down, suddenly concentrating on slipping batteries into a sleek black remote he'd extracted from a plastic bag.

Ed shook his head, trying to think. "I don't know. I just— something made me think of them last night, I guess."

"Meg, maybe?" Charlie tried. His brother sounded careful, like he was trying not to spook him.

"No," Edward replied. "It's just…" he gestured weakly, not wanting to explain. But they sat there looking at him, and he felt his mouth moving to fill the silence. "Sometimes everything is all mixed up in there," he continued, swirling his fingers next to his head. "I can't be sure what any of it is, only pictures of random things and ideas that don't make sense."

George nodded, then pointed the remote and turned on the flat screen. The picture was amazing, crisp and bright. Once the setup finished running, Edward blinked at the sudden image that flooded his view: a tampon commercial. Excellent. George muted the television and turned to him.

Charlie looked between his older brothers, and asked "Like what?"

Edward shook his head and drank more coffee. It had cooled to the perfect temperature and seemed to be working wonders with both his pulsing headache and his swirling stomach. Eggs. He could probably stand some eggs, though he didn't feel like cooking them.

George studied him. "Does your head still hurt?"

"A bit," he admitted. "Nothing a few aspirin won't cure." So Edward turned to grab a couple from the cabinet near the sink.

"Ed," George prodded.

"Yes?" He popped the tablets in his mouth, washing them down with the last of the coffee. Then, eyeing the depressingly empty bottom of his mug, he turned back to the machine for a refill.

"What was it, specifically, that made you think there was someone else, besides Meg?" George asked. His brother, the bloodhound, was sniffing along for clues to solve the mystery.

"I told you," Edward demurred. He didn't feel like getting into it again. His brain was still reeling from the notion that he might have remembered something from last fall, no matter how insignificant. Desperately, he tried to think why it had happened, and how to make it happen again.

"No, you didn't, actually," George frowned. "I should have asked sooner, come to think of it."

"Wait, what?" Charlie bleated, eyes wide. "Ed was cheating on Meg?" Charlie turned to Edward in outrage, but George silenced him with an upraised palm before he could draw breath again.

"No," George grouched. "He only *thinks* he was."

Edward shrugged at that. It was debatable.

"Why?" Charlie breathed, looking at his eldest brother with betrayal in his eyes.

Edward blinked at them. Last night, Meg had dumped *him*. He had been so sure that he was right about that mystery fiancée, that he'd gone and told her he'd been messing around behind her back. Or maybe he'd only been partly sure, and had been hoping to flush Meg out if she knew something? Regardless, Meg had then, quite rightly, sent him packing. But what if he was wrong? What if he'd been putting the puzzle pieces together incorrectly and had come to the wrong conclusions? Edward felt defeated, suddenly. Wildly inadequate to conquer this mind fuck he was enduring. He'd been so sure he could navigate it alone, so sure he could figure it out himself and spare his family any more grief and trouble. But he couldn't anymore. And suddenly, he didn't want to. He wanted help, damn it.

"I found things," Edward told his brothers haltingly. "In my stuff…after, you know, they released me from the hospital. And then, when I got here and started poking around, I found more."

"Show us," George instructed, getting to his feet and dusting off his jeans. "Right now."

Charlie was already standing at the ready, looking more like a Burberry model than a design school student. He nodded at Edward, encouraging him.

Edward sighed. "All right. Come on, then." He led them up to his room, and to his closet. He stood at the entrance and gestured to the shelf, indicating the neat piles of women's clothing. The pajamas that he had let Meg wear were laundered and folded right on top. Charlie edged in next to George, and the two of them rifled through all of it, examining each item with a critical eye. Edward had meant to put it all away, in a bin somewhere. He couldn't think, at the moment, why he hadn't yet.

Charlie turned to glare at him. "You do realize this is all Meg's size, *right*? Her colors, her style? All of it?"

"I suppose," Edward hedged. "I'm not the fashion expert in the family." Of course it was Meg's size. He'd known that before he'd ever lent her something from the pile. And, naturally, the one thing she'd worn had looked spectacular on her.

"For fuck's sake, you blithering idiot. You fancied the pants off her," George said, exasperated by Edward's reluctance to concede the point.

Charlie held up a pair of black knickers with lacy white trim. "Looks like literally," he added wryly.

Ed squeezed his eyes shut, avoiding the thought of Meg in those panties and nothing else.

"What? *Ed.* You have to tell us everything if you want us to help," Charlie insisted.

"I keep seeing them. In that big bowl in the front parlor," Edward choked out.

"What, knickers?" George asked, chuckling and taking them back from Charlie to lay on the pile.

Edward nodded, shamefaced. This was more painful than he'd imagined. They were going to have him committed, locked in some institution where they threw out the keys.

"Likely tossed them in there when you were shagging her on the sofa, you hound," Charlie laughed.

Edward could feel it, the edge of something teasing his mind, but no amount of mental exertion would make it come out into the open. He scrubbed at his face.

"Jesus, Ed. I know it's hard," George told him. "But it will happen. I know it will."

Edward had to ask. "*How* do you know? I'm not so sure. It's been months."

"Because..." Charlie said, drawing out the word, clearly hoping for inspiration.

"Because it's already started happening without you even realizing it," George finished eagerly. "Like with the ...with the sheets..."

"And the knickers!" Charlie finished gleefully. "Maybe I ought to go put these down there in that bowl right now. Jog your brain a little bit more, eh, Ed?" he teased.

"Please don't," Edward told him, smiling reluctantly back. "I'll forget they're there, and then George will bring some new client by who will think I'm some sort of deviant."

"There is nothing wrong with deviancy," Charlie intoned primly.

"Fine. A pervert then," Edward amended, sort of.

"You said you remembered sending Meg stuff, right?" George prompted. "Doesn't that count, too?"

"I thought so. But it could be anything. It might've been something I wanted to get mum for Christmas, for all I know," Edward sighed.

"Okay," George said officiously. He clapped his hands. "We'll just take it easy, shall we? You'll let us know if you think of anything else strange, and we'll let wee Meg have a break from you. For now."

"But what if she hooks up with some other bloke?" Charlie asked worriedly. "Someone from the new office, or…some guy she meets on the T?"

Ed shrugged, resigned to more shitty outcomes at this point. It would be his own fault if that happened.

"I'll call her," George offered. "I'm not sure what I can say, but I'll think of something."

Both of Edward's brothers turned to leave, probably eager to get back to that flat screen now inhabiting his family room.

"Wait," he muttered grimly. "There's one more thing."

As a unit, they looked back at him. Edward moved back to his bureau, pulled open his sock drawer, and unearthed the small box hidden there.

"What's that?" Charlie asked. His naturally loud voice seemed even louder in the quiet stillness of the bedroom.

Edward opened the box and balanced it on his palm, holding it out for the other men to see. He found that he couldn't meet their eyes, so instead, he studied the floor near his feet.

"That," George said calmly, "Is an engagement ring."

"For whom?" Charlie squeaked, perplexed. George shifted sideways, shoving their younger, stupider brother a few feet over.

"That's quite a rock, Ed," George commented, looking up from the stone to glance at Edward's face. "Tiffany's. Classic."

Edward nodded. "I found the receipt. It seems I bought it in London the day before the accident."

George just shook his head. "Why didn't you say anything?"

"I wasn't sure—I thought maybe it was a favor for a friend or something," Edward admitted. "And then, because of all the other stuff, I thought maybe there was another woman, one I hadn't rediscovered yet. Someone I knew longer than Meg, obviously. I didn't know if I was some kind of schemer, or philanderer, or what."

"I'm still not sure how you came up with that," George admitted. He lifted the ring from its satin nest and peered at it more closely. Charlie reached for it, and he handed it over. "Was it because you and Meg…" he paused, searching for a way to word it diplomatically.

"Weren't hitting it off this time around?" Edward finished for him. "Yes, probably. I like her, you know, she's very easy to be around. I just don't think I'd want to *marry* her. It's hard to fathom." He shook his head, and his attention was snagged again, as it had been several times in the last few days, by Charlie's prints hanging over his bed. There was something about the right one. Something he was missing. He'd seen that image before, on someone's body besides his own.

Charlie did not appear to have been following the conversation. His eyes were glowing as he stared down at the diamond in his hand. "Oh my God, Edward," he breathed. "Meg is going to *love* this."

Chapter Twenty-Nine

IT WAS THE crack of dawn, but instead of sitting in her bedroom nursing a cup of coffee before work, Meg was fully dressed and camped out on a hard plastic seat in the middle of Logan airport. She'd finally allowed herself to wear some of the things Edward had sent her last Christmas—the new job had essentially necessitated it. Today, she was rigged out in an apple green sweater and navy-blue dress slacks. She had flip-flops on her feet, and a lovely pair of suede heels stashed in her bag for work. She felt very sophisticated, sitting there sipping a five-dollar cup of cappuccino while she saw off her international travelers. It was all part of Meg 2.0. No more loserness. Instead, all badassery, all the time. Maybe she'd even stop somewhere cool for breakfast before she headed in to work. Somewhere with croissants. And she'd take a cab this time, instead of hassling with the T.

Morgan, Owen and Oliver were headed back to New Zealand that day, after spending two weeks in Boston with her. Meg couldn't quite wrap her mind around it. She hadn't realized, for all those months, exactly how much she missed having her big sister nearby. Now that she was leaving again, Meg didn't know what she'd do without her. Then there were the boys: Meg was not ashamed to admit she was crazy about her new brother-in-law.

Owen was really that amazing—larger than life, and every inch of him strong and handsome, kind and good. Oliver, too, was incredible. One sweet, adorable, scrumptious baby, who could surely take over the world with his gummy little grins. Meg would have to come up with some way to go see them soon.

She forced the tears away and snuggled close to her sister's side.

"You'll be okay?" Morgan asked her quietly, stroking Meg's sleek ponytail.

"Yes," Meg assured her. "Molly and I are going out later, after work. Don't worry."

Morgan nodded, then leaned forward to fish a small, gift-wrapped package from her bag. "Here. This is for you."

"What is it?" Meg asked, frowning. She hadn't thought to get her sister anything.

"Just a little pep talk," her sister demurred. "Open it."

Meg unwrapped the small hardcover book and looked at the handsome woman on the front. "*A Woman's Power?*" she asked, frowning up at her sister.

She nodded. "It's a little corny, but..." Morgan shrugged. "I liked it. Maybe it will help."

"Okay. Thanks," Meg told her uncertainly. She hugged the other woman tightly and slipped the gift into her bag.

Morgan drew back. "Listen, Meggie. You've been, um... pulling your punches a bit lately. You're better than that." She gestured vaguely through the windows, "All of that. And one pesky little British amnesiac is not going to change that fact."

Meg glanced guiltily at Owen, but he was standing off to the side, bouncing Oliver on his hip and pretending not to eavesdrop. Her eyes filled with the tears she'd been trying not to let fall.

"I loved him, Sissy," she whispered. "It's been really hard."

"I know, honey," Morgan said. "And I hate to say this, but I still haven't ruled out the possibility of something changing for the better on that front."

Meg shrugged and shook her head. She was giving up on Edward. She *had* to, out of sheer self-preservation. Besides, if she started crying more than she already was, her makeup was going to get wrecked, and she hadn't brought anything with her to fix it before work. Morgan pulled her close.

"You know what to do, right?" her sister murmured in her ear.

Ah, yes. Her sister's age-old, pithy advice. It had gotten Meg through more fixes than she could count. Meg nodded, forcing a watery smile to her face. A middle-aged businessman strode by, doing a double take as he took in the sight of the two women clinging to each other. Meg looked quickly away, but not before she noticed Owen glaring at the back of the man's head. Her new brother-in-law was territorial, too, another thing she adored about him. He was perfect for her sister, who deserved such a man more than most.

"Say it," Morgan insisted, poking her in the arm.

"*Fake it till you make it*," Meg replied dutifully. It did make her feel a little better, she had to admit. It always did.

"That's right," Morgan agreed. "Give it a chance. You'll see."

"Okay," Meg said softly.

Owen had sidled back up to them, and now he cleared his throat. He paused a moment, allowing the flight announcements blaring over the intercom to play out. Both women stood up.

"Time to go?" Morgan inquired.

He nodded. Owen handed Oliver to his mother, then enveloped Meg in one of his big, tight hugs.

"You'll call if you need anything," he told her, pulling back. It wasn't a question.

Meg tried to smile brightly. "Of course." She really hated for him to think she was a pathetic mess, but perhaps that ship had sailed.

"Say goodbye, big guy," Morgan told Oliver. Meg's nephew blew her a wet kiss, then extended his arm out to her, offering his ratty stuffed elephant for her to kiss in return. Meg obliged, breathing in the sweet baby smell that clung to the matted gray fleece.

"Goodbye, Mr. Elephant. And goodbye to you, too, Ollie." She leaned in close and planted a loud kiss on his forehead that set the boy giggling and hiding his face in his mother's shoulder. Her sister handed Oliver back to Owen.

"Bye, Sissy," Morgan told her. "I'll miss you."

"Goodbye, Moo," she replied, using the nickname she'd coined as a baby. "Love you."

With that, the threesome gathered their gear and moved off, ushered into the shortest security line, reserved for the people with small children. Meg watched them as long as she could, but finally, with a quick glance at her watch, she knew she had to get going, too. She grabbed a quick bacon and egg sandwich from a kiosk on her way out of the airport, then ate it in the cab on the way to work. There was no time for croissants this morning, but soon, she resolved. Maybe even tomorrow.

By nine, Meg was scooting her fancy, high-tech chair up to her new desk, heels on her feet and a fresh mug of coffee cooling at her side. She was later than she'd intended to be, especially since she hadn't even worked there a full week yet. Meg booted up her company laptop and glanced cautiously around, no one seemed to have noticed. Only about half of the cubicles were occupied so far, but several of her new coworkers were striding around the office importantly, no doubt on urgent business. She exhaled, trying to relax and look like she belonged there.

For now, Meg wasn't being given anything critical to do. She lifted the few basic tasks sitting in her in-box and set to work on them. In her head, she reminded herself of people's names as they walked past her cubicle. When they made eye contact, she smiled pleasantly and tried to look smart and competent. And, as overwhelming as it felt, she kept reminding herself that soon it would all feel normal and comfortable. They would know her, and Meg would know them. She'd have more to do and would be able to offer opinions or assistance as needed. This was what she'd wanted, after all—a challenge, a chance to spread her wings, the opportunity to prove what she could accomplish. She would do her best and Meg would…fake it until she made it.

However, as optimistic as that sounded, by one in the afternoon she was ready for a break. Her new boss had called Meg into her office to teach her some things, and then had dragged her into to a long and mostly incomprehensible meeting. For over an hour, the other employees around the conference table had shot curious looks her way, obviously assessing her. Meg had found it excruciating trying to size them up in return, while still attempting to follow the thread of the conversation without zoning out. So now, instead of eating at her desk or in the building's basement cafeteria, Meg changed her shoes, grabbed her purse, and ventured outside.

She made her way down the sidewalk of Congress Street, searching for a place to sit where she wouldn't have to worry about schooling her expression or putting her best foot forward. She was startled, moments later, to come upon Faneuil Hall, and behind it, Quincy Market. The touristy spot was far closer to work than she had realized, but was relatively quiet at the moment. Meg snagged herself an empty bench under a shade tree with a happy sigh, settling in to eat her lunch and people-watch.

She lingered over her turkey sandwich from home, and a clump of red grapes that had seen better days. Traffic ebbed and flowed on the street, tires squealing and horns honking. A few students strolled by, enjoying the day. The businessmen and women were different: hurrying past her, focused and serious. A homeless man moved around the market too, pushing his cart and peering into the trash cans. Meg thought she'd like to buy him some lunch. She didn't have any money on her right now, but if she came back after payday she might be able to find him again. Meg nodded to herself. She would try. It was a good reminder to keep her perspective—because as sad as she'd been, she wasn't, in actuality, that bad off. Things could always, always be worse, and the truth was, she had a roof over her head, food in her stomach, and her health. So. The rest would come in its own time.

Meg took out a yogurt smoothie, something she enjoyed but hadn't bought much before on her old meager salary. Tilting her head back to drink, she noticed a familiar face across the street, heading toward the wide stone stairs that rose from Congress to the elevated plaza of Government Center. *Edward.* Outfitted for work in a dress shirt, slacks, and tie, he moved swiftly. He looked determined, all business, older somehow. Meg hadn't seen this side of him before—in the fall he'd always been so warm and conspiratorial with her. Longing for invisibility, she held her breath and watched him. He must have felt it—Edward glanced her way, expressionless as he trotted up the incline, but he didn't seem to recognize her from his vantage. Meg held still, waiting, but in moments, he was gone.

What were the odds? In this whole damn city, he had to cross paths with her *here?* Right when she was hoping for neutral territory? Meg released her breath, praying it was only a one-time, freak coincidence. Getting over him would be markedly easier if she wasn't faced with the guy on a regular basis. To be safe, though, she swiftly packed up her things to head back to the office a bit early. And just to be extra, extra safe, next time she'd head in the opposite direction when she went out for lunch. The homeless man would have to find a different good Samaritan to buy him lunch.

After her brief taste of freedom, the afternoon dragged. Meg was bored to tears, weary of acting chipper and trying to look busier than she actually was. But she was far too new here to risk getting caught surfing the internet or checking her personal email account. So, she checked and rechecked her work email, organized her filing drawer, and read through the online employee handbook for a third time. There seemed to be an inordinate number of friendly men who were finding reasons to stride past her cubicle as the day wore on. It was getting unnerving, and Meg found herself smoothing her hair back and wanting to check her makeup with disturbing frequency. With all her focus on the work and the salary, she hadn't really considered the fact that the new, larger office could be something of a meat market. And while she might be able to convince herself that she was through with certain members of the aristocracy…that didn't necessarily mean she was ready to face the rest of his deranged gender.

Molly began texting her by early afternoon, eager to plan their evening happy hour, and providing a welcome, if guilty, distraction. They settled on a location to meet, out near Molly's house. It was beyond Meg's skill set to feign confidence while wearing business slacks in a bar, surrounded by young, sexy coeds, so she coerced her friend into bringing along an extra pair of jeans for her to change into. If she kept on her heels and lost the cardigan, Meg thought she'd look adequate for their girls' night out. With a couple shots under her belt, she might even find it within herself to faux-flirt a bit. When Molly was her wingman, anything was possible. Lord knew, the girl attracted men like flies, never more so than when she was trying to avoid them. And Molly had sworn that this night was all about Meg, no dudes allowed. They were sure to be inundated.

Finally, Meg decided that she had lingered at her desk long enough. She checked in one last time with her boss, grabbed her things and stood near the bank of elevators, trying not to look too eager to flee. But the truth was, she couldn't wait to leave. With each ticking minute in the crowded elevator, descending and stopping on every other floor, Meg wanted to scream. Finally, freed from that confinement, she hustled out of the lobby and up the street, to join the burgeoning sea of workers flowing into the T station. When she could finally wedge herself onto a train car, she was pressed against the wall with nothing to hold on to. With every jerk and sway of the car, her nose was smashed into the gabardine lapel of the suited man beside her. Meg supposed it was a good thing she hadn't had any powder to reapply to her face today. If the man was married, his wife would likely have suspected something unsavory. It certainly felt a lot more intimate than Meg was comfortable with.

The T rose through the tunnel after Kenmore and surged onto the above-ground tracks. Meg turned slightly and watched the buildings of BU Central pass by. Stop by stop, the workers were replaced by scruffier and rowdier students. Meg felt impossibly formal in her work clothes, and painfully dowdy. As soon as she reached her stop, she pushed her way toward the door and hurried down the steps. She dropped her bag right there on the filthy concrete between her feet, stripped off her cardigan and shoved it deep inside the tote. Feeling a little more casual in her sleeveless cotton top, she waited for a break in the rush hour traffic, then ran across the street. Her phone pinged and she glanced at it—Molly had already arrived and commandeered them some stools.

The bar was filling up for happy hour—a short line had already formed on the sidewalk out front to get in. Meg peered inside the dark interior, trying to spot her friend in the crush of people. As she moved forward, she readied her ID, then flashed it at the burly, stern-faced bouncer. He took an extra moment to study hers alone, looking between the card and her face a few times as she held up the line. Meg shifted on her feet impatiently before he finally smirked and returned it to her. He had large black spacers stretching his earlobes and a thick silver ring dangling from his septum. He scratched at his scraggly beard with thick, stubby fingers.

"Have a nice night, Madam Flynn," he drawled, looking her over. "Try not to bust any balls in there, all right?"

Meg rolled her eyes and sighed, pushing past him as he chuckled. Molly was waving enthusiastically from a stool near the back. Meg zig-zagged through the crowd and the waitresses hoisting trays of beers, letting the thumping music loosen her tense muscles. A small knot of guys was gathered next to Molly at the bar, surreptitiously darting looks her way. When Meg reached her friend, she dropped her tote, snagged the grocery bag Molly was holding out, and headed for the ladies' room in the corner. The dart games were already starting, but so far, only one pool table was occupied. Meg wended her way through them, pushed into the restroom, and locked herself in a dim, graffiti-covered stall to change into Molly's jeans. They were too tight—a skinny, distressed pair that Meg was reasonably certain her so-called friend had chosen on purpose. If Meg so much as thought about bending over, half her ass would be on display.

She sighed, bagging up her work pants and standing at the sinks. Meg stared at herself in the smudged mirror, not liking the expression on her face. She looked aged and grim. She looked…like her mother. God, that thought made her furious. Whatever else she did with her life, she refused to turn into her damn mother. Meg stomped out of the bathroom, not even caring what anyone thought of her or her attitude.

When she neared Molly, it became clear that two of the neighboring men had detached themselves from their group to chat up her friend. Apparently Meg's arrival had been enough enticement for the move—at her approach, they turned to her with avid anticipation. Four shots were now lined up on the bar, where before there had only been Molly's pink girly cocktail. Meg took in the guys' appearance at a glance. They held themselves with equal measures of confidence, clearly the alphas of the pack. Neither had any expectation of rejection, and for some reason that chafed. She didn't like the thought of being such a foregone conclusion, right then.

They were interchangeable, as far as Meg could see. Both had medium brown hair, sticky with gel or mousse and not looking like anything a girl might want to touch. They were marginally attractive, she supposed, though there was nothing distinctive about either of them. One wore a faded Bruins t-shirt, and one a Red Sox jersey. Nothing challenging there, either. When Molly cleared her throat, Meg turned to her, eyebrows raised in inquiry. Like a bad joke, she told Meg their names.

"Meg, this is Peter," she said, pointing at the Bruins fan. "And that's Paul. Guys, this is my friend Meg."

"I'm Paul," Bruins corrected, sticking out his hand and glancing quickly at Molly. His palm was damp, and Meg fought not to cringe as she grasped it.

His friend must have seen something on her face though, because he ran his own hand down his thigh before he reached out to her. "Pete," he confirmed, and though his hand was dry, it still felt too warm. Too doughy. Meg pulled away quickly. She looked at Molly, who shrugged and gave her a tiny smile. *Who cares?* she seemed to be saying. Meg felt a smile stretch her lips wide, her old party-girl persona slipping over her face like a mask. She reached between them to grab a shot, clinked glasses with Molly, and tossed it back before the others could even contemplate a corny toast.

"To robbers," she said, after she swallowed. Molly snorted, the only one to get her joke. Molly's father, after all, was the one who'd always complained that Molly's student loans were the equivalent of "robbing Peter to pay Paul." They'd never been able to unravel the logic of it, but there it was.

"We thought we could play doubles, Meggie," Molly said, gesturing toward the pool tables with her shot glass before downing it. "You in?" Molly watched Meg's face carefully for clues about what she wanted to do. They had said no boys tonight, but keeping the boys away from Molly was like trying to beat a cloud of gnats off with a baseball bat. Meg opened her mouth to speak, but then her cell phone began buzzing in her back pocket. She held up a finger and turned away. Meg frowned, pulling it free and doing a quick mental calculation. It was too soon for Morgan and her family to be home yet. Which meant...

Meg clutched the traitorous device, afraid of what she'd see when she turned it over. It was both better and worse than she feared. The screen, when she finally looked, showed a grumpy little cartoon boy in a backwards ball cap. And the name read: *George Hughes.* Meg knew what she did in this moment was critical. Everything hinged on whether she answered this call. She could either wallow forever in a fantasy that was never going to come true, or she could keep some small shred of her self-respect, no matter how ill-fitting it felt. Meg peeked over her shoulder to find Molly staring at her, waiting. And then, without her having to decide a thing, the call was bumped into voicemail. Meg took a deep breath, held the button down to turn off her phone, and shoved it back in her pocket. She nodded at Molly, who popped off her stool and called,

"All right! Let's do this."

By some predetermined agreement, Paul moved closer to Meg, placing a proprietary hand low on her back and steering her toward a free pool table.

"I hope you know what you're doing," Meg muttered, not at all sure whether she was talking to her new admirer, or herself.

"You better believe it, Hot Stuff," he replied. He smacked her on her ass, handed her a pool cue, and shot his buddy a barely veiled, smug look. Meg winced. It was going to be a long fricking night with Handsy McFeely. He'd be lucky if she didn't crack him over the head with her stick.

But somehow…it wasn't. The drinks kept coming. The guys managed to not be too obnoxious. And the faux flirting happened as if Meg was on autopilot. She didn't mean a word of it, but it rolled right off her tongue like it used to, and Paul just ate it up. He touched her arm every chance he got, doling out winks and innuendo like a champ. The guys let Meg and Molly win in turns, and finally, *finally*, it was time to go home. Paul asked for her number, naturally. Meg had known he would, but she hadn't yet come up with a way to turn him down, woefully out of practice as she was. She stood awkwardly, searching for words, when Molly stepped in. She took Paul's phone, then typed away on it with a coy grin.

"So, I'll talk to you soon," he said warmly into Meg's ear, pulling her in for a quick half hug. Meg gave him a fake, sickly smile, grabbed her bag, then pulled Molly out of the bar.

"Tell me you didn't give him my real number," she groaned.

"Certainly not," Molly protested, affronted. "He was a total tool."

"Then…?" Meg prompted.

"Taco Bell," Molly said, pleased with herself.

"That was mean," Meg told her, though she couldn't find it within herself to feel that guilty.

"Don't worry," Molly reassured her. "It's the 24 hour one. They deliver."

"Oh, well that's okay then." Meg laughed, feeling…lighter. A bit.

"Yeah, I thought he might appreciate that. Hey, were they trying to grow moustaches? What was up with that?" Molly snorted.

"I have no freaking idea," Meg giggled, laughing harder. Okay. It was going to be okay. She could totally do this.

Chapter Thirty

EDWARD WAS DRIVING back into the city from Newton, where he'd gone to visit possible new clients. The couple had purchased a lovely old farmhouse on a nice parcel of rolling, tree-dotted land. The men had not minded "living rough" so far, as they'd termed it, but they had just been cleared to adopt a set of three siblings from the foster care system somewhere in town. Now that the paperwork was going through, they wanted to restore the home and get it functioning well for family life before they picked the children up and brought them to their new home for good. It was exactly the kind of commission Edward liked best—no egos getting in the way, no questions about his father, a sensitivity to historical accuracy, and a home filled with kindness and love. The added bonus being, of course, no trashy wife to foul things up with her machinations, like their last big job. The compressed time frame didn't even bother him, not with all those pluses.

Trashy, naturally, reminded him of the evening he'd spent with his brothers the night before. They'd dragged him to some new nightclub on Lansdowne Street, very close to Fenway and crawling with students and fake IDs. Edward had taken one casual lap around the place, noting the Russian exchange students holding court in the side room like some sort of junior mafia, the frat boys hugging the bar watching a hockey game rerun, and the sorority sisters gyrating together on the dance floor. He'd deemed himself safest on the perimeter, landing a spot at a small table against the wall, where he could keep an eye on his brothers and not be molested himself.

Charlie studiously pretended not to check out the preppy college boys. George was fixated on his new woman, who had shown up moments after them—he shadowed her on the dance floor, where she moved sinuously against him to the music. Given his brother's bulk, Edward had been mildly surprised by how much rhythm he appeared to have, but a cloud of threat still clung to him, of danger. Edward had wondered if the girl knew she was playing with fire, if she was taunting George purposefully. If so, she had to realize that he was about thirty seconds away from burying himself in her body, up against a dark wall somewhere. Whether he managed to get her tight black pants around her ankles first or not.

Edward had to look away, uncomfortable with the display. He had nursed his lukewarm beer and turned his attention to the female half of the clientele. That was, after all, why they'd purportedly brought him here. If Edward was going to be so cavalier about letting Meg slip through his fingers, they reasoned, perhaps he ought to get a good, close look at what he was giving her up for. Perhaps he ought to remind himself exactly why Meg had seemed like such a good catch last autumn. Edward met the eyes of every single girl and woman who walked past him. Waiting for a flash of recognition. A flare of desire. Anything.

But the whole evening had passed, and the only thing that happened was the moment Edward had looked down at his feet and remembered, clear as day, the shoes he'd been wearing on the day of the accident. As breakthroughs went, that had to be the most pathetic there was. Only that: an image of his leather wingtip shoes, laced on his feet, on the floorboard of their rented car. And not a damn thing else. His expression must have been something to see, because after that not a single person met his eyes any longer, male or female. Edward sat and stewed, and eventually his brothers had deigned to go home.

He'd just hit Commonwealth Avenue and was driving through the outskirts of the Boston University campus when he saw it—a small café with a large plate glass window fronting the street. He did a double take, feeling just the faintest shiver of recognition. Edward slowed and changed lanes, and about a block up ahead saw another car pulling away from the curb. With only a few angry honks aimed his way, he slipped his car into the free spot and got out. He hadn't had time for more than coffee this morning, and he'd been sleeping poorly again, too. No doubt that was why this little place had caught his attention—some lunch and some more caffeine seemed just the thing. He stood on the sidewalk and looked around. It all seemed *very* familiar. Edward knew he hadn't actually gone to BU, but perhaps he'd known someone who had? He shook his head. This place, this block, felt right to him. He'd been here before.

Pushing inside, he took in the décor. Artsy, colorful—just the sort of thing you'd expect around here. The tables were only half full though, which surprised him. He'd been certain it would be crowded, but when Edward checked his watch, he saw that he was a touch early for the lunch rush. His luck, he supposed. Behind the counter was a tough-looking punk girl, sporting black hair streaked in vivid turquoise and cats-eye glasses with little rhinestones in the corners. She seemed to be working the fifties pinup angle, maybe crossed with a colorful rockabilly look. Edward sniffed. She was cute, but that wasn't his thing. She was also blowing bubbles with her chewing gum and looked bored out of her skull. He did a cursory review of the menu board over her head as he approached, but when he opened his mouth to order she grinned and cut him off.

"*Ha*," she said, looking him over. "I knew it." Punk Girl looked smug.

"Sorry?" Edward murmured, perplexed. Had he missed something? He stared at her face, and a shimmer of recognition passed through him. He knew her. She was… *Christ*, Edward thought she might be George's new girlfriend. Fuck buddy. Whatever. This was getting complicated, suddenly.

"Don't bother saying a word. I know exactly what you want," she told him, holding up one imperious hand. Edward blinked. Obviously he'd been here before, but shouldn't he at least have the opportunity to diverge from the path? Or was it just that she thought she knew him because she knew his brother? He ought to clean George's clock, since he'd clearly been telling tales.

But…Edward was feeling expansive after his excellent morning meeting. Why not see what she came up with? What would be the harm, to have a small window into what *before* had been like? It wasn't like there was anything in particular he disliked on the menu here.

The girl, *Poppy* her name tag read, was gesturing with an impatient hand. Where had he seen a poppy recently? A big, blowsy red flower, somewhere…

"C'mon, dude. You know the drill. Eight seventy-five," she said brusquely.

Edward fumbled his wallet out of his back pocket and handed over the money. Receipt in hand, he drifted toward the back of the café, to a table in the middle that looked inviting. Poppy kept shooting him satisfied looks, and he wondered what he'd done that she had found so predictable.

Soon after he settled at the table, she brought out his latte.

"By the way," she said, looking down at him. "Your kid's really cute."

He shook his head. "I don't have a kid," he explained. She'd obviously confused him with someone else, which suddenly seemed to explain a lot.

"Hmm," was her only response. She arched a disbelieving brow at him, then moved off.

Edward sat and drank the coffee, looking around the place and absorbing the feel of it. It was nice here. He supposed this was the sort of place at which he might have hung out, even though it wasn't overly convenient to his house. Maybe he'd worked a job out here, or had a friend nearby. A different girl delivered his food, and he eyed the plate with curiosity. An everything bagel, it seemed. With a lot of *stuff* on it. How odd. He tucked into it anyway, surprised a little by how tasty it was. Of course, as hungry as he'd been, a shoe might have tasted as good. And he was feeling sentimental today. Nostalgic. Those men this morning had worked some sort of magic on him, making him feel kinder to the world around him than he'd felt in months. Edward made a mental note to bring Charlie along to his next meeting. After all the kid had been through, he'd like him to have a view of the possibilities his life could hold.

Edward liked the music in here. They were playing some indie rock, with a dark, thumping, edgy beat to it. He should ask what it was, he should…Edward put his bagel down. His drifting gaze had snagged on a girl sitting against the far wall of the café. His eyes roved over her form, her table, settling finally on the fair, unblemished skin of her neck. Soft, downy hairs had escaped her ponytail, tickling her nape every time she moved her head. Edward felt the strangest urge to go to her, to touch those fine strands. And more. He didn't just want to touch her, he wanted to press his lips to her skin, too. He wanted to taste her, just there, behind her delicate ear. As he watched, she slammed her binder closed and slipped it into her backpack. A student, likely too young for him.

Still, when she rose to go, he did too, abandoning his table without a thought. When she started down the street, Edward did as well, following furtively at a distance, trying not to look suspicious. Her walk seemed wrong, bouncier than he'd expected. But he gave in to what seemed to be a harmless compulsion and waited to see where she'd lead him. He'd taken the second half of his bagel with him, and Edward took bites of it as he hurried to keep up with her. His mother would be appalled to see him stuffing food into his face on a public street like this. But she wasn't here just now, was she? Three long blocks later, the girl stopped beside a stone staircase. Laughing, she greeted a friend, and turned to enter the huge brick classroom building. Edward jolted when he saw her face, in that last second before she disappeared from view. He didn't know her. Her face was totally different than he'd expected it to be.

And then, somehow, he knew—she wasn't Meg. And he'd been *expecting* Meg. In that café, on this street, he'd been expecting Meg, wanting her here, with him. But that was crazy. Meg had broken things off with him. He'd seen her just the other day, sitting on a bench near Quincy Market, eating yogurt and swinging her foot back and forth. Her trousers had ridden up, her shoe had been dangling off her toes, and he'd noticed a tattoo on her ankle he hadn't realized was there before. The sight of it had made Edward uncomfortable, anxious in some undefinable way. But he'd been late for his appointment, so he hurried past without acknowledging her. Meg was just a girl, though, just someone his brother had conjured up from Edward's past who was comfortable to be around, but didn't set his world on fire. He felt doubt and confusion cloud his certainty. Wasn't she?

Edward kept walking. Through Kenmore Square. Cutting over to Newbury, he looked for the homeless woman and her painted wooden sign, but he didn't see her there today. His steps faltered, slowed. Edward closed his eyes, took a deep breath, and tried to relax. Tried to let the memory teasing him flow free. A heavy-set woman swathed in shawls. Chilly air. His navy-blue wool duffel coat. But that was all. He swallowed, feeling off. He'd head down Newbury Street, maybe stop in at Hathaway's shop, and then make for home. George could take him to pick up his car later, even though he would get a ticket for an expired meter. But as he walked, Edward thought maybe he didn't want to go home yet. On such a pretty day, maybe he ought to go to the park. Take a stroll around, get some fresh air. He had his mobile in his pocket. If he had some sort of episode, it would be okay—he could call for help.

In the porcelain dealer's shop, Edward shuffled slowly around, examining the items on display. Nothing had changed since his last visit, and after his usual genial greeting, Hathaway largely left him alone. But Edward was seeing things nonetheless: a small, soft, feminine hand, trailing fingers along the rims of urns and bowls, cupping round painted mugs in pretty palms. He was hearing things, too, a woman's tinkling giggle, teasing the edges of his hearing. Someone in the back room, perhaps? But no, it was closer than that. Right behind him, beside him, God—in his own head.

"Hathaway," he blurted out.

The man rushed over. "Yes, my lord?"

"Do you keep…" Edward stretched his neck, trying to think past the hazy snippets of images behind his eyes. A hand on his arm. A woman nearby, but not near enough. "Do you have records from last fall? What I bought from you, I mean?"

"Certainly, sir. Just one moment." Hathaway disappeared through a door behind his counter, emerging in moments with a thick black binder. "Here we are," he said cheerily, thumping it on the counter and leafing through. "What month did you want?"

Edward considered. He'd worn his wool coat, and brown suede shoes. "How about September. Beginning of September through…" His throat closed on him, but he forced the words out. "Through mid-December or so."

Hathaway nodded, turning pages, and Edward approached him warily. "Well, in September there was this order," the man said. "For that couple on Beacon Hill, wasn't it?" He turned the book toward Edward, pointing at the page.

"Whitfield. Yes," Edward said, his brain supplying the name easily. "May I?" he asked, laying his hands on the book.

"Certainly. All of your purchases should be right there in that section."

Edward just stood there, looking down with unfocused eyes. The engagement ring. All he could think of was that damned ring, and the heft of it in his hand. Hathaway interpreted his mood as a desire for privacy. It was just as well.

"I'll be in the back if you need me," the dealer said, slipping quietly through the door.

Edward nodded, and when the man had gone, he forced himself to turn the page. There was the bill of sale for his enormous pottery basin, dubbed in the paperwork as an antique holy water urn from a church in Amiens, destroyed during the first world war. Interesting. He hadn't recalled that detail. It cast his odd thoughts of knickers in that bowl in a faintly blasphemous light, come to think of it. The thing had been hideously expensive, Edward saw. He must have really loved it. He turned another page, and another, and there, only days later, was another receipt. One small bowl, and a handwritten note at the bottom in Hathaway's hand: "*Will pick up.*"

With a jolt, Edward could see it, the gray finish, the embossed gold bee at its center. He could see, clear as day, the box it sat in, the tissue paper protecting it, the bow he tied carefully around it. A gift, then, but for whom? It wasn't his mother's taste, which ran more toward Limoges, and certainly nothing he'd have given his brothers. It was the "satellite," he remembered. The moon meant to orbit his huge planet of a bowl. Edward pressed his fingertips to the thin page, willing himself to excavate more from the recesses of his murky brain, but whatever channel had been edged open was closed now. There was nothing else. Edward didn't bother looking at the rest of the book. Somehow he knew it didn't matter. Whoever he'd been with in the shop that day, he'd given that bowl to her.

He left the basement store without a word, not wanting to make any more small talk. He climbed the steep stone steps up into the sunshine. Out on the street, Edward turned toward the park again, but paused. Everything felt surreal, the reality of the noontime street, the warm spring day, the sunshine, the people. Just below the surface was another view, a transparent film laid under what was real: bare trees, his breath visible in the cold air, cars edging down the street, a warm cup of cider in his hand. A warm hand in his. Edward jumped, jerking his arm close to his body, but there was no one there. He forced his feet into motion, forced his expression into complacency. It wouldn't do to lose it here on the street. If he was going to have some kind of psychic break, he'd at least like to be sitting down.

He took off at a trot toward the public garden, hoping to find a free bench. The sensation of someone beside him wouldn't leave. He picked up his pace, tore across Arlington between the speeding cars, and entered the green lawns of the park. The willows trailed long fronds into the pond. Beds of spring flowers were everywhere. Edward's heart swelled at the sight, even as he worried he was having some kind of meltdown. A jogger brushed past him where he stood glued to the path. A homeless man sat on the nearest bench, his shopping cart pulled close while he dozed. Edward walked further, past tourists and runners. Past businessmen, and nannies pushing strollers.

One such woman was gathering her things at a bench facing the water. Edward hovered as she packed up a bag emptied of crumbs, small rubber boots, and a child's bucket hat. In lightly accented English, she called to her charge, a tow-headed tot apparently saddled with the moniker of Preston, and buckled him into the stroller. The boy acquiesced without complaint, more interested in his small toy train, and in Edward, standing nearby. When they'd gone, pacing slowly up the path that skirted the pond, Edward parked himself on their vacated bench. He sat off to one side, leaving enough room for a companion, even if it was a ghost. Edward looked at the water, let his eyes go out of focus, let his muscles relax, and waited. Something was there, lurking in the periphery, a wave hesitating before it broke and washed over him, something...

Beautiful.

The strollers reminded him of what the girl in the coffee shop had said. Polly, was it? No, *Poppy*. She'd said his kid was cute. Edward was certain that he did not have a child, but the words reminded him vividly of a dream he'd once had. Not long ago, at all. Just like that, he could see himself in his mind's eye, chasing a woman through his house. A lovely, lithe wife barreling ahead of him through the halls, their children laughing and giggling in other rooms. Running up the back stairs, racing after his woman, arousal and love, devotion, desire, all pumping through his veins, making his blood run hot. She was fast, the little minx, slippery. Edward couldn't catch her. Up two flights of stairs, breathing hard, he reached out his hands. His fingers brushed at the ends of her shiny, dark blonde hair. He stretched farther, hit the landing outside their bedroom, and wrapped his triumphant fingers in her shirt.

Even as that old dream played itself out like a movie behind his eyes, he knew with sick certainty who the woman was going to be. Still, Edward Allen Larrabie Hughes, 22nd Viscount Shurso and heir to the Earl of Westbroke, sat on a park bench in the heart of his adopted city, a man far from the place of his birth, and waited impotently for the blow to fall. The birds sang loudly all around him.

The dream had ended when he'd turned his wife in his arms and leaned down to kiss her. He was the conquering hero, and she was…she was his Meg. *Meg.* Not *just* Meg, the woman he had half-heartedly tried to date mere weeks ago, but *his* Meg. Even as Edward tossed up one last wall of defense, even as he wondered if his former life and current life had somehow gotten mixed up in his fractured brain, he knew the truth. Other dominoes began to fall, other memories unearthed from their hiding places, crowding rapidly to the forefront. Edward rubbed his hands over his face, and up into his hair. The Andersons, Carl and Anjelica and their hideously expensive tiled bath. Meg's old apartment. Perusing the catalogs he'd pilfered, lying in bed, dreaming of her. Stealing touches from her in restaurants and furniture stores. Edward started again at the beginning, sometime in September, and tried to run through the sequence of those missing months. It was all there, all of it, all of Meg and all of him. The slippery road, the gold sedan fishtailing before it hit them. And then, the hospital: his mother sitting staunchly in an armchair by the window, Freddy's voice loud, always too loud with Edward's concussed headache. And the worry over his father, first whether he would live, and then, whether he'd keep his legs or even walk again. Blanketing all of that winter was the terror Edward had felt, the terrible loss of something very, very precious.

Edward felt ill. He had been surrounded by clues. A ring in his bags, a woman's clothes in his home. Hell, once they'd found her again, his blasted family had even put the woman herself in front of him. For the love of all that was holy, Edward had *slept* with Meg—made love to her in the bed that they had chosen together! Even when presented with the sight of her tattoo the other day, so permanently emblazoned on his brain that he'd been able to describe it from memory to his brother Charlie *after* the accident, stupid, blithering Edward had not been able to figure it out. He was such a bloody fool.

In a panic, Edward hastily reviewed all of his interactions with Meg since his return to Boston and their reintroduction. His knee jumped up and down in agitation. He'd been a disinterested, cold prick. Oh, God. Sweet, forgiving Meg had tried so hard, tried until she couldn't bear it one second longer, and he'd done nothing but go through the motions. As perceptive as she was, it had probably been obvious to her. Edward tortured himself a little further, thinking of what Meg must have gone through for all those months without a word from him. She must have been broken-hearted. *He* was broken-hearted, just sitting here imagining it. Sitting here. On a park bench. In the public garden. How had he gotten here?

What the *hell* was he doing just sitting here?

With a curse, Edward jumped up and took off running as fast as his legs would carry him.

Chapter Thirty-One

HE'D STOPPED AT home briefly, and then, checking the time, had picked up his car from the coffee shop and headed to Meg's office, hoping to catch her as she was leaving for the day. Except then, Edward had been intercepted by Meg's boss outside the building, who starchily informed him that Meg was no longer employed there. Of course, Edward had known that. She'd told him about the new job herself, but somehow, in his confusion and desperation, he'd forgotten that salient little detail. Oddly, now that the lost months were restored in his brain, all of the recent information seemed sketchy, at best.

Edward stood on the sidewalk frustrated and trying to regroup. Where would she be, right at this moment? Not here, and not at her old apartment, which, with sudden clarity, he knew was several blocks further up the street. No, she'd either be at the new job, working late—likely somewhere near where he'd spotted her eating lunch the other day, or…he glanced at his watch again. The new apartment, that sublet room in the stark, modern high-rise, only short painful minutes from his brownstone. He'd been there. If she'd left work on time, and had encountered normal rush hour traffic, Meg could be there already.

It took an age to work his way back into town, an accident near Kenmore Square snarling the roads for several blocks in two directions. By the time he'd found a parking spot where he could ditch his car, it was early evening, the sun hanging low in the sky. Edward wanted to scream. No one was answering the call box, despite him pressing the button over and over. The doorman eyed him balefully, refusing to even approach the door, much less open it for Edward. He'd tried calling and texting Meg, but given the speed with which his messages were rolling over into voicemail, he suspected she had either blocked him or just turned off her phone altogether.

Edward was getting ready to turn away and plant himself on the bench to wait for her, when through the glass doors he spotted Meg's roommate emerge from the elevator. She was wearing a dangerously short schoolgirl skirt, sky-high platform heels, and incongruous fuzzy black cat ears on her head. The girl met his gaze, and must have recognized the desperation on his face, because her steps faltered, then slowed to a stop. Her painted red lips formed a stunned little O.

Suddenly, the doorman was there, up in Edward's face and blocking his view of the lobby. He had a thick island accent that was a little difficult to unravel through the thick glass doors. Normally, Edward would know his name by now. But when he called him by the moniker on his nametag, *Pierre*, the man looked startled, then baffled, before peering down at his chest and pulling the tag off in annoyance. He pushed open one door, the only positive development so far.

"Not me," he growled, using his body to edge Edward further back from the threshold.

Edward strained to see over Not-Pierre's shoulder, trying to get another glimpse of the roommate. *Mayu.* She was called Mayu.

She had turned to the side and was talking to someone, pointing toward Edward with her short, pink-tipped fingernails. And then he noticed her, *Meg*, peeking out from a small side room with a pile of mail in her hands. She stepped warily out into the lobby, and he drank in the sight of her—sleek and elegant and very professional in her skirt and heels. Edward swallowed hard against the rush of emotions that washed over him—pride, desire, fear, love. Above everything, love. Oh, God.

Meg froze, staring at his face. Out of the corner of his eye, he could see Mayu shifting on her feet uncertainly, and the doorman looking between them with his walkie-talkie at the ready. But Edward only had eyes for Meg.

"Please," he croaked out, begging her. "Please let me in."

Meg blinked furiously, but she didn't move. Poor Meg. Scared and confused and not wanting to be vulnerable again. Edward ached for what she must be feeling. She looked away.

Edward blinked too, feeling his lashes grow wet, but he didn't care. The only thing he cared about in this whole world was breeching this God-forsaken door so he could get to her. Right this second, if not sooner. The doorman placed a firm hand on his chest, holding him in place where he stood.

"Miss?" Not-Pierre inquired over his shoulder. "Do you want me to…"

But Meg had turned back to him and taken a hesitant step in his direction. Edward felt hope unfurl in his chest, but still, he held his breath, waiting to see what she would do. "Edward?" she asked. He didn't hear it, only saw her beautiful mouth form the word. His name, a breath on her lips.

Any words he could have said lodged in his throat. Instead, he nodded. Fast. Another interminable moment, and she came two steps closer. Edward refused to take his eyes off of her, willing her to believe him. To believe *in* him.

"Let him in," Meg whispered, her expression stunned.

Not-Pierre, the doorman, clearly did not agree. He turned to her, astounded.

"Are you sure, Miss? Because I can…"

"Let him in," Meg replied more firmly, sparing the other man a quick look. "Please."

And then, like magic, the way was clear. Edward flew over the polished marble and crushed her to him, scattering the mail she held around her feet. His arms wrapped around her, he buried his face in her hair and just inhaled her scent. In his head Edward prayed, formless desperate pleas, over and over. *Don't let me be too late. God, please. Don't let it be too late.*

MEG STOOD THERE in shock as Edward clung to her like a second skin. She wasn't sure, exactly, why she'd let him in, only…there had been something on his face. Something new and desperate that she hadn't seen before. It seemed like wishful thinking to admit it, but Edward's eyes, just then, had looked *normal* again. As if he'd been wearing a mask for the last few weeks, and had finally taken it off. Meg tried not to hope. Tried not to read too much into it. But, *why* in the hell was he here, now, clutching her close and murmuring into her hair? What had happened? She pulled back a little, and Mayu caught her eye over his shoulder.

"Are you going to be okay?" her roommate asked, looking both perplexed and concerned.

Meg nodded. Whatever Edward was at this moment, he was no threat to her. She shifted in his arms to look at the doorman too, who hovered nearby, radio at the ready.

"Thanks, Percy," she told him. "I appreciate your help."

He narrowed his eyes at Edward's back, accepting his dismissal, but only grudgingly. Percy shuffled slowly back toward his podium with several pointed backward glances, and he didn't look happy about it.

"Edward?" Meg asked, a little afraid of what he'd say. It wasn't anything she expected.

"*Percy*," he hissed, looking swiftly from her to the doorman. Mayu was gone, apparently having made a discreet exit somewhere along the way. Finally, he refocused on her.

"Can we go somewhere private?" Edward pleaded softly. "I really have to talk to you," he begged.

"Is everything okay?" Meg questioned. His whole demeanor was beginning to worry her.

"It is now," Edward answered cryptically, blinking down at her. "At least, I hope it is." He looked traumatized.

That, as much as anything else, made her stomach flip. Meg took a deep breath and gestured toward the elevators. "Do you, uh…do you want to come upstairs?"

Edward nodded, bending to help her gather the mail she'd dropped when he tackled her. "If that's okay," he said. He was being very deferential, Meg thought. Like he was scared of spooking her.

She tried to stay calm, to walk to the elevator just opening and discharging its passengers, as if nothing was amiss. But the truth was, her hands were shaking, in little fine tremors, and her legs felt like they were made of water. Edward's gait looked funny, too, kind of stilted and awkward, and Meg started to feel just the tiniest bit afraid. Not of him, precisely, but of what he might be about to say to her. Her mind raced ahead, supplying a variety of unsavory possibilities. A horrendous, contagious disease. Someone in his family dead. A child with another woman. His missing fiancée, reappeared?

When Meg peeked at him, Edward was gripping the waist-high bar of the elevator with white knuckles and staring up at the digital floor numbers like he could will the elevator faster with his mind. His jaw was clenched in a grim line. Edward gave the impression of a man just barely holding himself in check. Meg swallowed, the sound of it seeming deafening in the small space.

When the doors slid open on her floor, Meg bolted down the hallway, not even checking to see if he followed. Silently, he trailed behind her, and when she unlocked the door, he stalked into the center of the living room. It was growing dim now in the failing evening light. Edward stood there, quiet and still, and watched her. Meg placed the mail on the kitchen counter, and centered her bag carefully on top of it, but still he remained inert. A silhouette, framed now by the city lights coming on outside the uncovered windows.

Heart pounding, she approached him, leaning close to hit the light switch on the wall. The lamps on the end tables flared to life, and Edward blinked rapidly. His eyelashes, Meg saw, were wet. He was crying? Why was he crying?

"Edward?" she asked again, trying to quell her rising panic. "What's going on?"

He cleared his throat, but then shook his head, seeming, for the moment, unable to speak.

"Edward, you're starting to scare me." Meg told him.

"Meg," he forced out, looking her in the eye.

Meg faltered back a step, staggered by what she saw there. It couldn't be. There was no way, it could *not* be happening, it...

"Meg, darling, it's me. I'm here. I'm...back," he said, his voice so utterly agonized she had to gasp in a huge breath to try to steady herself. She stared at his face, his desperate, tortured face.

"You," she began, but couldn't come up with what followed that.

"*Me,*" he assured her. "Not the zombie that's been walking around pretending to be me, just...*me.*" He nodded, but held back, seemingly afraid to come closer.

Meg didn't want to say it out loud, in case she was misunderstanding him. But still, "Are you saying that you..."

"Remembered," he agreed. "Yes." His voice sounded odd. Strangled and raspy.

"Everything?" Meg squeaked, horrified at the frantic timbre of her voice, which must have betrayed every riotous emotion swamping her in this moment.

He nodded quickly.

"And?" Meg managed, not even daring to think about what this might mean. He'd come to her, surely that was a good thing, right?

Across the room, Edward sank down to his knees on the floor, gazing up at her with tormented eyes.

"And…I don't know if you can ever forgive me," he told her. "How could you? Oh, God, Meg. I'm so damn sorry. For all of it. I've made a wretched mess of things."

Meg took a step closer. "Edward, it wasn't your fault," she whispered. Gingerly, she knelt in front of him in her skirt.

"Still," he protested. "It doesn't make it hurt any less."

"No, it doesn't," she agreed. Edward slumped onto his heels, hanging his head in misery, his hands resting on the glossy wood floor beside him. She ached to comfort him, but there was a distance between them now that she didn't know how to cross.

"What…" Meg said, then quailed when he looked quickly up at her. But Edward looked so hopeful that she found that she did have the courage to go on, after all. "What do you want to do?" she inquired.

He answered without pause. "I want to fix everything I've broken," he vowed.

Meg's stupid, fragile heart stuttered in her chest. She scooted back on her knees and stood again, needing a little space. "What else?" she prodded.

"More than anything, I want to kiss you," Edward told her, searching her face.

Meg swayed on her heels. "Edward, please get up," she said softly. He pushed himself to his feet, still studying her carefully.

"I think you need to sit down," he countered, considering her. He scanned the room, then her. "Come with me." Edward took her gently by the hand, then tugged her down the hall to her bedroom.

He turned the shiny brass builder-grade knob, looking down at it with what Meg imagined must be distaste. He'd always been so fond of the original bronze fixtures at his place. Once she followed him into her bedroom though, Edward's brow furrowed as he surveyed it.

"It's awfully sterile in here, isn't it?" he commented, then looked swiftly at her. "Not your things, I don't mean that. But it's hard to picture you living here." Edward gestured in an all-encompassing wave, then guided her over to sit on her bed.

Meg looked around too, having known *real* Edward would feel that way. Somehow, zombie Edward had never noticed it. That, as much as anything, seemed to signal his recovery.

"It was only going to be temporary," she explained, slipping out of her heels. "Until I got on my feet. Now that I have a better job, I'm hoping to move again."

He nodded, but his expression turned inscrutable. He clearly had an opinion on that, but obviously didn't want to share it with her right now. Meg wasn't used to real Edward obfuscating, and it immediately put her on guard. Naturally, he noticed.

"No, no—don't worry," he reassured her. "I'll tell you everything, I promise. But..." He looked around again. "What do you think about coming back to my place, instead? Would that be okay? Grab a couple things to bring with you, and then...come with me."

Meg paused. What *did* she think of that? Allowing him the change in venue? Just picking up as if nothing had happened, and traipsing off after him like an agreeable little puppy?

Again, Edward was very aware of her, seeming to read her mind. Exactly like before.

"Please come," he implored her. "I think it will be good for us to be there while I explain. To be in a place where we were so happy. Also," At this, he hesitated. "I have something I want to show you there."

Meg felt like the worst sort of pushover, but she went. While he waited in her living room, she changed her clothes, then grabbed a few things to carry her over, in case…well, just in case. The ride to his house was quiet, each of them lost in their own thoughts, the fine German engineering of his shiny black car humming beneath their feet. She couldn't quite bring herself to hold his hand. Edward kept glancing at her, as if to assure himself that she hadn't evaporated into thin air.

Meg tried not to get weepy as he led her upstairs from his now-pristine garage. It would have been worse if she'd had to enter through the foyer, she mused. Even more memories to contend with there, like that lovely front room of his, with its well-loved chaise and big pottery bowl, and its sunny view of the street through the huge bay window. Instead, he sat her in the unfamiliar great room at the back of the house, which had largely languished forlorn and empty all the times she'd been here before. Now it boasted deep leather couches, recessed lighting on dimmer switches, and an enormous flat screen television on the far wall. Perched on a wide armchair, Meg watched him as Edward sat at an angle on the couch, as close as he could get to her without invading her space. He popped right back up again, though, looking antsy.

"I forgot," he faltered. "Can I get you anything? Something to drink, or…?" he trailed off.

Meg shook her head. "I'm okay," she told him. And the longer she watched him, the more okay she felt. Edward was even moving differently than he had the last time she'd seen him. He was holding himself differently, and his voice was softer. It had lost the clipped edge, the supercilious tone that he'd acquired this spring. In infinitesimal increments, Meg was beginning to believe that her ghastly nightmare might actually be ending.

Edward sat back down. His gaze drifted over her face and her body, caressing her. And, in halting, soft words, he began to tell her everything. His trip to London with his father. The predictably horrible weather. The accident. And then: the hospital, the house in Cambridge, and finally, here in Boston. Edward's words were laced with pain, and Meg swallowed against the tears clogging her throat. Whatever she had suffered, hearing his rendition of his recovery was a fresh torment. He explained about the photos he found in his study, and the clothes he'd found in his closet. He talked about his pervasive, nagging sense of loss. And then he recounted his wild speculations and terrifying fears.

By the time Edward began describing the events that had led to his memory returning, he was nearly as overcome as Meg. How fitting, she thought, that it should be their coffee shop that had triggered his recollections. How appropriate, that those beautiful old willows in the public garden, trailing their fronds across the lake, should stand witness as Edward's life and love were returned to him. He told her that he had begun dredging up little tidbits of memory days ago, maybe longer, but that nothing had made particular sense or had seemed terribly important. He told Meg that, to him, nothing would ever be as important as being able to remember *her*. Being able to remember *them*. Meg sobbed. And she believed.

The sight of Meg's tears seemed to push Edward past whatever reticence he'd been feeling about touching her. He reached forward, took her shaking hands, and pulled her to him. And Meg, lurching toward him and all the safety and comfort he had ever represented, ended up curled in his lap, kissing him like her life depended on it. His tongue tangled with hers as she clung to him, desperate, deep, and possessive. It lasted for seconds, or maybe for hours. Meg didn't care. But suddenly, Edward pulled his mouth from hers, and in one graceful motion, stood and lifted her in his arms.

"Come upstairs with me, love," he breathed in her ear.

"Yes," Meg told him, tears falling again in fresh rivulets down her cheeks. "Yes, please."

Chapter Thirty-Two

EDWARD KISSED HER for the first time in months without that hazy veil between them. And this kiss was so different, so pure and undiluted, that it jolted through him like a bolt of lightning. Arrowing through his chest and heart and straight to his groin. Suddenly, Edward *wanted* her. *All* of her, desperately, right *now*. He didn't want to comfort, or be comforted. He wanted to *possess*.

He hoisted Meg into his arms, and only barely managed to secure her acquiescence before charging up the back stairs with her like a man on fire. He was burning for her, it was true. But the fact was, he was more marauding conqueror than lover aflame in that moment. He had what he wanted in his grasp, and Edward would be damned if any man tried to take her from him now.

He held Meg close in the narrow stairwell so she wouldn't bump her head or her legs on the wall. But he had to keep stopping on the way, again and again, not because he was tired, but because he was starving. Hungry for the taste of her mouth again, her tongue and lips that kept peppering his neck with fervent kisses. By the time Edward managed to shoulder his way into his bedroom, he'd had to shift Meg around for both their sakes. She clung to him now like a passionate vine, legs wrapped around his waist, and arms wound tight around his neck.

He set her down next to the large antique bed. As Meg's body slid down his so she could put her feet on the floor, he felt every exquisite inch of her. Edward shuddered at the sensation, and imagined that they must resemble two boxers in the final round of a bruising bout: clinging to each other, swaying and half-drunk, barely keeping upright. He felt battered, God knew.

In this house, in this room with Meg, Edward suddenly bore the brunt of every last second they'd been apart. The sorrow of it cut through the fog of desire he was in, wrapped meaty hands around his throat, and squeezed. He didn't want her to see him choke, not now. He didn't want to wreck this for her, the sweet reunion that Meg deserved. Edward turned away so she couldn't see his face, then pulled off his shirt to gain himself an extra moment. He was wearing a faded charcoal grey Henley that he had chosen specifically because he remembered, actually *remembered*, Meg liking it on him.

Facing the windows, his jaw set and shoulders tense, he struggled to find his footing again. The pain must have shown in his posture, the self-recrimination he felt creeping in, wounding his soul. Edward was a fool to expect her not to notice. From the first moment, Meg and he had always been in tune with one another, and now was no different. She slipped her arms around his waist and laid her warm cheek against the hard planes of his back. Her palms rested lightly against his bare stomach and he pressed them there with shaking hands.

Edward turned in her arms and crushed Meg to him, needing that reassurance. When he could stand it, he moved back just a touch, grabbing her hand and pressing her palm to his heart. To his tattoos, inked with colorful precision on his pectoral muscle. His large hand covered hers and held her to him until she could feel his heart beating fast in his chest, below the layers of skin and bone protecting it. Tears stood in his eyes, and Edward knew his anguish must be obvious as he looked down at her.

Meg's throat moved as she swallowed, and he wished he could spare her this part of himself. But as often as he'd tried to do that with his family, it hadn't worked at all. He'd only succeeded in bolloxing things up, epically.

"It's okay now," she whispered to him. "It's all going to be okay."

He shook his head. "I almost…" His voice caught in his throat for interminable seconds before he soldiered on. "I almost ruined everything. What if I had…" Edward couldn't continue, blinking furiously at her, and doggedly refusing to give in to the tears that threatened.

"But you didn't," Meg said, matter-of-fact now. "You didn't, and I didn't. But…"

He shook his head, unable to endure a single qualification. Meg smiled, reaching up to cup his cheek with her free hand.

"While I hate to admit this, I think we kind of owe your brother," Meg told him.

Edward gasped out a startled laugh. "George!" He inhaled hugely. "He's always been the most obstinate bastard I know."

"Thank God," Meg said through watery eyes.

Edward dropped his forehead against hers. "Yes. Indeed." If George hadn't kept mollycoddling the both of them, throwing them at each other over and over, none of this might be happening. Edward *did* owe his brother—he owed him everything.

He looked over Meg's shoulder at the wall and was struck by a sudden idea. He parked her on the side of the bed, crouched down in front of her, then placed her foot on his thigh so he could bend to look at her ankle. There, right on the inside of her leg, just over the rounded knob of her ankle bone, was her tattoo.

"What is it?" he breathed, not daring to say it, himself.

"You don't remember?" she teased him. It should've stung, that reference to his memory loss, but he couldn't believe Meg meant anything cruel by it.

"I do," he admitted. "I just want to hear it from you." His thumb stroked over the design, back and forth.

"That, my dear noble friend, is clan Flynn's coat of arms," Meg grinned. "And so is *that*." She jerked a thumb over her shoulder at Charlie's excellent rendition of the image, wolves, gold coins, and all.

Edward smiled, too, feeling lighter, somehow. *Unburdened.*

"And so, my fetching Irish lass, is *this*," he told her. He grabbed her hand again and placed it against his chest, covering the symbols of their two families entwined over his heart. His gloriously happy, humble, beating heart.

She pulled him up as she scooted herself farther back onto the mattress. Edward stretched his frame over her, brushing her hair off her face and smiling down into Meg's shining eyes.

"I love you," he told her.

"And I love you," she retorted, running her hands up and down his sides.

It was all the encouragement he needed. Edward bared her skin inch by inch, reveling in each and every part of her that was revealed as he divested her of her clothes. He was struck dumb by the feel of her skin sliding against his, the heat and silky smoothness of it. The scent of her, making him drunk. And those soft little sighs Meg always made for him, which still drove him wild. He tried to keep his head, he did. He wanted this to be perfect for her. But when Edward stroked his hand down from her breast, over her hip, and through the slickness between her thighs, he was utterly, irrevocably lost.

He was out of his trousers and buried inside Meg in moments. Hard as stone for her, Edward squeezed his eyes shut at the way her body felt. The warm, velvet way she surrounded him and held him tight.

"Meg, love," he forced out, needing to acknowledge the moment in some way.

Her response was inarticulate, gasped into the pillow beside her face. But as Edward pushed into her as far as he could go, then pulled away just as slowly, again and again, he needed to see her. Propped on his elbows, he used his hands to frame her face, forcing her gaze to his. And what Edward saw there, the incandescence limning every beloved feature, turned all of the sorrow and regret into joy. Rebirth. A wonderful, giddy, second chance for the future.

He smiled, allowing that happiness to fill him, and he made love to his woman, making sure she felt it too.

Meg cried out softly with every thrust. She was getting close—Edward could feel it. But his darling girl was not about to leave the outcome to chance.

"More," she gasped in his ear. "Please."

Edward's smile stretched wider. "Like this?" he inquired calmly, pushing deeper, but keeping his pace tortuously slow. Meg's head craned back, exposing her beautiful neck for him to kiss as she strained for release. But as much as he was enjoying her, he was only a man, and he had his limits.

When she dug her nails in his back, tilting her hips and urging him faster, he had to give in. Edward had never been able to deny Meg anything, and he wasn't about to start now.

"Marry me," he gasped out, knowing she was just at the precipice. "Marry me, soon."

Meg's adorable squeak of surprise was quickly cut off as she convulsed around him, and the pulsing squeeze of her body pushed Edward right off the cliff, too. He couldn't take his eyes off of her. When they could both breathe normally again, he asked her once more.

"Will you marry me? Please, Meg?" Edward begged her. He still had her pinned beneath him, and he didn't intend to let her up until she agreed. As right as the world felt in this moment, he expected he could stay here, like this, for *days*, if need be. He didn't want to have to spend a single moment without her ever again.

Meg was the one getting teary now. "Really?" she asked him, looking unbearably soft and sweet.

Edward rolled his eyes. "Are you daft? Of course, *really*," he chuckled. "What? You thought I'd let you get away *again*?"

Meg giggled, shaking her head.

"Then you'll do it? You'll be my wife, Meghan Flynn? For better or worse?"

"Yes, I will," she agreed. "For all of it."

Edward felt like his face was going to split in two, he was smiling so hard. "Brilliant," he told her, reaching deep under one of the pillows. "Then you'll probably want this." He leaned up, straddling her waist, and cracked open the small light blue box. He couldn't look at the ring that had given him so many hours of angst over the last several months. Now that he had his life back, he knew it was perfect for her, and he didn't want to miss a single second of Meg's reaction to it. Her eyes went wide, and the smile faded from her face.

"Oh my God, Edward," she exclaimed, looking a little distressed. All right, so he might have gone just a tiny bit overboard, but...

"Too late now," he told her cheekily, reaching for her hand to slide it on her finger. "You already said yes. No do-overs."

Meg stared down at the rock on her hand, then gaped up at him. He took a deep breath, feeling very, very smug all of a sudden.

"This is the one?" she asked softly. "The ring you've had since...before?"

Edward nodded, sliding off her to stretch alongside her lovely, fetchingly bare body. He traced a finger gently down her arm. Meg must've noticed the glint in his eye, because she shifted away, pulling the blanket at the foot of the bed up and over her. Edward smirked.

"If you don't care for it," he told her, reaching for her hand, "We can always return it. Switch it out for something you prefer."

Meg snatched her hand away, holding it protectively against her chest. "It's not that," she said quickly, and he couldn't hold back his smile of triumph. "But...doesn't this have bad memories for you? I'd hate for you to feel uncomfortable every time you see it."

Edward took her hand, then, and looked. Really looked. He thought about choosing the ring, and the way he'd felt in that London jewelry store. He thought about the anticipation thrumming through his system, knowing he had a secret and dying to get back across the pond so that he could share it with her. He studied his ring, sparkling from Meg's finger so perfectly it looked like it had been made for her. As she was made for him, and he for her. Edward shook his head, kissed her hand, then rolled toward her.

"No," he told her, dropping small soft kisses across her forehead and nose, her chin, her cheeks, and finally, her lips. "No more bad memories for me."

"Ever?" Meg smiled mistily.

"*Ever*," Edward confirmed.

Epilogue

Four Years Later

THEY WERE GATHERED in Violet's family room, a cloud of expectation hanging heavy in the air.

"Is everyone ready?" Edward called out merrily. His mother was having a very difficult time holding herself still, her usual poise cast off in her excitement.

"Where's Dad?" Freddy asked.

"Don't worry, he's coming," the countess said dismissively. "Now can we get on with it?"

"With what, mum?" Edward asked insolently.

She swatted him on the arm. "Don't you start that with me, young man. Just…" she gestured around, careful to encompass Meg in the motion. "Do what you came to do."

"All right, if you insist." Edward stopped to smile at his wife. "Meg and I have an announcement."

Violet exploded into motion, crying out "Are you having a girl?" When Meg burst into laughter, his mother exclaimed, "Oh my Lord, you're having a daughter!" She clutched Edward in a death grip, emitting an odd sound that was half laugh, half sob. Pippa barked and jumped around their feet, her tail wagging madly.

"Aw, come on, mum, we weren't *that* bad," complained Freddy.

"Says you," smirked Charlie.

Edward had to pry his mother off his chest so that he could retrieve the ultrasound photo he'd stashed in his shirt pocket for safekeeping.

"*Daughters*, mum. Plural," he told her carefully. She didn't look at the picture, only collapsed into his arms and cried harder.

George slipped the little square photo from Edward's fingers, and frowned down at it. "This appears to be a hydra," he commented archly.

Edward glared at his brother. "Hydras have *nine* heads," he pointed out, as if that was important.

Meg snorted, reclaimed the photo from George, and handed it back to Edward. He disengaged from his mum and put the snap carefully into the countess's hands. Her elegant face went slack with shock. When the ultrasound was over, and he and Meg had sat there in stunned disbelief, the radiologist had stuck two tiny pink stickers on the photo, helpfully placing a bow on each little head. They'd thought it silly at the time, but Edward had to admit now, it was pretty effective as a visual device.

Violet recovered quickly, though, and immediately began showering Edward's face with kisses, murmuring, "Brilliant boy," to her oldest son, over and over.

Eventually, she broke off to turn to Meg, who she held by the arms and examined fondly. His mum patted her on the cheek. "You, too, darling, of course," she said weepily. "But then, we knew *you* were perfect right from the start, didn't we?"

Meg burst out with a startled laugh. Edward blinked, uncertain if there had been an insult buried in there somewhere. "Wait. What?"

At the sound of heavy thumping making its way down the hall from their father's study, all heads turned to watch his arrival.

"Hullo," he said warily, leaning on his cane as he cleared the doorway. "I heard a commotion. What's going on, then?"

Violet launched herself at him. "Baby girl, Alistair!" she cried.

"*Girls*," Meg interjected.

Violet didn't miss a beat. "Girls! Baby girls, Alistair," she cheered, clapping her hands with glee. "Little pink baby girls in bows," she elaborated, lest anyone in the room miss her point. She snatched the photo from Charlie—who had somehow surreptitiously gained possession of it without her noticing—and handed it to her husband.

He peered down at it, then looked up at Edward and Meg with an expression of amazed, undiluted joy.

"Well! Good show, you two," he said. He thumped his cane in emphasis, and Violet deftly moved her dainty foot aside just in time.

Freddy was eyeing Edward with a sour, betrayed expression on his face. "Now look what you've done, Ed."

Charlie, with his usual short attention span, had disengaged from the festivities and was sketching furiously on a pad he had produced from under the coffee table.

George was hugging Meg tightly, whispering something pithy in her ear that made her blush and tear up. When he turned to Edward to hug him and clap him soundly on the back, he shook his head morosely. "You poor bastard," George said quietly. "You poor, poor bastard."

Edward chuckled. "In more ways than one, I imagine," he agreed.

"I suppose you'll be wanting me to make two of everything, won't you?" George asked. "Two cradles, two rocking horses, two…"

Charlie had marched back over to them, and now he shoved a drawing under their noses.

"Here. Just do this," he ordered briskly.

Mapped out in clear sketches were the blueprints for a whole suite of baby furniture. In duplicate. There were curved edges and pretty cut-outs of forget-me-nots worked into each side.

"For the hydra?" George asked dubiously, studying it.

"For the *twins*," Meg smiled, gazing at Edward.

"Even sea monsters need naps," he informed his wife, grinning.

Violet, delirious in the kitchen and chattering away to her husband, popped the cork on a bottle of champagne.

"I know!" she called out. "We could name one Evie! I've always adored that name. And the other…Louisa," she decided.

"We?" Meg mouthed to him, true alarm beginning to creep into her expression for the first time.

"I love you," he told her. And then again, "Really. Totally adore you."

"And don't you forget it," she whispered back, her eyes going watery as she gazed at him.

As it always did with Meg, the rest of the room seemed to melt away. Edward promised, "Never again."

Review

Did you enjoy **Finding Love**? If so, please consider leaving a review at the retailer where you purchased this title.

Book reviews can be as simple or as detailed as you wish, but all of them help authors sell more books, and assist other readers in finding the stories they want to read.

Almost any book can be reviewed by simply logging into the website where you purchased the title, then scrolling to the bottom of the title's product page to find an area called "Leave a Review."

Up Next

Lost in Love (*Lost & Found, Book 2.5*)

If you read *Finding Love*, then you know…
some characters are unforgettable.

George Hughes never minded being the spare heir—at least, he didn't mind until his brother and father almost got themselves killed six months ago. He might be brawny and good at fixing things, but without his older brother's charm or cleverness, what good is he? Then George meets a woman whose problems he can actually fix, and he knows he can't just walk away. Not when she might hold the key to his brother's recovery, and especially not when she looks and acts like his dream come true. As luck would have it, George seems to be exactly the right man for *this* job.

Poppy Whitlock can usually take care of herself, but these days she's got problems on top of problems: a less-than considerate roommate, a petty faculty advisor determined to sink her career hopes, and a looming health issue making everything else feel perilous. But then a gorgeous British man with a knack for saving the day barrels into her life, offering not only his help, but his heart—and going it alone doesn't look nearly as inviting. When Poppy saddled him with the nickname *Burning Love*, she never could have guessed how accurate it would turn out to be.

If you loved *Finding Love*, then you know…you just have to learn what happens when George and Poppy get **Lost in Love**.

—

Includes the bonus short story **Lucky in Love**!

Two men, two bars, and one very big secret—Charlie Hughes is about to find his perfect match, and it's going to change everything.

Lost in Love

Chapter One

CALL IT AN occupational hazard, but Poppy Whitlock had a teensy problem with nicknames: she just could *not* help doling them out. Working in a coffee shop on a college campus would do that to a girl, she supposed. The customers might or might not give Poppy their real names, and she might or might not decide to use them. But if they were memorable enough, or maybe just came into the café often enough, sooner or later Poppy had christened them with some appropriate nickname or another. Or *inappropriate*, as the case may be. It was the same in her classes. Nearly every piece of artwork that depicted a human being ended up with a Poppy-ism, and even some that didn't. People on the T, people on the street…when she considered it, no one and no thing was really safe from her naming habit.

Given this propensity of hers, it was no great surprise when a thick, muscular arm spun her around on the dance floor and her brain sputtered out, *Who's this hunk of burning love?* Once she took the guy's measure, the moniker may as well have been carved in stone. *Burning Love*, indeed. The look in his eye was enough to singe off her eyebrows. The bigger surprise, however, was that she sort-of knew him. Well…in a manner of speaking. Poppy had spotted this intense hulk of a man across the bar only moments before, sitting next to two of her favorite regulars from Jazz & Java, and based on his face, he had to be a relation of the dude's. In Poppy's world, grad student and teaching assistant by day, coffee shop manager by night (or, wait—was it manager by day and student by night? She shook her head. Yet another tricky definition in her life.), she didn't exactly get the chance to interact with many of the people she supposedly 'knew'. She was too busy for actual friends, and she had a weird window-shopping kind of relationship with her customers, especially the regulars. She made up names for them, and, truthfully, she made up lives for them, too. Burning Love's two buddies over there just happened to be one of Poppy's only true success stories, where real life actually mirrored her own mental fiction: she'd fixed them up in her head, and then they'd fallen for each other for real. Something had happened between those two, she knew, some kind of trouble in paradise. But here they were, together again, even if they seemed a bit more awkward than they had in the past. She'd known they would hook back up eventually. They'd been too crazy in love not to.

And here, up close and personal, was their friend and probable relative. Poppy had to hand it to him: for a guy that was built like he was (namely, like a freaking house), BL had some *moves*.

"Hey, Sweetheart. Mind if I join you?" he yelled.

"Why not?" she asked, all unconcerned sass. But Poppy was just dying to know what this could possibly be about. When she'd decided to blow off some steam tonight, meet up with her roommate and his boys and pretend she didn't have a ton of shit to do, she hadn't anticipated *this*.

"So, my friend says she knows you," he explained, leaning in to be heard and giving her a delectable whiff of his cologne. He pointed across the bar to the table he'd just vacated, where the café lovebirds were looking gob-smacked to see her, to say the least. And sort of like they barely knew each other, which was pretty weird. Must've been one hell of a fight.

"Um, yeah, I kind of know both of them," she admitted.

"What?" he yelled, brow furrowing. He was doing fine dancing, but trying to do that *and* have a conversation in all this racket was clearly going to be a challenge. The band playing McGillicuddy's tonight seemed to be approximating Irish rock, but truly, they were all over the map. And not shy about that fact.

"I said, *I kind of know both of them*," Poppy tried again. She looked back and forth from him to the table. "Hey, are you two related, or what?"

He shook his head, clearly not having picked up on what she'd said. In exasperation, Poppy looked around the place, then spotted a corner that seemed slightly more empty and quiet. She pointed it out, then grabbed his hand and towed him with her. His very large, very warm paw. And Burning Love was totally on board—he didn't resist in the least.

Once they'd reached the corner, she realized it was a much smaller space than she anticipated, what with him crowding his bulk up in there with her. She gave him another once-over. He wasn't dressed like a lot of the other club-goers. Not bad, just…not flashy. Which was a point in his favor, come to think of it.

"Now, what were you saying?" he asked, leaning a shoulder against the wall, and dropping his head down toward her.

"I just thought maybe you and that guy looked alike. Are you two related?"

He looked taken aback, but he nodded. "Yeah. He's my brother," he explained.

Poppy nodded too, and then they just stood there. Burning Love seemed to be at loss about what to do next, and Poppy wasn't nearly tipsy enough to give him any pointers. Finally, he cleared his throat.

He rattled off something incomprehensible, his words obscured by a particularly loud guitar flourish from the stage, then grinned.

"I'm sorry?" Poppy yelled, wincing.

"So do you come here often?" he enunciated carefully, then shook his head, disgusted. "It sounded much cheekier when I didn't have to scream it twice."

Poppy laughed. "What's your name?" she nearly screeched, going up on her toes to put her mouth closer to his ear. His arm slipped around her waist way too easily, helping her keep her balance. He seemed reluctant to let go, once she was flat on her feet again.

"George," he told her, sticking out his hand almost formally. She took it and shook, but then Burning Love didn't let go. Instead, he used it to pull her closer to him. "And you?"

"I'm Poppy," she called out, fully expecting to have to explain further. It wasn't the most common name in the universe, and to this day she had no idea how or why her fairly sedate parents had picked it.

But instead of being perplexed, BL just smiled at her. "Like the flower," he agreed, stealing her usual explanation. His palm stole around her waist again, then spread across her lower back, licking heat across her skin. Poppy blinked. Sure, she didn't get out that much, but the way she was reacting to this guy—it was as if she'd never run across a red-blooded male before.

George gazed at her for a long moment, then glanced around the bar again. He seemed hesitant, but then he leaned down to her again.

"Hey, you want to go outside for a little bit so we can talk?" he asked her. His lips were warm, and brushed faintly against the shell of her ear. Poppy shivered.

She pulled back and thought about that. She'd checked in with her roommate Furby and his buddies when she first got here, then left them entrenched at the bar doing shots. They'd never miss her. And just outside McGillicuddy's was the busy area of Quincy Market, lined with shops and other bars and restaurants. If she stayed close to the entrance, she would be reasonably safe. Besides, BL wasn't giving her any hinky vibes. Poppy usually got feelings about people, and George here wasn't raising a single red flag.

"Sure," she told him. "C'mon."

To read more, please purchase *Lost in Love* from your favorite bookseller!

FREE BOOK

Get a glimpse of Morgan, Meg, Molly and Mina—*before* their happily ever afters take place!

Sign up for the author's Reader's List and get a free copy of the Lost & Found prequel novella "Girls Night Out."

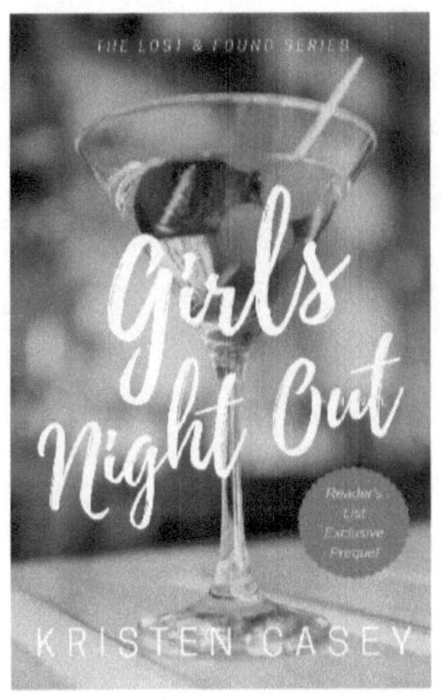

Visit Here to Get Started:

http://eepurl.com/ctGk1j

Also by Kristen Casey

The Triple Threat Series

The Titan Was Tall

The Doctor Was Dark

The Hero Was Handsome

The Masquerade was Magic

The Hero's Brother

The Triple Threat Box Set

The Black Watch Security Series

False Flag

Heat Seeking Missile

Brothers in Arms

Fight or Flight

Search and Destroy

Squared Away

Acknowledgements

I am so fortunate that I get to spend my days doing what I love, and I'm even more lucky that I have such great people surrounding me and cheering me on.

Once again, Deborah Bradseth at Tugboat Design has my heartfelt thanks for her lovely cover design. Her advice and insight on other book-related matters continues to be invaluable.

Helen Snay remains God's gift to authors. As my beta reader and editor, her eagle eye and helpful suggestions make my writing better. Any errors that persist are mine alone. As my dear friend, her laughter and support make my life better. Plus, she's a lovely human being and a joy to be around.

I could thank Kathleen Oristian for her exceptional work on my headshots—she'd certainly deserve it. However, her unflagging enthusiasm for my entire career might be the thing I'm most grateful for. Everyone needs a friend that will carry the torch at those times when it feels too heavy to carry on one's own—and Kathleen is my cheerleader, therapist, drill sergeant, and comic relief, all rolled into one person. If it weren't for her, I might never have told a single soul I'd written anything. If you enjoy my books, you probably ought to thank her. God knows I do.

That brings me to my family. My husband and children never doubted for a second that I could do this, and their faith in me, their utter, unwavering belief that I would not only succeed, but thrive as a writer, made me believe it too. Needless to say, I love them to an irrational degree.

Lastly, I want to thank the family and friends who became some of my very first readers. Your enthusiasm and praise have been such a tremendous gift. I hope I continue to make you proud, with each and every book I write.

About the Author

Kristen Casey writes the kind of heartfelt, steamy books she loves to read—full of relatable characters and delicious dialogue. She lives in Maryland with her husband, kids, and assorted cats, and in her free time, she enjoys all things crafty—especially projects she finds on Pinterest.

Sign up for her newsletter to receive exclusive free content and the inside scoop on sales and new releases—all emailed right to your inbox.

You can also follow her on social media for behind-the-scenes tales, character and setting inspiration, book reviews, and more:

Goodreads: Kristen_Casey
Facebook: AuthorKCasey
Twitter: AuthorKCasey
Pinterest: KristenCase0461
Instagram: Kristen.Casey.Books
BookBub: Kristen Casey
TikTok: KristenWritesRomance

Reading Order of Kristen's Books

The Lost & Found Series

Girls Night Out (Prequel exclusive to subscribers)

Finding Home (Book 1)

Finding Love (Book 2)

Lost in Love (Book 2.5 – Includes *Lucky in Love*)

The Flynn Sisters Box Set (Includes *Christmas in Cambridge*)

Finding a Husband (Book 3)

Finding Forever (Book 4)

Forever and a Day (Book 4.5 – Includes *Forever Starts Now*)

The O'Connell Sisters Box Set (Includes *Heroes & Husbands*)

The Triple Threat Series

The Titan was Tall (Book 1)

The Doctor was Dark (Book 2)

The Hero was Handsome (Book 3)

The Triple Threat Box Set (Includes *The Masquerade was Magic* and *The Hero's Brother*)

The Black Watch Security Series

False Flag (Book 1)

Heat Seeking Missile (Book 2)

Brothers in Arms (Book 3)

Fight or Flight (Book 4)

Search and Destroy (Book 5)

Squared Away (Book 6)